Praise for
THE MOST DANGEROUS PLACE ON EARTH:

'If you are cruising for a quality read that's also an unputdownable
quickie, reach for Lindsey Lee Johnson's debut novel . . . a high-
wire high school drama.'
Elle US

'Gripping . . . Each chapter offers a vignette into a more compli-
cated interior life – ones that involve inappropriate student-teacher
relationships, cheating on SATs, drugs, sex, and house parties . . .
Lindsey Lee Johnson works a convincing assortment of different
voices into her debut.'
GQ USA

'In Johnson's excellent debut, her sharp storytelling conveys an
authentic sense of the perils of adolescence . . . Johnson allows these
dramas to unfold through various shifting perspectives . . . Readers
may find themselves so swept up in this enthralling novel that they
finish it in a single sitting.'
Publishers Weekly (starred review)

'In sharp and assured prose, roving among characters, Lindsey Lee
Johnson plumbs the terrifying depths of a half-dozen ultraprivileged
California high school kids. I read THE MOST DANGEROUS
PLACE ON EARTH in two chilling gulps. It's a phenomenal first
book, a compassionate *Less Than Zero* for the digital age.'
Anthony Doerr, author of *All the Light We Cannot See*

'An astonishing debut novel, THE MOST DANGEROUS PLACE
ON EARTH plunges the reader into the fraught power dynamics
between (and among) high school teachers and students with both
nuance and fearlessness. With a stunning constellation of characters'
voices and a fiercely compelling story, it's impossible to
put down, or to forget.'
Megan Abbott

'[An] alarming, compelling and coolly funny debut . . . Ms
Johnson's characters are unpredictable, contradictory and many
things at once, which make them particularly satisfying . . . Here's
high school life in all its wonder . . .

THE MOST
DANGEROUS
PLACE
ON EARTH

LINDSEY LEE
JOHNSON

HODDER

First published in the United States by Random House,
an imprint and division of Penguin Random House LLC, New York.

First published in Great Britain in 2017 by Hodder & Stoughton
An Hachette UK company

1

A CIP catalogue record for this title is
available from the British Library

ISBN 978 1 473 66126 4

Printed and bound by Clays Ltd, St Ives plc

Hodder & Stoughton policy is to use papers that are natural,
renewable and recyclable products and made from wood grown in
sustainable forests. The logging and manufacturing processes
are expected to conform to the environmental regulations
of the country of origin.

Hodder & Stoughton Ltd
Carmelite House
50 Victoria Embankment
London EC4Y 0DZ

www.hodder.co.uk

For Susan and David Lee Johnson

The pot at the end of the rainbow is not money. I know because I have it.

—Marin County woman featured in *I Want It All Now! An NBC News Special Report*, 1978

The mind is its own place, and in itself can make a Heav'n of Hell, a Hell of Heav'n.

—John Milton, *Paradise Lost*

Nobody talks to children.

—Jim Stark in *Rebel Without a Cause*

CONTENTS

Eighth Grade

THE NOTE   3

Junior Year   31

THE LOVERS   50
THE STRIVER   87
THE ARTIST   115
THE DIME   142
THE RIDE   169
THE DANCER   201

Senior Year   235

THE PRETTY BOY   237
THE SLEEPING LADY   255

Eighth Grade

THE NOTE

Cally Broderick lingered in the doorway of the resource office, waiting to be noticed.

She would have been easy to overlook. She was short and skinny, and her dirty-blond hair had begun that year to wave and shine with oil. Her hazel eyes were pretty, though too wide-set, her nose thin but too long. Every four weeks her face produced a constellation of pimples that loomed and gleamed when she turned her cheek to the mirror, disgusting and enthralling her. Her face was a question she considered daily, widening her eyes in the mirror on the inside of her locker, sucking the flesh of her cheeks between her teeth. Her mother said—or used to say—that Cally was "striking looking," a description Cally rejected: it was not only vaguely violent sounding but also patently untrue.

She was a restless girl, anxious to rewind her life or jump it forward. In service of the latter goal, she'd made a list of skills to learn before adulthood—how to swallow pills without gagging, to buy tampons without blushing, to shake the hands of her father's friends without giggling and glancing away. But as the years passed, the list only grew longer: life presented more questions as she lived it, more and more doors to unlock. These questions she didn't share with anyone. She wrote them in a battered journal, then stuffed the journal in a pillowcase and shoved it under her mattress lest someone—her brother

Jake—find it and expose her. She would not even show it to Abigail Cress, her best friend. Prior to Abigail, Cally would have said her best friend was her mother, but that was now impossible, for a multitude of reasons too complex to explain. In fact there was little about her life that Cally Broderick could explain, to herself or to anyone else. She was a girl in middle school. She was thirteen years old.

The resource office at Valley Middle School was small and dim—the resource teacher, Ms. Flax, had a moral objection to fluorescent lights, preferring to squint in the amber glow of a ceramic lamp—and stank of mold, and of the pesto pasta that steamed at the teacher's elbow as she marked papers at her desk.

Ms. Flax, over thirty but under fifty, had an apple-shaped body that she wrapped in hippie scarves and tunics and long mud-colored skirts. She was not pretty, Cally decided, but prettyish, with featherweight hair and deep brown eyes that turned down at the corners, making her look on the verge of tears even when she laughed. Across from her sat Tristan Bloch, who flipped through a stack of shiny colored papers on the desk. He was fat and pale with blond hair buzz-cut so close she saw bits of scalp through the glistening bristle; on sunny days at recess his head would glow as if on fire.

Everyone knew that Tristan spent hours in Ms. Flax's office, during homeroom, study hall, sometimes recess and lunch. No one knew what they did in there for all that time. Probably she helped him with his work, but it seemed just as likely that he helped her with hers.

"Ms. Flax?" Cally said. "I got this note? You wanted to, like, see me?"

Ms. Flax started and looked up. "Oh, yes," she said, shifting her weight, and the chair cushion squeaked and farted beneath her. This embarrassed Cally. And it happened every time—pushing hair out of her face, Ms. Flax would pretend not to notice the noises as she begged Cally to change her ways, as if Cally's "applying herself" would determine the course of Ms. Flax's own sad life. "Come in, please. Have a seat."

"No thanks," Cally said. She knew what Ms. Flax was like: to step inside, to sit, was to condemn oneself to an inquisition.

"Cally, please."

Seeing no way out, Cally relented, stepping into the room and taking the seat next to Tristan Bloch's.

"Mr. Hoyt says you've been copying algebra homework," Ms. Flax said. "You are an extremely bright girl, Calista Broderick. Why would you do this?"

"I don't know," Cally said. She looked to see if Tristan was listening, but he did not react. Hunched over the desk, he was folding a sheet of silver paper again and again. All the while he tongued the corner of his mouth. His white T-shirt was tucked into the oversized sweatpants he wore every day, in colors that seemed chosen to assault the eyes: apple red, lime green, and even, horror of horrors, yellow. He wore yellow now. Fruit punch stained his thigh, the splash darkened to a sick bluish gray. Cally's mother would have told her it was rude, but she couldn't stop staring at that spot. It was like one of those inkblots psychiatrists showed you to see what kind of crazy you were.

Everyone knew that Tristan didn't have a father, only a dumpy mother with his same squinty eyes and an aura of frizzed red hair. She'd find any excuse to come panting through the halls, bringing Tristan homework assignments, sweatshirts, Slurpees. At least once a week she'd stride into the front office, hot cheeked, indignant, to yell at Principal Falk about Tristan's special academic accommodations. Then she'd trudge down to the resource room to conspire with Ms. Flax, as if they would be able to turn Tristan into a normal human being just because they wanted to. But Cally knew what Tristan's mother didn't—she was only making his situation worse, she was exactly as weird as her son, what he needed most in life was to get away from her.

If Cally did end up motherless, she thought, at least she'd never have to worry about her dad trolling the halls of her school.

"This isn't you," Ms. Flax insisted.

Cally shrugged. Of course she could do the homework herself, but there were more interesting things in the world. There was her best friend, Abigail, and their afternoons behind closed blinds. There was Ryan Harbinger's body as he stretched to field a ball, and the current that jagged through her in English when he palmed her bare right thigh under the desk, then squeezed it hard enough to bruise, grinning when she screamed. There was sprawling sideways on her bed with her head dangled over the edge, picturing velvety blood as it seeped to the top of her brain. Everything was more interesting than algebra, but she couldn't say that to Ms. Flax, who had probably done all her own school assignments before her teachers even thought of them. And look at where it had gotten her—stuck in middle school for the rest of her life, with Tristan Bloch.

Tristan's silver paper had transformed into something tiny, sharp, and shining—a spear, a crown, Cally couldn't tell. His eyes narrowed to slits and his tongue worked its way to his top lip, sucking at it, revealing the pink gloss underneath.

"Oh, honey," Ms. Flax said. "Talk to me. How are things at home?"

"What?" Heat surged in Cally's chest and face; she felt it making her ugly.

Ms. Flax shifted in her chair, began again. "Since your mother has been ill, I know it has been difficult. It's all right to feel sad, even angry. I wish you would share your feelings, rather than acting out in this way."

Cally thought, Abigail was right about Ms. Flax: she made you think she wanted to help, but underneath she was a total bitch. "Just because I don't care about eighth-grade math doesn't mean there's a problem," she said. "It's not like it matters. None of this does."

Ms. Flax's eyes widened, and for a second it seemed she would cry. How awkward that would be. Unbearable. "Look," she said, "I'm on your side here, Cally. But I can't help if you refuse to be honest with me."

Cally crossed her arms. Beside her, Tristan Bloch picked up his folded silver paper, pressed it to his lips, and blew. Then he set it on the desk—a tiny, perfect crane—and nudged it toward her.

This was when Cally made the mistake. She should have ignored him like most people did. But instead she reached forward and plucked the crane from the desk. She set it in her palm and raised her hand to her eyes. The bird had a sharp beak, a scissor neck and tail, two precise, glinting wings. It seemed to float in her palm. In that moment it seemed possible this tiny bird could fly—out of this stifling room, out of this school and this town and away. She smiled at Tristan then, and Tristan smiled back.

"What a lovely gift," Ms. Flax said. "Calista, don't you think you should say thank you?"

Mercifully, Cally's iPhone buzzed in her pocket. Abigail always knew when she needed saving.

"Do I have detention or not?" she asked.

Ms. Flax sighed. "Three days. And you'll make up the homework for Mr. Hoyt."

"Fine." Cally stood and turned to leave, the paper bird between her fingers.

That night, Cally curled on her narrow bed to text with Abigail.

Abigail never came over to Cally's house. It was an unspoken agreement between them. It was partly because Cally's room was small and plain, with a west-facing window that admitted scant light. Directly outside the window was her mother's rose garden, which permeated the walls; no matter how emphatically Cally spritzed her own fruity perfumes, she could never quite cover the room's damp soil smell. Beyond the garden, the view swept across to Mount Tamalpais. Under the window was a small wooden desk that Cally rarely used. She preferred to do her homework on her bed, which she'd piled with pillows and pushed against the wall. The wall itself was papered in a pattern chosen for the child who had had the room before her: faded yellow balloons floating upward to the ceiling. In places, she had outlined the balloons with marker, had drawn on faces and hairstyles, torsos and hands. At the seam she'd scratched the paper back, exposing strips of ancient glue.

The walls of Cally's house were thin, and the sounds were layered: as she lay there clutching her phone, she heard her dad shouting at the TV, her brothers fighting in the bedroom next door, the steady silence from her mom's room on the other side. Since Cally's mom had gotten sick, her dad had stayed home to care for her and fight with the insurance people, and now he camped out in the living room every day, his paperwork spread over the couch. He slept there too, TV blaring into the night. Cally barricaded herself with pillows but could not drown out the noise of the stupid late-night show, or her dad when he yelled at the commercials: "Oh right, sure, whose house *looks* like that? Assholes."

Cally was hungry, but to get to the kitchen she'd have to pass her mother's room. Her mother would be shrouded in bleached blankets, sleeping. A slight form sinking in the center of the bed. Cally's dad would tell her, "Go on in, just sit with her, spend some time." But whenever her mother woke, her eyes weren't right and Cally didn't want to see them. Her mother's eyes were once a bright, unclouded hazel—like Cally's own, but kinder—and this was the memory she wanted.

Her brothers didn't go in either. Erik was a sophomore at Valley High and walked to school each morning with razor blades in his pockets. Jake, nineteen, should have been out of the house but wasn't smart enough to go away to college, and in Mill Valley there wasn't much for him to do but bus dishes at High Tech Burrito and smoke weed under the redwoods in the park. Jake was the one who came into her room to steal the allowance and birthday money she'd stashed under her jewelry box or rolled into the lace cups of her bras. She'd begged for a lock on her door, but her dad said it was "inappropriate," a meaningless word adults used to shut down ideas they didn't like. He just didn't want to pay for it.

Cally turned over in bed, pulling the sheets over her shoulders. She and Abigail were discussing Ryan Harbinger, who sat next to Cally in English so he could squeeze her thigh under the desk, and copy what she wrote about the books he never read. For the past two weeks he'd been pursuing Cally in PE class, pulling her into the willow trees to make out while they were supposed to be running the mile at Bayfront Park.

OMG you slut, Abigail texted. Tell me more!!

What do u want to know?

U know. When's he going to make you his gf?

???

Come on. U know u want it!

> I think he likes Elisabeth Avarine

That bitch. No way

> She's so pretty I think

^ Obvi
Looks aren't everything
U have to make him want u

> How???

Hmm well u don't want to be too clingy. U don't
want to be that girl.

> No, Cally agreed. Definitely not!

Cally understood that Ryan was too busy to care about things like schoolwork or novels or the volatile feelings of girls. He was captain of the baseball team, and in the hot afternoons of late spring she and Abigail and Emma Fleed would go in their skinny-strap tank tops and miniskirts to watch him play, singeing their thighs on the bleachers. When Cally's bra strap fell down her arm, she wouldn't bother to hitch it up. She'd already been dress-coded three times that quarter, but she didn't care. She would train her eyes on Ryan, tracing his body against the green blare of grass, and when she closed her eyes at night she'd be able to keep seeing him, an afterimage burned onto the insides of her eyelids, her very own personal beautiful thing.

The next afternoon, PE class was at the pool. Aquatics and Safety Training. Cally stood with the other girls in their ugly one-piece bathing suits, squinting against the silver swimming pool, shifting on their feet and rubbing toes on calves. The boys were on the bleachers across the water.

Cally hugged her chest and looked around for Ryan Harbinger. Instead her eyes alit on Tristan Bloch, who emerged blinking from the locker room in blue trunks and white T-shirt. Cally became suddenly, intensely aware of her own semi-nakedness, how the spandex swimsuit molded to her nipples and cut into her thighs. She felt a vague, unsubstantiated panic about pubic hair. As Tristan scanned the pool deck, she ducked behind Abigail and Emma. She was hiding there when she heard Ryan's voice at her back:

"Cally Broderick! You gotta go in!"

She turned and he was there, suntanned and bare-chested and grabbing at her, trying to throw her in the pool.

"Ryan! No!" she shrieked, but he didn't stop. Terror could sound exactly like joy. Cally ran forward, evading Ryan's grasp; the other girls scattered like birds. She glanced over her shoulder just as Tristan Bloch knocked Ryan into the water and crashed in behind him, splashing her. Cally stopped short at the edge of the pool and rubbed the sting of chlorine from her eyes. She felt mascara smudging on her face and tried not to let it worry her.

Both boys surfaced.

"The fuck are you doing?" Ryan yelled across the water.

Tristan struggled to stay afloat, arms chopping. His T-shirt bubbled around his face and threatened to swallow him.

Ryan streamed through the water, rose, and barreled down on Tristan's head, plunging him under. It happened so fast. It went on forever. Cally was steps away, conceivably she could do something, but it felt like watching TV. Everyone gathered around the pool and stood there, waiting to see how far Ryan Harbinger would go.

Finally Tristan pushed out from under Ryan's hand, gulping the air, panicked, like a lost little kid. Abigail and Emma yelled at Cally to get away from the edge, but she couldn't move a single limb.

"Want more, faggot?" Ryan pushed Tristan under again.

"Stop it!" someone, not Cally but Dave Chu, yelled.

"You like it, fag?" Ryan was grinning at Cally now. "You like it?"

"Please," she said, too quietly to matter. She backed away to huddle with Abigail like they were nothing more than spectators.

When Mr. Gifford charged out of the locker room, eyes on his clipboard, Ryan released Tristan and vaulted out of the water. He was back with the boys before the teacher looked up. Tristan broke the water's surface, heaving for air.

"Tristan Bloch!" Mr. Gifford yelled. "What the hell are you doing in the pool?"

Everyone laughed, so Cally did too. She guessed Tristan would regret having given her the silver crane, would be disappointed at the kind of girl she had turned out to be. She'd saved herself.

Cally found the note in her locker the next day after school. A sheet of binder paper folded into impeccable quarters, her initials neatly printed on the front in pale blue ink. The handwriting was not what she'd hoped for: Ryan's hurried scrawl.

She unfolded the note.

> Dear ~~Cally~~ Calista Broderick,
>
> You might not think I watch you but I do.
>
> Every day in class, and at recess, and when you come to Ms. Flax's room when I'm there because of my acommodations. In PE I see you when you run the mile around the marsh and you cut through the long part and go into that clump of trees with that asshole Ryan H. (I'm sorry Calista but he really is an Asshole.)
>
> You might not think that anyone in this School sees you but I do. I mean sees you really. Did you know that you have the World's most beautiful skin. It smells like rasberries. And you have the smallest softest blondeish hairs on your arms. I know this because I touched you one time, in algebra remember? You were reaching for a fresh pencil and I reached across at the exact same second and Boom!! I touched your bare skin. You might of thought that was an accident Calista, but what if it wasn't?
>
> ~~Sometimes when I'm watching you I think about~~
> I think that you are Perfect. People say Elisabeth Avarine is prettier than you just because she has a better nose but you shouldn't beleive them, I don't. First of all your hair is longer and wavier than Elisabeth's. And second, when you look at you, you can

tell that you aren't Brain Dead. I mean I can tell that you think about things, like I do.

Calista, sometimes when I'm watching you I think about this day back in sixth grade. We were all standing on the flats during PE and looking up at the ridge of Mount Tamalpais, The Sleeping Lady. You know the Legend: The Mountain Witch sent her daughter Tamalpa to cast an evil spell on a Miwok warrior who went up the Mountain alone. But Tamalpa stole his gold headdress and all his power. The warrior didn't care because he was already in love with her. Tamalpa fell in love with him too. She couldn't help it. But she knew that she would only destroy him, so she poisoned herself with Deadly black blossoms. Then three girls came and covered her with a purple blanket, and the Mountain changed itself into her shape. Like a wizard. Or a ghost.

You know how the Mountain is always Beautiful, but it's hard to remember its Beautiful because it's always there? It's like a poster that you hang up in your room because you like it so much, but after a while you don't see it anymore. And when someone asks you what does it look like, you have to think. So that day in sixth grade we were trying to see it. The Mountain was deep green like jewelry. The sky behind it was bright blue. We were squinting to see The Sleeping Lady's nose, boobs, waist and legs. You said, "Why do we call her Sleeping when everybody knows she's Dead?" Everybody laughed but I liked it when you said that. Because no one else in Mill Valley would even think of it.

Calista, the Truth is sometimes I don't know if I can stand to stay here in this Town. Miss Flax says I am smart and special and can be anything I want. But the thing teachers never explain when they say that is, How do you find out what you want? When the

Lawyer people become Lawyers, is it because that is
what they always wanted to be? When they were in
Kindergarten playing with their Legos, did they day-
dream about Lawyering? If they did, then I am even
weirder than people say. I must be like an Alien or
something. Because I never thought about being a
Lawyer, or a Doctor, or a Top Executive. I mostly
think about how the Universe is these forever blues
and blacks and blinking stars, how it looks like the inside of a big open umbrella but in actuality goes on
forever and swallows everything, my house and my
street and Mill Valley and California and America and
the Earth and the Sun and all the Planets and the
Galaxies—I think how the universe is this huge
forever-big and at the same time small enough to fold
up in my brain like an Origami box, where I can
imagine it all. I think, how is it that these opposite
things could both be True? I guess this is what Miss
Flax is getting at when she tells me that I'm Special. I
guess I know she doesn't want to be mean to a kid
and that is why she chooses to say Special, which is
really just a nicer way of saying Alien. I wonder if you
think about things like this too. There's no way to
explain it but I feel like you do.

Calista I want to talk to you. Every day I think
about talking to you, but you're always with Abigail
Cress walking to her house after school, or else
you're stuck in the middle of that whole big group of
other girls who are Nothing compared to you.

Calista I Love You do you think you could love
me back? I could help you with your algebra homework sometime. If you wanted.

                                        Tristan Bloch

The blue words blurred on the page. Cally's breaths came shallow
and fast. She was dizzy, and wondered if she should stick her head in a

paper bag. (She had seen this on TV.) Tristan Bloch had called her Calista, which was her real name, private, and only for her mother to use. He knew about her and Ryan. He knew that she went to Abigail's every day after school. Had he followed them? Had he peeked in the window while she and Abigail and Emma Fleed lay head-to-foot and pumiced each other's calluses or stuffed their faces until they puked or debated who Ryan was going to choose as his girlfriend, Cally or that bitch Elisabeth Avarine?

Cally did not know what to think about the note from Tristan Bloch; she did not know what to do. If her life weren't what it was, she might have asked her mother.

She took the note to Abigail. While privacy was a fantasy at Cally's house, at Abigail's they had nothing but. Abigail's vast bedroom had turquoise wallpaper and a queen-sized bed and a mini-fridge stocked with Cokes and her older brother's beer that they'd steal and share outside, in the dank space beneath the deck. The beer was bitter, but she loved its buzzing at the base of her skull and the backs of her knees, and she loved scooting close to her friends in the dark and conspiring. She was grateful for Abigail, for her giant, echoing house and parents who were always at work. ("They're on New York time," Abigail explained, which made no sense, but Cally was happy to be in a house like Abigail's, so she kept her mouth shut.) If the Cresses did come home, they'd say hello and click off to their master suite across the house, not caring what the girls were up to as long as they were quiet.

Sometimes they all went to Emma Fleed's house on the mountain, but Emma was often busy with ballet class and rehearsals and couldn't truly be counted upon, as Abigail liked to say meaningfully to Cally when Emma wasn't around. At this Cally would feel a proprietary thrill: she was Abigail's, Abigail hers.

That afternoon, in Abigail's bedroom, Cally sat beside Abigail on the queen-sized bed as Emma stretched on the floor. It seemed perfectly safe for Cally to pull the note from her pocket and hand it over.

When Abigail read the first line, she laughed out loud. She was the only person Cally knew who actually said "ha" when she laughed, barked it. "Ha! Oh my God, dude," she said. "This is hilarious."

"Yeah," Cally said. The note made her stomach turn, but if Abigail thought it was hilarious then it probably was.

Emma stood up and grabbed the note. "What's this crossed-out part?" she said. " *'Sometimes when I'm watching you I . . . '* Nasty."

"Don't read it out *loud*. God." Cally felt as responsible for each sentence as if she'd written it herself.

Abigail pushed on. "You know what this means. You're what he thinks about. When he—you know—"

"Gross."

"In his room at night," Emma said, "after that creepy mom of his tucks him in—"

"Okay, I get it."

"Maybe he does it at school! Maybe you're running the mile and he's sitting there watching you, hand down the front of those sweats, going at it." Abigail squeezed her eyes shut and gaped her mouth, acting out a strange kind of pleasure-pain that Cally had never felt.

Emma shrieked with laughter. Cally blushed, hid her face in her hands.

Abigail asked, "What do you want to do?"

"Forget it ever existed? Is that an option?"

"It kills me how innocent you are," Abigail said. "Do you think *he's* going to forget it?"

Cally shrugged.

"What if he, like, comes after you?" Emma said.

"He wouldn't."

"He wants you. What if he won't take no for an answer?"

"I don't know." Cally remembered Tristan's gaze, his thumbs stroking origami paper to life, what he wrote about her *bare skin*. What if he wouldn't?

"Well," Abigail said. "You know what you have to do."

Ryan Harbinger answered the door in dirt-smeared baseball pants and sweat-sheered T-shirt, and he didn't ask them in.

"Who is it, honey?" his mother yelled from inside.

Cally and Abigail stood together on the stoop; Emma had abandoned them for a late rehearsal. Mothers had a way of hating Cally and

Abigail on the spot, but Cally believed if she were Ryan Harbinger's official girlfriend, his parents would learn to like her. She'd spend weekends at his house—his mother would cook waffles shaped like Mickey Mouse and his father would ask pointed yet encouraging questions about her future, as though college were next week and not a million years away.

Ryan looked them over. "Nobody!" He palmed the back of his head. "'Sup?"

"You have to see this." Abigail nudged Cally, who held out the note.

As he took it from her, his thumb grazed her skin, but he didn't look at her. He never did, exactly. He looked at her earlobe or the top of her head, and when he was kissing her amid the willows by the mile loop, his eyes stayed closed, his eyebrows worried, like it hurt.

You think about things, like I do, Tristan Bloch had written. "Yeah, he thinks about fucking you," Abigail had said, and Cally had shoved her and told her to shut the fuck up, yet the picture clicked stubbornly into focus: Tristan's face contorted in the pleasure-pain Abigail had shown her, hips thrusting against her—sweatpants didn't have buttons or zippers or anything . . .

Ryan laughed. "*Calista.* What the fuck." His eyes were merry, golden-flecked. "Moron got your name wrong."

He read on. He was gorgeous to watch. There were little lines around his mouth, and dark gold tendrils of hair against his temples where sweat had curled it.

"No fucking way." His laugh jumped higher, and Cally burned happily. She had given him this pleasure—it belonged to her.

"Tristan fucking Bloch," he said. "Is he serious with this shit?"

"It was in my locker," Cally told him. "I just, like, found it." She did not say, *I wanted it to be from you.*

"What a fag."

"So, what should she do?" Abigail asked. They'd discussed this in Abigail's bedroom—they'd find out what he thought because *Cosmo* said guys liked when you asked for direction, it made them feel important.

"No worries. I got this." Ryan leaned into Cally for a kind-of-hug that veered sideways as his mother yelled in her anxious pitch, "Ryan! I need you! Right! Now!"

"Okay, Jesus, calm the fuck down!"

As he pulled away, Cally realized she'd been holding her breath. He had crumpled the note in his fist. She wanted to grab it back, but he had closed the door.

Cally and Abigail walked from Ryan's to the 7-Eleven on Miller to buy Red Vines, Tostitos, Reese's Pieces, and Big Gulps.

In Abigail's bedroom they closed the blinds and ate until the sugar made them giddy. This was their secret. Only the Red Vines would they ever bring to the baseball field—they would loop the vines around their fingers and tongues and every boy would stop to watch.

"Let's see if he has a Facebook," Abigail said.

"Who would friend him?"

"Just his mom."

"And Ms. Flax."

"Oh my God, they're probably doing it!" Abigail screamed, delighted. "She probably takes him into that little room and fucks him all through seventh period."

"Get your mind out of the gutter," Cally said, but she was laughing too.

Cally and Abigail sat shoulder to shoulder in front of Abigail's computer. They found Tristan's profile in two seconds. "What the fuck is this picture?"

"You can't even tell it's him, his face is all blurry."

"Oh, it's him," Abigail said. "Check out those pants."

Cally laughed again, in a hard way that made her throat hurt. In the photo Tristan wore his trademark yellow sweatpants and white T-shirt. His skin gleamed with sweat, and his nipples pricked under the shirt as he stood in hero pose—leg hitched, chest puffed, arms extended—atop a boulder on Mount Tam. The day was bright, and he squinted into the camera, grinning.

Abigail turned and looked at her, so Cally said, "What a freak."

"Let's friend him," Abigail said.

"You have to do it," Cally said. "If I do, he'll think he has a chance. He'll, like, show up at my house tonight or something."

"With a wilted little condom"—Abigail was cracking herself up—"that he keeps in his pocket just waiting for the day when the hot, sexy, beautiful *Calista* Broderick—"

"Shut up, you're such a bitch."

"Ha, you love me," Abigail said. It was true. If not for her, Cally would be alone with the note, rereading it, waiting for its curious horror to fade. She'd have to feel what Tristan's words opened in her, the shame that became a kind of pleasure, nothing like the anxiousness she felt when Ryan kissed her, or when he flicked his thumb over her nipple like he flicked quarters during the boring parts of algebra. It was a discomfort she'd tried to will to pleasure because it was meant to feel good, she was meant to want it, she was thirteen and pretty and it was the only logical thing to want. If not for Abigail, Cally would've kept the note, read the words again, traced them with her fingers: *No one sees you but I do. I mean sees you really.*

The note was like Ms. Flax's office, a stifled room where she was trapped with Tristan. It occurred to her that Ms. Flax might know about the note. Maybe she'd even told him to write it. Teachers like her were always encouraging hopeless kids like Tristan to inject themselves into the social scene with ridiculous gestures—declarations of love, blind stabs at friendship—as if middle school were a safe haven in which to conduct these experiments, when in fact it was the most dangerous place on Earth.

"Okay. I'm gonna do it," Abigail said, and clicked *Add Friend*. Seconds later, she yelped. Tristan had approved her immediately; he clearly didn't understand the concept of waiting so as not to seem desperate.

It turned out he did have Facebook friends—not his mother or teachers but kids from their grade who would not have said one word to him at school. There was, incredibly, Emma Fleed. And Elisabeth Avarine, Dave Chu, Nick Brickston, Damon Flintov, and even Ryan Harbinger, approved just twenty minutes before. On Tristan's Facebook page they read:

> **Tristan Bloch** and **Ryan Harbinger** are now friends.
>
> **Ryan Harbinger:** hey yo trisstan wut the FUCK
>
> **Tristan Bloch:** ?
>
> **Ryan Harbinger:** yu know wut im talking about
>
> **Damon Flintov:** ya triSTAIN u no wut hes talking about dont u
>
> **Tristan Bloch:** I am sorry I don't.
>
> **Ryan Harbinger:** CALLIE fuckin BRODRIK mutherfuckr

Cally caught her breath. Her name online, more permanent than ink.

> **Damon Flintov:** hey trisss nice pic u think callies seen it yet?
>
> **Ryan Harbinger:** ha ha thats sum sexxxy shit
>
> **Damon Flintov:** callys fuckin wet now bro
>
> **Abby Cress:** omg lolz

"Abby!" Cally said. "What are you doing?"

"It is fucking funny, Cal," Abigail said. "You have to admit."

"Don't write anything about me, okay?"

> **Abby Cress:** Cally says don't talk abt her ok?

"What the fuck?" Cally slapped Abigail's arm. "Now they know I'm here!"

"Fucking chill," Abigail said.

> **Ryan Harbinger:** tristans the one talking abt her rite TRISS?
>
> **Ryan Harbinger:** u might not think I watch you but I do
>
> **Ryan Harbinger:** u have the world's most beautiful skin
>
> **Ryan Harbinger:** calista i love u do u think u could love me back?

Damon Flintov: awwwww

Tristan Bloch: Hey guys will you please not.

Ryan Harbinger: u said it trisSTAIN

Ryan Harbinger: i have ur note, callie gave me it

Ryan Harbinger: callie sez tell u ur a fat fuckin loser

Ryan Harbinger: and ur notes fuckin hillarious btw

Ryan Harbinger: calista i think that u r perfect

Jonas Everett: LMAO

Nick Brix: wut the fuck

Emma Fleed: Cally Broderick is Hott!!

Steph Malcolm-Swann: callie brodrick is a Bitch u guys

Tristan Bloch: Where did you get that.

Tristan Bloch: I didn't write that.

Emma Fleed: and hes a liar to? lol

Damon Flintov: fuck this fag

Dave Chu: guys ur being kind of mean now.

Ryan Harbinger: hey yo trisstain were just telling u the truth

Damon Flintov: trisstan block is a fat freak perv

Jonas Everett: he he

More and more new comments flashed onto the screen.

"This is getting harsh," Abigail said cheerfully. "Ryan Harbinger must really want to fuck you."

Once when Cally was a kid, her family had gone water-skiing at Lake Tahoe. When it was Cally's turn, her mom had jumped in too, floating beside Cally in the cool water as she guided her feet into the skis' slick rubber fittings and handed her the rope. Then her mom had swum to the boat, climbed aboard, and leaned over the stern to grin and wave so energetically it seemed that she would crash into the lake. Cally had clenched her teeth and waved back, believing she was ready. But when the boat took off, she was paralyzed, unable to stand, unable to release the rope. The water coursed over her body, flooding her nose and her mouth, and she knew it then: the world was going to drag her where it wanted. When the boat stopped and the water subsided, she coughed and gulped the air and was surprised to find that breathing was something she was still allowed to do.

She might have set this in motion, but now it was dragging her behind. She watched the comments fill the screen.

> **Damon Flintov:** hey triss. if i had a face like yours
> id shoot myself
> 👍 13 people like this post
> **Ryan Harbinger:** bwa ha ha
> **Elisabeth Avarine:**

Cally curled up on Abigail's bed. "Turn it off."

"What's your problem?" Abigail said. "They're defending you. Ryan Harbinger is defending you."

"Maybe I shouldn't have shown it to him."

"Oh, come on. That note was disgusting. It was like sexual harassment or something."

"I think I ate too many Red Vines." Cally got up and went into Abigail's bathroom, which was newly remodeled in expensive white marble. Like magic, the bathroom had transformed into a shrine, but Abigail hardly seemed to notice it. To her it was just a place to pee in the middle of the night.

Cally leaned over the toilet. She saw Tristan's crane and Ms. Flax's sad eyes and her own name inked in delicate blue. She wanted to puke but couldn't. She told herself that Abigail was right—the note was disgusting and she'd had every right to report it. And Tristan Bloch had brought it on himself. He'd laid it all out on paper, for anyone to read. What did he expect to happen?

She moved to the sink, rinsed her mouth and hands with water from Abigail's brushed-chrome tap. In the mirror her eyeliner looked suddenly clumsy, a painted-on frame around little-girl eyes. Her cheeks were wan under their bursts of blush.

In a line beside the sink stood three washcloths folded into origami fans. This sight made her queasy again, so she shook one fan open and scrubbed it over her face. She picked up the other two, shook them, and folded them in sloppy squares like the washcloths in her bathroom at home, which made her feel better and worse at once. Even if she'd wanted to, she had no idea how to refold them. There was someone who'd know how, but to talk to him would be to lock herself into that airless room forever and throw away the key.

"I thought you fell in," Abigail said, spinning toward her in the desk chair, when Cally returned to the bedroom.

Cally grinned, remembering with sudden force that Abigail was her best friend in the world. "Let me," she said, and went over to Abigail and leaned over the keyboard to type:

> **Abby Cress:** Hey tristan I talked to cally and she says FUCK OFF you make her sick and fuck your gross note too NO THANK YOU!!!

When Abigail laughed, it sounded like mercy.

Then they went to YouTube to watch a cat try to scramble out of a claw-foot tub, its panic hilarious. They watched the clip five times, collapsing on each other in laughter, before Abigail sent Cally to the mini-fridge to find her brother's beers.

As she popped the tabs on the cold silver cans, Cally began to feel free. Powerful. She began to believe that Tristan Bloch would fade away, that already he was folded into that square of paper, pale and insubstantial as that barely blue ink. Already, he was almost nothing.

From then on, Tristan spent his lunch periods outside, walking the edge of the schoolyard where asphalt crumbled into marshland. He kept his head bowed, and when he came back inside, his ankles were purpled with mud.

Nobody bullied him at school. Nobody minded him at all.

And every afternoon, Cally and Abigail watched from Abigail's bedroom as the Facebook posts continued, flashing onto the computer screen at an inexorable pace, gleeful, hateful, now from people they didn't even know. Sometimes Tristan wrote back, defending himself angrily or desperately, but each comment he posted only renewed the energy of the attacks.

Someone would stop it, Cally thought. Tristan would close his account. Tristan would tell. Or some adult—his mother, Ms. Flax—would sense something wrong, venture into the Facebook world and see what was happening, pull them all back from the brink.

One foggy morning in June, five weeks after he wrote the note to Calista Broderick and one week before the end of eighth grade, Tristan Bloch woke early, at 6:00 a.m.

His bedroom lay at the end of a narrow hall. The small room was painted little-boy blue. Against one wall was pushed a twin bed with a Pokémon blanket and red metal frame. Stickers splotched the bars of the headboard, the top layer of each pried off over years by a plump, patient hand, so that only the white underlayers remained, the shapes of rockets and robots and snakes indelible, reminding the boy of his boyness every day, reminding him that he was still a child, in a child's bed.

He pushed off the covers and set his feet on the carpet. He wiped his eyes with the belly of his T-shirt. The shirt was warm and retained the sour smell of sleep.

Yawning, he went to the trio of wooden shelves beside the window. He cracked the blinds; lasers of white light hit the objects on the shelves. The Revell Wright Flyer model airplane, carefully constructed of balsa wood and glue. A four-by-six birchwood board with Boy Scout knots of thick white rope, each neatly labeled in his fifth-grade print: *Cat's Paw, Figure Eight, Square Knot, Bowline*. A tiny samurai with tiny sword, a thumb-sized bald patch worn on the crown of its black plastic head. A stack of books with brightly colored spines: *Harry Potter, The Hobbit, The Lightning Thief, The Boy Scout Handbook* (three years out of date), *The Official NASA Guide to Rockets*. A cherrywood box of origami folding papers, given to him by his father before his father disappeared. A broad, beige clamshell that cradled gleaming pennies. A wallet-sized school photo from first grade, his white-blond hair shaped into a shining bowl. A Matchbox car. A calcified branch.

Tristan blew dust from the lid of the cherrywood box, thumbed the head of the tiny samurai. If he could live just in this room, he'd be okay. But he could not.

Tristan undressed quickly, threw his T-shirt and sweatpants and briefs in the hamper and selected new ones from his drawers. He dressed and stepped into the hall. For a moment he allowed himself to pause, to press his ear against the cool painted surface of his mother's hollow door. An almost imperceptible sifting of sheets.

He crept downstairs and into the kitchen. He was hungry. There was a carton of organic orange juice in the refrigerator door. He tipped its mashed cardboard spout to his lips and was braced by its coolness, its tart, bright taste. Licking the last drops from the corners of his mouth, he set the empty carton on the counter. He found a Pop-Tart in the bread bin and ate it over the sink in four quick, crumbling bites.

The one-car garage was a cool, gray cave just off the kitchen. The car sat outside, while boxes and bins cluttered the dim space, plastic toys and scooters that Tristan had never much liked. Dust tickled his throat, making him cough. When he stopped, he listened for footsteps; none came.

Tristan found his bicycle and rolled it to a strip of empty floor. Kneeling beside the red metal frame, he examined it. The chain had fallen off the gear. He looped his finger under the chain and fit it onto the circle of metal teeth, rotated the pedals and watched it whir.

He stood. Grease stained his fingers. He couldn't risk going in the house again, so he swiped his thighs, leaving dark stripes like war paint on the yellow. Dutifully he picked up his helmet, which seemed to scream at him with its glossy neon plastic, and squeezed it over his head, taking the usual moment to tuck the tips of his ears uncomfortably inside, and snapped the nylon strap under his chin. Then he remembered. He didn't have to wear it.

He unstrapped the helmet and tossed it aside. Leaving the automatic door closed, he wheeled his bike out the side door and along a narrow, graveled alley to the street.

He pedaled under the wide arms of sycamore and maple trees, their leaves shaggy and bright against gray fog, their broad trunks draped with moss. He turned and rode along the empty street to the entrance of Valley Middle School. The large, modular building—its windows blackout, its siding painted penitentiary gray—sat on an ancient landfill at the edge of the Pickleweed Inlet and Bothin Marsh.

He kept riding: beyond the school's front entrance was Bayfront Park, where they ran the mile in PE, although Tristan himself had been spared this particular horror by virtue of weak knees and an indomitable mother. He'd spent hours on the splintered park bench, filling out worksheets on the rules of basketball or the tenets of weightlifting as he watched Calista Broderick cheat the course, disappearing into the willow trees with Ryan Harbinger. Ryan, who had made it his mission to prove that Tristan was unfit for this world. Calista, the girl with the magical name, an alien-princess name, and a distant look that sometimes crossed her imperfectly pretty face; Calista, the girl who he had sensed, or hoped, was like himself—*with* that Ryan-Abigail group but not *of* them—although he now saw how absurd that hope had been.

The air grew colder and damp as Tristan drew nearer the water. With no helmet, he felt the moist breezes whip over his scalp. He liked it. He steered onto the bike path that cut through Bothin Marsh. Before him stretched an expanse of green brush that turned to reddish reeds, and the water shone like mirrored glass. There were the echoing shrieks of gulls, the honks of pelicans. White egrets balanced on thin black legs among the reeds, stretched serpentine necks to watch him as he passed. Glancing over his shoulder, he saw the teal rise of Mount Tamalpais, its profile the body of the mythic Sleeping Lady, its shoulders shrouded in gently shifting fog, and the valley nestled beneath it. He could appreciate the beauty of this place now, without a hint of pain or sadness, because in his mind he had already done it: he had already made the decision. This was why he'd slept so soundly the night before, why he'd woken determined and hopeful. For the first time in a long time, he'd felt power in his muscles and focus in his mind, had felt compelled to climb onto that bike and ride.

He pedaled on. The bike path circled wide and slid under the Richardson Bay Bridge, a flat, unspectacular span that stretched over the water on concrete grates. On the other side, he took the road to Sausalito. As cars paraded by, he kept to the path between the water and the road. At a stoplight a woman in a pearl Mercedes looked out and glared at him, and for a moment he feared he would be stopped, found out—but then she tapped her head and shook her finger at him, and he remembered about his helmet. He shrugged. The light turned, and the car pulled ahead.

He biked on. This was farther than he had ridden possibly ever, and his bottom was sore on the hard, hook-nosed seat and his legs were growing tired. The sun was burning through the fog, and even without the oppressive squeeze of helmet, his head was hot and wet, salty sweat dripping down his temples and eye sockets and into his eyes and mouth. He squeezed the rubber handlebars for strength. Passed apartments that crouched on stilts over the water. Finally, parched and heaving, he saw the Golden Gate Market and slowed, craving the sweet ice of a cherry-cola Slurpee on his tongue. But his pockets were empty.

He rode on. The road began to wind uphill. To the left was a battered metal guardrail and to the right were houses, so many houses, crowded as teeth, fighting for a view of that water. Tristan's lungs tightened, his heart beat a galloping rhythm in his chest as the road slanted upward, and he was forced to slide off his bike and walk, leaning on the handlebars, the rubber hot now and slippery with sweat, to push the weight of both himself and the bike up the terrible slope. The pavement rolled beneath his wheel, glittering with glass and drifted garbage, debris of accidents already forgotten. To keep himself going, he tried a series of distractions. He thought of all the U.S. presidents in order. The prime numbers, starting with two. The times tables. The countries of Africa. Then Europe. The wars. The wiggle of shapes on the maps in his history textbook, with dark arrows of armies moving back and forth across.

An hour had passed and he was almost there. He got back on the bike and rode into the yellow-grassed hills. At a fork in the road he veered right. A green road sign pointed him forward: SAN FRANCISCO. When, finally, he reached Highway 101, the cars and buses blew by him in a noisome, furious rush. It was 7:45 a.m., and the working parents of Mill Valley were on their way to offices downtown. His mother, too, must be awake by now.

Turning to his left, he saw the red-orange spires of the Golden Gate Bridge, like masts of an enormous ship, like skyscrapers of an alien nation, like ladders to the sky. His heart beat frantically in his ears. Yet for the first time in a long time, he felt like he could breathe.

He got on his bike and skimmed along the path that sloped downward to the bridge. On the left side was the pathway for pedestrians, a narrow lane guarded by rust-colored bars to the height of his shoulders. He stepped off his bike and leaned it against the rail, not bothering to lock it. It was early yet for tourists, but there were some: mothers gazing over the water with sundresses whipped around their knees; fathers hiding behind large, expensive-looking cameras; kids running back and forth between their parents' legs, or trying to poke their small faces between the bars of the guardrail and failing.

You had to go over, that was the thing.

Tristan knew this because he had studied. He'd learned everything there was to learn about the Golden Gate. For example:

The bridge was 8,981 feet long.

Until 1965 it had boasted the longest main span of any suspension bridge in the world, at 4,200 feet.

It was made of concrete and steel and painted a color called International Orange, which enhanced its visibility in fog.

Its weight was supported by giant cables, each cable made of 27,572 strands of wire.

It was held together by approximately 1,200,000 rivets.

It was 746 feet above the water.

Cally's father read the newspaper story aloud. Tristan Bloch, age thirteen, had gone to the Golden Gate Bridge and jumped.

He'd left his bike against the rail, leaning where the tourists came to pose for pictures.

Tristan's mother came to school to gather his things. She drifted through the halls, slack, rudderless.

In the eighth-grade pod, Cally pretended to search her locker while Mrs. Bloch worked herself up to opening Tristan's. Ms. Flax and Principal Falk and the janitor clustered around her, murmuring. What could they possibly be telling her? There was nothing they could have done. They couldn't have made Tristan less awkward or strange, or stopped him from writing that note and sending his heart into the world for everyone to cut a piece of. Couldn't have stopped Cally from giving the note to Abigail and Ryan Harbinger. After Tristan had jumped, Ryan and Damon Flintov had been suspended for a week, Abigail and a few others for three days each. Cally had been questioned, but she and Tristan weren't even Facebook friends; technically speaking, she'd done nothing wrong. So now she was supposed to go back to class, copy science labs and cheat on algebra tests as though nothing had happened.

Tristan's mother fell against the locker, pressed her forehead to the metal. Ms. Flax palmed circles over her broad back and murmured something that Cally, stepping closer, barely heard: "Gloria, we don't have to do this now. We can wait, as much time as you need."

Cally knew she should leave, hide, but she couldn't. From down the row of lockers, Ms. Flax noticed her and glared. The teacher must have understood the truth: that this was Cally's fault and no one else's.

Finally Tristan's mother stepped back and the janitor clipped the lock with bolt cutters; the hollow clang made Cally gasp as if it were her own dark heart being cut. She stopped herself from crying out. It seemed wrong to go through someone's locker, even if they were dead. She expected Tristan to trudge around the corner and shout at them to get out, which, after all, would have been his right.

Tristan's mother opened the locker, and as the adults peered in to assess its secrets, a rush of origami cranes, red and blue and green and gold and silver, paper wings rustling, tumbled forth and floated to the floor.

"It's just a bunch of paper," the janitor said. He and Principal Falk looked at each other and then at Tristan's mother, as if waiting for an explanation.

"Calista Broderick," Ms. Flax said flatly. "Shouldn't you be in class?"

Cally had come too close. Words dried up in her throat like leaves.

"Well? What are you waiting for?" said Ms. Flax.

Cally knew that she was going to be found out, Ms. Flax was going to expose her—but then again, that would be a kind of blessing. She stepped closer to Tristan's mother. "Mrs. Bloch? I just wanted to say. I'm sorry."

Clutching a silver crane, Tristan's mother gazed back at her. Her eyes, small and watery blue like Tristan's, asked, Who was this girl, what was this effusion of beautiful paper, what did any of it mean?

The newspaper said that Tristan had left no note.

"Calista," Tristan's mother said. "Yes. Tristan mentioned you. You were a friend to him—he never said it, exactly, but I could tell." She smiled. The sudden light in her face was strange and hard to look at. Did she not realize that Cally was the girl Tristan had written to? Did she not care? "Thank you," she said.

What Cally felt then was more than guilt or sadness. It was like the pleasure-pain that Abigail had shown her, a connection that cut you and thrilled you, a sharp, exquisite opening.

She smiled back at Tristan's mother. And understood:

She thought he had a friend.

Junior Year

Even in January, the classroom was crowded, clamorous, and hot. Sunlight pulsed through tall arched windows at the back, intensifying the stew of smells—pencil shavings, whiteboard marker, old food and young bodies. Teenagers filled five rows of five desks each. The first row was populated, unsurprisingly, by girls. To Molly Nicoll, they betrayed no hints of the awkward vulnerability, the blushing, blemished, essential discomfort with self, that had plagued her own teenage years: rather, they slouched in their seats, dangled legs over chair-arms like gymnasts, and typed into their phones with agile, furious thumbs. They wore tasteful makeup, and blouses with skinny jeans, or logoed fleece jackets and yoga pants. Their eyes flashed up at Molly, questioning whether she had anything remotely interesting to offer—and judging, presumably, that she did not, they returned to their small screens. Behind these girls was the co-ed hubbub of the middle rows, and in the back were boys—with sideswept hair and polo shirts and boat shoes, or buzz cuts and hoodies and giant, gaudy sneakers—who talked or yelled or threw small objects back and forth or stared out the windows or slept. They were juniors, six or seven years younger than Molly herself—a gulf of time and experience that seemed suddenly impassable.

Nevertheless, from the front of her new classroom she addressed them, waving her arm in the manner of a desperate hitchhiker:

"Hi, everyone! Hello? Can we quiet down, please?"

The students hushed and looked her way, and she felt a swell of tenderness toward them—*They listened! They liked her!* And yet she was unnerved. Her own teachers had given her theory and pedagogy, heuristics and state standards. They had not told her how to stand before these privileged, unfamiliar faces, feeling in her tight blazer and wool trousers as foreign and enormous as she had when she was a teenager herself.

She was twenty-three years old, recently graduated and newly credentialed, and until a week ago had never lived anywhere but her father's cramped, two-bedroom ranch house on the outskirts of Fresno, in the nowhere place between beige strip mall and brown farmland.

"My name is Miss Nicoll," she began, glad that she'd rehearsed. "I'm really excited to meet you. I understand your teacher had to leave kind of suddenly. That must have been hard for you guys." The students did not blink. She pressed on. "We'll pick up where Ms. Frank left off. We're going to look at great works of American literature, and discuss some social and historical themes that these works explore. I'm looking forward to hearing your ideas in class and reading the essays you'll write at home. And if you ever have any questions or concerns, I hope you'll talk to me. My classroom door is always open." As if to prove this openness, Molly beamed a smile around the room.

It was impossible to tell how much of her message, if any, was reaching the students. But they seemed, if not inspired, willing to go where she would take them, and for that she was grateful. She ran through the roll quickly, remembering what names she could, then uncapped a pen and wrote in large, looping letters across the whiteboard: *The American Dream*.

"What is the American Dream?" she asked them. "What do American authors have to say about it? And what does it mean to us today? These are the questions we're going to explore."

The front row nodded; the others stared. Several girls took out sheets of lined paper and wrote *The American Dream* across the top, then looked up at her for more. Finally a hand crept up in the front row. Its owner, Amelia, had rapidly blinking eyes and a frown of bangs over her forehead.

"Yes?" Molly asked hopefully.

Amelia looked at her phone and recited, "The American Dream refers to the equal opportunity for every American to achieve success through ingenuity and hard work."

Molly had been warned about this: apparently the modern teenager preferred to live outside of knowledge, or to skim along its edges by way of Wikipedia, Yahoo Answers, and the basic Google search. She nodded. "Okay, yes. Thanks. Can we put the phones away for a minute? What I want to know is, what does it mean to *you*?" Again they said nothing, merely shifted in their seats. "What are some things that one would aspire to achieve or attain?"

"Good grades?" guessed a girl in the front.

"A Lambo?" asked a boy in the second row.

"Maybe a personal assistant?" another girl offered. "Who follows you around all the time and, like, does stuff for you?"

"A private jet!" called a back-row boy, and another sang out: *"Fly like a G6!"*

The class laughed, the room relaxed. Molly said, "So we're thinking of lots of material things. That's interesting. How about a safe home? A rewarding career?"

"Obviously," said Amelia.

"Now, do you think every American has the *opportunity* to have these things?"

"If they get a job," said a boy in the middle.

"Well . . ." Molly had been trained not to lecture her students, but to use the Socratic approach, questioning them until they reached true insights on their own. In theory this approach was noble; in practice it was a little exhilarating and a little terrifying, like steering her subcompact through a storm. "What kinds of jobs are available to most people?"

"Whatever kind," Amelia said with a shrug. "If you want something, you just have to go for it."

"I don't know what Ima do, but I'll be successful at it," a back-row boy called out, apropos of nothing.

"I'm gonna be a lawyer," said another. "They make bank."

"You know you have to know how to read to get that job, right?"

"Ha-ha. Shut up, chach."

"Okay, that's enough." Molly took a breath and began again. "We seem to be a little unsure about the state of the American Dream today. That's fine. That's good! Let's continue thinking about this as we look at Fitzgerald's critique of the Dream in his era. You all have your *Gatsby*s, right?" Before more could be said, she split the students into groups and asked them to locate a relevant passage in chapter one. Soon the classroom hummed with conversations, the front-row girls tugging the rest along. It felt like a minor miracle. Engaged with the literature, the students must have been feeling what Molly had felt in the rare unlonely moments of her childhood: when discussing *Gatsby* in an English class, or reading *Jane Eyre* by flashlight, the gears of her life would click into place, the lock release, and she would be revealed, simply and wholly herself. But after five minutes, the groups began to dissolve—books were down, phones were out, boys were stabbing one another with pencil ends. She quieted them.

"Now, I need one person from each group to tell us about the ideas you've come up with. Who'd like to go first?"

At the front of the room, a girl raised her hand and stood up. She was skinny and short, with a governess face (narrow, gray-eyed) and a gorgeous riot of black curls.

"Yes, thank you?" Molly said.

"Abigail."

"Thank you, Abigail. What did you guys come up with?"

Abigail explained that she'd finished reading the book over winter break and so was prepared to speak beyond the first chapter. Before Molly could stop her, the girl launched into a monologue explaining the problematic revisioning of the American Dream in the twentieth century as related to the parties at Gatsby's mansion. She spoke with the uninspired authority of a SparkNotes entry, projecting dutifully to the room in a voice that never wavered or changed in pitch, pointing out precisely the passages that any English teacher would have chosen, making exactly the arguments that any college English major would make. Her own group members watched her, impressed and perplexed by all the ideas they'd supposedly discussed. The rest of the class clutched their iPhones resentfully or rested their chins on their fists.

At last Molly had to interrupt her: "Excellent, Abigail. Thank you so much. Why don't I read one of those passages out loud, so we can all see what you're saying about the rise of materialism?"

Abigail shrugged and returned to her seat. The room exhaled. At the whiteboard, Molly opened her book and began to read. She loved to read aloud, the way the words, pronounced, surrounded and sheltered her:

> "By seven o'clock the orchestra has arrived, no thin five-piece affair, but a whole pitful of oboes and trombones and saxophones and viols and cornets and piccolos, and low and high drums. The last swimmers have come in from the beach now and are dressing upstairs; the cars from New York are parked five deep in the drive, and already the halls and salons and verandas are gaudy with primary colors, and hair shorn in strange new ways, and shawls beyond the dreams of Castile. The bar is in full swing, and floating rounds of cocktails permeate the garden outside, until the air is alive with chatter and laughter, and casual innuendo and introductions forgotten on the spot, and enthusiastic meetings between women who never knew each other's names."

She was deep into the rhythms of the language, almost forgetting the twenty-five kids who were watching her, when the banging began. Startled, she paused, then continued more forcefully, but the banging grew louder, and soon threatened to overtake the cheerful timbre of her voice.

In the back row, a pale, burly boy was kicking the leg of his desk. He wore an oversized T-shirt of cherry red and a matching flat-brimmed cap. His eyes were wide and the blue of bathwater; a silver stud gleamed above each eyebrow; his thick lips curled in a sneer. It was the absolute worst possible scenario that the offending noise should come from him.

"What's that tapping?" Molly said finally.

Instantly—it felt instant—the banging was louder. Relentless.

"Can whoever's doing that please stop?" she asked.

He did not stop.

She was gearing up to confront him—day one was too soon for an enemy, especially an enemy like him—when Abigail set down her *Gatsby* and spun to the back of the room. "God, Damon, would you shut the fuck up? What is wrong with you?"

"The fuck is wrong with *you*?" the boy hurled back.

Energy stirred in the room, the excitement palpable, and now a second boy, Ryan something, jumped eagerly into the fray. "Yeah, Abi-*gail*," he said, his tone twisting her pretty name into an insult, "why do you gotta be such a bitch?" He and Damon laughed together, in a hard, unbridled way.

"Fuck you both," Abigail said calmly, and picked up her iPhone with all the graceful disdain of a French film star palming a cigarette.

Molly shouldn't have allowed foul language in class—*Maintain at all times a learning environment of positive language and mutual respect*. But in truth she admired the girl. She raised her hand. "Hey, guys? Can we all calm down, please, and watch our language?"

This failed to impress Abigail, who rolled her eyes and continued to text. Damon and Ryan smirked in satisfaction, and the rest of the class turned reluctantly back to their books. Molly pressed on with the lesson. When she dared to look at Damon once more, he was disemboweling a red Swingline stapler. He glared at her. She had the sense he might spring forward to stab or staple her where she stood, and her toes curled painfully inside her tight and pointed heels.

This was when she noticed the girl who'd been sitting beside him all along. She was the only girl in the back row. She looked like a lost soul from Haight-Ashbury: wavy hair, placid face, gauzy top, cutoff jeans. Her feet were flip-flopped. Her desk was bare but for a single book spread open. The book was too thin to be *Gatsby*. Molly guessed it was poetry, something appealing to teenage girls. Dickinson? Plath? The girl was reading, fingering the pages. This simple act made Molly smile—here, finally, was something to relate to, a familiar gesture in a foreign land.

• • •

Valley High was prettier than public school had any right to be: it resembled a small university, with various halls all stuccoed Creamsicle-orange, generously windowed, and radiantly trimmed. Out front, iron gates embellished with scrollwork cordoned a manicured lawn from the street. At the center of campus, the clock tower—a century old, timelessly tasteful, with art deco numerals and narrow arched windows—posed against the cerulean sky.

This was Mill Valley, which *Smithsonian* magazine had recently declared the Fourth Best Small Town in America. The town itself—fewer than five square miles nestled below Mount Tamalpais and Muir Woods—had been a vacation destination for elite San Franciscans at the turn of the twentieth century and a haven for hippies after the Summer of Love. In 1970 it was made famous by its theme song, "Mill Valley (That's My Home)." Performed by Rita Abrams, a pigtailed, orange-muumuued schoolteacher, and her fourth-grade class, the song was recorded by a local producer and played on the radio nationwide. As Abrams's song chirpily described, Mill Valley's beauty was extravagant. The town was endowed with not only green mountains and gold hillsides, but also redwood forests, canyon waterfalls, wetland preserves, the Pacific Ocean, and the San Francisco Bay. And people paid for this extravagance—by 2013 the average home price had soared well north of a million dollars. It felt worlds away from Fresno, from whence Molly had fled the moment she was offered the sudden, mid-year position at Valley High.

The faculty lounge turned out to be an arena of cliques not unlike the cafeterias of Molly's youth. There were the advisers to the much-lauded drama program, who huddled together to plan their student shows. There were the would-be science fiction writers, who sat around a table in their short-sleeved dress shirts and black jeans, conversing in their own pop-cultural code. There were the older, tenured teachers who cruised in and out just to check their mail, never making eye contact lest they be asked to join a committee; in their own minds they were already retired.

The room itself smelled of bag lunches. Fluorescent lights buzzed overhead. Three large windows overlooked the front lawn, but their blinds were tilted to block most of the sunlight and slice the view of students walking by. There were laminate tables, molded plastic chairs, a droning refrigerator, and a crumb-speckled microwave. In one corner, a kind of faux living room had been arranged, with an aged armchair and abused vinyl sofa, a lunar scar where its cushion had been gashed and sewn. Wooden mail cubbies lined one wall, and wedged beside them was the copy machine, where at lunch on the Friday of her first week Molly stood making handouts for Monday's class.

She was midway through her copy run when the machine jammed. As her colleagues looked on, she commenced the humiliating dance of pushing buttons and clattering drawers. She was ready to unplug the machine from the wall when she was nudged aside by a woman with sculpted blond hair and boot-cut jeans whose pockets sparkled with dark glitter. Without looking at Molly, she pressed two buttons, opened a tray, pulled out the paper, pressed a third button, and set the copier humming once more.

"Thanks," Molly said over the noise of the machine. "I hate these things."

"You mustn't let it see you scared," the woman replied. Her eyes were very blue and her blouse very white, and her skin had the tanned, rind-like quality of a regular marathon runner. She stuck out her hand. "Gwen Thruwey. Advanced Algebra, Calculus AB."

"Molly Nicoll."

"You're English, right?"

"I've got three sections of American Lit."

Gwen nodded as though this merely confirmed what she'd read in Molly's file. "Must be nice. I'm doing four sections of Advanced Algebra plus the one of Calculus *and* running the crew program. Why I say yes to these things, I'll never know."

"Wow. You must be exhausted."

Gwen gave her a smile. "You don't know the half of it."

The next moment, Molly found herself in the unprecedented position of sitting beside the most popular person at the lunchroom's most popular table.

"Everyone, this is Molly Nicoll," Gwen announced. "She's the English person taking over for Jane Frank. Nice of Jane to up and quit on us smack-dab in the middle of the school year."

"Hello," Molly said.

Gwen's disciples were Jeannie Flugel, a salon blonde who taught World Cultures and Contemporary Social Issues; Allen Francher, a barrel-chested, unilingual lacrosse coach who'd been coerced into teaching French and Spanish 1; and Kristin Steviano, an Integrated Science teacher who looked like she'd just stepped off the Pacific Coast Trail, wearing a vaguely ethnic sweater and hiking shorts, although it was winter.

"You know how Jane left, right?" Jeannie said conspiratorially. "In the middle of first period, she bursts into tears, then runs straight to Katie Norton and says she's never going back into that room. She never thought she could hate a child, but they made her do it, she said. They *made* her hate them."

"I don't know if I could hate my kids," Allen Francher said, "but then again, if I were hit by a bus, they'd probably be thrilled."

"I can't believe that's true," Molly said.

"You wouldn't believe a lot of what goes on around here."

"What's that saying?" Gwen asked. "The inmates are running the institution?"

Everyone laughed, so Molly did too. Kristin turned to her and shrugged. "Welcome to our weird little world."

After several moments of conjecturing about Jane Frank—maybe she was clinically unbalanced; maybe her students had made fun of her mustache—the teachers moved on to discuss a reality TV show Molly hadn't seen. What she gleaned from their conversation was that some contestants on the show appeared to be genuine and sweet, while others were competing "for the wrong reasons."

"Just look at Alana H.," Allen said. "It's obvious she's only in it for the fame."

"She treats it like some kind of game."

"Well, he's not going to choose her. He couldn't. He loves the other one."

"Just wait," Gwen said. "She'll get him into the fantasy suite, and *true love* will go right out the window."

"But no one really falls in love on those shows," Molly cut in. "I mean, how could you? You'd have to be insane."

No one responded. In the uneasy silence that fell over the table, Molly's colleagues exchanged glances.

"About Alana H.," Jeannie said, turning toward Gwen. "Did you hear, just last year she was trying to get a hosting job on *Access Hollywood*? There's an audition tape going around online."

"Well," Gwen said, "that proves it."

In this way, almost indiscernibly, the conversation moved forward without Molly in it. Molly felt herself shrinking, a figure on the platform as the train pulled away. The feeling was familiar. In elementary and middle school she'd been largely invisible. In an effort to be seen, she'd shown up to ninth grade with a new pixie haircut, a bold disaster: with her too-large eyes and too-wide nose, she had looked like an unpretty boy. For months afterward, wherever she went in her high school she'd heard giggling, whispering, directed at the newly bare nape of her neck. And she'd realized there was something worse than being ignored; there was being a target. By senior year, she'd grown her hair out, learned to walk with her head down, and made herself invisible again.

Molly's colleagues fell silent. A new teacher had entered the lounge. The woman glided rather than walked, with chin slightly raised. Salt-and-pepper hair was cut squarely at her chin. She wore a midnight-blue sheath dress and brightly patterned silk scarf, and carried a slim leather folder that did not appear to have anything in it. Molly had glimpsed her before, settled on an outdoor bench with a salad and a book of Alice Munro short stories, as relaxed as if reclining on a beach.

She stopped at the copy machine, over which Molly's papers were strewn, and turned to ask the room, "Who belongs to these?"

Molly stood up. "Sorry, let me take care of that."

"Beth, this is Molly Nicoll, our new English teacher," Gwen called out from her seat. "She's replaced Jane Frank. You remember the Jane disaster."

"Do I?" the woman asked.

Gwen smiled tightly. "Molly," she said, "this is Beth Firestein. She directs our AP English program."

"It's great to meet you," Molly said. She hurried over to Beth Firestein and offered her hand.

Beth was petite, although she didn't seem so. Straight bangs framed a heart-shaped face with features that were small and finely drawn: dark eyes winged by crow's-feet, delicate ears, and a serious mouth. Her handshake was firm and dry. Molly noticed that her fingernails were manicured, shell pink, impeccable.

"You are a fan of Lawrence," Beth said coolly. Her eyes were on the handouts Molly had made—Lawrence's "Give Her a Pattern," an essay she intended to use as a launching point to discuss Gatsby and Daisy and the romantic ideal.

"Oh, yes."

"Conrad says that the novels of D. H. Lawrence are nothing but obscenities and filth."

Molly hesitated, gathering her papers. Finally she said, "If depicting women as real human beings is obscene, then I guess he is. But I think he's wonderful. No one, except maybe Woolf, wrote more beautiful sentences."

"Yes," Beth said, nodding. "You are right about that."

Molly beamed. Not since college graduation had her literary opinions been sought out and approved of.

Beth withdrew a sheet of paper from her leather folder and began her copy run. "How are you settling in?"

"All right, thanks. I had some trouble setting up my email account, but that's the only glitch so far."

"Oh, I don't do email."

"Aren't we required to? In case our students need to get in touch with us?"

Beth waved Molly's question away; the question was a fly that annoyed her. She pulled another paper from her folder and placed it on the tray. "Where did you say that you studied?"

"Fresno State," Molly answered. "Where I grew up."

"And the Fresno schools aren't hiring?"

"I needed to try out a different place. I mean, I needed to be different."

Beth did not answer. As the machine hummed, spit out papers, she squared off the copies and slid them into her leather folder. Molly hugged her own bale of papers to her chest. She saw she had been too honest, revealed too much, as she always seemed to do.

Finally Beth said, "It's only geography, dear."

Molly nodded respectfully at this, but inside she bristled. If a person's life could not change—if a person could not change—then what was the point of it all? Maybe Beth, admirable as she was, had been worn down by years of service, had grown complacent. Maybe Molly would remind her what was possible.

In the following weeks, Molly woke each day at six-thirty, arrived at school by seven-fifteen, checked her mailbox in the faculty lounge, made copies, and opened her classroom before the students arrived. She tested her lessons on her Period One class, which had become her favorite by virtue of being her first; she told many jokes that didn't go over and a few that did; she paced madly in front of the whiteboard with the purple marker in her grip (like that line she loved from Eliot, "a madman shakes a dead geranium"); she scribbled. After her lectures she split the kids into discussion groups and then circled the room, weaving around the desks, pausing to rest a hand on a student's shoulder, to lean down and listen in, to throw a question or opinion into the mix. At times she felt she and her kids were truly connecting: at times she felt they were understanding not just the books they were meant to be reading but Molly's own secret heart, and she wanted to weep with joy. Just as often, there was defeat. There were times Molly heard herself lecturing about a passage, her voice sliding from authoritative to appreciative to rhapsodic, saw the smirks on the kids' faces and felt as if she'd read her diary out loud. There were kids, like Abigail Cress, who seemed to have no love for learning yet badgered her constantly for A's. There were kids, like Damon Flintov, who never, ever did their homework, no matter how many extensions she granted. There were kids, like Amelia Frye, who texted all through class, and believed her blind enough not to notice or callous enough not to care. Sometimes a student (Ryan Harbinger) would actually fall asleep, and Molly would feel responsible for having bored him, and also hate him and then hate herself for hating him. There were moments when all was calm and quiet, kids reading at their desks, and then the class would dissolve in laughter and she'd have absolutely no clue why. These moments would haunt her lonely weekends, would wake her in the silence of her studio apartment in the middle of the night. In some ways, her students knew so much more than she did, possessed vast, secret stores of information, codes and connections, that she felt helpless to understand. When she circled the room, she'd peer over their shoulders at the phones in their palms, catching flashes of photos and texts. What were they doing? she wondered. What lives were they living on those little screens?

She spent the breaks cleaning up her classroom and listening to students' excuses for the homework they did poorly or not at all, or traversing the campus on invented errands, mostly avoiding the faculty lounge. She ate lunch while marking papers at her desk, stayed after school to hear more excuses and requests, then hurried to the conference room for the various meetings to which she was called. Finally, at five or six in the evening, she drove home to resume what was without question the worst part of her job: the Sisyphean tasks of grading and emailing. After dinner of salad or soup at her kitchen counter, she graded assignments and quizzes for an hour or two, then logged in on the district-provided laptop to answer emails from her students and, more often, their parents, tutors, and educational consultants.

Generally speaking, the parents were displeased. Their missives ranged from the mildly threatening to the openly incensed. They were annoyed about the homework—she gave too much or the wrong kind, or the directions were unclear or the deadlines were unreasonable. They were angry she'd forgotten which of her students had Individualized Education Plans and academic accommodations, and more than happy to send her their privately obtained, highly detailed psych reports and to educate her about the district's legal obligations. They were uniformly certain that their kids deserved high grades:

> Hello Molly,
>
> My son Wyatt tells me you are new to town and to
> teaching. I'm sure it's the same in Fresno but here

we expect our students to perform at a certain level. If you have any questions please ASK, I like to be very involved with my son's education.

Good luck.

Tessa Schuyler-Sanchez

Dear Ms. Nicoll,

I'm not trying to tell you how to do your job but this homework is really out of line. Three chapters in one week??? You know these kids have other classes too. Please be reasonable!!! Also I see my son Ryan Harbinger received a C+ on the reading response that he wrote for you about color themes in The Great Gatsby. He put a lot of time and effort into that assignment, and he is DEEPLY upset and heartbroken about the grade. I know you will reconsider.

Cordially,

Ellen Harbinger

dear miss nicoll

just wanted to let you know jonas will be unable to complete the essay due on friday as he has a very important game coming up for baseball and this will take all of his focus this week. jonas is a very gifted kid i'm sure you can see that and i'm sure you will understand and give him a pass on this. thx.

kevin everett

Her students, too, sent rambling emails that they never seemed to proofread:

Hey Miss Nicoll,

Sorry I don't get this homework are we supposed to just free write about what we think or do we have to use quotes from the book? And if you said 3 pages does that really mean 3 or if we do 2 and a half is that OK because that's really all I have to say? Or do you want me to add a bunch of random stuff in their to make it three?

Also I was absent on Friday b/c I had to go skiing in Tahoe with my family, did I miss anything?

Sincerely,
Steph Malcolm-Swann <3

When Molly had exhausted her patience for emails, she returned to grading, then reviewed her lesson plans for the following morning, when the whole routine would start again. She became accustomed to falling asleep with a pen in her hand, and slept without dreaming.

Molly was locking her room for lunch one day when she felt a strange hand cradling her elbow. She turned to find Doug Ellison, who taught government in the classroom next to hers. They had nodded to each other from across the hall but never spoken, and he seemed an enigmatic figure, avoiding other teachers, remaining with kids in his room during the lunches and breaks. He was probably ten years older than Molly, slender and slope-shouldered with thinning strawberry-blond hair. He seemed kind; she'd noticed him standing at his classroom door at the start of every period, greeting his students one by one.

"Miss Nicoll, I presume? Doug Ellison."

"Molly. Nice to meet you finally." She offered her hand.

He took it. "I hope you didn't dress up for my benefit."

Blushing, she glanced down at her outfit—a sage-colored sweater, pencil skirt, nylons, and heels. She shrugged. "I can see you didn't dress up for mine."

Doug chuckled and hitched his jeans, which were held up by a frayed and braided leather belt. "Well played."

She smiled too. Then he asked her to join him for lunch.

It was a friendship she hadn't expected but was happy to fall into. Soon they were eating together most days, at his desk or hers, sharing the sandwiches and sodas and potato chips they toted in brown paper bags, a habit they'd both carried over from their own school days, while almost every one of their students bought lunch off-campus. She found that she liked him. He was someone of whom Bobbi, her father's elderly secretary, would have said, "Bless his heart, he means well." Despite his lame jokes and flirtations, Molly thought Doug Ellison did mean well. She liked how he shook his students' hands before class, and the easy way he joked with them, even the awkward ones, in the hallway during break. She liked that he seemed, like her, to care more about kids than test scores, and more about fiction than friends.

Soon they moved from commiserating about their work to talking about their lives. She told him that her father, who operated a small construction business out of their garage, had wanted Molly to stay home forever, to help run the business once she was, as he put it, "done with school"—as though her education were merely a tiresome childhood phase. She told him how every time she stepped into her father's office and wove her way through dusty piles of his things, her lungs would start to close. How she'd calm herself by curling in a cracked vinyl chair and hiding inside the story of someone somewhere else. "Sitting around with her head in a book," her father used to complain to Bobbi when Molly was right there beside her, thinking, *If my mother had known how to do this, she wouldn't have needed to leave.*

Doug told her that he was from the Central Valley too, the small town of Visalia. His mom was a teacher; his dad was a cop. His two older brothers were amateur wrestlers, or believed themselves to be, and when they were kids their favorite ritual was to wait until the smaller, weaker Doug had fallen asleep, then attack: while one held down his arms, he told her, the other would sit on his head, and he would lie helpless against the barrage of fists and knees and elbows—it was frankly impressive the way they would manage it, flattening him to the mattress and keeping him quiet while they pummeled his body and their parents slept soundly in their room down the hall. He'd learned, eventually, to prop a chair under his door handle, and to hide his favorite novels in the laundry hamper, lest his brothers find them and rip out their pages for sport. As a teenager, he'd found refuge at school, staying late to run track and edit the newspaper and practice the trombone, and when he'd earned a full-ride scholarship to Berkeley it had been as if the low, mold-speckled ceiling of his life had cracked open and sunlight had poured down. At Berkeley he had been happier than ever before or since. He'd majored in English, completing an honors thesis on the failure of the masculine ideal in *The Sun Also Rises* that was widely admired among his professors. Molly saw the value in Hemingway, she told him, but preferred the British modernists— Joyce, Lawrence, Woolf. Their novels were so mournful and musical; when she read, she felt the prose vibrating her body like song. She expected Doug would laugh at this confession, but he didn't.

He and his wife, Lacey, had recently separated—a secret, he said, that almost no one knew. He'd met her in a seminar the spring of his senior year, and married her six months after graduation. "She was the most beautiful girl I'd ever been with, and she loved me, and I didn't want her to leave me, so I asked," he said. "I remember feeling life was blowing by like a tornado and I needed to grab hold of something, anything I could. Our families came, we had a live band, a big cake, the whole nine. At the end of the night, I vomited in the bushes. That was the first time I disappointed her, definitely not the last." Molly was amazed by how easily he opened up to her, the unflattering depths he was willing to plumb. She saw that his failed marriage was a tender subject that he still found hard to talk about, and she liked that he trusted her enough to tell her this. Most of all, she liked that the two of them could avoid the faculty-lounge cliques together and tell themselves it was a choice.

THE LOVERS

At seventeen, Abigail Cress knew she wasn't beautiful. She wasn't modelesque Elisabeth Avarine, trailed down Miller Avenue by grown men in Lexus sedans. She wasn't even ordinary-pretty like Cally Broderick, her former best friend. Although black hair fell in glossy curls over Abigail's shoulders, beneath it were small gray eyes and a thin sharp face and a nose that would have been too big on a boy. In her track uniform—a red sports bra stretched flat across her chest and silky blue shorts that ballooned around her hips—her body was skinny and hard as a coin.

She believed unprettiness was something to atone for, so she made herself an A student, track captain, president of the Valley High chapter of the National Organization for Women, editor of the yearbook. She enrolled in Mr. Ellison's class to prep for the June SAT, and on weekends wrote out careful, color-coded flashcards for the vocabulary words she didn't know. She believed high school was easy: you just did the work. She believed love was bullshit, teenage boys idiotic. She made plans: Dartmouth for college, or another competitive school on the East Coast, where she believed she would fit in better than she ever could in Mill Valley, California. Where her life would click into focus and her unprettiness transform to specialness, or glamour.

She shopped. Bluefly.com, Piperlime, Nordstrom, Saks. Her parents paid her credit card bill each month without comment. She accumulated stuff she didn't even want. James Perse T-shirts ($65 each) and J Brand skinny jeans ($169). Tory Burch "Aaden" ballerina flats ($250). A Marc Jacobs "Eugenie" quilted-leather clutch ($495). She'd once spent $500 on black satin lingerie from Agent Provocateur just to see if they'd notice; while waiting for the package to arrive, she'd drifted to sleep each night to the image of her bedroom door bursting open in a flurry of outrage, her father's gray suit rumpled, her mother's black hair frizzed. But they'd never said a word about it. Her best friend, Emma Fleed, had seen it hanging in the closet with the tags still on and made such a big deal about it, Abigail had told her to take it all.

She was grateful for Mr. Ellison: thirty-two years old, tall, with sloped shoulders and a barely noticeable paunch over his belt. When he taught, he wore striped dress shirts, Gap jeans, and a braided leather belt that had started to fray but held some special meaning for him—Abigail teased him about it once, offering to buy him a new one from Michael Kors or Ferragamo, and he pouted until she changed the subject. He wore square-rimmed glasses over his hazel eyes. His hair was strawberry-blond and thin and his face clean-shaven. There were little nicks of blood around his jawline and neck. His teeth were straight, his fingers freckled and strong. He had a degree in English literature from Berkeley, which was a hard school to get into, and his favorite book was *A Confederacy of Dunces,* written by some guy who'd killed himself before the book was published and won the Pulitzer Prize. Mr. Ellison talked about this story often, seeming to cling to it in a way that made no sense to her.

He was the yearbook adviser. He edited her write-up of the drama program, and she liked to watch as he scrolled red pen across the page, striking through lazy phrases, lassoing commas that had no place.

She liked to watch him pace around the yearbook room in the afternoon light. The walls were cream, and the ancient windows, arched and warped, sealed them in a golden heat. The building, Stone Hall, was over a hundred years old and always smelled like something baking. It was her favorite place.

Mr. Ellison asked for her number at the beginning of junior year, in case important yearbook issues arose.

In September and October, their texts were strictly business: *When is football article due??* and *Editorial mtg Tues 3pm.*

Their dialogue evolved gently, slowly. By November: *What r u up to?* She'd text, *In pjs in bed still studying,* just enough to make a picture in his mind. By January he'd begun to text her deeper questions:

> What do you care about?

> > I don't know. Grades I guess. College. Beating my
> > sprint time. Making the best yearbook ever!!

> Is that your answer?

> > > What do u mean?

> I don't believe you. I think there is more.

> > > Maybe . . . do u rly want to know?

> What do you want?

> > > Why r u asking?

> What have you never told anyone else?

> > > I don't know.

> Tell me.

> > Ok. Here's something. I've always hated summer.
> > Since I was a kid. I'm already dreading it.

> I thought kids were supposed to love the summer?
> No homework, slip-n-slide, hot dogs, &etc.

> > Exactly. All year there's hw and tests and so much
> > to do u can't even think, then one day a bell rings
> > and it's like stop everything, go outside, here's this
> > piece of plastic and some nasty boiled meat on a
> > bun, time to have FUN!

> I'm not sure I understand. I want to.

There's too much time. U just float around in it like
a speck. Sleep in. Hang out. Watch tv. Go online.
Go to the beach. Get burned. Eat shitty fast food u
don't even like. What's the point?

Is that what you do? Or, what do *you* do with all
that time?

                                    Nothing . . . think.

:) What do you think about?

                          U don't really care abt this do u?

I care about you.

It's stupid. Just . . . Is there something more to me
than all this stuff I've been given? What if there's
                                                    not?

Talk to me, he wrote. Tell me a secret.

One afternoon in early February, Mr. Ellison took Abigail into the
clock tower to research a yearbook article about the school's history.
Students weren't allowed up there, but she was an exception.

He unlocked the door and guided her through the dusty dark to a
steep wooden staircase. She began to climb, cobwebs clinging to her
wrists and hair. She coughed. Mr. Ellison followed, his breathing heavy
in the close space.

Finally she climbed out onto splintered floorboards, blinking in the
sudden light. The belfry was a small, square room with arched windows that had looked dollhouse-sized from the ground but now revealed themselves to be enormous. It no longer held actual bells; to
mark the hours, the secretary played a recording of bell-like sounds
that had been donated by the class of 1978.

Mr. Ellison emerged behind her, and bent to catch his breath. After
several uncomfortable seconds he straightened and smiled at Abigail,
wiped the sweat from his forehead with the back of his arm.

"I can see why people don't come up here much," he said.

"Yeah," she agreed, pulling a sticky string of cobweb from her hair. But she was interested. She began to circle the room, running her hand over the scribbled yellow walls. Paint flaked and powdered in her palm. The walls said:

THE OPPOSITE OF LOVE IS NOT HATE BUT IN-DIFFERENCE.

DEFY THE LAWS OF TRADITION.

DROP ACID NOT BOMBS.

It was afternoon, and sunlight slanted through the windows. Directly below them, on the school's gated front lawn, kids sat cross-legged on the grass or sprawled dramatically across one another's laps. They looked like toys. The sun made their skin gleam like plastic; their backpacks were comically small. Above them, and farther out, were rooftops, treetops, an azure sky that softened and blanched as it stretched past the Bothin Marsh and over the bay to San Francisco. The city's white and ash-gray towers shadowed to slate against the sky. At the waterfront, the rectangles of the Embarcadero Center skyscrapers, where her parents worked—her mother managing stock portfolios on the thirty-second floor and her father trading futures on the thirty-eighth—stood clearly against the horizon, but she couldn't make out the details of windows or stories or lights.

Mr. Ellison moved behind her, reaching over her shoulder to point to the city. His body pressed heat against her back. "Isn't it strange," he said, "how close it is and yet how far away?"

"We can see the world," she said, "we're just not allowed to touch it."

"You're allowed to do anything you want to do," he told her.

She smiled. At the same time terror licked up her spine and made her neck begin to sweat beneath her hair. She wanted to turn and look at him, but didn't.

Outside, a bird's small head bulleted toward them—thudded against the window. Abigail shrieked and jumped. Mr. Ellison steadied a hand on her hip. The bird reeled back and disappeared.

Heart pounding, Abigail peered out the window to see where it had gone—was there any chance it lived? She shouldn't have cared, and yet she did, intensely. Pressing her cheek to the sun-warmed glass, she saw it, a pigeon, lying side-splayed on the roof like something sleeping. Its gray eyes glossed open. Its belly shaded by the protective fold of a wing. Abigail flinched. Turned away from the window, and into Mr. Ellison's arms.

She pressed herself against him, her cheek to his chest. His cotton dress shirt lay soft against her skin. He smelled unexpectedly like sandalwood, and she realized that he had anticipated this moment—in his bathroom that morning, he'd stepped towel-wrapped from the steaming shower, shaved his face, swiped deodorant through the hair under his arms like it was any other day, but in the last instant he had paused, thought of this moment, her, Abigail, and dabbed his neck and wrists with this cologne.

When she craned her neck to see him, he smiled a gentle, closed-mouth smile. Tucked her head back down and vised his arms around her. His heart was kicking at her ear. It was a human heart. It was not a teacher. It did not know or care about the yearbook or the SAT. It belonged to her.

Through the rest of the winter, their problem was simple: they had nowhere to go. His apartment was off-limits. He had a wife—Abigail had seen her pacing the aisles of Mill Valley Market—with smooth, nut-colored hair and high cheekbones, a ballet neck and a Pilates body. She would wander around with nothing in her basket but a jar of organic lingonberry preserves and a square of dark chocolate, as though the abundance of actual food overwhelmed her. Abigail wanted to feel bad for Mrs. Ellison, she seemed so sad and lost, but she was too beautiful to sympathize with.

Because there was no place for them in town, Abigail and Mr. Ellison began to take drives together. He picked her up behind the Dumpsters at Starbucks and drove her up Mount Tamalpais toward Stinson Beach or Bolinas Ridge. They parked on the desolate edges of cliffs or in groves of eucalyptus that shuddered in the fog. They touched hands, and talked. They talked forever. He opened her with questions, eased his way in. Until one day she made the move. So for the rest of their relationship they would be able to say that she'd started it.

He was her first. They did it in the cramped backseat of his hatchback or took a picnic blanket from the trunk and lay down in the car's grassy shadow. She was always on top, his hands clamped around her hips. She liked to see his face, his grateful silence and closed eyes, and then to lean down and press her cheek against his neck and feel the throb of a pulse that needed only her. In the same moment, she liked to imagine herself pulling away from him, fleeing, and all the pretty things he'd say to call her back. She stayed, arched back, and told him that she loved him. He said he loved her too, collapsing his hand inside her dark nestle of hair, gripping until it pulled the skin from her skull and releasing, kissing the tip of her ear. Her ears were beautiful, he told her, small and white as shells, which she'd always known was true, but which no one else had ever noticed.

They traded fantasies. He would quit his job and follow her to college, perhaps enroll himself, go for a Ph.D. as he had always planned to do; she would forget college and live with him instead, learning to cook and to iron, making his apartment her whole world.

He loved her. She knew he had a wife, but thought that was just one of the names we put on people. She had a brother she hadn't talked to in six months, and parents she wasn't sure were in or out of town. Only she and Mr. Ellison were real.

One afternoon in mid-March, Abigail and Mr. Ellison sat side by side at a computer in the yearbook room, editing a fall sports layout. They crossed pinkies over the mouse, and then, for one second forgetting what their love story would look like to the rest of the world or that the rest of the world even existed, she kissed him.

They parted, and Abigail turned to see Cally Broderick, her former best friend, standing in the doorway. Cally stared for a moment, then fled.

Abigail found her in the girls' bathroom. Unlike the remodeled sections of the school, this room showed its hundred years, with walls of dull white tile and floors of scuffed linoleum. A chemical stench overwhelmed the smells of human beings. A mirror, slashed by lipstick and black marker, stretched the length of four porcelain sinks smeared with yellow soap. There was one frosted, crosshatched window painted shut. On the far wall hung a battered metal tampon dispenser that, as far as Abigail knew, no Valley High girl had ever deigned to touch. Beside it, an ancient hand dryer, turned on and abandoned, roared air into the empty space, then exhausted itself. Two stall doors were open; a third was shut.

In a clatter of metal Cally emerged from the closed stall and, without looking at Abigail, walked to a sink and turned her hands under the water.

Abigail went to the sink beside Cally's. In the mirror Abigail's eyes looked charcoal under the fluorescent lights, her skin aged and gray.

"You can't tell anyone," she said over the stream of water. Her voice echoed off the tile, and she glanced over her shoulder. "Seriously."

Cally stared back. Her wide-set hazel eyes were glossy and pink, and Abigail thought not for the first time that this was not the same girl that she'd loved in eighth grade. They'd gone to different elementary schools but met in sixth-grade homeroom, and for a period of two years and nine months they were inseparable. They'd spend hours in Abigail's bedroom, sometimes with Emma Fleed, eating junk food or sneaking her older brother's beer or painting each other's toenails or watching YouTube videos or Facebooking or curling up together on her bed and combing fingers through each other's hair and laughing and laughing and laughing about nothing at all. When Abigail allowed herself to think about this time, she knew it was the happiest she'd ever been. Emma was Abigail's best friend now, and Abigail loved her but not in the same way. Everyone knew that Emma was more devoted to dance—she was training for Juilliard or someplace like it—than to any friendship.

In the months after what happened in eighth grade, Cally had stopped coming to Abigail's after school. In high school, she'd started to call herself Calista. She'd let her hair grow to her waist; the tips faded from honey brown to blond, and the ends split. Instead of wearing designer clothes that they'd shopped for together, Cally would come to school in ripped jeans and peasant tops from the Salvation Army, or flowery dresses with men's vests and shoes. On sunny days she often wore no shoes at all. These changes had made Cally cooler to some people—her new friends were Alessandra Ryding and the Bo-Stin slackers, hippies' kids who were bused to Valley High from Bolinas or Stinson Beach—but as far as Abigail was concerned, Cally had transformed herself into an alien.

Cally shut off the faucet and shook the water from her hands. "He's *old*," she said.

"He's thirty-two."

"He's our *teacher*."

"He's different."

"Are you having *sex* with him?"

Abigail was silent.

"What is he, like, a child molester?" Cally said. "What's wrong with him that he can't find someone his own age?"

Abigail pushed aside the disconcerting thought, and what it implied—that there was something wrong with her. She said, "You don't have to be so fucking judgmental."

"You're fucking seventeen years old."

"So are you," Abigail said.

"*I'm* not fucking an old, child-molester teacher who can't find someone his own age." Cally turned and punched the hand dryer to life, and they waited through the white noise without speaking. What was there to say? Would Cally keep quiet if she understood what Mr. Ellison meant to Abigail? How their relationship wasn't what it seemed? There was the messy business of sex, yes—there was Abigail's shame the first time Mr. Ellison discovered her open and wet, and the sticky embarrassment of condoms, how she'd hidden her face in her hands as he ripped open the package and shielded himself, how he had pushed into her body and she'd bitten her lip till it bled, how even now, when they made love, she had to ride the wave of pain until it crested to pleasure, and how sometimes, if he was too hurried or she too distracted, it never did, and she felt him come with a dry awareness that disturbed them both—there was all of this, yes, but all of this was not the point. There was something greater holding them together, some force that seemed to shift each time she tried to name it.

As the hand dryer faded to silence, Cally crossed to the door. With her palm on the handle, she turned. "He's married, right?" she said. "Doesn't that bother you, like, at all?"

"He loves me," Abigail insisted. "Love is love." These were Mr. Ellison's words, and she hated how they sounded when she said them: generic, babyish.

"Seriously?" Cally said. And she left Abigail alone.

By April, Abigail was haunted by the fear that Cally Broderick had exposed them. Conversations seemed to halt when she entered the girls' bathroom—but she could have been imagining this. Kids whispered to each other when she entered Mr. Ellison's SAT class after school—but they could have been talking about anything. In Miss Nicoll's class, Ryan Harbinger and Nick Brickston would smirk at her, but then they'd always enjoyed antagonizing her. Cally—*Calista*—continued to avoid her altogether, because she was guilty for spreading rumors, or angry about their fight, or stoned. As Miss Nicoll read aloud in first-period English, Abigail would stare down the cover of her *Gatsby*—the starry blue, the leonine eye—and turn the question over in her mind. On the one hand, Cally had no loyalty or love for Abigail, their best-friendship having ended years before; on the other, it seemed unlike Cally to spread rumors out of malice, especially after the way she'd fallen to pieces over Tristan Bloch. No, Abigail decided, Cally wouldn't tell. She wouldn't dare.

Then Nick Brickston posted the picture on Instagram.

Nick had been in the Gifted track with Abigail through elementary and middle school—she suspected he was smarter than she, although his insistence on treating school as one long practical joke made it impossible to know for sure. Regardless, his Photoshop skills were unimpeachable. In the picture, Mr. Ellison's head, cut from a yearbook staff photo, topped the naked statue of David; Abigail, cut from a track-and-field action shot in sports bra and shorts, ran toward him, her outstretched hand cupping his crotch. Nick had faded the Frankensteined photo to an even black-and-white, neutralized the background, shaved the space around each of Abigail's fingers so they melded seamlessly into the stone flesh of the David. It looked uncannily real. Even Mr. Ellison's face—eyes blinked shut, grin wide open—projected an ecstatic release that Abigail recognized.

She replied with a comment: *You guys are so fucking IMMATURE.*

"We have to deal with this, Abigail. This Instagram thing. What are we going to do about it?"

"Nick Brickston is an asshole."

"But have you—I mean, is there any way he really knows?"

"I haven't been texting him my deepest secrets, if that's what you mean."

"Please calm down. I'm only asking."

"I am fucking calm," she said, and hugged her ribs. For a moment they were quiet, staring at the dark road ahead.

It was Friday night. Abigail had met Mr. Ellison at the Dumpsters behind Starbucks, and he'd driven them up to Mount Tamalpais State Park and parked his black hatchback on the dirt shoulder of the highway.

They were past the city limits. Here, houses were distanced by acres. Hikers found shelter when the sun set. There were no streetlamps, just the road that twisted through the mountain's curves and deer that skittered across the road in threes and telephone poles that leaned into the sky. Redwood and oak and madrone trees were black masses hovering at the edges of the road. Below them, Mill Valley twinkled blithely, the soft darkness of greenery punctuated by the bright lights of people at home. Like her parents, who were already sleeping, living as they did by New York hours. Her friends who were doing homework, or not. The San Francisco Bay was a slick strip between the valley and the city; the moon dipped its silver trail over the water. But the mountain was black.

Headlights veered into the dark car, and Mr. Ellison shoved her toward the floor. "Whoopsy daisy," he said.

"What the fuck, Mr. Ellison?" But she was yelling into cheap upholstery that stank of polyester and Corn Nuts. She'd suggested he get a new car, one with working heat and air and soft, dove-gray leather seats like her own Mercedes E-Class, but he had only laughed.

Now his fingers tightened on her skull. "Don't call me that, remember?"

"Sorry," she said. "Doug." The word was ugly in her mouth; it reminded her of the pumpkin-colored freckles on his scalp that she'd noticed one night and had been trying not to see again.

"All clear," he told her, and tugged her up by her hair.

"Ouch," she said. "Jesus."

He smiled. In the dark it was just a shape shifting on his face. "I didn't really hurt you, did I?"

She turned to look out her window, but she was not on the view side and the road fell to blackness below.

After a moment she said, "My friends think I'm hooking up with this loser from Redwood I can't even stand."

"What do you tell them?"

"That my parents got me an SAT tutor and he, like, comes to my house every Friday night to quiz me. It's the dumbest lie ever, I can't really blame them for not believing." She tugged at her shorts; the nylon of her track uniform clung uncomfortably to her thighs.

"You should study for the test," he said. "It's important."

"Oh, are you going to tell me what's important now?"

"Abigail. Sweetheart. It's just that I've been through all this already. You can benefit from my experience."

"Whatever," she said. Her phone buzzed and she pulled it from her backpack. On the screen was a text from Emma:

> Wut up beez. get ur ass up, im done w/dance class
> and im comming ovr!! xox

"When I was in high school, we didn't have cell phones," Mr. Ellison said wistfully. "We didn't even have email. If you wanted to talk to your friend, you had to call their house and ask for them."

"That sounds really fucking depressing," she said, typing into her phone. "Emma wants to know what's up. She wants to come over to my house."

"What are you telling her?" he asked, his voice pitching upward so he sounded less and less like Mr. Ellison, more and more like Doug.

"I told her I'm sitting in a car in the dark with you and we just made out and you pulled my hair, and next we're going to climb into the backseat and fuck like bunnies. Oh, and studying SAT words."

"Please be serious. I don't think you begin to understand the ramifications of this."

"Ramifications," she echoed. "That's one."

"It means consequences."

"No shit."

"I wish you wouldn't swear."

She rolled her eyes.

"You understand why you can't talk to your friends about us. We discussed this."

"I *know*," she said.

"They think you're just like them. They don't want to think about how far beyond them you already are. And to your parents, you'll always be a little girl."

"Yeah, right," she said, and was quiet. "I *have* been studying, you know. I'm not an idiot."

"I believe you."

"No, really. Quiz me."

"Abby. I don't want to—"

"Just do it. I'll start. *Unconscionable.* Unrestrained by conscience. Unreasonable. Excessive."

He smiled. *"Egregious."*

"Egregious. Awful, terrible. Outstandingly bad."

"Good," he said. *"Ubiquitous."*

"Too easy. *Ubiquitous.* Being everywhere at the same time."

"Or appearing to be. Yes. Excellent."

"Now you," she said. *"Ephemeral."*

"Ephemeral," he echoed. "Transitory, or fleeting. *Evanescent."*

"Vanishing from sight or memory. Short-lived. *Convergence."*

He set his hand on her knee.

"Hedonistic," she said. *"Aesthetic. Intrepid. Perfidious. Parched."* He was Mr. Ellison again and she was kissing the words against his ear.

He pulled away from her. "What about your friend Calista? How do you know she hasn't told?"

"She's not my friend," Abigail said, although in the bathroom she had thought, for a moment, maybe—

"Well then," Mr. Ellison said, "probably she has."

Abigail shook her head. "She's not an idiot. She knows what would happen if she did."

"What would happen to us, you mean. You have to talk to her."

"You don't have to freak the fuck out."

"Don't you realize what the school will do to me if they find out? Or don't you care?"

When Abigail was silent, he went on. He said maybe she wanted the whole school to find out, maybe she didn't love him as he loved her, maybe all this time she'd been planning to destroy him.

She squeezed his hand over the gearshift and without warning he began to cry. Little strangled sobs. If this was all out in the open, he said, it would be the weight of the world off his shoulders. But if Abigail left him, he would have to jump off the Golden Gate Bridge.

When she told him how fucked up that was, he said he didn't mean it. "I'm such an idiot," he told her. "I don't know what I'm doing. I don't know what I thought my life was going to be. . . ."

Abigail tried to listen, but in her palm her phone flashed with new texts from Emma, a rapid succession:

> U dont answer ur phone??
> OK im comming ovr anyway . . .
> Dude where R U?!?

"I don't deserve you," Mr. Ellison said. "You should leave me. Forget I ever existed."

Abigail set the phone in her lap. She lifted his hand and pressed her lips to his palm and the palm to her breast.

"No," she said. "I love you. I don't love anything as much as you."

He seemed to calm then, and smiled as they kissed. But something shifted—for a few terrifying seconds she could not feel anything at all, and he was just another human body that was much too close to hers.

When her phone buzzed again, she pulled away and stared into the glowing screen.

OK fine, Emma's text said. L8r.

Abigail started to text back, but Mr. Ellison took the phone from her hand. He said, "You know, if they find out, it's my life that's going to be ruined."

She knew what he meant: divorce, unemployment, lawsuits, prison. Yet his statement felt unfair, even untrue. She felt there was much more for her to lose, and told him so, although when he challenged this, she stared into his hard eyes and had nothing to say.

When Mr. Ellison dropped Abigail at Starbucks later that night, he suggested they avoid each other until the rumors died down. At school she'd steer clear of his classroom except when absolutely necessary; they wouldn't be seen flirting in the yearbook room or laughing in the hall. On weekends their lives would revert to what they'd once been. For her this meant weeknights and Sundays spent alone in her room, doing homework and eating takeout from D'Angelo's and Sushi Ran, Saturdays shopping and going to parties with her friends. She went along with this scheme because she wanted to protect them both. But after only a week, she was called to Principal Norton's office.

The room was small, a cubby on the ground floor of Stone Hall. It had the same yeasty smell that permeated the entire building, but here the odor mixed with the faint perfume of the fuchsia roses that Ms. Norton had scattered in hopeful bursts around the room. Ms. Norton had cropped auburn hair, warm brown eyes, a pixie nose, and mauve lipstick that might have been fashionable in 1995. Behind her wide birch desk she gave off, even to Abigail, the impression of a little girl playing Office. She was small, in a red skirt suit and low-heeled black pumps that looked like Naturalizers or some equally revolting brand advertised with words like "affordable" and "comfortable." As she beamed at Abigail, waiting to begin the official business of the meeting, she levered her heels in and out of the pumps beneath the desk.

Abigail liked Ms. Norton and pitied her, given all she had to deal with at that school—crazy parents like Dave Chu's who thought their mediocre son was God's gift, juvenile delinquents like Damon Flintov who were always one bored afternoon away from setting the teachers' lounge on fire. But now she perched awkwardly in one of three chairs opposite Ms. Norton's, heart pounding in her chest as she gave the vaguest possible answers to the principal's inane questions about her AP classes and the upcoming SAT. Never in her life had Abigail been summoned to the principal's office—but she knew why she was there now.

On the desk, Ms. Norton's iMac was turned toward Abigail, cocked at an angle that allowed her to distract herself with scrolling photographs of the principal's other life, that is to say her actual life. There were family photos in which she was, astoundingly, not the mother but the daughter, and Abigail realized she had no idea how old Ms. Norton actually was. She could be Mr. Ellison's age, or closer to twenty-six or forty. In the photos, she sat in the shadows of two silver-haired parents, their hands on her shoulders, and then swam alone in a black one-piece, face obscured by a snorkeling mask, thighs abstracted in sapphire water. She posed in a strapless wedding dress, shoulders bared and a peacock-feather fascinator in her hair, its delicate white netting draped over her face as she smiled with mouth wide open, as if shocked by her own capacity for joy. These photos disturbed and unsettled Abigail. She had once run into Ms. Norton at the Mill Valley Health Club and felt actual physical discomfort, a twisting in her stomach, at the sight of the principal's body in spandex shorts and sports bra, her belly crunching on the sweat-slicked mat. Abigail saw the irony in this revulsion, given her own situation, but the rules that governed student-teacher relationships were meant for other people, not for her.

Ms. Shriver, the secretary, opened the door behind Abigail. "The parents have had to drive in from the city," she said. "They're running late." Some deranged helicopter set was swooping in to handle their kid's latest hiccup, Abigail thought.

As the secretary shut the door, Ms. Norton sighed. She tapped her fingernails on the desk. "Well, it looks like we'll have to get started just the two of us."

"Wait, *my* parents are coming?" Abigail said. "Are you serious?"

Fear surged through her, and yet the corners of her mouth were twitching up. The idea of not one but both of her parents leaving work in the middle of the trading day, extracting their cars from the parking garage and driving out of the Embarcadero, over the Golden Gate Bridge, and back into Mill Valley in order to meet with sweet Ms. Norton in this pathetic little office was so farfetched that the whole situation began to feel hilarious.

"Quite serious," Ms. Norton said. "Abigail, I'm afraid there's something we need to address."

Abigail tried to focus on Ms. Norton's face—she was usually excellent with administrators, appearing quietly respectful yet alert.

Ms. Norton pulled a sheet of paper from a desk drawer. After a second's hesitation she laid it face-up on the desk. "Will you tell me what you know about this?"

Abigail caught her breath. It was a printout of the Photoshop picture Nick Brickston had posted on Instagram—Mr. Ellison as the naked David, herself as the girl with her hand on his crotch. "Where did you get that?" she asked. The account was supposed to be private.

"I know this is difficult," Ms. Norton said. "You are such an excellent student, mature, clearheaded. Before proceeding with anything, well, public, I wanted to hear it from you. I feel we can speak as adults, Abby. I believe you will be truthful with me."

As Ms. Norton spoke, she looked so distraught that Abigail did feel like the adult in the room—as if it were her job to protect Ms. Norton from the world's harsh truths and not the other way around. "Sure," she said.

"What is the nature of your relationship with Mr. Ellison?"

Abigail stared back into Ms. Norton's eyes. But her mind went elsewhere, parsing the question the way she'd learned to parse reading comprehension questions on the SAT. The key word was "nature," meaning *character, type, temper, or the vast force that regulated everything in the physical world*. That was it—a vast force had caught Abigail and Mr. Ellison, controlled them from the start.

Ms. Norton sighed. "Look, I shouldn't tell you this. But I feel you need to know."

"What?"

"Unfortunately, this isn't the first time we've heard these kinds of rumors about Mr. Ellison. Nothing definitive, nothing has ever been proven. But if you are keeping secrets, if you are trying to protect him . . ." Her words hung in the air, and Abigail tried to make sense of them. Nothing had been *proven*? What had been alleged?

The office door opened and Abigail's mother rushed into the room, her Ferragamo heels clicking furiously over the linoleum. She wore a sleek black suit and a Bluetooth headset that latched like an insect to the side of her face.

"You're still not hearing me," she said. "How many times do I have to go over this with you? Is it possible for a human animal to be more clear?" Then she clicked off the headset and tucked herself into the chair next to Abigail's, brushing invisible lint from her skirt. "Hello, sweetheart," she said, "Principal Norton. Please, tell me everything I've missed." As she adjusted her hair, Ms. Norton slid Nick Brickston's picture back into the drawer.

Abigail's father entered next. He wore his usual charcoal suit with a starched dress shirt and the Burberry tie Abigail had bought him for his birthday last June. With one thumb he texted into an iPhone that gleamed darkly in his palm.

"Sorry I'm late, jam-packed day," he said. He took the chair on the other side of Abigail, patted her knee. "So what are we doing here? That secretary wouldn't tell me anything." He pressed a button on his iPhone and laid it ceremoniously on the desk.

Abigail focused straight ahead, on Ms. Norton, who leaned forward in her chair as if to confide a secret. *Nothing definitive. Not the first time.*

"We are prepared to launch a full-scale investigation," she said. "But I wanted to hear from Abigail first. To discern what is fact and what is fiction."

Abigail's parents turned and stared at Abigail like she was one of those picture puzzles at the Exploratorium, narrowing their eyes to see the hidden shape within.

"Investigate what?" her dad asked.

Ms. Norton stared at Abigail as if trying to unpeel her. "Has Mr. Ellison crossed the line with you, Abigail? You really must be truthful with us. Has he taken advantage?"

Abigail gripped the sides of her chair. She didn't know what to say, but it didn't matter because in that instant her parents accosted her from both sides.

"What does she mean, honey?"

"Which one is Mr. Ellison?"

"Abby-girl, what is she talking about? Did somebody hurt you?" Her father's voice lowered and gentled. His small gray eyes mirrored her own and she wanted to say yes. She wanted to fold herself into his lap as she had not done since she was six and feel the power of his arms and his money and his ability to sue. She wanted to cry like a baby and tell him, *Yes, it was all his fault. That horrible man. That teacher. And please hold me and love me and remember that I was your girl first.*

Instead she lied. "I don't know what you're talking about."

Ms. Norton cocked her head. "Abigail, are you sure?"

Her father's phone buzzed and shuddered on the desk and he made no move to answer it.

"Mr. Ellison is my teacher. That's it," Abigail said. "Plus he's, like, super old. You actually think I would *do* something with him? I mean, talk about gross." As she spoke, she hated herself for how the words sounded—the ditzy singsong of the syllables. She was thankful Mr. Ellison wasn't there to hear it.

Abigail's father exhaled. He reached over and squeezed her palm, a gesture meant probably to reassure her but which seemed to reassure himself: Abigail was the same predictable, reasonable daughter he'd always known. She was still a girl, not a woman, judgment sound and body undiscovered, whose desires—a collection of objects, pretty things—were easily paid for and contained. He wouldn't have to think of her in any other way.

He released her hand. "Principal Norton, my daughter always tells the truth. I think we're done here." He plucked his iPhone from the desk, and both he and Abigail's mother stood up. Abigail stood too.

Ms. Norton nodded. She got up and walked around the desk and opened the office door to show them out. "Well," she said, hesitating with one hand on the doorknob, staring at Abigail. "Thank you for coming in. I'm sorry to have taken your time."

Abigail's father was turning something over in his head. He said, "You know, Ms. Norton, I have lost half the workday, as has my wife"—Abigail's mother nodded in solidarity—"but that's fine. I don't care about that. I'm just not sure what you were thinking here. Pulling my daughter out of class, accusing her? Like she's some kind of juvenile delinquent?"

Ms. Norton closed the door again. She steepled her palms. "Mr. Cress, no one is accusing—"

"Where is this teacher, anyway? I'm just wondering. Why don't you drag *him* in here for questioning?"

"I have spoken to Mr. Ellison."

"And what does he say for himself?"

"His statements align with Abigail's."

"He denies it?"

"Yes."

"I want to talk to him."

"I don't think that would be a wise course of action at this time—"

"I don't see why not. I'm here already."

Ms. Norton looked miserable, out of her depth; Abigail almost felt sorry for her. "I'm sorry, Mr. Cress. If Abigail said nothing happened, if she is telling us the truth—"

"Of course she's telling the truth," Abigail's mother said. "Do you know our daughter at all? She doesn't even care to date boys her own age. The fact that she even has to *hear* about something like this—"

"Get your things, Abigail, we're going," her father said, and opened the door himself.

Ms. Norton trailed them to the hallway, prattling uselessly. "Let's no one leave angry," she said. "I feel we should pause for a moment, reflect . . ." Abigail couldn't believe the principal was so naïve as to think everything would be so easy to fix, like "I Statements" were actual problem-solving strategies and not just the nonsense that the Conflict Mediation Club posted on its Facebook page.

Ignoring Ms. Norton, Abigail and her parents hurried down the hallway toward the exit. The fluorescents formed a tunnel of light.

Abigail's father's phone buzzed again, and this time he sped ahead to answer it.

Abigail's mother walked close beside her, pressing at the small of Abigail's back. They were silent except for the clicks of her mother's heels, which echoed through the hall. She wore the same Chanel perfume she'd worn forever; its jasmine mixed with the sharp scent of the damp silk blouse beneath her suit and Abigail could not remember the last time she'd been close enough to her mother's body to smell this smell.

Mr. Ellison's classroom was the fifth door on the left. Three doors from where they were. The door was open.

Abigail slowed her steps. She could run back to Ms. Norton's office, lead her parents down a different hall—but no, it was too late. Mr. Ellison's voice carried far. He was talking to someone—a boy. What was he saying?

As they came closer, she recognized the voice of Dave Chu. It sounded desperate.

Mr. Ellison was reassuring him about something. He was gentling his voice the way he used to do for her. And suddenly she hated Dave, who still got to be soothed by Mr. Ellison, who still got to believe in love and teachers the way that she did not.

When they reached the classroom, she stopped.

Seeing her, Mr. Ellison stood up behind his desk; his chair scraped the floor. He swallowed, his Adam's apple jumping in his throat. With arms by his sides, he clenched and unclenched one fist. It was the hand with his wedding ring, the silver titanium he'd let her weigh in her palm that first night in his car, to let her feel how light it was. How insubstantial. How he could slide it off and on and off again. Facing her in his blue striped shirt and jeans, his square-framed glasses and stupid braided belt, he was all the layers of the man she knew. He was Mr. Ellison and Doug and Mr. Ellison again.

She wanted to run to him, to claim him. She wanted him to claim her, to tell her parents all the wonderful things about her that they had never bothered to know, things she herself had not known, that she could be not only smart and self-sufficient but loving and kind and sweet—even, in the right light, beautiful.

But the main thing, the important part, was how he looked at her. The rash of shame on his cheeks. His worried brow. His fear. Not the fear of what might have happened to her, not the fear even of losing her, which he'd professed so many times, his freckled head rolling in her lap, but the fear of getting caught. And she understood, or rather felt, that everything Ms. Norton hinted at was true.

Love is love. What did it mean?

"Abigail?" he said, and his voice tore on the edge of her name. "Did you need something?"

"Abby?" her mother said. "Honey, who is this? Is this him?"

Abigail shook her head. Her brain strained to catalog, organize, everything he'd ever done or said. Real: When he pulled her hair, and the shivers down her body made her gasp. Not Real: When he told her, *You're the one I didn't realize I was waiting for. You're a miracle, Abby, you're mine.* Now his eyes begged her to leave and she told herself, *Nothing he has ever done or said to you, none of that happiness, was as true as this is.*

Her mother's phone rang and she stepped away to answer it.

Abigail stood in the doorway, weighing her power in the palm of her hand. It was the weight of a stone she could hurl at his head, watch it strike the thin skin at his temple, watch as he jolted and bled. He was right—she could ruin him.

What had Ms. Norton called it? *Taken advantage. Crossed the line.*

Yes, she had crossed over.

Several weeks into the semester, Molly sat in her apartment with a round of *Gatsby* essays on her knees and an exhausted red pen in her hand.

The apartment was in fact a converted toolshed attached to the circa-1910 Mill Valley home of Justin and Julie Smythe-Brower, a pair of corporate lawyers with three towheaded children under six. It had a separate entrance she reached like a burglar, following a trail of slate stepping-stones around the main house. Its ceiling was low and its walls paneled in a glossy maple, giving the studio a vibe both groovy and claustrophobic, like a 1970s ski cabin or Scandinavian sauna. The single window's glass was thick and warped; tawny spiders skittered over its sill. But she cherished it, because it faced onto a redwood grove, lush and dark—a view unattainable by even the most privileged people in the place where she was from.

Now, outside her window, the redwood grove had blackened and blurred. The fog dripped desultorily on her roof, pattering its wooden beams. She curled up in the corner of the love seat and draped her comforter around her shoulders. In a large house, on such a night, she might have felt her loneliness acutely, but the small apartment fit her perfectly. The family in the main house sent happy sounds across the yard, but these were almost imperceptible to her and not quite real, like a distant radio transmission.

Her students' essays disappointed her: mediocre efforts peppered with one or two competent, if soulless, endeavors; two or three unmitigated disasters; and three or four thinly disguised plagiarisms from the *Great Gatsby* entry on Wikipedia. (Couldn't they at least bother to change the font?) Where was the passion, the connection? How could they read a book like that and come away with nothing?

And yet: toward the bottom of the stack she found a paper that made her set her red pen down.

Calista Broderick
Period 1 English

Great Gatsby Essay

"I hate careless people." This is what Jordan Baker says to Nick when they are driving together. Careless, what does it mean? The dictionary says, "Not giving sufficient attention or thought to avoiding harm. As in, 'She had been careless and left the window open.'" The truth is, everyone is careless. In Mill Valley, most people leave their doors and windows unlocked all the time. No one thinks anything is going to happen. No one thinks at all.

Here is something that I think about.

Let's say your window's open on a cold, damp, foggy day and a strange man happens to be walking down your street. He's not even meaning to do anything, but he sees the sliver of open window and suddenly gets the idea, hey, there's a nice little space to worm into. Why not. Let's say he decides to open the window the rest of the way, then sucks in his stomach and slips inside. The house he's slipped into is warm and cozy and he wants to see more of it. Let's say he goes from the living room where there's no one to the kitchen where it smells like bacon. A mom is there, cooking breakfast. She has her back to him and she can't hear anything but the crackle of the bacon on the stove and the pan spitting hot grease on her hands that hurts in a way that she's used to. She cooks this breakfast every Sunday. Let's say her husband went out for bagels and her three kids are asleep in their rooms upstairs. They could sleep through a thunderstorm, or a 4.0 earthquake. (In fact, they have. They dream they're on sailboats, carnival rides.) Let's say the man is standing there in the kitchen, looking at this mom who has left the window open so carelessly, who has not "given sufficient attention or thought to avoiding harm." The man thinks, Nobody ever cooked bacon for me. The man thinks, Well I'm here now, there's a knife.

Let's say it wasn't actually the mom who left the window open. She isn't a careless person, she is a mother, always shutting cabinet doors behind the dad who leaves them open for people to bang their heads on, always double-checking locks behind the kids who think locks are something the mom invented to nag them about, because none of their friends ever lock their doors. They live in Mill Valley, and most of them have never been anywhere else except for St. Barts and the Seychelles and Hong Kong and Vail, on vacation. They think, All the bad and interesting things happen in the East Bay or The City. Nothing happens here.

Let's say it was the mom's youngest kid, a girl. The girl was so small and meek and unspecial you'd never think she'd do anything that mattered. Let's say the night before the man came, she was sitting by the open window, reading a poetry book. She liked to listen to the fog dripping through the trees, a sound that was softer than rain. She liked the fresh, minty smell of it—some of the trees were eucalyptus. On those nights with the fog in the valley everything outside smelled good, even the dirt on the ground. It smelled like things growing and she liked to be reminded of that, that even when the world was shit and she hated everyone in it, most of all herself, that there were still things growing, all the time, in the dirt beneath her feet. Let's say she fell asleep with her book splayed open on her chest, then woke up hours later and stumbled to bed. Let's say she left that window open, not all the way, but just enough.

When the mom is lying bloody on the kitchen floor and

her bright insides are staining the linoleum, when the man has been hauled off to prison to spend his life thinking about something he hadn't even known he'd do, when the dad has had to learn to shut the kitchen cabinets on his own, and when the kids have woken up on the third day without their mom, on the fourth and the fifth and the seventeenth day, the twenty-fifth and the thirty-seventh, and realized as if for the first time that she is never, never going to barge into their rooms to wake them up again—the question is, when all of this has happened and you're looking for someone to blame, who is it going to be?

The point of this paper is: Jordan Baker is right. I hate careless people too.

Calista's essay was not technically an essay. How could Molly impose on it a teacher's judgment or brand it with a grade? It was a missive tossed over the transom, or a secret sent through a chink in the stone wall between them, like promises whispered by Pyramus and Thisbe. The girl was trying to reach someone; the someone was Molly.

From the first day, when she'd seen her reading poetry rather than paying attention, Molly had guessed that there was something special in Calista Broderick. She was gratified to be proven right. Now that she knew, she could help Calista, mold her talent and encourage her interests, bring her books from the library and train her to organize her ideas into paragraphs, papers. She'd once read a report in *National Geographic* about the largest caves on Earth, in China, each so large that it was like its own world. Maybe Calista's mind—maybe Molly's own—was like this. An immense space, at once apart from the world and embedded within it, a secret place that was strange and dark and vast enough to make its own weather.

The story was metaphorical, had to be—murder simply wasn't done in Mill Valley. Maybe something else had happened to Calista's mom. Maybe Calista feared or, in the reckless destructiveness of teenage desire, wished it would.

Molly remembered this intensity of feeling. At sixteen she'd spent her days walking in circles, warm wind carrying dust over the sidewalk to rasp in her lashes, and with it the smell of the Central Valley, of sun-baked manure and smog. The houses on her street were stuccoed, pale as ghosts, alike except for the details meant to convey the illusion of personal taste—a square or curved front door, a pewter or copper light fixture, a trim of white or brown or cornflower blue. Around the community (for "community" was what they called it) wrapped a high cinder-block wall. There were so few colors there, no tall trees—as a teenager she'd felt alien and alone with her Bob Dylan T-shirts and her Doc Martens rip-offs and the claustrophobic rage that she could not explain to anyone, because her sister was little and her father was working and her mother was gone and there was no clear reason why she should be in any particular moment so furious, so bored.

The next day, Molly was sitting down at her desk for lunch when Calista floated past her open door in a white cotton dress and white woven sandals. She was alone.

"Calista?" Molly called. "Come in. I want to talk to you."

Calista hesitated. Molly understood. As a kid, she'd clung to door-ways too; she'd liked the safety they offered, the option of being nei-ther in nor out, neither here nor there. But then Calista came inside, and slid into a chair opposite Molly's. She wouldn't look at Molly, quite. She wouldn't commit to looking anywhere. Molly glanced back over her own shoulder but there was nothing—just the whiteboard, blank, with rectangles of fluorescent light reflecting off its surface.

"Your *Gatsby* paper," she said. "There were some interesting ideas in there, really compelling stuff."

"Really?" In Calista's face Molly detected a flicker of interest, or hope.

"Definitely. But the thing is, it was more a stream of consciousness than an essay. Did you realize that?"

Calista crossed her arms and gazed vaguely away. Molly saw the error she had made. She said carefully, "What happens in this story, is it something you worry about? Something happening to your mother?"

"What do you mean?" Calista said.

Molly paused. "You know, my mother left when I was twelve."

"You don't know where she is?"

"No," Molly said. This wasn't strictly true. Her mother had never stopped sending her emails and postcards, even misguided birthday gifts, from the various cities she passed through: L.A. and Portland and Austin and Vegas, Nashville and even New York. Molly accepted these scraps of love but sent nothing in return. And her mother continued to roam, hunting for something she'd probably never find. She wondered if it had been worth it.

"My mom almost died," Calista said suddenly. She reached out to skim her hand along the edge of the desk. "Breast cancer. I was in middle school. It was like, we kept waiting for her to die, but she just kept getting worse and worse. That's what no one tells you, how slow it is. It takes forever, and eventually you just want it to be over with, one way or the other."

Calista had never before uttered so many words in a row in Molly's presence. Molly's heart quickened; she stopped herself from reaching for the hand that trembled just slightly on the other side of the desk. "I'm so sorry, Calista. That must have been so hard on you."

Calista shrugged. "It's okay, she got better. It was weird, though. No one told me she was going to die, and no one told me she was going to live."

There was nothing to say to this, other than: "It must have been a great relief, to have everything back the way it was."

At that, Calista's eyes shifted into focus. Her irises were startling, stippled with gold. She said, in a voice that was cynical and strangely weary, weary of Molly, weary of all the adults in the world who could not, or would not, understand her, "Nothing ever goes back."

What did it mean? Molly wanted Calista to believe she'd been right to confide in her, to know that she saw her. But communicating with Calista Broderick was like shouting through a block of ice. If only Molly could find the right thing to say, she might break the ice and release the girl from herself. She set her elbows on the desk, leaned in. "You are such a perceptive, intelligent person, Calista. You could do anything you set your mind to, but I see you just floating along. Why not try?"

Calista looked down at her arm, where green marker spiraled over the skin like a tattoo gone rancid with time. Her hair, long and wavy, fell across her cheek and hid most of her face. "I don't know."

"You don't know?" Molly wanted to take the girl in her arms and soothe her, tell her she should know how lovely she was, how rare. She wanted to buy her a sweater, a copy of *The Awakening,* and a fortifying meal. She wanted to be a person in her life with the power to do any of these things. But she could think only of what her own father used to say to her when he found her incomprehensible: *Is that all you have to say for yourself?* Because she could not say this, she said nothing, and could only sit by, helpless, as the moment closed. They were back where they'd started: teacher and student, nothing more.

Molly had been teaching for six weeks when Damon Flintov vanished from her class. Principal Norton delivered the news in a hushed hallway encounter one morning in mid-February: the boy had some legal troubles and would not be returning for some time. Molly was not to discuss this situation with anyone. She was to move the class forward without him.

As soon as Molly walked into class that morning, she saw this command would be impossible to heed. Her kids launched straight into gossip.

"Drugs," Steph Malcolm-Swann announced. "They arrested him at some party."

"He's not arrested, he's in rehab," said Jonas Everett.

"Just because his dad made a deal with the judge," said Amelia Frye. "Otherwise, who knows."

"Lockdown for life," Wyatt Sanchez said mournfully.

"Real," said Steph.

"Oh my God, no one gets life in prison for drug possession," said Abigail Cress. "Plus he's a juvenile. Don't be retarded, you guys."

And suddenly they were competing for Molly's attention, sitting up in their desks, shouting over one another to share their rumors and theories, asking what she thought. She wasn't supposed to discuss it, and they were delaying the commencement of classwork, but she didn't mind. It was clear the kids knew far more about whatever had happened to Damon than she did. And there was a magic in it. Somehow the loss had forged a bond, and Molly felt the thrill of being one of them, if only for those twenty minutes, as interested as they in all the dirty details and as willing to be distracted.

It was only later, grading quizzes in her empty classroom after school, that she was brought down by a tugging sadness. It was strange: during the time that she had known him, Damon Flintov had consistently provoked and annoyed her. He'd tapped, he'd banged. He'd dismantled office supplies and drawn on desktops. During Silent Reading he would click his pen again and again, artillery fire, and when she asked him to stop, click on with heightened aggression. He'd plug in earbuds and play his music loud enough to send an angry, steady buzzing through the room. One day, out of nowhere, he jumped up, said, "Fuck this," and stomped into the hall. (Molly stood, baffled, in his wake.) On other days he showed up grinning but reeking of marijuana, gazing at her with bloodshot eyes—she was ashamed to admit that she preferred him this way. Now he was gone. His father's money might have saved him from a blemished record, but what had happened was more disturbing: the vanishing of Damon Flintov had been conducted with terrible swiftness and efficiency. His absence was a scandal to the kids, a relief to the adults. Molly herself was relieved. It was like Damon had been settled in a rowboat in the dark of night, pushed out to sea. Without him, his world went on. As Molly's world did, back home in Fresno, without her.

She communicated with her former life by way of her little sister, Lisa, with whom she Skyped once or twice a week, and who sent her emails that were at once intensely loving and vaguely threatening: a *Cosmo* article that directed young women to catch husbands early lest they end up thirty and alone, competing with the ceaseless parade of twenty-two-year-olds behind them; a fertility chart captioned only *Food for thought, xoxo*. These emails annoyed her—why did married-with-children people feel so compelled to pull her into their web?—yet she couldn't help wondering about the life she might have had if she'd stayed and given Josh, her college boyfriend, what he wanted: the Central Valley version of the life her landlords were living, brightly and blondly, just across her yard.

It was easier to think about Damon. What more could she do for the kid? A flock of bad ideas flew through her brain: write an email, phone his parents, find out where he'd been taken and show up there. She had enough sense not to make these mistakes. Instead, she invited Doug Ellison over for dinner.

Molly didn't see quite how small her studio apartment was until Doug Ellison was standing inside it. She offered beers; he hovered behind her as she bent to pull them from the mini-fridge. They went to the love seat. The room was intimately lit, and her bed asserted itself, making its presence known like an alpha male spreading his legs in a bar, as they sat together sipping beers.

Finally Molly turned to Doug and asked, "Have you ever had a student disappear?"

He laughed. "Wishful thinking."

"Be removed, I mean," she said. "Legal issues."

"Sure, why?"

"I'm not allowed to talk about it."

"Now, Molly. If we only did what we're allowed to do, would we ever have any fun?"

She rolled her eyes. "I keep thinking the strangest things. Where he is. What he's doing right this minute. I keep seeing him in one of those awful orange jumpsuits they make them wear, behind barbed wire or something. Don't laugh."

"You're sweet."

"I keep thinking, what could I have done? What could I have done to make it different?"

"Don't be so hard on yourself," Doug said. "You know, these kids have resources you and I can only dream about. Damon Flintov—of course I know who you're talking about—he's got a mansion, a Beemer, parents with more money than God."

"What does that have to do with anything?"

"Just saying, he'll be fine. Damon Flintov may be a belligerent moron, but trust me. In ten years he's living the high life while you and I are still droning on about the five-paragraph essay."

"You say that like it's a bad thing."

"Isn't it?"

"I became a teacher in order to teach." As soon as she heard this, her voice tight with righteousness, she knew it was untrue. "I wanted to help them. I wanted books to save them the way they saved me."

Doug nodded. "I might've felt that way once. But there are other aspirations."

"Like what?"

Doug took a swig of his beer. "Look," he said. "Some people get what they want. Some people don't. We tell kids life is fair, hard work, bootstraps, et cetera, but you know, and I know, that it isn't. The deck is stacked. You and I, for example. We're smart, we did well in school, we work hard. And our kids' worst nightmare is to end up like us."

"You're wrong," Molly said.

They were quiet. Molly could see, on Doug's jaw, where he'd nicked himself shaving, a small, dark bead of dried blood. She had the urge to push him out of her apartment—her hand closed around her beer bottle as if it were a weapon. But why? He'd made no threats.

Or every threat. He was scanning her garnet bedspread, her stacked books, the single framed snapshot on her bedside table. Her college graduation, on the sun-browned lawn of Fresno State. In the photograph Molly was flanked by her sister and her dad, her black gown open in the heat. "You look like a baby," Doug said.

"It wasn't that long ago."

He leaned forward, squinting at the picture. "That your guy?"

"Who, my dad?" In the photo Molly's father hunkered unsmiling, eyes shielded by dark glasses.

"The other one."

"Oh. That's Josh." Her ex-boyfriend was there, she realized, at the edge of the photo, grinning into the sun. The frame cut off his right ear. He wore the same wraparound sunglasses he always wore, as though his life were one long river cruise on the San Joaquin. Maybe it was, now that she'd gone.

"You broke his heart, didn't you?" Doug said. "Crushed it. Ground it into tiny little pieces."

She winced. He'd hit a tender place, one she hadn't known was still vulnerable to thoughtless blows. She said, carefully, "I couldn't give him what he wanted."

"Go on." Doug set down his beer and stared very seriously into her face, as though plotting to pry her open with a churchkey. His glasses magnified his eyes. She saw the teenager in him, nerdy and guileless.

"We met my sophomore year of college," she explained. "Josh was outgoing, popular; I guess I intrigued him. We were happy when we were alone. But at parties, we were strangers. He'd make instant friends with everyone—it was so easy for him—and I would want to join in but I couldn't, somehow. Then we'd fight. Of course he got fed up with me. 'Why do things have to be so heavy all the time?' he'd ask. 'Why can't you just be happy?' I'd tell him, 'I hate parties, you know that.' But I couldn't explain what I wanted instead."

Doug nodded. After a moment he said, "Well, he looks nice. Not for you, though."

"What's that supposed to mean?"

"I see you with somebody different, is all. Less Mr. Nice Guy. More like—"

"You?" she ventured.

"More like you, I was going to say."

She drank her beer. It had gotten warm. She set the bottle on the floor. "What am I like?"

He turned toward her. His knee nudged hers. He smelled of sandalwood cologne: alcohol, pencil shavings, cream. There were freckles on his knuckles.

"Do you want to know a secret?" he asked.

They were manuscript pages, printed in Courier and scrawled over in red pen. *The Beauty and the Darkness, A Novel by Douglas F. Ellison*. He was watching her face as she read.

> Most of Professor Brent Cumberland's students at the University of Northern California admired him, many harbored secret crushes, but in the end only one of them made any difference.
>
> It was a Monday morning in September and the clock was striking nine. Cumberland stood in front of his class. Today he was giving a lecture about his own award-winning

novel. He was comparing it with Ernest Hemingway's *The Sun Also Rises*. (It was not Cumberland himself but numerous literary critics who had introduced this comparison.) *A Beauty* was his first published novel but it had been enough to earn him a large advance and launch him from the wilds of public high school to the ivory tower of University. Now he had everything. Successful career, full bank account, attractive wife. But when he was alone he wondered: What was the point of it all? What did it all mean?

Cumberland paced in front of his whiteboard. A former athlete, he was tall and broad-shouldered. He had full dark hair and a neatly trimmed beard. He wore stylish jeans and a tweed jacket and a braided leather belt that had been the best he could afford after his college graduation ten years before. His students gazed up at him. Some of them were like adoring fans and others were like deer in the headlights. The girls wore short skirts and ponytails. They leaned over their desks to show their cleavage and bounced their bare legs under their desks. They must know what they are doing, Cumberland thought. Girls like that always knew.

Midway through his class the door opened and a girl barged into the room and took a seat in the front row. Flushed and panting. She was pretty, Cumberland thought. But in a way you had to think about. Her hair was blonde. Her eyes were gray. She had the lithe graceful body of a ballerina. He could wrap his hands around her wrist or neck and snap it like a twig. He did not know—yet—that this was something he would want to do.

After class the girl approached him at the podium. He braced himself for the usual fawning. "Can I ask you something?" she said hesitantly.

"Of course my dear," Cumberland said grandly. She seemed nervous and most females found it comforting when he spoke this way. "How can I be of service?"

The girl bit her lip. "I wanted to tell you how much I love your novel. Especially the love interest. Rosalie." When she talked she leaned closer to him. Her breath was lovely although a little rancid—laced with black tea. He pictured her in a disheveled student apartment, on a bed strewn with velvet and silk, reading his book. When she spoke about Rosalie it was clear that this young girl understood him better than his own wife did and better than any critic. The girl was inspired by his words and he was inspired by her passion. Now she put her hand on his arm. Innocently white.

Cumberland cleared his throat authoritatively. "Oh. Yes. Thank you, Miss . . ."

"Angelica."

"Angelica," he intoned in a deep bass that gave her pleasure. He was pleased too. "Call me Brent."

She giggled. Her gray eyes danced. This girl was young and free. She was not run down by life. Had he really once been like her, so young and unafraid?

Angelica. The name was quite appropriate. He felt his spirits lifting just being near her.

"So?" Doug asked Molly. "What do you think?"

In that moment there was no force on earth that could make her lift her eyes from the manuscript pages to meet his gaze. What could she possibly tell him? *Doug, this story is not just technically incompetent, but pathetically implausible.*

And yet—Doug's story was so vulnerable, like a brash child's handwriting wobbling over a page of lined paper. Amid the delusion and misogyny there were just enough glimmers of intelligent sensitivity to pique Molly's interest: she wondered which aspect of Doug Ellison's being would win out in the end. It was like a brief affair she'd had her freshman year of college, with a guy who'd played bass in a campus rock band—ninety-five percent of what she'd known of him had told her she should run the other way, yet she was held captive by the five percent that suggested deeper waters: an impressive vocabulary, a volume of E. E. Cummings poems on the nightstand, the tender way he would pronounce his mother's name. Now Doug was waiting to talk about his book, wanting to know what Molly thought. Because she could not possibly tell him what she thought, she kissed him.

His kisses were clumsy, or hers were. His breath was beer-bittered, as was hers. They kept missing each other—they clinked teeth, bumped noses, she tongued the corner of his mouth. They caressed each other's elbows, gripped each other's shoulders like eighth graders dancing. She wasn't small, and he seemed not to know what to do with her. He tried to pull her onto his lap; her shins banged the coffee table. She yelped. He apologized, she forgave. She wanted to help him. She stood and led him to the bed.

They sat side by side on the edge of the bed and slid off their shoes: her black flats, a skin of nylon stockings underneath; his battered loafers revealing the surprise of silk socks, finely striped navy and green.

"So fancy," she teased, pointing toward his feet. "Trying to impress me?"

He looked at her as though she'd caught him shoplifting. "They were a gift," he said.

Now they were awkward; their kissing seemed wrong and so did the way that they sat there, inches apart on her pilled red comforter, avoiding each other's eyes. Molly sensed that she'd caused it, although she didn't know how.

"Should I put on some music?" she asked finally.

"Sure."

She reached down to click on the CD player she kept under her bedside table. This relaxed him, and he laughed: "Didn't think they made those anymore." What played was a Green Day CD from her high school days, a sentimental favorite. It was wrong for the moment and she offered to change it, but Doug said no, it was perfect. He kissed her again, and they lay down together. It was nice to have him on her bed, she felt, although strange. It was nice to be touched, although strange. He'd brought condoms. Hot pink. She recognized them as the ones the HIV Awareness Club gave out at school and thought, *He wasn't willing to buy his own?*

She said, "Presumptuous much?"

"Once a Boy Scout," he said, grinning.

As their bodies moved together, she remembered being sixteen, when all she'd longed for was to kiss a boy and cuddle. She remembered being twenty, when Josh's arms around her had felt thrilling and safe and not stifling hot. She wanted to ask Doug Ellison to lie beside her without speaking. She wanted to ask him to leave. She wanted him to feel familiar, she wanted him to be someone she wanted and knew. But he was only someone.

THE STRIVER

In the front row of Mr. Ellison's SAT workshop one sunny April day, Dave Chu leaned over his desk, neck craned, eyes blinking. His forehead was curtained by a shining swoop of black hair. Whenever he looked down at his notes and then back up, the swoop fell forward and he jerked his head to flick it out of his eyes. This happened approximately every twelve seconds. He would have cut it, buzzed it to the scalp, but his mother said his hair was the only part of him that looked like her.

His mechanical pencil scratched across the page. He wrote everything Mr. Ellison said, even the jokes, the stories and asides, even as around him kids like Emma Fleed and Ryan Harbinger were staring at their phones or dozing at their desks, as beautiful Elisabeth Avarine sat silent and still in a halo of sunlight at the back of the room.

In the middle of his lecture, Mr. Ellison stopped by Dave's desk, smiled, and told him, "You don't have to remember everything I say. Just write down what feels important."

Dave stared back. This was ridiculous advice. How was he supposed to know what was important? Maybe in math class these distinctions could be made—*here are the relevant formulas, here are the steps to solve the equation*—but in English everything was random. Even the rules were not rules. In SAT prep, Mr. Ellison would say, "Here are the rules about prepositions," and then, five minutes later, "But remember—when it comes to writing, there are no rules!"

These contradictions were slowly driving Dave insane. He had written them all in his meticulous notes. Crisscrossed the pages with arrows, underlines, exclamations that were inadequate to express the madness in his head.

He wrote:

Mr. Ellison does not like semicolons! But you can use them sometimes.

Pronouns: Mr. Ellison does like He. He does not like You.

There is a rule about They. It is bad for some reason. Choose He or She instead!

"But," Dave said, his hand crawling uncertainly into the air, "excuse me, Mr. Ellison, what if you don't know if it's a he or a she?"

"Check for the Adam's apple, Dave, everyone knows that," Mr. Ellison chuckled. Dave wrote:

?!?!?!???

Mr. Ellison said that adverbs were bad except when they were not. One adverb that was bad was "run quickly." Mr. Ellison had once told Dave's class that he'd run track in high school but had been cheated out of first place in the all-county track meet his senior year. Perhaps this was why Mr. Ellison disdained this particular phrase. Perhaps it raised a secret pain that he tried to cover over with his brave pacing through the classroom and big block letters on the whiteboard, his attempts to flirt with Abigail Cress, who sat upright in her desk next to Dave's.

Dave wrote:

One adverb that is good is "carefully worded accusations."

This is from a book that Mr. Ellison likes called Confederacy of Dunces.

This book is good because Mr. Ellison likes it.

Other books (Twilight) are bad because Mr. Ellison does not like them.

Mr. Ellison first read this Confederacy book in college at UC Berkeley.

UC Berkeley is a very prestigious school.

Mr. Ellison said, "*Very* is the most useless word in the English language." Dave wrote: *Do not use very.* Mr. Ellison said the good news was that *very* would not be tested on the SAT. So never mind. Dave scratched through his notes. The *very* rule was not important.

There was already too much to remember.

He had to prepare for the fill-in-the-blank questions on the SAT Critical Reading section. He had to learn the Master List of 100 Most Common SAT Vocabulary Words: *abstinence, abstract, aesthetic, alleviate, ambivalent, apathetic, auspicious, benevolent, candor, cogent, comprehensive.* There were eighty-nine more Most Commons. Dave would Google them later. He wrote:

Remember to make flashcards and memorize and use them in a sentence!

Remember that on the actual test there could always be more.

Mr. Ellison said, "If you're struggling on the SAT, just use the strategies!" At this Dave felt a tug of optimism, the string of a high-flying kite.

Mr. Ellison said, "The most important strategy is Process of Elimination." Mr. Ellison was about to explain this (Dave's mechanical pencil hovering over the page, his fingers vibrating with anticipation), but then he forgot because Abigail Cress was asking about the word *hedonistic.*

"So, would you call that a negative-tone word or a positive-tone word?" she asked, crossing and uncrossing her skinny legs. Mr. Ellison chuckled, although what Abigail said was plainly not funny.

Dave knew that he was missing something. He wrote:

To Google: is hedonistic good or bad?

Mr. Ellison said, "A second strategy is to follow the checklist for grammar questions." He pounded the whiteboard with capital letters, blood-red:

1. SUBJECT VERB AGREEMENT.

2. PRONOUN ERROR.

3. PARALLELISM.

4. ADJ—

From the hallway came a racket: the thunder of feet and laughter and the smack of something heavy hitting the floor. Dave stopped writing. Mr. Ellison went to the classroom door and opened it: there were Cally Broderick and Alessandra Ryding, crouched on the linoleum where a backpack's contents had spilled.

Dave watched the back of Mr. Ellison's head. The teacher was still for a moment, and when he spoke it was not in his classroom boom but a voice that was smaller, startled:

"Calista Broderick? What are you doing out here?"

Cally came slowly to her feet, pushed her overgrown hair behind her ears, and glared. She was nothing like the girl Dave remembered from middle school, the type who'd care about something practical and normal like the SAT. Dave was the exact same person he had been in eighth grade, seventh grade, fifth grade, third grade, just with larger polo shirts and sneakers. What had happened to her?

Cally said, "Nothing, Mr. Ellison. Sorry." But she didn't sound sorry at all.

Alessandra Ryding got up from the floor and sidled beside Cally, a woven backpack dangling from her shoulder. Alessandra was willowy and olive-skinned and president of the HIV Awareness Club. Dave couldn't help but wonder how often she had sex—he guessed it was often—and with who. She was even flirting with their teacher: "Calista's a bad, bad girl, Mr. Ellison," she said. "Do you think she should be punished?"

Alessandra collapsed in laughter. Cally elbowed her ribs. Dave couldn't see Mr. Ellison's face, but the teacher shifted on his feet. This startled Dave. It made him remember with sudden, embarrassing vividness the Photoshopped picture of Mr. Ellison and Abigail Cress that Nick Brickston had posted on Instagram. In the picture, Mr. Ellison was naked and his eyes were closed and Abigail was in her track outfit, touching him right there. To this point, Dave had mostly ignored the rumors that Mr. Ellison and Abigail were doing it, thinking such things only happened in the movies. But now he wondered.

"Mr. Ellison?" Hannah Jones called out. "I have a question? About this modifier thing?"

Mr. Ellison cleared his throat. "Ladies, why don't you move along? Your peers are trying to learn something here."

Alessandra answered for them both—"Peace and love, Mr. E."— and the girls carried on together down the hall.

Mr. Ellison sighed and shut the classroom door. With the interruption, he seemed to have forgotten about the rest of the grammar checklist. Instead he replied to Hannah, mentioning something called a "dangling modifier." This relaxed him, and he began to chuckle. He said, "Dangling modifiers are the funniest parts of grammar. You'll see."

Dave wrote:

Mr. Ellison thinks that there are funny parts of grammar.
Google this. Google everything.

Dave sat at his mother's wide glass dinner table and vocabulary swam in his brain. They weren't words to him yet, only letters jumping in and out of line.

Mr. Ellison had said, "Make a picture for each word—this is how we remember what we read." As Dave chewed string beans and watched his father slice into a steak—his father's eyes dark under heavy eyelids and speckled brows, hair a peppered gray—his brain struggled to conjure pictures for the Hundred Most Commons. But all he saw was Mr. Ellison's bald spot as he pounded nonsense on the whiteboard, Abigail Cress's foot tapping in her track shoe because it was all so easy for her, and Elisabeth Avarine glowing, silent, in the sun at the back of the room.

"You are distracted again," his father said. "Why?" The knife in his hand jabbed toward Dave. An exclamation point.

Dave shrugged. "Tired, I guess."

His father's eyebrows narrowed. "You are not yourself."

His mother, in her chair between them, laid her fork on the glass table with a deliberateness that seemed rehearsed. She turned to Dave. "David Alexander, have you been doing ecstasy and raves?" she asked, pushing her black swoop of hair out of her eyes. "Your parents are not stupid. We've heard what goes on at that school."

Dave laughed. He had never even touched a cigarette or tried a sip of beer. When had he ever had time for such things?

His parents took this laughter as proof there was something wrong with him. His father said, "What are these teachers teaching you? This disrespect."

His mother said, "This is not the boy I raised."

"I don't know what we're paying these teachers to do," his father said. "Has Mr. Ellison graded your practice SAT yet?"

Dave shook his head.

"You must score over 2100 if you expect Berkeley to consider you."

"I am aware of this," Dave said.

"What is this attitude?" his mother said. "UC Berkeley is a very fine school."

"For some people," Dave said. He didn't know why. He opened his mouth to insert another string bean, and the words fell out. He knew nothing about Berkeley, really. It was as if he'd suddenly decided to have a vehement opinion about artichokes, which he had never eaten, and now he'd have to explain the opinion and defend it.

"What does that mean?" his father said.

"*I* went to Berkeley," his mother said. "Your *father* went to Berkeley."

"It was a privilege," his father said. "Our parents didn't have the opportunity to go to college. Our parents had nothing. And when they gave us something, we appreciated it."

"I do appreciate it," Dave said. But he sounded unconvincing even to himself.

His father clattered his fork on the glass. He leaned over his plate. "It's not easy to go to college when your parents work in factories," he said, stabbing the knife toward Dave's mother. "It's not easy to become a doctor when your parents are strangers in this country, when your only path is hard work and scholarships and loans." This time he stabbed toward himself.

"I know," Dave said.

"You do *not* know. You do not know anything, because we have given you everything. You don't know that you are exceptional—we tell you and tell you and yet you refuse to see it. When are you going to see it?"

Dave cut a cube of steak and chewed. The meat was salty and rare. His brain groped for the Most Commons to describe the reddish flesh that quivered on his plate. It was *florid, querulous.* It *extenuated.* These words sounded right to him although he sensed that their meanings were wrong. He swallowed, raised his head. He knew that already he had gone too far, yet he couldn't stop. He said, "I *do* want to go to a good college. It's just, I was thinking, maybe I should take a gap year first."

"What is this, a gap year?" his mother asked.

"It's like . . . I don't know. Time off after graduation. To, like, think, travel, whatever. Like a vacation, I guess." Dave immediately regretted the word. It was not what he meant. In those dinner table conversations he never said the right thing; it was like trying to remember the Hundred Most Commons when the proctor started the timer in the fourth hour of the SAT. Hopeless.

But Dave's father did not yell. Instead his face brightened and relaxed. He laughed. "Your whole life is a vacation."

Dave was aware that the only thing holding him back was himself. His father was a vascular surgeon at UCSF Medical Center. His mother, who had stayed home to raise him, had been prelaw at Berkeley. Dave was their only child. He was everything.

Dave's parents believed he took after his father. It was true that they looked alike. Both were tall and slim with skin that showed the webs of blue-green veins at their temples and wrists. Dave had his father's heavy-lidded, almond eyes, sparse brows, and nose whose broadness made him a little less than beautiful. The long neck. There was even a small mole, flat and black, above his lip that exactly resembled the mole on the ridge of his father's cheek. But this was where the similarities ended. He was not like either of his parents, really.

He was unremarkable. He had no diagnoses. No dyslexia or numerophobia or even ADHD, which at least would have earned him time-and-a-half on the SAT. According to the official records, he had a normal attention span. Average math skills. A moderate interest in history and science—he was in chemistry now and felt a quiet fondness for the periodic table printed on the inside cover of his textbook. There was an order to it, a totality, that reassured him. He hated English, which was all opinions and loose ends.

At school, he was well aware of all the ways in which he was not enough. For example, in history class it was not enough for him to know the basic components of President Roosevelt's New Deal. He was expected to grasp its nuances, its causes and implications. More than this, he was expected to have an opinion—to be like Abigail Cress, who could articulate a fully formed thesis about any topic imaginable. He had heard her debate the New Deal, the Cuban Missile Crisis, the Sunnis and the Shi'ites, evolution versus creationism, the proper technique for dissecting an earthworm, the literary merit of *Harry Potter,* and the superiority of Lancôme mascara. He was in awe of her, and a little afraid. He knew that in his parents' eyes he ought to be like her. If only he would work a little harder.

On his report card, it was not enough to have that hard-won column of B-pluses; in his parents' eyes he might as well have failed. In group presentation projects, it was not enough for him to do exactly his share of the work (three slides, two references, two minutes on the Key Components of the New Deal) and no more. Yet this was what he did. He left it to the Abigail Cresses and the Nick Brickstons to show off—Abigail did this by making seven extra slides with historical photos from an expensive Internet archive and delivering a memorized speech aided by color-coded notecards, Nick by patching together a single slide with nothing but jokes about President Roosevelt's wheelchair and Mrs. Roosevelt's horse face and then charming their teacher by stretching his allotted two minutes into six with what could only be described as a last-chance audition for an improv troupe, as Abigail seethed behind him.

After school, Dave played soccer. An average member of an average team. Every afternoon, he arrived at practice on time with his shorts and jersey clean, cleats tied. He ran the warm-up lap and drills knowing he was not the fastest or the slowest, not the preternaturally graceful Ryan Harbinger yet not a klutz. He rarely scored goals but happily assisted other, better players in the mad pack-run down the field. Most of his friends were on the team, and he loved to practice. But he hated the games, because his parents attended. As soon as he felt them there, he had to strive for points, elbowing opponents and herding the ball toward the goal line, all the while sweating under his oppressive swoop of hair that he could not cut because to do so would be to break his mother's heart.

• • •

After dinner Dave retreated to his room and closed the door, but his mother pushed in anyway.

She stood on the square red rug in the center of the room, which was lit by the gentle glow of Dave's soccer-ball desk lamp. The room had light blue walls, bare except for one Ansel Adams poster—a black-and-white photograph of Muir Woods redwoods reaching into gloom—that had hung above Dave's bed for as long as he had slept there. The bed's beige comforter masked Superman sheets. Beside it sat a small maple desk, so close that he could roll out of bed and into the black desk chair with hardly a step between. His desktop was bare except for the soccer-ball lamp, a Mason jar of mechanical pencils, a tray of paper clips, and a laptop computer.

Dave's backpack slumped on the floor by the desk, yawning to reveal a crowd of books and binders. His desk drawers were full as well—of papers tumbled and dog-eared and torn; broken sticks of lead and crumbles of eraser; movie-ticket stubs; scribbled-on school pictures; four *Harry Potter* figurines and a pack of Batman Silly Bandz from when he was a kid; a hot-pink condom handed to him by a member of the HIV Awareness Club on the first day of his freshman year; a crumpled picture of Kate Upton in a white bikini, ripped from the *Sports Illustrated* Swimsuit Issue that Jonas Everett had brought over; a pile of metallic origami papers from sixth grade; a half-drafted love note to Elisabeth Avarine that would have looked to anyone at first glance like a list of SAT Most Commons (*abundance, adulation, impetuous, inevitable*) and which, after what had happened to Tristan Bloch, he knew better than to send—but these were Dave's secrets. The drawers were shut.

"David?" his mother said. "Why are you hiding here? We're not finished with our talk."

Reclined against the maple headboard of his bed, Dave shrugged. His mother was small, compact, yet there was no room for her in there. He was too old for her to curl beside him on the bed—if she'd even perched on the edge, it would have embarrassed him. They were used to seeing each other over tables spread with food, or sitting in her Lexus in their separate leather seats, listening to the radio, looking at the road.

It still felt strange to him, this distance between them. When he was a kid, they'd spent hours, days, years alone together. When his father would leave for work, the air in the house would seem to lighten and expand, and she'd sit with him on the vine-laced living room rug playing Thomas the Tank Engine and then cook him butter noodles, warm and plain just like he liked, and fold him into bed at night with stories about heroes who were always brave and always saved the world. And just loved him. And there was nothing that he'd had to do to earn it.

Dave's mother arranged herself in the desk chair, pointed her knees toward the bed. "We are not understanding each other," she said.

Dave shrugged.

"You think we don't love you? We don't care? You're the most important thing in our life, David. Number one."

"I know," he said. What she'd said was supposed to be a compliment, but it made the acid lurch in his stomach.

Dave's mother wrinkled her forehead. Her eyes were liquid brown. The skin around them had feather grooves in which the black gunk of her makeup had smudged. She said, "All we ask is that you realize what you are."

"What I am," he echoed.

"You know you could do so much better, you could do anything. If you'd only try." His mother's voice was firm, emphatic. He was going to throw up. Did she really believe these things? Did she believe he hadn't tried?

He had nothing to say to her. He pulled his legs to his chest. His socks were bleached and his toes banded by a thin gold thread.

In his silence his mother said carefully, "You know, I have always wondered what it would feel like to have really done something."

This confession had come out of nowhere. Was he supposed to respond? He couldn't. He felt he had intruded on a private moment she was having with herself. Yet she seemed to be waiting for him. Her gaze fell to her hands; her hair swept into her eyes and she tucked it self-consciously behind her ear. It was not her usual harried brushing away. It was something a girl would do.

"What do you mean?" he asked.

"Nothing." She smiled, waved him away. The moment was over. "It's just, I don't want you to regret. You have so much potential. You can be anything you choose to be." She placed her hand on his shoulder and squeezed.

Dave looked into her eyes. What he saw was not anger or disappointment or righteousness but simple human need. She had given up her life to be his mother. Because he was special. Every report card had told her otherwise, that he was little more than "a hard worker" and "a pleasure to have in class," yet she had kept her faith. He had the potential, he *could*, and one day—at the right time, with the right class, the right teacher—he would. This was the story she'd told herself; it was his job to make it true.

It was hard, he thought, to be responsible for all this happiness. He was angry but he was also sorry.

"I'll try harder," he told her. "I will try to be better."

Drifting to sleep that night, Dave imagined another life in which he was allowed to wear happiness in the simple way that felt native to him. He thought of his future secretly, as if his parents would peer through the crack of his open bedroom door and deep into his brain (he usually left the door open because closing it triggered a string of questions he couldn't stand: "Why do you need to close this door? What are you doing in there?"). He saw not a high-powered job, not a doctor's white coat or a lawyer's striped suit, but himself, Dave Chu, in chinos and polo shirt, in the middle of an ordinary life. Some job. A home. Enough money to see the newest superhero blockbuster every Friday night, not at the art-house theater in Mill Valley but at a strip-mall megaplex with stadium seating and IMAX screens. He wanted the hero to get the girl. He wanted to eat Milk Duds and popcorn and sip Sprite from a straw that he shared with his girlfriend or wife.

Dave could not help but imagine Elisabeth Avarine in this role, a girl he'd never talked to but who was so unearthly gorgeous that it was difficult to look at her. She had sugar-blond hair that hung straight around her face and down the narrow space between her shoulder blades. She had eyes like sea glass, skin like milk. Dramatic, dark blond eyebrows. A little divot in her pink lower lip. She was tall, as tall as Dave himself. At school that day she'd worn a thin white T-shirt slung wide over her shoulders, revealing a strip of collarbone, and cutoff jean shorts. The shirt had shrugged up as she'd crossed the classroom, her belly button winking beneath the shadows of the cloth. She'd slid into her desk and the hem of her shorts had pressed into her thighs. She'd crossed her ankles and the bones there were delicate, flanked by fine grooves. A gold chain draped over one ankle, dangling two small hearts. This was all the jewelry she needed. Her feet were naked but for a pair of brown thong sandals slid through little crooked toes.

With closed eyes, on the cool cloth of his pillow, Dave watched Elisabeth as she bent to rifle in her backpack. The sun caressed her shoulders, white and soft. Her hair swung like a movie curtain over her cheek, and a bra strap, pink as a shell, unhitched and fell down her arm. Seeing him, she cocked her head and smiled, waved him over—

People said Elisabeth was a bitch, stuck up, but Dave sensed a sweetness lying deep within her, like the black-cherry filling at the bottom of a yogurt.

In his dream-life, Elisabeth would tuck her hand into the crease of his elbow as they walked into the movie. He'd never had a girlfriend, but when observing other couples, he was fascinated by this easy intertwining, wondering how it felt and whether Elisabeth would sense the nervous sweat that lined the crease of his elbow beneath her hand. Was it possible she would feel the sweat with her slim, clean, pink-polished fingers and simply wouldn't care?

Elisabeth would kiss him, muss his hair. They'd have two children, maybe three. A house filled with small clothes and toys and the pleasant hum of voices in the other room. He thought of this, treasured it, a wish he knew could not come true.

He told himself that his parents knew best. There was something about living that he didn't understand yet; there was a reason that the small life that he wished for was not right. Perhaps it was true—as when in childhood he'd desired nothing more than the simple sweetness of vanilla ice cream but his father urged him toward the rocky road—that Dave did not know what he wanted, that the happiness he yearned for would elude him, until he learned to dream of more and better things.

That Thursday, Mr. Ellison handed back the results of the practice SAT. After class Dave approached the teacher's desk, clutching his score report. Mr. Ellison was slicing someone's essay with red pen—as the teacher himself liked to say, grinning conspiratorially at whichever class he happened to be in front of, he was "making it bleed."

Dave rustled his score sheet. "Excuse me, Mr. Ellison," he said. "Can you tell me, what are the tricks?"

"Tricks?" Mr. Ellison slashed out a paragraph of the essay on his desk.

"I need to score 2100."

Mr. Ellison put down his pen. He looked up, blinking behind his glasses. Dave's face made him sigh. "At some point, Dave, you have to say you've given it all you've got. You just have to know the stuff, or at least have a sense for it."

"A sense?"

"Instinct. And your score has already gone up two hundred points, hasn't it?" Reaching over his piles of papers, he pulled the report from Dave's hand. "Yes. You're at 1750 now. That's very respectable."

"I need at least a 2100. That's the cutoff."

"Cutoff?"

"For Berkeley!"

"Aren't you being a little hard on yourself?" Mr. Ellison leaned forward in his chair, projecting humanness instead of teacherness. It made Dave uncomfortable.

"If you will tell me the tricks, I can learn them," Dave said. He was startled by his own voice, loud and pleading. "Please."

"Okay. How about this? Stop by tomorrow before class. We'll sit down and go over your test together."

Relieved, Dave started to thank him, but Mr. Ellison stood up abruptly, looking past Dave to the open classroom door.

Dave turned to see what he was looking at. There, in the doorway, stood Abigail Cress. She was staring hard at Mr. Ellison and her cheeks were white and she looked like she might cry, or scream. There was a lady with her—tall, important-looking, with black hair like Abigail's and a black suit and a black Bluetooth headset blinking at her ear.

"Abigail?" Mr. Ellison said. "Did you need something?"

"Abby?" the important-looking lady said. "Honey, who is this? Is this him?"

Abigail shook her head.

Then the lady's phone buzzed and she answered it, clicked back into the hall.

"I could have," Abigail said to Mr. Ellison. "I could have, but I didn't."

"What are you talking about?" Mr. Ellison said, glancing at Dave. His voice canted, face like chalk.

Dave knew he was not meant to see this. Some aspect of the rumor was true, and he did not want to know what. He wanted to excuse himself, but the air was ice and he sensed if he spoke he would shatter it.

"I wanted you to know," Abigail said evenly. "I could have told them, and I didn't, and I still could. If you ever try to talk to me again."

Then she turned and left, and Mr. Ellison said that he would see Dave in the morning.

The following day, Mr. Ellison's classroom was dark and a sign on the glass-paned door said, SAT WORKSHOP CANCELLED. The SAT was only two weeks away.

Dave faced the door and fury rose in his chest. Where was Mr. Ellison? This was nothing short of abandonment. The teacher had led him to the cliff's edge, dropped him into the abyss. He was gone, with no explanation and no excuse, and Dave Chu's choices had narrowed to one.

From behind the counter of the 7-Eleven on Miller Avenue, the old man in the red vest watched teenagers push in and out of the swinging glass doors.

At home, their parents served them three squares a day: heaping plates of quinoa and kale, sustainably farmed chicken and sustainably fished fish, steel-cut oatmeal for breakfast, mango slices for dessert. But here, he gave them what they wanted.

Big Gulps. Slurpees. AriZona Iced Tea. Flamin' Hot Cheetos and Kettle Chips. Jalapeno Cheese Taquitos, glinting with grease. Top Ramen steaming in its Styrofoam cup. Armloads of candy.

A kid was complaining to the old man about the five-dollar minimum on credit card purchases. "Who carries cash?" the boy said.

"People who don't have credit cards," said the old man.

"Who doesn't have credit cards?"

The old man sighed. "There are fees," he said. "You still want your Dr Pepper?"

The boy nodded. He added four dollars of candy to his order, swiped his card through the machine, and pushed out the door into the parking lot.

It was 4:00 p.m. Nick Brickston stood at the edge of the lot. He was just to the side of the glass doors, where the 7-Eleven man couldn't see him. Slim, dark-haired, he wore a black T-shirt, jeans, and the limited-edition baseball cap he'd bought at the ballpark when the Giants won the World Series. He leaned against the trunk of a redwood tree. The tree was so thick, and Nick Brickston so skinny, that it would take four of him to match its girth. Its branches smothered him in shade.

Nick did business here almost every afternoon. The world's last remaining pay phone was stuck to the side of this 7-Eleven, but he didn't use it. He was a drug dealer, sure, but he took calls on his iPhone like a normal human being.

Dave trudged down the sidewalk, bowed under his backpack's weight. He hauled all his books to school each day, just in case, and the pack strained at the seams. He wore his everyday outfit: pressed chinos and polo shirt, sneakers with clean white soles. When he reached Nick, he set his pack on the ground and flicked the hair out of his face. Sweat slid into his eyes; he pushed the heel of his palm over his brows. Regarding Nick, he thought how strange it was that the two of them, and Tristan Bloch of all people, had for six months in sixth grade called each other friends. It had all been orchestrated by their mothers, and had ended when Dave and Nick swapped knot-tying and origami for sports and girls and movies. Tristan had called them traitors and kicked them out of his house, all the while crying like a baby, a slug-trail of snot leaking from his nose.

All Dave asked Nick was: "How much?"

Nick rested his head against the tree trunk, squinted into the sky. "Seven hundred."

"Seven hundred dollars?" Dave said, trying to calculate sixteen years of allowance, Christmas money, and birthday money in his head. "That's a lot, isn't it?"

Nick shrugged. He had so many customers he could afford to be casual. "That's what it is. I guarantee over 2200, every time."

Dave digested this. Nick, who was not even taking the SAT prep class at school, promised to earn a nearly perfect score. "How do you do it?"

Nick grinned. "Don't worry 'bout it. Skills."

"Well, I only need 2100 to get into Berkeley."

"Whatever," Nick said. "Seven hundred for my services, plus fifty for the fake ID. You sure you want to do this?"

"I can get your money," Dave said.

The safe in the basement contained the sixteen years of birthday and Christmas money that Dave had never been allowed to spend.

Each birthday, he opened the card from his parents and the brand-new hundred-dollar bill fluttered out. He was allowed to hold it, the bill like a feather in his palm. He was allowed to examine its face: the obscure seals and numbers like an ancient code that maybe everybody knew but him; Benjamin Franklin's odd disappointed eyes, nestled in flesh; the strange, scrawled signatures at the bottom. He was allowed to inhale the bill's faint ink smell and press its cool cotton-linen paper to his cheek. Then he had to give it back.

"You do not need another toy," his father would say. "Someday, there will be something worthwhile to spend this money on. You'll see." And his mother would take it downstairs to the safe.

Now Dave opened the door to the unfinished basement and ducked inside. He crept downstairs in the dark, breathing air gritted with dust.

As he flipped on the overhead bulb, the dust settled on his white sneakers. This worried him briefly—when his mother came home she would see it—but he pushed on.

The dim room was piled with storage boxes, each filled with artifacts and sealed and labeled in his mother's elegant print. The safe sat in the corner, behind a box called *DAVID Classwork & Report Cards, K–3*. He pushed the box aside, cardboard scraping the concrete floor, and silky cobwebs stuck to his fingers. The safe, revealed, reflected yellow light.

He grasped its metal dial. Recalled the numbers his mother had made him memorize when he was eight. "In case, unexpectedly, we die," she'd explained at the time, turning the dial in the series her fingers had seemed to know by heart. "In this safe, we keep the deed to the house, the security passwords, the bank account numbers, keys." The safe had swung open and she'd removed each item, displaying it like one of the *Price Is Right* ladies on TV. "This is my mother's jewelry box with the diamond for when you propose," she'd said. (*Propose what?* eight-year-old Dave had thought.) "This book has the phone number of our attorney, our accountant, all the important people. See this paper? These are the terms of the living trust. This is what says that everything belongs to all of us, and that after your father and I are gone, everything will just belong to you. It helps with the taxes. Do you understand?"

Eight-year-old Dave had nodded. He'd known that he was supposed to pay attention to these details, to remember—*diamond, living trust, taxes*—but as his mother had busily arranged the contents of the safe, one phrase returned and echoed in his brain: *In case unexpectedly we die.* What had his mother meant by this? Were his parents going to die? When? And what was going to kill them—a sickness, an earthquake, a man with a gun? And would Dave survive this disaster if he remembered the numbers that opened the safe? If he forgot the numbers, what then? Would he have nothing? Would he have to find some other parents to take care of him?

His mother had not finished. "David?" she'd said, jostling his arm. "Are you listening to me? Look, this is where all your money will be safe until we can trust you to do the right thing." The manila envelope had crinkled in her hand. It was flat at the ends but bloated in the middle, like a snake that had swallowed a mouse. In black marker it was labeled *DAVID*. It did not look like much; Dave imagined with tender longing all the superhero figurines and soccer jerseys and vanilla ice cream cones he could have bought with all those birthdays.

He had not visited the safe in the eight years since his mother had revealed its contents, but he'd memorized the numbers. Now he clicked the wheel right to the first number, back to the second, then forward again, and so on, just as his mother had, until he felt the final click and release. The safe swung open. It was not like safes in movies. There were no thick gold bars or winking piles of coins. Only a stack of papers, five black velvet jewelry boxes, and a ring of keys. He held his breath like he was going underwater. Reached in, and shuffled the papers until he found what he was searching for. This part did feel like a movie. Blood drummed his ears. His hand shook. Over the years, the envelope's belly had distended. Crouching in the gloom, he flipped the envelope, pried up the clasp's metal wings, and unfolded the flap. He reached in slowly, imagining the fat black widow spider that would tiptoe up to bite him for his crimes.

But there was no spider, just the stack of bills his mother had for sixteen years collected in his name.

Slowly, carefully, he counted it.

One hundred dollars per birthday for sixteen birthdays.

Twenty dollars per Christmas for sixteen Christmases.

Ten dollars per Easter for sixteen Easters.

Five- and ten-dollar bills, assorted, from his grandparents and from aunts and uncles he hardly remembered or hadn't met.

In total, there was $2,525 in the envelope marked *DAVID*. He'd always known it, yet he couldn't believe it. He was rich.

But he couldn't take it all. He didn't want to. The money scared him, the bills so vulnerable. They could be torn, they could be cut with scissors. They could fly out the window and flap away on the breeze. He could lose the money, or be seized by the sudden, irrepressible urge to find out what it smelled like when it burned. Such things— carelessness, destructiveness—were not in his nature, yet he could not trust himself. He was a teenage boy, as his parents had reminded him so many times—left to his own devices there was no way of knowing what damage he might do.

Dave exhaled. Unlicked eight hundred dollars from the stack. Seven hundred and fifty dollars was for Nick Brickston. The other fifty was half a birthday, just for him.

On May 4, a Saturday, Dave's father woke him at 6:00 a.m. Dave threw off the covers and stumbled to the bathroom, showered and toweled off, combed his shock of hair until it shone. He brushed and flossed his teeth. He examined himself in the mirror, zooming in closer and closer until his face abstracted and his eyes were black tunnels shifting in his skin.

He dressed. Nothing special. Blue polo shirt and chinos, white-soled shoes. Then he loaded his backpack with supplies: one admission ticket, printed from the Internet; one plastic card that identified him as the one and only David Alexander Chu, Student, Valley High School; two number-2 pencils, sharpened, and one soft eraser; one graphing calculator; two extra calculator batteries, just in case; one watch without audible alarm; two peanut butter granola bars; one ripe banana; one canteen of filtered water. And in his front pocket, folded and tucked against his thigh, eight hundred dollars in cash.

His mother made him gluten-free toast and turkey bacon and fried three eggs sunny-side-up. "The SAT book said you'll need lots of protein to get you through," she told him.

Dave thanked her and ate it all, cleaned his plate, although he hated how the eggs quivered and glared at him like eyes.

When it was time, his mother drove him to a high school in San Francisco. To get there, they had to cross the Golden Gate Bridge. On the span Dave conducted his silent ritual, holding his breath between one orange spire and the next and trying to imagine those final, suffocating moments in the life of Tristan Bloch.

They passed through the toll booths and merged onto Nineteenth Avenue. In the driver's seat Dave's mother said, "It's too bad we have to drive all the way into the city. I still don't understand, you couldn't take the test at your school?"

Dave shrugged. "All the spots were taken." The lie flowed from his mouth, so easy, surprising him.

"Too bad," his mother echoed, and was quiet. Then she asked, "Are you nervous?"

The money in his pocket was a steadying force, a strange power. He shook his head. "I think I'm really ready," he told her. It was the least that he could do.

At the curb she turned and smiled at him; he turned and smiled back. Then he jumped out, his backpack, lighter now, hanging from one shoulder.

The car pulled away from the curb. The school, St. Antony's, was a massive gray building with an iron gate at its entrance and a dark, enormous cross upon its face.

Nick Brickston waited in their meeting place, around the side. "'Sup."

Dave nodded back. He rustled in the backpack for his wallet, then slipped it into the pocket of his chinos. Nick had brought the school ID card he'd made, with his own smiling face next to Dave's full name. "But my last name—won't they know you're not me?" Dave had asked when he first saw the fake; "Naw, man, trust me, no one wants to be the racist prick that starts that conversation," Nick had explained. Now he handed everything to Nick—the backpack with both pencils and the calculator, the erasers, the granola bars, even the banana. He was thirsty and thought about keeping the canteen for himself, but didn't. In the end, he gave it all.

The scores were posted early on a Friday morning three weeks later. Dave's parents had punched the release date into their phones, so the phones trilled and beeped at them when it was time. They hurried into Dave's room and hovered behind him as he logged on to his College Board account. His mother at one shoulder, his father at the other.

As he typed in the password, his mother said, "I cannot look." But she did. She set her hand on his shoulder and squeezed. *Assiduous,* he thought. That was what his mother felt like when she did this. He knew the word was wrong but suddenly no longer cared. It was almost over. When he clicked the button, it would be done.

It was clear that Molly and Doug Ellison had ruined a perfectly good friendship with the play at intimacy that neither of them had enjoyed. Now Molly was determined to avoid him. She'd arrive at her classroom just after the morning bell had rung so she wouldn't see him greeting students in the hall; she'd lock her room and walk around the campus during break so she could disappear into the crowds of kids; she'd leave at the start of lunch, hurrying away with a brown bag and a book, to eat unseen in her car. Yet his presence remained: she saw his students grinning as they exited his classroom, she heard the dull reverberation of his voice behind the wall, the banging of his pen upon the whiteboard next door. She prayed that her students did not notice her blushing. She knew she was being ridiculous, but she worried she'd get stuck with Doug in awkward silence, struggling for words as the eddy of kids pressed them closer and closer together. She worried he'd ask her to read more of his book. She worried, perversely, that he might also be avoiding her. But most of all, she dreaded looking into his face and seeing his regret.

And then, one day at lunch, Molly went to the faculty lounge and discovered she could stop her dodging and hiding.

"Just quit," announced Gwen Thruwey. "No warning."

"And he's actually gone?" asked Kristin Steviano.

"Just like that?" asked Jeannie Flugel.

"Just like that."

The teachers were blocking the mailboxes. They stepped aside for Molly, but went on gossiping as she reached for her pile of memos and paystubs.

"Sleeping with a student," Gwen said. "Can you believe it?"

"Such a cliché," said Jeannie. "You never think it happens in real life. I wonder what his wife thinks."

"He told me he was separated," said Kristin.

"Lacey is as much his wife as she ever was. She's gorgeous, too. She goes to my gym."

"Can you imagine, being married to someone like him?"

"But do you really think he did it?" Kristin asked.

Gwen paused grandly. "I always knew there was something off about Doug Ellison. The way he looked at those girls."

As Molly listened, her heart was pounding in her chest. Now, at his name, there was a sickening feeling, a cool turning beneath her ribs. "What are you talking about?" she asked.

Gwen turned to face her. "Oh, Molly. You and Doug were so close. Surely you must know." Gwen's blue eyes stared through her, implicating Molly and her heap of papers in whatever crime Doug had committed, judging her, somehow, for the whole sleazy mess.

"No" was all that Molly could manage to say. The bell rang, and lunch was over.

Hurrying into the hallway, Molly ran into Beth Firestein.

"Are you all right?" Beth asked, lightly touching Molly's arm. Beneath her manicured hand, Molly's skin looked allergically splotchy and red. "You don't look all right."

Under the elder teacher's cool, intelligent gaze, Molly could not lie and could not tell the truth. "My kids are waiting," she said, and pulled away.

She went into the hall. Here the students were swarming. Their sounds were all around her, the squeaking of sneakers and the echoing clanging of lockers slammed shut. A hand-painted banner drooped overhead: FEAR, MADNESS, GREED—VALLEY DRAMA DEPARTMENT PRESENTS—TOM STOPPARD'S "DARK SIDE OF THE MOON." And the world through which she moved seemed curiously loosened, unfastened—she grew dizzy in the crowd of faces, a stretch of mopped linoleum slippery beneath her feet, and she paused and pressed her palm against a locker to steady herself. Her heart went on hammering in her chest, a little wildly, and there was a trembling in her fingers and a lightness in her legs and a cold, dull weight at her core. The faces around her, baby-cheeked, pimple-spattered, belonged to kids she didn't know. Her thought was a drumbeat:

Which one?

Which one?

The kids went into classrooms; the classroom doors shut. Each one she passed had a small window at eye level, and past these portholes floated other teachers' disembodied heads. Molly's afternoon class was gathered outside her door at the end of the hallway, waiting to be let in. They huddled in circles or sat on the floor with their backs against the wall. Seeing them, she felt her body jangling with nerves as it had not since her first day. She had the feeling of one waiting in the wings to start a play, having forgotten every line. At Doug's door she paused, peered through the porthole. Gwen was right, he was gone: his students milled among the desks, a substitute teacher flailed for attention. Molly recalled how Doug had greeted his students in the doorway every day, how he'd patted their backs and reached for their hands. It had charmed her. Now his desk was deserted and bare.

For the rest of the afternoon, as her students buzzed around her, Molly scrutinized her relationship with Doug Ellison as if feeling for a slipped stitch. She remembered his novel, with its chauvinistic teacher and nubile student. It had disgusted her, but it was only a story, and to condemn a man based on fiction alone would be to betray her own principles. What about *American Psycho*? *A Clockwork Orange*? For God's sake, *Lolita*?

And there was the day she'd reached out to Calista Broderick— how strangely Calista had acted, how damaged she'd seemed. Was it possible—of course it was possible—that Calista had been the one?

Soon another scene rose to Molly's mind, one she'd previously tried to block out. Several weeks before, she and Doug had been finishing lunch when a few kids trickled into his classroom. The first among them was a tall, uncommonly beautiful girl, not her student, named Elisabeth Avarine. She'd settled in a back-row seat and stretched her arms over her head. She was somehow clumsy and graceful at once, like a colt staggering from the womb. Molly had openly stared; she just could not imagine how it felt to look like that. She'd turned to Doug and he was watching the girl too, curious and yet more than curious: hungry.

It was four o'clock when Molly got home, and the main house was undergoing its daily changing of the guard: the Range Rover in the driveway, the daytime nannies handing off to the evening staff, the children running inside to trade school clothes and backpacks for soccer shorts and flute cases. The nannies were hurrying the kids in Spanish, the kids responding in English and nonsense. The little one, Archer, stood on the front stoop in only his diaper, desperate not to put on his pants. "I don't wanna go!" he was wailing. Then: "I don't wanna stay!" Molly understood him. The world was such a wrong place—how could one go, how could one stay? She forced herself to smile and wave as she circled around to her studio, then let herself in and locked the door.

The sight of the bed was more than she could stand. She went to the bathroom and ran the shower, undressed quickly, puddling her clothes on the floor, and stepped under the water. She shivered. Hot water needled her shoulders and back. But she wanted to be scalded— the best part of sunburn was peeling.

Under the steaming water she tried to black out the images that came to her, of Doug and the girl—whoever it was. Calista? Elisabeth? Another student Molly didn't know? How had he done it? Had he rented a room in some seedy hotel? Had he pulled her into the world of dusty ashtrays and sour sheets, cellophaned soap, hangers handcuffed to the rod? A Mill Valley girl would never have been in a place like that before. He would have opened her eyes to the unclean world, undone in one sordid night sixteen years of her parents' careful tending.

Molly knew what girls needed: he had told the girl he loved her. She must have thought she loved him too.

She recalled how he'd twisted his hands in her hair, pressed her head toward the band of his boxers; how he'd stroked her neck while they kissed on her love seat; how he'd pulled her chair out in his classroom, its metal feet scraping the floor. Had he really thought he would get away with it? Cheating on his wife with Molly, with a sixteen-year-old child? Or—God—cheating on the child with her.

The following morning, Molly avoided her teaching duties in the classic way—by asking her students to edit one another's papers. This allowed her to sit at her desk, pretending to update her grade book as she watched the kids mill around the room. They flirted with each other, sent signals. The girls preened, the boys swaggered. They committed tiny acts of violence imbued with the promise of sex. Of course she had known, in the abstract, that they were sexual beings (she'd been a teenager not that long ago), but it disturbed her to think of them that way. Disturbed her to notice how Ryan Harbinger strutted over to Hannah Jones, squeezed the flesh of her arm to make her shriek. Calista Broderick tugged her hair to one side, exposing her suntanned neck to Jonas Everett. Wyatt Sanchez inked purple spirals on the wrist of Samantha Aster, who flushed with pleasure. Abigail Cress seemed to focus on her work, but even she was agitated by the room's strange heat, thumping her bare legs beneath the desk. The girls were beautiful, the boys were beautiful. Even the ugly ones were somehow beautiful. Doug could have chosen any one of them.

They were also children. The depth and breadth of what they did not know astonished her. They'd mostly never heard of James Dean, Ronald Reagan, Virginia Woolf, Donald Rumsfeld, Bruce Springsteen, Rodney King. They were babies on 9/11. They loved to point out to her all the things they learned in school that they *would not ever use,* yet they had no idea what it was to be a grown-up person in the world, what one would use or not use in the span of a lifetime. Their lives had not even begun.

The peer edit did not last long. Ryan Harbinger derailed the lesson from the back row, hollering at Molly over his classmates' heads: "You're tight with Mr. Ellison, right?"

"Tight?" Molly asked.

"You hang out," explained Steph Malcolm-Swann, who was in the desk next to Ryan's, blackening her nails with a Sharpie.

Molly set aside her grade book. It was clear where they were going and even clearer that she shouldn't go there with them. But it was also flattering and pleasing and, honestly, surprising that they should care about her private life. "Why are we talking about this?"

Ryan nodded knowingly, as though she'd let slip crucial information. "So you know he took off."

"I know it's time to continue with class." She picked up her copy of *Death of a Salesman* and waved it at them. "Books, everybody?"

"Do you talk to him still?" Steph asked.

"I heard he got moved to a school in the city," offered Hannah Jones, who was in the front row typing into her iPhone, thumbs uninterrupted.

"I heard he got fired," said Amelia Frye.

"I heard he got wrapped," said Ryan.

Steph put down her Sharpie. "He wasn't fired, they made him quit."

"Wrapped for what?" asked Jonas Everett, who seemed to have just woken up, from a middle row.

"You know what." Ryan shook his fist and tongued his cheek, creating an obscene visual that made Molly feel queasy all over again.

"Baller," Wyatt said, grinning.

The class laughed.

In the front row, Abigail Cress had taken out her own *Salesman* and was staring determinedly at its cover. Molly could see they'd hit a topic about which Abigail had none of her signature confidence. And for the first time, Molly liked her. She and Molly were together in their miserable discomfort, the only ones in the room who wanted the conversation to end.

Their common opponent was Ryan, who willed it to go on and on. "So, Miss Nicoll," he said, stretching tanned arms over his head. "You and Mr. Ellison."

"We saw you together," Steph said, looking delighted and a little guilty.

"All those private lunches," said Ryan.

Molly stood up and took her place at the whiteboard. "Okay, guys, that's enough."

"What's he like?"

"Do you know where he went?"

"Did he tell you he was leaving?"

"No," Molly said, a little too forcefully. The room was silent, and she realized that she *had* been hurt by this small slight, that he had not thought enough of her to tell her goodbye.

"That's cold," said Nick Brickston, aptly; she supposed that he had read it on her face. Nick had been silent to that point, lounging in his seat in the corner of the room, splaying his long legs under the desk.

"I'd like to move on, please," Molly said.

Nick Brickston continued; the class turned to hear him. "All that time you hung out together? Then he just cuts out? You must be pissed."

"Hella," Ryan said.

Around the room were whispers and murmurs of assent. The kids had turned back to stare at her, with expressions both curious and pitying. Even Calista Broderick was watching her closely, her eyes unusually lucid, conveying something like compassion. Molly could see that it wasn't going to stop. And she didn't want to shut them down the way a typical teacher might—open dialogue was good for classrooms, and anyway there was kindness in their questions. Some buried thing within her, some long-subdued instinct, lunged for it. "Okay," she said. She leaned against the whiteboard, hugging her book to her chest. "Yes, we were friends. No, he didn't tell me he was going. Yes, it bothers me. Of course it does."

"But do you know—" began Samantha Aster.

Molly flashed her palm. "None of us knows what really happened, do we?"

In the silence that followed, Molly's kids glanced uncomfortably at one another. Molly had the sudden, horrible thought that they did know—they walked the same halls and heard the same rumors; they had heard, and maybe passed on, every sordid detail. They knew who the girl was when Molly did not. She had the thought that now they were protecting her.

Abruptly, in the front row, Abigail stood up. "I need the bathroom pass," she said.

"You know you don't have to ask," Molly told her, grateful for the interruption. She smiled meaningfully at Abigail while handing her the slip of purple paper. *Poor girl,* she thought, *she seems so mature in so many ways, but she's not ready for this.*

Abigail hurried out of the room.

"That's some fucked-up shit," Nick Brickston said philosophically as Abigail left, returning them immediately to the topic of Doug.

"That's enough," Molly told him, although she couldn't disagree. And liked him just a little more for having said, so bluntly and efficiently, what she could not.

THE ARTIST

This was how Nick Brickston got away with it.

Step One: Tell the client to register for the SAT at a distant location—a high school in San Francisco was best—where all would be anonymous.

Step Two: Make a fake high school ID with his picture and his client's name. His tools were few: iPhone camera, MacBook Pro with Photoshop, the laminating machine in his mom's home office.

Step Three: On test day, go to the school and wait. Flash the ID card and admission ticket. Keep the chitchat to a minimum, giving them no reason to ask questions.

Step Four: Sign his client's name on the line. (He studied each client's handwriting, then mimicked it—he'd heard that when test officials suspected cheating, they'd analyze the writing on the essay portion, and this, he thought, was a stupid reason to get caught.)

Step Five: Sit for the test. Open the booklet. Wait for the magic to start.

The essay test always came first. Nick told his clients ahead of time which historical and personal examples he planned to write about; that way, on the ride home, they could tell their parents how the test had gone and sound legit.

His current client, Dave Chu, had been mystified by this. "But how do you know what the essay prompt will be?" he'd asked.

"I'll tell you a secret," Nick had said. "Doesn't matter what it is. Any question they're gonna ask, you can answer it using World War II and fuckin' Martin Luther King. Then for the third example I tell a story, like how my little cousin Ricky got sick with cancer and how I helped him get through it and learned about the meaning of life or whatever. Trust me. The SAT eats that shit up."

"Is he all right?"

"Who?"

"Your cousin. Ricky."

"There *is* no Ricky, man. The SAT doesn't know that. Sympathy points."

Nick kept it casual with clients, but in truth he took pride in these essays, imagining the scorer who would read them: some apathetic English teacher, assessing essays on a Sunday for extra cash, would slog through the pile of asinine high school bullshit, growing bored, depressed, resentful even, before encountering Nick's thoughtful, elegant prose and becoming, well, entranced. Nick knew the risks of standing out; he simply couldn't help himself.

Nick was in seventh grade when his parents split up. Within a year, his dad had married someone else and bought her a big, sunny house in San Rafael, a few exits north on the 101 freeway. Right after that, he'd had new kids, twins, a boy and a girl with cherub faces and curly blond hair. They didn't look like Nick or his big sister, Amy, who were tall and lean with dusky hair and ink-drop eyes. They looked like the new wife.

On the day his dad's twins were born, Nick had gone to the hospital. In the private room, the new wife slept and Nick's dad cradled the girl twin, Addison, smearing tears out of his eyes. A nurse handed the boy twin, Colson, to Nick. He balanced the baby's body in his arms. Its eyes were closed, thin wet seams. It had flat cheeks furred with shimmery blond hairs, a Cheerio mouth, and a too-sweet reek, like buttermilk.

Nick grinned. "He's heavy," he said to his dad, and then to the baby, "You been eating fuckin' T-bones in there, bro?"

The baby struggled. Trying for a better hold, Nick jostled its head by mistake and it made a mewling-kitten sound that quickly surged into a screech.

"Hey, watch it!" Nick's dad said. "Be careful with him!" Laying the girl twin in the nurse's arms, he took the boy from Nick and hugged it to his chest, murmuring.

"Whatever," Nick said. He went to the window and slid down in a vinyl chair, plugged in his earbuds to listen to what looked like music but was actually words: an audiobook he'd found on iTunes.

Selfishness was holy, the book said. The only way. Nick wondered about this. It felt true. His dad bounced baby Colson around the room, hunching to coo secrets in his ear, and Nick listened to *The Fountainhead* by Ayn Rand and swiped through the Instagram feed on his phone, waiting for something to catch his eye. Anything happening. Any excuse to get out of that room.

His dad still asked him to visit some weekends—*"Cindi's got the guest room all ready for ya!"*—but Nick always refused. He could hardly stand to look at his dad's face. The man was so simply, stupidly, undeservedly happy—having spent Nick and Amy's childhood at the office, he wanted to try again with a new wife, new kids. Why should Nick be part of it? He and Amy didn't get to start over. That dark-haired, dark-eyed family, the one his dad had thought wasn't worth saving, was the only family they were going to have.

After his dad left, Nick had started running this scam on his mother. He'd say, "Mom, can you give me more than one snack for lunch tomorrow? I swear, I'm always starving. Guess I'm still growing!" Then he'd shrug and give her this big, sweet, *Leave It to Beaver* grin that always made her smile. She'd pack not two but three fruit snacks or bags of chips in the next day's lunch, and at school he'd sell all three to kids who'd left their lunches at home or didn't want to eat the nasty so-called health food they sold at the Valley Middle School Snack Bar. It's not like he was stealing. It was his food to start with.

He'd had a long career since then. When he was done with lunches, he started selling papers on the Internet. But that turned out to be too much work, so instead he started selling grade changes at school. For a fee, he'd hack into the online grading system—shockingly easy to do, people were so dumb about their passwords—and bump up a test score, adjust a project grade, mark a few blown-off homeworks as done. This year, he'd started selling fake IDs. Occasionally he threw parties at empty mansions that were on the market around Marin, hauling in kegs and charging every kid a fifty-dollar cover. Last year, he'd found a supplier in the city and started providing weed and pills outside the Miller Avenue 7-Eleven. Periodically he went to Silk Road online and bought bulk portions of Molly, a popular product to retail at parties. And then there was the SAT. In Marin County it was easy to make money—kids there didn't have allowances, they had bank accounts. And sometimes he did shit just because, to take a teacher down a notch or to shake up the dull day-to-day. The Photoshop of Abigail and Mr. Ellison had been like this.

After Nick's dad left, his mom had started working overtime to keep up with the mortgage. She left for work before he got up in the morning and came home after dark. Amy left for San Diego State. Nick took care of himself.

On Saturday morning in the city, in the fog that shrouded St. Antony's School, Nick waited to become Dave Chu.

He held the SAT admission ticket and ID and hoisted Dave's backpack on his shoulder. Inside were all these perfectly organized supplies his parents had probably packed for him—everything that the SAT website, playing on the last desperate hopes of low scorers, claimed would help—granola bars, a watch, a banana.

He was almost to the sign-in table when a girl from his school, Elisabeth Avarine, stepped into line behind him. What was she doing there? She wore tight black pants and flip-flops and an oversized UC Berkeley sweatshirt. Her face was bare, pillow-wrinkled, and her hair tied up, with blond wisps floating down. But she was still Shakespearean, a Juliet—*O, she doth teach the torches to burn bright*—and he saw why every guy wanted her. If she wanted him, he wouldn't turn her down. But this was impossible to imagine, because Elisabeth Avarine didn't exist in his dimension. She was like a hologram, shimmering, silent. At certain angles she seemed to disappear. Nick was more interested in someone he could touch.

"'Sup," he said, nodding.

Elisabeth gave him a small smile but then looked at the ground.

He wasn't offended. She always froze when teachers called her out in class, never spoke except in this whisper that wasn't a voice at all.

"Next!"

It was his turn to check in. He realized Elisabeth would hear him (presumably she could hear, even if she couldn't talk). She'd hear the lady ask his name and hear him say, "Dave Chu." But he couldn't turn back now. He would have to have faith.

Stepping up, he handed the ID and admission ticket to the lady behind the card table. She wore thick plastic glasses that magnified her eyes and made them swim in her face as she peered at the ID, at Nick, at the ID again. Nick held an easy smile, wiggled his toes in his sneakers, and steadied his breath while the lady stared at him, the ID, him, her eyes narrowing and widening, and he wondered if she'd bother to think this through, if she'd make herself ask the obvious question: *Is this Chinese boy really you?*

He waited for it. Almost welcomed it. It would be a new challenge to overcome—the scams had become almost too easy lately—but the lady just squinted again and asked him, "David Alexander Chu?"

"Yeah," Nick said. "I go by Dave, though."

Elisabeth made no noise behind him. The lady frowned; he could see her deciding whether to pursue this.

One thing Nick's career had taught him was that most people would rather go along than question—even when something terrible happened, a mass shooting, a suicide, and the news reporters swooped in to interview the bystanders, it was always, "I didn't know, he was nothing like this, of course there were no red flags, we couldn't see it coming." What these people meant, what they should have said, was that it had been easier not to look.

The lady sighed and pointed the way.

He glanced back as Elisabeth stepped up to the table and flashed her own ticket and ID. The lady at the table asked her something.

Elisabeth shook her head. The lady said something else and Elisabeth nodded, shifting from foot to foot, keeping her gaze on the table. Her eyes flickered up to meet his, unreadable.

In the classroom, Nick felt an uncommon flash of fear—was the proctor watching as he wrote Dave's name and address on the lines provided, penciled in the bubbles underneath?

Nick set down his pencil and stretched. Elisabeth had taken the seat behind his, and he turned toward her as casually as he could, searching her face for some affirmation—a nod, a mouthed *Don't worry,* anything—but she ignored him, hunching over her Scantron form, and with the heat of the proctor's gaze on his neck he turned forward again, squinting thoughtfully at a poster of mitosis and meiosis. His leg trembled under the desk and he stilled it, consoled by the fact that the shaking leg was as Dave Chuian a gesture as he could have possibly invented, easily explained by the anxiety of an inept test-taker facing down the Scantron, that firing squad of small, blank circles.

"Please turn to Section One in your test booklets," the proctor said.

Nick flipped the page.

Is it always advantageous to pay more attention to details than to the big picture?

He began to write. To focus, to settle into the rhythm of his breath and the sounds of pencils scratching, erasers squeaking, the world receding as he analyzed the words of Martin Luther King and the implications of the Holocaust for the fifty billionth time, all the while replicating Dave Chu's precise, small, blockish print, letters that hovered just above the line—and then the exhilaration as he finished the essay and worked his way through the math, the reading, the grammar, as he witnessed the incredible blinking circuitry of his own brain as it picked out patterns and called up formulas, skimmed dense blocks of text, unveiled the logic in the grammar of the sentences, dismissed red-herring answers and pushed toward the right ones, and honestly, it was hard to believe people had to be taught how to do this—that what he had, at least Sarah always told him, was a gift from God.

• • •

She wasn't exactly his girlfriend. She didn't demand a label, she seemed perfectly at peace whether he made promises or not, and she always looked happy to see him.

She was in school for dental hygiene and knew all there was to know about brushing and flossing and the names and positions of the teeth and the techniques for scraping off years of plaque with a tiny metal hook. But she didn't know about Nick's Mill Valley life. What would he get out of telling her?

Because here was Mill Valley lately: It was his mom at work and the housekeeper at home, running her vacuum through the living room, Nick tripping over the cord on his way out the door, taking the Audi and cruising around Marin for some kid to sell to or some girl to hook up with. And silencing his phone because his dad kept calling—not wanting to know Nick, just wanting him to visit the new family like some fucked-up guest of honor.

Here was Mill Valley. A dream made up to make eight-year-olds happy. You could tell Nick his own childhood had been a dream, and he might have believed it. All those grand redwoods. Tree-smelling skies. The mountain looming at the end of Miller Avenue, creased with trees and pearly-misted, or teal under torn-cotton clouds. The rich hippies parading along the triangle of avenues, congratulating themselves for buying Priuses along with their Range Rovers and getting their overpriced organic oranges at Whole Foods. And all the kids believing this was life. Kids like Tristan Bloch thinking they needed to die because otherwise there was no way out.

Nick could understand that.

After Tristan had jumped, the middle school teachers had cried and asked one another why. Tristan's mom had started wearing Anti-Bullying Awareness ribbons around town, and Nick's more earnest classmates had taken to wearing them too, each as shiny and ineffectual as a bit of Christmas tinsel. They'd made the kids write journals and stories and essays on the topic—*Tell us your feelings! Express yourself!*—as if the answer to a crisis was more homework. For the first assignment,

Nick had written the truth: that the eighth-grade boys were only act-ing sorry to get out of trouble, and the girls enjoyed making a drama of grief, sobbing and smearing their mascara for Tristan when they were really only thinking of themselves—*Did* I *have something to do with this? What if this happened to* me? And that none of them—not the students, not the teachers, except Ms. Flax—had wanted to deal with the kid when he was alive. When Nick's social studies teacher, Ms. Lamb, had read this, she'd sent him to the principal's office and called his mom in for a meeting. At the meeting, Nick was interrogated by the teacher, the principal, and the counselor, while his mom sat by sighing and rubbing her temples. And afterward, driving home, she'd told him, "I don't need this, Nick, honestly. Right now this is the last thing I need."

For the next assignment, Nick wrote a satirical story about Tristan Bloch as an angel in some vague, nondenominational Heaven, spilling grace upon Mill Valley and teaching all the eighth-grade kids to love one another and cherish life, "because all our souls are equal and con-nected through the generous and life-giving spirit of Mother Earth, just like we learned this year in the Native American Unit in Social Studies." Ms. Lamb gave him an A and pinned the story to the wall.

It was around this time—Tristan's death, Nick's parents' divorce, the specific hell of middle school—that Nick gave up the Gifted track. He began to treat school like a joke, or a game, because he saw that that was what it was: a game that kids could win or lose.

Tristan Bloch, for one, had lost. What made Nick different from Tristan was that he'd found a way to escape. He knew he couldn't do it out in the open, in front of everyone, in a town like Mill Valley—he wouldn't get ten steps out of his mom's house before someone pulled him back and set him up with some extremely expensive aura-cleansing therapy. No, he had to find a trapdoor somewhere.

First, he escaped in the one place he knew he wouldn't see anyone from school: the Fiction Room of the Mill Valley Public Library. There, as redwood branches brushed the windowpanes, he read everything his teachers didn't assign. (For what they did assign, that was why God invented SparkNotes.) Now he escaped by hopping a bus into the city—through the Headlands and over the Golden Gate Bridge and he was there, everywhere and nowhere. Anonymous. There, he could build his real life; freed from the tyranny of perfection, he could begin to be himself.

Sarah had long russet hair that trailed into his mouth when they lay in spoons on piles of blankets and rugs on the floor. Her eyes were the color of mint. Pale and clear. Wide open.

They'd met on Valencia Street three months before. The day was windy, fog scudding across the sky. He walked down the street in slim dark jeans, a black T-shirt and hoodie. The hoodie was two sizes too big, but he liked the bulk it lent him. Hunching against the wind, he pulled the hood over his head. But in the moment he saw Sarah, the wind whipped back, stirred his hair and shocked his ears.

She was passing out flyers on the street. Although she was short, her body looked curvy and full under an oversized apple-red sweater and two pink and gold scarves that wound in loose cowls around her neck. Her hair was tangled and her cheeks pink from the slaps of the wind. The papers in her hand were small and bright and she was giving them away. Smiling in earnest and walking up to people on the street, extending offerings to those who passed pretending not to see her or turned their heads to roll their eyes and smirk. No matter how many people walked by, she continued to smile with clean, white teeth.

Behind her stood a dingy, white-box building with colored paper flags strung over the threshold; the flags twisted in the wind and smacked against the edges of the door. A sign above read, HIS UNIVERSAL LOVE MINISTRIES. As Nick approached, the door opened, and yellow light spilled onto the street, along with the hum of people mingling inside. But Sarah was outside, alone.

Nick pulled his hood over his head. He'd been harassed by plenty of Jesus freaks in the city before, and wasn't in the mood to be indoctrinated. He fingered the plastic earbuds that he wore looped around his neck so he could slip them in at a moment's notice, block out the noise of the world. Sped up to pass her so he wouldn't have to be another asshole turning her down. He *was* that asshole, but didn't, for some reason, want her to know.

But she reached out to him, catching the edge of his sleeve. Her touch was slight, a small bird finding footing.

"Excuse me," she said. "Can I ask you something?" When she spoke, there was the smallest something wrong with it, a hint of a childhood lisp—it should have annoyed him but didn't. She gazed up at him and he noticed the daubing of freckles on her nose and over the tops of her cheeks. She said, "Are you happy?"

"What?"

"There is love all around you. You don't have to be alone."

Nick searched her face for a hint that she was messing with him, but her eyes were wide open, her gaze unwavering. "Are you serious?"

She smiled. "Why don't you come inside? There's coffee. And cookies, I think."

"Oh, fuck. Hold up. We talking Oreos? Or some, like, cardboard Nilla Wafer shit?"

She laughed, tilting her head back. The curve of her neck was creamy white. "I'm Sarah," she said. That lisp again. Her hands, as she took his and led him into the white-box church, were precise and small and soft, and he told himself, *She's blazed or crazy, walk away,* but something within him that was deeper than cynicism and deeper than embarrassment and deeper than fear said, *Stay.*

Nick went back to the church, again and again, until Sarah agreed to go out with him.

In Mill Valley, believing in God was something you just didn't talk about. But his friend Ryan's family was Christian, and once, when after a sleepover Nick's parents had been too busy to pick him up, Nick had gone with the Harbingers to church. And the pastor or reverend or whatever had trembled red and declared that God was their constant companion, and Jesus the Truth and the Light. There was a whole thing about how God was Jesus and Jesus was God that made no sense, but Nick didn't worry about that. He remembered instead the after part, when he stood in line with Ryan and his mom and dad and little sister, and when their turn came, the pastor gripped Nick's hand in both of his and told him, "Son, always remember that Jesus loves you. No matter what." Nick stared back, his hand trapped in the pastor's palms. Beside him, Ryan jabbed his ribs. Nick just stood there, the squeeze of palms so wet and close that he wanted to pull away, but, just for a minute, he didn't.

The first day he entered Sarah's church, he wanted to laugh. The mantras, the chanting, the sitting cross-legged on the dusty floor discussing God's abiding love—it all seemed so self-conscious, pretentious. The old guru in charge had taken the bits and pieces of religions that he wanted and left the rest behind. Nick couldn't believe in it. But he did believe in Sarah.

So he stayed. Removed his shoes and socks and sat beside Sarah and watched as she placed her palms on her knees and closed her eyes.

"There is nothing but this moment," the guru said. "We will close our eyes and feel the universal love move through us."

Nick stifled his laugh by fake-coughing.

The guru said, "Now we will make one sound together."

The people in the circle puffed their bellies, and then a low hum carried through the room, building power slowly, reverberating. Nick smirked and turned to Sarah, but she had her eyes squeezed shut and was humming as earnestly as all the others.

The rug they sat on was old and gritted and had bald patches in its oriental pattern. This was something his mother wouldn't stand for. He stared at it, at one space where the rug had been worn but not worn through, and as he stared he shook his foot, which kept tingling and falling asleep, and felt the presence of Sarah's body beside him and tried not to hear what the guru was droning on and on about. When the guru finally shut up, Nick closed his eyes and listened to the silence. The room smelled increasingly of feet. There was the occasional cough or sigh and, once, a low, whistling fart that cracked him up, but when he opened his eyes, he saw that the guru was staring at him and that no one else had laughed or even seemed to notice, so he made a straight face and forced himself to watch the worn spot on the carpet until after a year or two passed someone finally said,

"Amen. *Namaste.*"

The people bowed, then stood and stretched. Dazedly they smiled at one another, brushed off their pants and skirts.

"What did you think?" Sarah asked him as they walked into the open air.

"I think, where can we go now?" he said.

But she turned him down.

So he'd returned, again and again, each time forcing himself to sit through the entire service, staring at the objects in the room and holding his breath as much as possible and trying not to laugh.

One day he'd focus on the rolled edge of a flyer unpeeling from the wall. The next, the guru's weird bent toes, big and tanned with blond hairs sprouting, the nails clipped short and buffed to shine. Next time, it was the electrical cords that were tangled like briars on the floor in one corner of the room, and from there, a crooked outlet halfway up the wall, a small blank face with nothing plugged into it. And then, when he knew he could get away with it, he focused on Sarah's small hand as it cupped her right knee, her short, unpainted nails, the freckles on her fingers and the thin gold ring around her pinky, like something given on Christmas to a child.

The weeks went on like this. Each Saturday, she drew him in. Each Saturday, he sat and watched the objects in the room while the guru droned about love, forgiveness, God and meaning and universal truth, until they settled into that long and awkward silence in which Nick was supposed to feel something. And each time, he felt nothing but the wanting. Her. Afterward he always asked her to hang out with him, but she'd just smile and shake her head.

He told himself, *Forget her, give it up*. He didn't have to work so hard. There were plenty of girls in Mill Valley.

But then one day, for no apparent reason, she said yes. That morning he'd been made to see his dad and so was feeling particularly shitty; he'd asked her to dinner out of habit, not expecting to hear yes, not even really caring. They went for tacos and beers and he saw why she had been so careful—because as soon as she allowed herself to give him something, she gave it all. She told him everything, about her school, her friends, her parents and five sisters in Visalia—some dusty-sounding place between San Francisco and L.A.—and her religion, which she'd found a year ago, how she'd felt so lost in the city, anxious and alone, until she'd found His Universal Love Ministries and found herself, for the first time in weeks, able to draw a full breath.

Then it was Nick's turn to talk. He didn't mean to lie to her; the stories came so easily they were almost unconscious. He was in his second year at City College, majoring in English. He shared a shitty apartment in the Tenderloin with four guys from school, an apartment chaotic with comings and goings, where there was pot smoke in the air vents and pee rings in the toilets, trash in the hallway, moldy dishes in the sink.

"You wouldn't want to see it," he told her. "Where's your place?"

After taking Dave Chu's SAT, Nick went to meet his supplier in Dolores Park, and then on to Sarah's apartment. He knew it well by now.

She lived in a falling-down Victorian on Valencia. Painted red and pink with lacy wooden trim, it looked like a cake designed by a five-year-old. But he liked it, because it was ancient and crappy and no one had come in with a crew and a pile of money to fix it up. It was allowed to exist.

He climbed the stairs. The wood felt soft, gnawed on. Her studio was at the top, a wood-floored room with scuffed beige walls and tall ceilings, a sink and hot plate in the corner, a narrow doorway leading to a tiny bathroom tiled pink. In the main room were two huge windows she kept uncovered, and outside a view of Valencia, crowded stucco storefronts and patchwork Victorian façades, and Muni wires sketching geometric patterns on the sky. Packs of twentysomethings roamed in and out of taco joints and bars, and there was the steady thrum of traffic and people passing on the street. As night fell, fog settled over the city, misted the streetlights.

And Sarah. She sat beside him on the couch, which was draped by an ugly flowered sheet that looked a thousand years old and had the falling-apart softness cotton got when it had been worn and washed a million times, like his favorite T-shirts he'd had since elementary school that his mom was always telling him he didn't need and should let the housekeeper use as rags.

Sarah nestled into the corner of the couch and turned toward him. Unwinding her long gold scarf, she nudged her stockinged toes under his thighs. "This city is always so cold," she said. "Have you noticed that? Even when it's warm, there's cold underneath, like the fog is just waiting to roll back in."

"I'll keep you warm," he said.

She grinned. Pulled his face to hers and kissed his mouth, his cheeks, his forehead. He closed his eyes and she kissed each eyelid, then pulled his body over hers. He felt her moving underneath him live and warm and open and he could fall into this softness, he could disappear inside it. His blood resounded in his ears. She pushed him back, she laughed. Her laugh was loud and full, rolled over him, and he laughed too. There was no talk of love. With focused blood he unwound her layers of skirts and scarves like she was a present, her flesh glowing pink in the light of the lamp. Her freckles were cinnamon on the caps of her knees and along her arms and she was wearing nothing fancy, a white cotton bra and briefs that shouldn't have turned him on (the Mill Valley girls wore tiny lace thongs from Victoria's Secret) but did.

After, they lay together on the couch with their legs hanging over the edge, and he wanted nothing in the world but sleep. But she was restless.

"Wait, I've got an idea." She jumped up and ran naked to the bathroom, flesh bare and trembling. Seconds later she returned in white panties, hands up, dental floss stretched thumb to thumb.

It was weird, but he lay back and let her do it—rested his head on the arm of the couch and opened his mouth.

Sarah stood over him, frowning in concentration. Her hair waved over her shoulders and chest. "Close your eyes."

The glossy ribbon, laced with mint, slid between his teeth and wiggled into his gums. It felt good. It tingled. It hurt.

"Oh!" she said. "You're bleeding."

He ran his tongue over his teeth, tasted liquid metal. "Keep going," he said. He heard her steady breathing as she worked the floss between his teeth, pressing into the tissue.

After all those boring hours at her church, this was when he felt it: love was all around him. It was here, it was in this room. But only if he let it in.

He waved at her to stop, swallowed the traces of blood that had seeped from his gums. "Sit down," he said. "I have to tell you something."

"What is it? Are you okay?" She came and sat beside him on the couch.

"I'm, yeah, I'm amazing. I just have to tell you—I don't want any secrets—"

"You can tell me anything."

"I know." He hesitated. Her pupils were wide in the low light. "There's something you should know about me."

"What?"

"I want you to know me."

She smiled. "I do. What are you talking about?"

"No—I mean, you do, but not really. Not everything—"

"What are you trying to say?"

He'd come this far, so he let it all go, telling her everything, rambling, clumsy. "I don't go to City College. I don't live in the Tenderloin and I don't have roommates. I mean, I don't live in the city, period." He went on. It took just a minute to unravel it all.

"I don't understand," she said.

He had made a mistake. The moment of grace had passed, seemed suddenly stupid, and he heard the door close in her voice. Felt her turning against him. She took her sweater from the arm of the couch and covered herself.

He said, "I live in Mill Valley. I go to high school."

"High school?"

He nodded. "I come to the city to do the SAT—I take it for people, they pay me and I—"

"Who does? Wait. How old are you?"

"To get the right scores, so they can get into Stanford or whatever—"

"So, you cheat."

"No. I take it legit. I'm just, like, really good at it. It's easy for me, and—"

"Easy? To take some rich kid's allowance so he can cheat his way into college? And you're, what, sixteen? Oh my God." Clutching the sweater to her chest, she stood and backed away from him. "Where are my clothes?"

Her skirt was balled up at his feet. He handed it to her. "Sarah, listen, I'm still me."

"You're a liar, Nick." She stepped into the skirt, yanked the sweater over her head. "Of everything you've told me in the last three months, how much was true?"

Not much, he realized. "That I care about you, Sarah—that I had a, I don't know, fuck, like a breakthrough, now, tonight, and it's all because of you—"

"So none of it. Basically."

He'd have to play the last card he had left. "That I love you, Sarah, okay? I think I love you. And I think you maybe love me too."

She hugged her ribs. "I don't even know you. I don't have any idea who you are. Do you?"

There was nothing he could say.

"Get out," she told him.

He put on his jeans and hoodie. Slipped his iPhone into his pocket and looped the earbuds around his neck. She didn't move. He could feel her shivering, watching.

He opened the front door. Turned back to tell her . . . he didn't know what.

Sarah's eyes were red and wet. She shook her head. "What a fucking waste."

Then she shut the door behind him; from outside, he heard the bolt slide over and click into the jamb.

Hunching against the cold, he walked to the bus stop two blocks down. He understood that he had lost her. And yet, there was still the Nick that he'd invented—older, freer, living on his own terms. This version of himself, he knew, was not real now, but could be. And that was something to believe in.

At lunch on Monday, he found Elisabeth Avarine in the courtyard at school.

"Here," he told her, holding out three hundred dollars in cash. "Your cut." She looked confused, so he added, "Thanks for, you know, helping me out. Keeping this between us."

She cocked her head and stared up at him, like she was running through and vetoing ideas of what to say. Or judging him. Which was why most people had decided she was a stuck-up bitch years ago. "What am I supposed to do with this?" she asked finally.

"Whatever you want."

She furrowed her brow like this was a brand-new, strange idea. "What would you do?"

He couldn't tell her the truth—that he'd bank it and know that he was a few hundred dollars closer to freedom. Instead he told her something that would be easier for her to believe.

"You know me," he said, and grinned. "Get some refreshments. Host a function. Fuckin' rage."

That spring, a series of storms rolled through Mill Valley, and the days were made sunless and strange. All that distinguished the town in clearer weather—the steep hillsides, the glittering marshland, the redwood groves that had grown for a thousand years—now seemed dangerous. Streets ran to rivers. Downtown was a mess. Terwilliger Marsh, risen above the level of its reeds, seeped into the sixth-grade playground at the middle school. Redwood trees collapsed over Panoramic Highway and power lines cracked, threw sparks against the wind. Up on the mountain, the housewives were stuck in their driveways, their narrow streets blocked by felled lines. On campus, rain pelted the windows, flooded the landscaping, and streamed down the front steps. Because Valley High had no cafeteria, students crowded the halls during lunch, huddling in stairwells or eating cross-legged on the floor. This situation didn't seem to bother anyone but Molly. Her colleagues only stepped around the kids, avoiding looking down.

She began to leave her classroom door open at lunch. Soon kids were gathering inside—first her students, then their friends, then anyone who needed a dry desk to eat on. The room filled with smells of wet wool and sandwiches and sushi and chai lattes, and with the clamor of kids: kids talking and laughing and shouting, scuffling with one another, drumming on desktops, blasting music on iPhones. Coke cans and candy wrappers cluttered her trash bins. Rain-dampened backpacks were strewn across her floor. She didn't mind. She had given the kids a place to be. And they had begun to talk to her—about their homework and their grades but also about their lives, their one-act plays and sailing regattas and soccer games. They complained to her about their other teachers. They waved to her in the hallways. In class they chattered happily, as though they actually wanted to be there.

Yet Molly's classroom still looked, mostly, like Jane Frank's domain. It was time that she made it her own. She went in on a Sunday, when she would not have to explain what she was doing. First she broke the rows of desks—they conveyed rank and opposition where camaraderie was wanted—and arranged them into two concentric circles. Then she pushed her own desk to the side of the room. On the desk—which to this point had held nothing more than her grade book and office supplies and three or four outdated, official-looking handbooks—she stacked novels she intended to read or recommend. She displayed a porcelain cougar that Bobbi had sent upon learning it was Valley High's mascot and a bouquet of paper dahlias that Steph Malcolm-Swann had made for her in art class. Next she brought out the prints that she'd stored in the trunk of her car, having never gotten around to hanging them at home: a photograph of Joan Didion smoking a cigarette, cover art from Dylan's *Highway 61 Revisited*, a Rothko that had always evoked for her the threadlike line between heaven and hell. All these and more she pinned to the corkboards on which Jane Frank had hung her passive-aggressive grammar posters and lengthy lists of rules. Finally she went into the storage room and found an olive-colored vinyl couch that seemed abandoned, dragged it noisily down the empty corridor. It fit perfectly under the windows at the back of her room. There she rested, pleased with her work. The classroom felt like home—a truer home to her, anyway, than any she had claimed.

A strange energy had begun to build in Molly's blood, a deep and relentless curiosity. She wanted to know her kids. She wanted to defend them, if she could—from predators like Doug Ellison who would hurt them, from the expectations of their parents and the cruelties of their peers. She'd sit across from perpetually spaced-out Calista Broderick, who was her most compelling student and the hardest to reach, and long to ask all manner of impossible questions: *Why are you like this? What is your house like? How can I help you? What do you want?* She'd notice Elisabeth Avarine passing by her open classroom door, always alone, her slender body shrouded in loose T-shirts, her shoulders hunched in what might have been misery, or shame. And again, she would wonder.

But it was not Calista or Elisabeth whom Doug had chosen, or any of the prettier girls at school. It was Abigail Cress.

When she first heard her colleagues whisper the girl's name, Molly was shocked. How had Doug managed to seduce such a smart, driven student? And how had it affected the girl? Setting aside her own feelings about Doug, Molly began to watch Abigail closely, searching her face for signs of psychic damage. Catching her eye in class, Molly would offer what she hoped was a reassuring smile. Once she knelt by her desk and said, gently, "If you ever need someone to talk to, Abby, I'm here." But the only discernible change in Abigail Cress was a renewed impenetrability. She was the kind of student to whom a teacher was neither a confidante nor a kindred spirit, but an insensate dispenser of assignments and grades. Eventually Molly had to accept the truth: that Abigail did not want her, that for this girl, in this case, there was nothing she could do.

One afternoon, Amelia Frye, the girl who'd read an answer off her phone on the first day, broke down crying at Molly's desk. She sobbed into her fist. Her shoulders were shaking. Her bangs were strewn over her forehead. The cause of this breakdown, as far as Molly could tell, was the C+ she'd been given on her *Death of a Salesman* essay. It lay between them, unloved, on the desk.

"Amelia, I'm sorry. I know it's not what you wanted. But we can talk about how to make the paper better. I can even help you plan a rewrite, and you can turn it in again for extra credit. How's that?"

This offer seemed only to refresh Amelia's anguish—she squeezed her eyes shut and let out a new string of sobs. *"I'm . . . so . . . stressed . . . out."*

"It's going to be okay, I promise."

"But it isn't okay. Everything is fucking terrible. I got in a fight with my best friend and she's still so pissed at me. And I didn't even do anything *wrong*."

"Oh," Molly said.

"And I'm never going to get into UCLA, my SAT score is fucking pathetic and my grades suck this semester and I don't even know why, and I can't show a C to my parents, they'll flip their shit, they're such fucking *assholes*!" Here she paused to breathe. Molly could see where acne bloomed beneath her makeup; a frenzied pink mottled her cheeks. She looked up at Molly with red and smeary eyes, and in a voice that was startling in its softness asked, "You know?"

Molly did not know, yet she did. Somehow, without exactly meaning to, she had slipped into a real, human moment with Amelia Frye. All she knew for sure was that she did not want to lose it.

"You know what?" she said. "Forget it. I can see you really tried here." She pulled a pen from the desk drawer, crossed out the C+ on Amelia's paper, and wrote a B in its place.

Seeing this, Amelia transformed: she stopped sniffling, her skin calmed, her eyes brightened. "Oh my God! Really?"

Molly smiled back. "Life is hard enough, right?" She reached across the desk and touched Amelia's hand.

It had been a risky impulse, but the girl didn't flinch. "Thank you," she said, giving Molly a broad and genuine smile. "This is totally going to save my life."

That night, Amelia Frye sent Molly a friend request on Facebook. Molly received the request over email—she hardly ever visited the site. The few photographs of her there, posted by her sister, were almost embarrassingly benign: she posed stiffly at her college graduation, forked cake at her niece's birthday party. By contrast, Amelia's page was crowded and alive. There were photos of her from every imaginable area of her life. She was there as a baby, sitting between young, attractive parents in a field of wild lupine. As a toddler she screamed with shut eyes, clenching a doll's neck. At eight or nine she made a clamshell with her tongue. At twelve, strapped to a snowboard on a chairlift, she grinned, swung her feet over the white void below. At thirteen she flexed her palm at the camera. More recent pictures showed her stretched by a backyard swimming pool in a chevron-print bikini, grinning in a pile of her peers on an overstuffed couch, and posing in black satin with a lime lawn behind her, narcissus blooms tumbling over her wrist, wearing a practiced, closed-mouth smile. There were status posts and links to videos and comments and comments on the comments that were posted. And there were glimpses of Molly's other students—Abigail Cress in the track-and-field team photo, Nick Brickston in the background of a party.

After a moment's hesitation—was there something in her contract about this?—she accepted Amelia's request.

Driving home one stormy Friday afternoon, Molly noticed the lanky figure of Nick Brickston under a redwood tree in the 7-Eleven parking lot. There was an elegant slump to his shoulders, a large black backpack at his feet.

She rolled down her window and shouted to him through the rain.

He acknowledged her with a quick but perceptible lift of his chin, which she took as a welcoming sign. She waved until he slung his backpack on one shoulder and came to her passenger window. His face was glistening. His skin looked slightly bluish in the rain. Water was dripping off his San Francisco Giants cap and drenching his hoodie and backpack. She worried, briefly, about the well-being of his books.

"What are you doing out here?" she said. "Let me give you a ride."

"That's okay."

"You can't stay out in this. I couldn't live with myself." She reached across and unlocked the passenger door. "Come on, I'll take you home."

Nick opened the door. "You sure?" he asked, glancing with uncharacteristic anxiousness over his shoulder.

She felt a flicker of paranoia—was someone watching them?—but covered it with a smile. "Get in."

Nick shrugged off his backpack and folded into the car. The pack was a brick at his feet, his knees high. He must have been over six feet. He didn't seem this tall in her classroom—but then, he was usually confined to a wrap-around desk, she on her feet at an appropriate distance.

"Do you want to toss that in back?" Molly asked, pointing to the backpack. She glanced in the rearview and immediately regretted the offer—evidence of her humanity was strewn with embarrassing abandon over the backseat: a Target circular with cut-out coupons, a potato chip bag spilling crumbs, a sports bra.

"It's all good," he said.

"So, where are we going?"

"Into the labyrinth," he said, and pointed her into Sycamore Park.

The maze of narrow streets was drenched and gray, the sidewalks bare except for a smattering of mothers who were bundling their children into European SUVs. The rain drummed the roof of Molly's Honda and shuddered down the windows. The heater whooshed hot air at their feet, intensifying the smells of his soaked cotton hoodie and cigarettes and her damp hair, her too-sweet shampoo, candy-apple, bought on sale.

Nick stared out the passenger window. Teenagers never felt the social burden of small talk; that was one thing Molly had come to like about them. But his silence was excruciating; she was compelled to fill it.

"So, how are you liking the class so far?"

He shrugged. "It's cool."

After a moment she offered, "Your *Salesman* essay was very insightful. I was impressed."

He nodded. "Yeah." Spectacular, the confidence of teenage boys! They took compliments like points they were owed—unlike the girls, who were surprised, or eager to say she was wrong.

"I think the other students would really benefit from your ideas. It would be nice to hear more from you in class."

"No doubt," he said, smirking, then pointed left. "Turn here."

Molly turned in to Tamalpais Park, dismayed by how easily she had reverted to talking about school, because at the age of twenty-three she still had absolutely no clue what boys wanted her to say to them. Behind the silvery wash of the rain, she made out tasteful Craftsman and ranch houses, picket fences slick and white. Giant redwoods, oaks, and sycamores. Along the narrow streets she saw nothing garish or overlarge, nothing ugly or out of place. In some ways it was absolutely ordinary. It was disconcerting, and somewhat depressing, to know that no matter how successful a teacher she was, she could never afford to live on these streets, in this neighborhood Nick Brickston knew as home.

Then, without warning, he spoke. "You know who you remind me of?"

"Who?"

"I'm tryna figure it out. I know. That girl from that book."

"Which? *Gatsby*?" She thought foolishly, *Let it be Daisy*.

"Naw, the one from last year. About the governess and that crazy bitch in the attic."

"Oh. You mean *Jane Eyre*." She must have frowned, because he seemed to make a calculation, then said,

"Yeah, like Jane. But also, that girl who was in *Titanic*. Rose whatever. Kind of like Jane Eyre and the girl from *Titanic* had a baby."

"Kate Winslet?"

"That's it."

The water streamed steadily around them. She was aware of Nick's body in the close space. Without wanting to, she thought of Doug Ellison, the hotel room, the girl. Was this how it started? As easily as pulling over in a rainstorm, unlocking a passenger door?

She cleared her throat. "So you do read the books. I was beginning to wonder if anyone did."

"When I feel like it."

"And you read on your own as well? You must."

Nick shrugged. Now he seemed embarrassed—he jutted his chin and she noticed his skinny, razor-burned neck, and the blackheads that muddled the grooves of his nose. She saw that she had pushed into a tender place, to witness something he spent most of his waking hours ensuring no one got to see.

"Stop here," he said.

She pulled in front of a two-story yellow Craftsman with a BMW in the driveway and a basketball hoop over the garage. It had a wide white porch and a front door flanked by outsized windows. The blinds were open, and through the rain Molly made out the form of a little girl, nine or ten, who was staring at them through the window, pressing her palm to the glass. What was she looking for?

"Is that your sister?" Molly asked Nick.

"That's just Nell," he said.

"Lovely home."

He looked at it like he'd never thought of it that way, or any way at all. "I guess," he said. "Hey, thanks for the ride, Miss Nicoll."

"Call me Molly," she said automatically, and they both were startled.

"Okay?"

She couldn't take it back, somehow. "See you in class."

Nick stepped out into the rain and slammed the car door behind him. She waited until he'd loped up the slate walkway and knocked at the front door. When at last the door opened, Ryan Harbinger was on the other side. The boys knocked fists, then turned to squint at her car through the rain. She sat there in confusion. This was Ryan's house? Why had Nick brought her here? Why hadn't he told her this was where he wanted to go? Was there any limit to the list of things she didn't know? Both boys waved and she pulled her car into gear; she had forgotten, briefly, that she was visible.

That night, there was a friend request from Nick Brickston waiting for her on Facebook. She hesitated for only a moment before accepting. She liked Nick, and anyway she'd already said yes to Amelia Frye.

Molly sat on the love seat in her little apartment and looked into Nick Brickston's world. She saw him bleary-eyed at parties, cheery with his mother, brooding at the mountain's edge, and shirtless (pale and skinny) at the beach. She read what he wrote on his friends' pages (much of it nonsense, none of it about her) and what they wrote to him. She saw him playing video games in Damon Flintov's bedroom and smoking a cigarette at Ryan Harbinger's baseball game. She read his friends' complaints about all their other teachers and all their other work, and was quietly thrilled to be the one they liked, the one who understood them and didn't assign work over holiday weekends, or when there were tests in other classes, who in fact hardly assigned work at all.

Jane Frank's curriculum called for *The Scarlet Letter*, but Molly chose *A Clockwork Orange* instead. She knew her kids: Hawthorne would not stand a chance. But the boys in her class would be braced by *Clockwork*'s violence, while girls like Calista might find the poetry inside.

On a foggy Monday morning, Molly greeted her class and handed out the paperbacks, then sat atop an empty desk, resting her feet on a chair and her book on her knees. The kids settled back in their seats. On the couch at the back of the room, Ryan Harbinger sprawled with his head thrown back on the cushion, Samantha Aster tucked under his arm. Jonas Everett sat wide-kneed on the other end, and Steph Malcolm-Swann and Amelia Frye spooned on the center cushion; Steph was French-braiding Amelia's hair. Molly began to read aloud. As soon as she started, five or six kids rested their heads on their desks, a few closed their eyes. She didn't mind. She knew that they were listening, like little children. She believed that, despite all the optimistic theory she'd been taught, in the end this was the best she could do for them: to let them hear the language.

After several minutes she was interrupted by the squeaking open of the classroom door. Katie Norton peered into the room. Her eyes traveled with evident concern over the circles of desks, the couch crammed with kids in the back, the collage of posters, and the mess of the teacher's desk, and landed on Molly.

"Good morning, Miss Nicoll. Sorry to interrupt. I have someone here who's very eager to join you." The principal turned and whispered urgently to a figure in the hall, then turned back and pulled the person in. In the principal's grip, bare-headed and flush-faced, was Damon Flintov.

On seeing him, the class erupted in hoots and cheers. Ryan Harbinger jumped up from the couch to pump his fist and shout, "Yo, yo, yo! Flint in the motherfuckin' building!"

"Free at last!" yelled Nick Brickston.

"Fuck yeah, bitches!" Damon hollered back.

"Hey!" Katie Norton snapped. "Is that the kind of language we use in here?"

"Of course not," Molly said. "Come on, guys. We're all just excited to see Damon." Damon was grinning with his ruddy, chubby cheeks, the silver stud glinting over each eyebrow. But his blue eyes were luminous and clear, and a little uncertain. He was only a kid, after all. One of hers. Why had she been so afraid of him?

"We're glad to have you back, Damon," she said now. "We missed you." As she said it, she realized she meant it. In a rush of good feeling, she stepped forward and embraced him. He smelled powerfully of boy: cigarettes and menthol deodorant and undertones of sour laundry. His chest was broad and fleshy and shielded by a T-shirt and she felt the queasy sensation of her breasts pressed against him, a fact of a hug that she remembered too late. His arms hung at his sides as she squeezed him. She heard him breathing. She felt him hesitate. She patted his shoulder blades and let him go.

Pulling away, Molly realized Katie Norton was watching them, arms crossed over her chest, on her face a contemplative frown. Months ago Molly might have rushed to Doug Ellison to debate what this meant. Now she knew better. She was trusting her instincts. She was doing her job.

THE DIME

Elisabeth Avarine ate lunch alone, on a low stone bench among orange trees, in a sun-baked courtyard. Her companion, in that little-populated corner of the school, was the small stone statue of a girl who sat atop the fountain in the center, gazing mutely with her head inclined. Perhaps it was the statue that drew Elisabeth here, day after day, or perhaps it was the faint citrus fragrance in the air, or the clock tower above, its arched windows revealing occasional flickers of light and ghosts. Perhaps it was that she simply found it easier to spend her lunches here, away from the groups on the front lawn and the smoking circles in the back parking lot and the crowds at the shopping center across the street. She had no obvious place in this complex social matrix nor the drive to insert herself within it. She preferred to be here—to tuck herself into this secluded, sunny courtyard, communing with a sixty-year-old statue, her small, contemplative face of stone, safely out of sight.

Nick Brickston, a person to whom she had never really spoken, stood before her, extending a wad of twenty-dollar bills and telling her he owed her. Telling her to take the money and spend it on, of all things, a party.

Elisabeth took a moment to process this. Squinting up at him, she saw a boy who was tall and thin with a sharp, narrow face, a boy who associated with slackers and tried to pass as one himself but whose eyes betrayed him, quick, intelligent, and dark. In response to these eyes Elisabeth's mind went blank, as often happened when she was given the imperative to speak, converse, parlay, *be normal*—in short, she was afraid.

Finally she said, "I can't take this."

"Sure you can. You did your part. Our secret, right?"

Our secret. The phrase sent a rare thrill through her body: she felt as if a gate were cracking open, she was being led inside. At the SAT, the registrar had asked her about Nick and she'd denied knowing him, not out of any sense of loyalty but because it was her nature to say nothing, to remain safely uninvolved. Now she saw that her decision to keep quiet meant, potentially, much more. She told Nick, "With or without the money. I wouldn't tell."

He sat down next to her. Casual, close. He smelled like cigarettes. He sat the way boys did, legs spread wide so his knee nudged her thigh. Warm, assured, he pressed the wad of bills into her palm. "Look," he said, "it's cool. I want you to have it."

"I can't have a party," she said.

"Of course you can."

"What I mean is, I don't—" she began, then stopped herself. Dipped her gaze to her lap, where her hands were clenched and knuckles white. How could she explain to someone like Nick Brickston, a boy who felt entitled to be everywhere, with anyone, *I don't have any friends*? To know this fact was one thing; to say it, impossible.

Nick was watching her closely—she felt his gaze on her neck. But it wasn't the kind of gaze she was used to. He was seeking something deeper. She didn't know what he hoped to find. She was desperate for him to leave and desperate for him not to. She could not think of a thing to say, and her silence stretched, terrible, between them.

Finally he saved her. "You know what? I'm gonna help you out. I've got some fuckin', what, expertise in this area. You got a house in the canyon, right? Your mom ever go out of town?"

All the time. Napa, Tahoe, Santa Barbara, Vail, depending on the guy. "In a few weeks, maybe? I'm not sure." Her voice sounded small to her ears, unsteady.

"That works," Nick said. "I'll put the word out." He pocketed the money. As he took out his phone and began to text, over Elisabeth's body rolled a sickly wave, as if she were boarding a puke-inducing roller coaster advertised as fun.

A clatter of metal turned Elisabeth's head—a small crowd was pushing through the doors, tumbling into the sun. They were Bo-Stin beach kids: Alessandra Ryding, Jess Steinberg, Kai Alder-Judge, and Cally Broderick. They had hair that waved to their waists or shaggy mops or dreads, cutoff shorts or ripped flared jeans and thrift-store tank tops or thin-strapped cotton dresses without bras. They went sockless in men's oxfords or flip-flops or no shoes at all.

Elisabeth could not help staring at Cally Broderick, who danced into the sun in a gauzy white sundress and bare feet. Her caramel hair tangled and waved to her waist and she squinted and laughed on the sun-bleached stones and she carried no bookbag, no books, just a small woven purse that could not have held more than a pencil. Cally—or *Calista,* as she called herself now—wasn't a real beach kid. She lived in a Mill Valley condo, as boring as the rest of them. In fact, she used to be joined at the hip with Abigail Cress. But after eighth grade, Cally had made a miracle happen. To Elisabeth it was almost unbelievable. She had wanted to become a different person, and then she did.

Before Elisabeth could talk herself out of it, she turned back to Nick Brickston and agreed to go along with whatever scheme he wanted, poured her faith into his hands.

Elisabeth lived in the hundred-year-old house her mom had won in the divorce.

Her parents' serious fighting began when she was eight. They fought and broke up and made up and broke up and made up until Elisabeth turned fifteen and her mom told her dad it was finally over. He moved to San Francisco. She said it would be easier for everyone. Elisabeth didn't get a say; she was only a kid. In the fifteen months since, he'd been traveling around or staying at their Hamptons house; she'd seen him only a handful of times. He'd sent her weekly emails and monthly checks addressed in this oddly formal way—*To Miss Elisabeth Madison Avarine.* On her sixteenth birthday, a new white Audi appeared in the driveway with keys in the console and a card on the dashboard. *Happy Birthday to My Special Girl,* the card said, but her dad wasn't there. Now he was like a ghost, haunting the big house in the canyon where their family used to live.

The house was gorgeous and huge, perched on an acre of steep, wooded hillside in the canyon behind Old Mill Park. It was worth at least three million dollars. But lately it had begun to reveal its frailties: hairline leaks in the sloped and shingled roof, strange clogs and clangings in the pipes, wood rot at the edges of the deck. Slowly but steadily, Elisabeth believed, the house was crumbling to pieces. Eventually it would surrender, retract its claws from the hillside, and slide into the dark.

Elisabeth's mom didn't fix things; she redecorated. After Elisabeth's dad moved out, each room was given a makeover, a color, and a name. Elisabeth's was the Purple Room: lilac walls, amethyst curtains, a lavender bedspread with heliotrope pillows. Her mom had the Blue Room, periwinkle with accents of cerulean and steel. There was the Red Room, where, when it was still white, her dad once retreated to manage the money—now it was a guest suite with rose-petal walls and ruby pillows, although no one ever came to stay.

The kitchen was her mom's studio, a blank slate. It was vast and bright and a skylight stretched across its ceiling, spilling pale light over birch cabinets and bamboo floors. Redwood branches swept across the skylight, shedding needles at the edges of the glass. Jars of paints and brushes and her mom's easel and canvases filled the room where normal people might cook food. Her mom had started painting right after the divorce. Landscapes, still lifes, twisted self-portraits. In real life, Heather Avarine was a true brunette with highlights of henna in her hair, smooth olive skin, neatly arched eyebrows, wide green eyes; in the paintings, her skin was cornflower blue, hair twists of indigo, eyes violet gleams. Though these paintings embarrassed Elisabeth, they were also her favorites. She liked to stare into the violet eyes and imagine what the shadow-mother on the wall was really thinking.

The kitchen opened to the White Room, where the walls were papered with bleached linen. Glass coffee and side tables floated on plush white carpet. There was a snow-colored couch and love seat. The accent pillows were white and there were white chenille throw blankets that Elisabeth and her mom would tuck over their toes when they curled up to watch Molly Ringwald movies from when her mom was in high school, or *Project Runway,* her mom's favorite show. Her mom always knew immediately which designer's outfit was the most fabulous and which one had no style and was doomed to go home. "In fashion, Liza-Belle, the worst thing you can be is boring," she explained. "It's the same in life. Even ugly is better than boring."

In the White Room a wall of bare, floor-to-ceiling windows faced the redwood deck and the forested canyon below. When her mom went out at night, Elisabeth would sit alone on the love seat and scan the dark canyon for signs of life. She knew any hiker could look in and see her. Strange men might peer through the glass, knives glinting. Kids from her school, hunting for a secret place to smoke. Wild animals. One night, when she was waiting for her mom to come home from yet another date, a deer appeared just outside the window. The deer stood sideways and pressed its brown flank to the glass, cropped hairs flattened and fanning out, like it would push through if it could. It turned its head toward her and stared. Ears perked and flicked, nostrils trembled. It seemed to know her. Trained its gaze on her like it had something crucial to tell her. But what? Elisabeth stood and stepped nearer to the window. The deer spooked, and clattered down the wooden steps into the dark.

Despite Elisabeth's pleas, her mom refused to fit the windows with curtains or blinds. She said the view made the house. She said, "Don't be silly, Liza-Belle, there's nothing out there but trees."

The most important room in the house was the Gold Room, her mom's dressing room. It had cheetah carpeting in tan and white, light yellow walls, white shelves edged in shimmering gold leaf. There were racks for dresses, skirts, blouses, pants. White drawers, gold-handled, for her lace and satin underwear. White velvet boxes for her jewels. Shelves of shoes with toes pointed down: flats, sandals, pumps, low boots, tall boots, over-the-knee. One pair of flip-flops for yoga, slim black thongs to flaunt red-polished toes. No sneakers. Nothing that Elisabeth's mom did not love. There was an oversized ottoman upholstered in gold fabric. A trifold set of full-length mirrors like in the dressing room at Nordstrom, and a small white pedestal to stand on.

There was no black anywhere. Nothing Elisabeth's dad might deem reasonable.

When creating the Gold Room, Elisabeth's mom had seemed to be pursuing something bigger than Elisabeth could understand. "For the first time in my life, I am going to have exactly what I want," she'd said, as if this explained it all.

"Okay," Nick Brickston told Elisabeth. "First rule, hide everything."

It was Saturday afternoon. She had waited until her mom left for a wine country weekend with Steve, an anchorman from the local news. Now she stood with Nick under the skylight in her mom's studio-slash-kitchen, trying desperately to seem at ease as he hauled in the last case of alcohol and stacked it with the others on the floor. White fog eddied over the pane of glass above their heads, and redwoods smacked drops of wet onto the glass. Nick palmed a delicate green glass vase that her mom had bought at the Fall Arts Festival. "Anything break-able. Anything valuable." He turned, assessed the room. "Hide the easel, the paintings. Plus the paints and brushes and shit. Who knows what fucked-up ideas people are going to get."

Elisabeth nodded.

"Do you have any money around?" he asked. "Cash, credit cards? Your mom's jewelry? You should get it out of here."

"Okay."

"Okay. Then there's the weird shit. The shit you wouldn't think."

Elisabeth followed him across the kitchen. He opened the refrigerator. Inside, along with the milk and condiments, were two liters of Smartwater, a takeout box from Sushi Ran, a bag of raw spinach, and a watermelon. "Will your mom expect all this to be here when she gets back?"

"Are you saying," Elisabeth said slowly, "that someone is going to steal this *watermelon*?"

Nick shrugged. "Last month Jonas Everett got wrapped over a missing crate of farmers' market strawberries. He's allergic—when he said he ate them all himself, his mom knew he was full of shit."

"Hide the watermelon, then, definitely." Elisabeth had hated wa-termelon ever since she'd puked it all over Mr. Hamilton's sixth-grade social studies classroom during her oral presentation on ancient Chinese foot-binding.

"Now the most important thing." Nick lifted the phone off its receiver on the kitchen counter. "Where can this go?"

"The phone?"

"Trust me, the last thing you want is this thing rings and some drunk asshole picks it up to say hello. Get it?"

"I think so. And we're going to keep everyone out here, right?"

Nick nodded. "Kitchen, bathroom, deck. No one goes down the hallways. No one goes in your room or your mom's room."

"Or the Gold Room," Elisabeth said, blushing as soon as she heard herself say it. No one knew about the room names and no one should. "I mean, my mom's dressing room. It has to be off-limits."

"Sure," Nick said. Then he grinned, draped his arm across her shoulders. "You know, you're gonna have fun tonight, girl," he told her. "If it kills you."

There were 175 kids in the junior class. Most of them didn't like her.

Since middle school, girls had pricked up around her, as cats prick up at danger, and edged away. Once, when she was in seventh grade, three eighth-grade girls had cornered her behind the snack bar, surrounded her and pressed her to the wall, so close she felt their hot, sweet-and-sour breath against her neck, and demanded to know why she thought she was so *fucking* superior. When she hadn't answered, the biggest of the three had smiled calmly beneath her dark, center-parted hair, braces glinting, then reared back and slapped her face. A sting that mellowed to an ache. Loose tears. That night, a plum-colored bruise had bloomed high on her cheek, and she'd wished that it would make her ugly by the morning, but it hadn't.

She didn't make such wishes anymore. But she knew what boys thought of her. The dime. The bitch. If they did talk to her, it was just to ask about her mom in a way that made her skin crawl.

Everyone liked Elisabeth's mom, who was pretty and fun and trendy in her skinny jeans and knee-high boots. She worked in a local boutique, and after closing took Elisabeth to dinner at downtown restaurants where divorcés hovered by the bar in designer jeans and dress shirts, or polos embroidered with the scrolling logos of Palm Springs golf courses and Napa Valley wineries. Elisabeth looked just like her, the men said when stopping by the table to be friendly. Those gorgeous, sea-green eyes. That skin. Elisabeth's mom always grinned and thanked them, radiating warmth as if to assure them that her beauty meant nothing to her. That she was not even aware of it.

The anchorman, Steve, was bolder than the rest. He pulled a third chair to their table without asking, flashed bleached teeth. He wore makeup for his job on TV, and orange foundation crusted in the folds of his eyelids and the grooves of his nostrils.

He leaned over the table and winked. "You know," he said, "when you grow up, you're going to be a knockout."

Elisabeth's mom beamed and patted the back of her hand, a reminder to be gracious.

Elisabeth clicked her teeth shut. Made a small, closed-mouth smile. "Excuse me," she said.

As she stood, Steve's eyes traced her height. Five foot ten in flats. As she walked through the restaurant in her scoop-necked sweater and jeans, three old men in a booth grinned at her with mouths full, jousted at her with their knives. She passed the clanging kitchen—two busboys, leaning by the open door, swiped their palms on their aprons and trailed her with their eyes. She bowed her head. If she looked at them, she'd have to smile, pretend she liked it. If they talked to her, she'd have to say hello, act flattered like her mom would, make small talk, which she was so painfully incapable of doing. So she raised her chin and stared ahead. Her body was a long elastic and she held it taut.

When she got back from the bathroom, her mother was sipping a martini and laughing and Steve was sitting close beside her, stroking the ridge of her thumb, whispering secrets into her hair.

People said Elisabeth was beautiful. Her mom said she was lucky, with a golden complexion and a body built for clothes. But the beauty was foreign to her. She wore it like expensive jewelry she knew was dangerous to own.

It seemed that she had always felt this way. She remembered a Memorial Day weekend when she was six or seven years old, at the Mendocino Valley ranch where Mill Valley parents went to play. The ranch crowned a hill at the end of a long dirt road that corkscrewed up through madrone and manzanita trees. Around the house was a clearing, and beyond that, hills of grass tall enough to hide in.

During the day adults would hike around the hills or sprawl in chaise longues by the swimming pool or pass out on towels on the lawn with paperback novels and bottles of beer. And inevitably, in the blaze of a late afternoon, Elisabeth's mom would wake red-bellied and howling for aloe. Elisabeth would bring her the bottle. She'd squirt the cold green gel into her palm and rub it over her mom's belly, chest, shoulders, and neck, skin hot to the touch and goosebumps rising, angry red.

"I didn't mean to fall asleep!" her mom would moan. "Why didn't you wake me, Liza-Belle?"

"Stop flinching," Elisabeth would say. "The gel will help. It always helps."

Her mom would laugh, tears glistening in her eyes. "My sensible girl. Where did you come from? How did you come out of me?"

When dusk fell, the crowd would gather at the fire pit. The adults smoked sweet-smelling cigarettes, flames playing on their faces, orange against the blueing dark, and laughed at jokes that Elisabeth didn't understand and so stopped listening to. She stepped closer to the fire, bracing against waves of heat. Above the flames the air rippled like warped glass, and gold sparks spit and sizzled in the sky.

Then hands gripped her waist and she was pulled back, settled onto a man's lap. He was a friend of her parents and didn't have kids of his own. Everyone had been swimming and she still wore her one-piece, pink with small black polka dots and a short, wavy skirt around the hips. Damp, it stuck to her body. On the man's lap she pulled the fabric from her skin with a sucking sound, creating a bubble of air, and then popped it against her belly. The man laughed. He said her hair smelled like lemonade. From across the campfire her mother explained that she squeezed lemon in Elisabeth's blond hair so the chlorine wouldn't turn it green. The man held her close against his chest, big hand blanketing her belly, heart beating fast against her back. Her swimsuit pulled against the secret place between her legs and there were sudden little stars bursting all over her body that made her face burn and she thought if she stayed absolutely still maybe nobody would notice and she would not have to explain.

Then the grown-ups wanted to have grown-up time, so the kids had to go to bed. They slept in tents on the lawn; there weren't enough rooms in the house for everyone who wanted to shower and change and sleep, and grown-ups needed privacy more than kids did. So Elisabeth changed clothes in one of the tents, quick quick, no lock on the door—not even a door, a half circle of shiny nylon, so thin, and the zipper dangled there at the end and there was no way to hold it closed and change at the same time. She could only stand and watch the zipper as she peeled the damp swimsuit from her body. Her skin was cold and clammy underneath and her thin hair crunchy from its lemons and its hours in the sun. Her dry clothes, a purple T-shirt and shorts and pink cotton underwear dotted with tiny panda bears, lay on the sleeping bag beside her. As she reached down for the underwear, there was the shriek of the tent unzipping. The friend was there, looking. She froze with her panties in her hand. What was she supposed to do? Scream?

But he acted like there was nothing wrong, he saw her there and he didn't say *Excuse me* and he didn't leave. He told her to hurry, her mother wanted her, it was time to toast the marshmallows. She didn't answer. She thought that if she didn't break her silence this thing would not be real, this thing so small it almost didn't happen.

During middle school, the greater world began to pursue her more aggressively, and in response she clung more stubbornly to her policy of silence.

There was the time her dad took her to visit the properties he owned in the city's Sunset District. When he had to meet with a tenant, she went to get a soda at the convenience store he promised was just around the corner.

The store was nowhere. There was no store. She was wandering the sidewalks, counting blocks and squinting at street signs, when a strange voice lapped the back of her neck.

"Your back is real straight," the voice said. "You work out?"

She glanced over her shoulder. The man was skinny and short and wore a tank top: thin white cotton over scarred white skin. He was loping along like a wounded deer and staring at her and sliding his tongue over his teeth. "Where you work out at?" he said. "Around here?"

"No," she whispered. She closed her elbows around her ribs and hurried, but the man caught up to her and now they were side by side.

They walked for a few seconds more, the man considering something.

"You're cute," he said finally. His eyes ran down, up. "Very cute."

Sweat broke out on her palms and under her arms. The smell of her own orange-flower perfume released from her skin, and she willed it back like a scream he must not hear. She scanned the street for a store or restaurant to duck into, but there were only more and more stucco houses, windows latticed and barred. "I have a boyfriend," she said finally, quietly. When she reached Taraval Street, she turned.

The man turned too. "He's a lucky guy. Very lucky."

Her throat felt strangled. Her breath too loud. Her T-shirt shrugged up in the heat and she could not move her arms to pull it down. She tried not to look like she was hurrying.

"You could be more lucky, though," the man said, showing crowded yellow teeth. He reached, and pinched the bare flesh at her hip.

She jumped. A small yelp escaped. But she couldn't speak. There was a tingling behind her nose and tears in her eyes.

The man laughed and sauntered off, and she pushed into the first open storefront she could find. After, she told no one. If she told her mom, her mom would blame her dad. If she told her dad, he'd want to find the guy and kill him, or—maybe worse, maybe more likely—he wouldn't do anything at all.

When she turned fourteen, modeling scouts began to call the house. There was one who saw her in the city one weekend and wouldn't quit until she agreed to a test shoot. Elisabeth didn't want to go, but her mom insisted: "This is your time, Liza-Belle! You have to take advantage of every moment." She said this with such conviction that Elisabeth wondered when her time would be over, and what would happen then?

At the studio, the stylists swarmed around her. Sitting still under the lights, she watched in the mirror as the hairstylist back-brushed her hair and wound it on hot rollers. The makeup girl spun her away from the mirror. "Keep your eyes closed, sweetie," she said. "This stuff is, like, industrial." Elisabeth obeyed. A machine growled to life and spit cold flecks of makeup over her forehead and eyelids and cheeks, her chin and her neck. "Once this foundation sets, it won't come off unless you scrub like crazy—you'll have to take off, like, three or four layers of skin." The other stylists laughed. "Relax, I was only kidding."

Eventually her skin was thick and poreless, eyelids glittered and heavy with lash glue, lips gummy and red. The stylists removed her robe and stood her in front of a silver clothes rack in nude thong underwear and five-inch platform heels. They never stopped talking. They told her she was gorgeous, so lucky. So young. "I'd kill for your thighs," one confided. "Fourteen, fuck, it's so unfair."

The photographer posed her on a white backdrop. In head-to-toe black he hunched, aimed his huge lens at her head. He never stopped talking. He said, "Put your shoulders back, honey, stand up straight, honey, give me your sexy look, look like you want this. Now smile. Not like that. Like you mean it, honey. Like you almost didn't want to but I was just so funny. Natural, sweetheart. Be yourself."

Elisabeth tilted on the five-inch heels and her limbs angled everywhere and the corners of her mouth trembled when she tried to hold the smile.

He kept telling her to close her eyes, then open them. "Look down, then look up. Don't stare, honey, no, don't squint."

When they got the photographer's proofs, the girl in the pictures did not even look like her.

Her dad didn't like them. He said, "Look at her, Heather, she's miserable."

Her mom yanked the proof sheet out of his hands. "Don't touch it, you're getting your oily fingerprints all over. Anyway, that's how she's supposed to look."

Elisabeth didn't want to listen to them fight, or to argue her side: she'd already decided never to set foot in front of a camera again. She went to her bedroom and shut the door. Back then the walls were plain, the furniture white, the bedspread a lime-green stripe she'd picked out herself. Settling at her desk, she opened her MacBook and plugged in her earbuds. She could click around on Facebook, scan through random pictures, but this would only leave her hollow, wanting more. What she needed in times like this was actual escape. She clicked over to YouTube.

She liked the videos of a spiritual healer who performed deep chakra cleansings with no tools but his just-washed hands: he placed one hand at the base of the patient's spine, the other at the location of each chakra, a spinning disk of energy and light that hovered in the air several inches from the skin. Then he circled his hand to spin the chakra faster, sloughing off the toxic residue the patient had accumulated through the simple act of living. The idea was to cleanse the patient's energy fields in order to fix what had gone wrong inside. People said it was a hoax, but Elisabeth wanted to believe it. The concept was simple, complete: spin out the bad stuff, and the rest of the body would heal itself.

She liked this idea of healing. She could be a surgeon, maybe: she wasn't sure about the med school part, but could see herself slicing into a body, in search of the source of the pain. She would specialize in heart surgery: crack the sternum to open the bones, reveal the jumping, fist-sized muscle, meaty and red. She loved that this human machine could be opened, examined. Could be held in the palm of a hand. Revealed, repaired, even replaced, encased in its jewel box of bone and sewn closed, and the person's whole life would be different. All her old problems would cease to exist.

Now it was happening, Saturday night: Elisabeth's house was full. Kids crowded the deck and the kitchen. Her mom's easel, paints, and brushes were stowed away; alcohol cluttered the counters instead. To Elisabeth's surprise, many had brought their own racks of beer or handles of vodka. Still, Nick commandeered the cases of hard lemonade and Red Tail Ale that her three hundred dollars had paid for and sold the bottles one by one, pocketing the cash.

He opened one for Elisabeth. She drank and the bitterness coated her tongue. Wincing, she tried to pass it back.

"Just drink it," Nick said. "You'll like it eventually."

She sipped. More and more people pushed into her house. She hid in the kitchen and watched as they paraded through the White Room, followed the trail of celery-colored towels she'd laid across the white carpet to the kitchen and the deck.

Dave Chu came in with some guys from the soccer team and picked carefully over the towels toward the deck. He was tall, like her. He wore a red polo shirt with a little embroidered horse logo and chinos and clean white sneakers. As he walked, he flicked his shining black hair out of his eyes. She was surprised to see Dave. He seemed too anxiously well behaved to have any fun at parties. On the other hand, he had paid Nick Brickston to take the SAT for him, so he must be more than the compulsive front-row note-taker she saw every day in class. As she shook out a garbage bag and began to fill it with used cups, she felt him watching her.

Abigail Cress came in with her best friend, Emma Fleed. Emma was short and baby-faced in a ballerina skirt of tiered chiffon, and Abigail was skinny and stylish, with a black silk top and tight dark jeans and a black quilted purse over her shoulder. They paused in the doorway and it was strange to see Abigail so quiet, so still. Wary. Everyone had been talking about her and Mr. Ellison, who'd disappeared the month before. Elisabeth herself had always felt funny around Mr. Ellison—there was something strange about the way he lingered by the girls' desks in SAT class, reaching down to mark answers on their test sheets, cresting his arm over theirs. And Elisabeth had seen him with Abigail once, she thought, while eating her avocado sandwich in the courtyard— squinting up at the clock tower and spying through the narrow, arched windows the figures of a man and girl embracing. Elisabeth herself hadn't even kissed a boy since Ryan Harbinger in eighth grade—when, in an empty classroom one afternoon, Ryan had out of nowhere grabbed Elisabeth and kissed her, a kiss quick and alien and wet, an anxious tongue darting around her teeth as if probing for something hidden there. Then, just as suddenly, Ryan had pulled away. Burning with embarrassment, Elisabeth had seen, gaping in the doorway with a Slurpee in his hand, Tristan Bloch. From then on, the rumor had circulated that Elisabeth had "stolen" Ryan from Cally Broderick; no matter the fact that Elisabeth and Ryan never again kissed or spoke, this rumor refused to die. Was it Tristan who'd started it? She'd never know.

She wondered if Abigail Cress had really gone all the way with Mr. Ellison. Had she seen him naked, and allowed him to see her? No wonder, she thought, that Nick Brickston had turned the affair into a joke. If you took it seriously, it would make you sick.

As Abigail and Emma followed the trail of towels to the deck, the Bo-Stin beach kids crowded in behind them, laughing and reeking of weed. They paid no attention to the towels. Cally, who she knew had always hated her because of Ryan, padded her pink and dirty feet across the carpet.

The storm surprised them, pushed everyone inside. The rain was fierce, drilling the rail of the redwood deck. The guys cursed, crushed cigarettes under their heels and sheltered plastic cups beneath their arms; the girls screamed and palmed the sky above their heads, ducking to save their hair. Only Cally Broderick and the beach kids welcomed the storm; they laughed and arched their faces to the sky, danced and tried to catch the raindrops on their tongues, embraced the falling water until their shirts sheered through, clung to their bellies and breasts.

The party spilled into the White Room. Elisabeth saw them coming, a rolling tide, and knelt to straighten the trail of towels. To save the white carpet was a hopeless effort; she knew this even as she tried. Abigail Cress and Emma Fleed ran in first, apologizing as they stumbled over Elisabeth but laughing too, so it was clear they didn't mean it. Then Damon Flintov and Ryan Harbinger were yelling and knocking people out of the way to claim the white couch and love seat in the middle of the room. After them came everyone, freshmen, sophomores, juniors, seniors, a mass of kids and yet somehow divided, the familiar groups and cliques of school asserting themselves as Ryan, Damon, and Nick dominated the couches in the living room, Abigail and Emma corralled the junior girls around the kitchen counter, and freshman girls circled on the carpet to share a bottle of vodka, drinking and passing with dizzying speed. Dave Chu stepped in from the deck, lingered near the windows as if looking for his assigned seat. The soccer team was playing flip cup at the dinner table, but he didn't join them; instead, seeing Elisabeth, he began to trace the room, collecting abandoned red cups and carrying them one by one into the kitchen.

Nick Brickston yanked Elisabeth's mother's iPod from the speakers on the sideboard and plugged in his phone; a rap song pounded out like a train that would run them all over. The beat vibrated the coasters on the glass coffee table and the lampshades on the lamps, and Elisabeth—who had given up on the carpet and stood backed against the far wall—felt the bass line humming in her teeth. Timidly she went and turned the volume down, strained to hear through the hum of fifty concurrent conversations angry neighbors who might be approaching the house, dreaded police officers' pounding at the door. None came— instead just more and more kids spilling through as the music grew louder and louder again, as if of its own accord. The rain was growing louder too, a rhythmic pounding on the roof. The branches of redwood trees nodded and thrashed at the windows, water streaking down the glass, and beyond them the hippie kids twirling and spinning. Inside, some sophomores opened a window and curled against it smoking cigarettes, exhaling into wind that blew the smoke back inside.

On the love seat Ryan Harbinger stretched, grinned and dimpled his cheeks, splayed his giant feet on the armrest where her mom usually placed her elbow or her half glass of white wine. He wore basketball shoes with red slashes and black soles, and they would ruin the white couch but it was too late to say anything. He set his forty on the coffee table—not, as Elisabeth's mother had taught her, toward the center on a coaster, but directly on glass at the edge. He lay back and giggling girls tucked into the spaces around his body or sat at his feet and hugged their knees. Freshman girls perched on the edge, arranging their smiles. Ryan draped an arm around one girl's waist but gazed away, as if the gesture were an accident.

Damon Flintov dropped his beer on the side table and sprawled on the couch, grinning and nuzzling a white chenille throw blanket to his cheek. He had a big head with buzzed, light brown hair, watery blue eyes, eyebrows pierced with silver studs. A wide, fleshy nose, chubby fingers. His belly bulged under an oversized purple T-shirt. He had this overgrown-infant look about him, yet he terrified her. He and Ryan both. She remembered, even if no one else did, what they had done to Tristan Bloch.

Elisabeth kept drinking and the front door kept opening and more kids kept cramming into her house. Kids she didn't recognize. Kids who didn't live in Mill Valley. Kids who didn't live in Marin. She sensed the night was splintering. It was no longer a linear series of hours leading to their natural conclusion but a grotesque collage of impossible events that had started nowhere and were leading nowhere clear; it seemed to Elisabeth that the party might simply go on forever like a movie on a loop, refreshing itself over and over, until something snapped.

Emma Fleed set up beer pong on the whitewashed kitchen table, arranging red cups like bowling pins and pouring beer into each one. She was a waitress, a hostess. How did she know how to do this?

Elisabeth knelt and scrubbed a beer stain on the White Room rug. From the love seat behind her, Ryan Harbinger yelled, "I see you, Dave Chu! I see you looking at this girl like you're gonna get some ass tonight. Man, this is Elisabeth Avarine—I wouldn't fuckin' hold your breath!" She turned and Ryan was grinning and Dave Chu walking away and Damon Flintov prying the battery cover off the remote control and doing this kind of choke-laugh, shaking his head like he couldn't believe he was friends with such an asshole, but loved him anyway.

Girls were sitting in circles on the floor sharing handles of vodka—passing and giggling and swilling into oblivion. Then they were up and dancing with one another, grinding hips and swinging hair, pouting at cell phone cameras and setting off flashes, collapsing in laughter together. They were laughing about nothing, as far as she could tell.

On the couches and chairs were couples making out, older guys with younger girls cradled, strange creatures sharing breath.

A girl was crying in the designated bathroom. Her friends rushed into the room with her, flanked her, locked the door. When Elisabeth knocked, a girl she didn't know stuck her head out; her charcoaled eyes were streaked with tears. "Give us some fucking *privacy*!" she yelled, and slammed the door in Elisabeth's face.

From then on, Elisabeth couldn't stop people from wandering through the house, looking for another place to pee. They disappeared in the maze of dark hallways. Where was Nick? Strangers kept going to the Purple Room—hers—and locking the door.

One guy—six feet tall, basketball-jersied, San Rafael High—she followed.

"Excuse me!" she called after him. "People aren't allowed down there!"

But the guy just laughed and kept walking. "Who are you, the fuckin' security guard?"

"Wait! Where are you going?" She tried to tamp the desperation in her voice.

He didn't answer. He flicked his fingernails against his shoulder, she the speck, the lint.

She followed and watched as he opened the door: there was a circle of kids on her bed, and on the floor, on their knees, Cally Broderick and Jess Steinberg were performing some kind of surgery on Elisabeth's precalculus textbook: Jess crushed a pill with a butter knife and cut the powder into rows, then Cally shut her eyes and lowered her nose to the book, closed one nostril and inhaled. Opening her eyes, she looked at Elisabeth. Elisabeth stared back, knowing she shouldn't yet unable to move or look away. Cally's pupils were wide and black yet impenetrable, and Elisabeth was amazed that someone she had gone to school with all her life could still be such a stranger. Elisabeth had so many questions to ask her—Why had she forced this total change upon herself? And how had she pulled it off?—but she could not fathom where to begin.

Elisabeth retreated. Noises were coming from the Blue Room. There, some freshman on her knees and her face in Nick's lap and she still had her clothes on and he was gripping her hair in his hands. Elisabeth turned away. Why had she expected more from him?

She went back to the White Room, which now felt, perversely, like the safest place. People there were gathered at the windows smoking blunts and someone had set up a glass bong on the coffee table and people lounged around it, passed it back and forth, and she thought, for a brief, hopeful moment, that things were winding down.

Then Emma Fleed started dancing on the coffee table. She swayed and shimmied to the music, flipping her skirt of tiered chiffon and whipping her dark hair and grinning, her confidence astounding even as the camera phones went up around her, even as she tipped forward and flashed the room. She didn't seem to be part of this place, as if she were performing for a full house only she could perceive, an invisible, adoring sea.

Damon Flintov peed in the kitchen sink.

Ryan Harbinger found the green glass vase and smashed it, not even angrily, just because.

By now the White Room was soiled and stained and it smelled like weed and cigarettes and spilled beer and B.O. A crack split the glass coffee table like a fault line. Still it wasn't over. The speakers bumped and buzzed—she didn't know rap music and every song sounded exactly the same, the beat relentless—and the room hummed with people in every corner, the rain having eased yet not stopped altogether, and outside the Bo-Stin hippies had multiplied to fill the deck. Cally Broderick stumbled out to join them, crawled up onto the railing and started to walk across it, dipping her toes and twirling like a gymnast on the beam, tilting and wavering as her friends cheered loudly, joyously, from below. As she tightroped on the wet and narrow rail, Cally teetered from side to side—on one side, the relative safety of the deck, on the other, the stretch of dark canyon that yawned down to the creek far, far below—in an exquisite tension that Elisabeth felt in the meat of her ribs.

Inside, Emma Fleed's skirt was twisted up around her thighs and she was drinking from a forty on the White Room couch. Another girl crouched beside her, trying to take the bottle away, but Emma kept shouting, "I *do* want it! I want it! Don't tell me what I want!"

Damon Flintov found the watermelon in a cabinet above the stove and hurled it at the White Room wall. Its pink guts exploded across her mother's perfect linen wallpaper.

Elisabeth froze. Fragments of green rind made a hideous mosaic on the linen, and pink juice descended in long, slow drips. The pink guts were her tightly packaged heart exploding. The people were falling down laughing around her, thrilled, entertained, and behind her she heard one boy dare another to lick it. She fell to her knees on the sullied carpet, raised the roots of her hair with her fingers. What would her mom say? What would her mom do? *How would her mom's face look when she saw it?*

The party around her revived itself. Elisabeth went into the kitchen, picked up the first forty she found, and uncapped it. It tasted rancid, but with each sip, she cared a little less. Cared less about the taste and less about everything else. In fact she liked it.

She stumbled down the dark hallway, searching for a quiet place to breathe. To her right she found an open door, a wedge of yellow light. She pushed inside.

A familiar scent enveloped her: vanilla, almond, bergamot orange. Her mother's perfume. A wave of nausea overtook her and she fell to her knees on the cheetah print carpet. For a fleeting yet real moment it seemed plausible that she would die. It was then she realized where she was: the Gold Room. Looking up, she took in the impossible sight of Damon Flintov and Ryan Harbinger scrambling in her mom's underwear drawer. Terror hurled her heart against her ribs. Even through her haze she understood that she was powerless to stop them. Damon pulled out a lacy fuchsia bra, which he stretched across his fat chest, looping the straps over his shoulders, and in the trifold mirrors he began to dance. Ryan laughed with his whole body, bending over, stumbling around. Elisabeth struggled to process this. They didn't seem to notice her, or didn't mind the audience.

Damon danced on the little stool and pushed his forty to his mouth and sucked, the amber liquid sloshing in the glass. He was jerking his big body around on the stool, posing in the mirrors. He pointed to the cheetah carpet. "This shit looks like a strip club, yo!"

"You fag," Ryan said, laughing.

Damon paused and puffed his chest. "What did you just call me?"

Ryan grinned, the lines deepening at the corners of his mouth. "I said, fuckin' faggot."

"Say that over here, bitch-ass motherfucker. Lemme hear you say that one more time."

Ryan slid his palm over his face to make it serious, like someone doing an impression. He crept to Damon on the stool and raised his chin. The boys' faces were as close as they could be without kissing.

"Mother. Fuckin'. Faggot," Ryan said, his face twitching to stay serious.

"You're dead, asshole."

But Damon fell into laughing and Ryan too, and then they were at each other like dogs. Damon lunged at Ryan and vised Ryan's head in his armpit and Ryan, bending over, his jeans sagging to reveal funny tight blue briefs, grabbed Damon around the waist and muscled him off the stool and they spun like they were dancing, grunting, Damon breathing hard, his face baby-pink and glowing, and Elisabeth released a scream as the two boys fell into the mirrors and Damon's body smashed the glass.

After, shards of mirror glittered on the cheetah carpet.

Puddles of malt liquor soaked into the floor.

Her mom's clothes had been rifled, tossed like streamers, stretched over strangers' bodies, torn. Some had been stolen. She had no proof of this last. She just knew.

"Be careful, there's glass," a voice said.

She looked up. Dave Chu was there. He knelt beside her.

She nodded. She started to cry. As Dave leaned closer, something shifted, and she fell into his arms. She did not even think.

His arms hesitated. His heartbeat accelerated against her ear. Then he hugged her to him. Her eyelashes matted and wetted his neck.

"It's so stupid," she said. "I thought someone would thank me."

"It's not stupid."

"My mom comes home tomorrow. There's no way to hide this. She'll see it, she'll see everything."

"She'll forgive you," he said.

Then they heard the sirens coming, a plaintive cry that echoed through the canyon, hurtling closer and closer to where they were.

"I'll stay with you," Dave said. "Don't worry, okay?"

Elisabeth cried. She did not know what she would tell the police, and she did not know what her mom would do. Maybe she'd be furious. Maybe she'd be proud. Maybe she'd blame all the others. Or maybe she'd realize that Elisabeth was the one who made this happen, who let the function grow and morph into a beast that would not stop until it tore this house apart.

"Miss Nicoll? Miss Nicoll? Molly?"

Molly awoke to find Nick Brickston staring down at her. She lay stretched across her classroom's vinyl couch, where she'd intended to rest for only a moment at the start of her free period. Now the afternoon sun streamed through the open window, bringing with it the scent of oranges rotting in the heat.

Nick Brickston cleared his throat; she sat up hastily. She was intensely aware of her untucked blouse and twisted skirt, the crust in her lashes, the staticky frizz of her hair. How long had he been standing there?

She sat up. "Nick, hi. I was just resting my eyes. What's up?"

"I just came to say hey." He sat down beside her on the sofa, creaking the vinyl; Molly tugged at her hem. For a moment they sat quietly together, the sun on their shoulders. Nick drummed his thumb on the vinyl. From there, the whiteboard looked very far away, Molly's cursive small and frenzied. Finally he said, "Oh, sorry about that reading-response thing you wanted me to do. Was that important? I could make it up if you want."

"Sure," she said, before realizing she didn't actually care. "I mean, no. It wasn't important. I know you've done the reading."

"Cool."

"But look," she said, "next time, if you need an extension or something, just text me." They exchanged numbers. Then they were silent. She waited for him to go, but instead he turned to her and said:

"I was thinking about something you brought up in class the other day."

"Really? What?"

"You told us everything we see is a signifier for something else. Something deeper. Like, the word *tree* signifies a tree, and the word itself changes how we think about the thing. Right? What did you call it?"

"Semiotics."

"Yeah." He leaned toward her. His eyes were dark and flashing, his breath tobacco-spiced. "Like, if we call someone a student, how does that change how we think about them? If we call someone a teacher, what does that mean?"

"Well, what *does* it mean?"

"It's crazy if you think about it, how arbitrary it is." His enthusiasm startled her; it transcended the cool in his voice. She recalled this thrill, its promise—when in high school her own English teacher had read from *A Room of One's Own*, and she'd realized that there was another way to see the world than how the Nicoll family did, an entirely different way to be. Now she had passed on this promise to Nick Brickston. Who knew what he would do with it? He shifted closer to her on the couch. "I mean, you're a teacher, and because of that we're supposed to think of you a certain way. But Ms. Thruwey's one too, and you guys aren't even on the same planet."

"What are you saying?"

"She's a *teacher,* but you're just Molly. A person you can, like, have a conversation with. Like one of us."

Molly couldn't help but smile at this. She wondered at the accidental power of this gangly teenage boy—how he knew to say what she most wanted to hear. "Nick, that might be the kindest thing anyone's ever said to me."

"It's the truth."

"Thank you for telling me the truth," she said.

• • •

That weekend, Molly's attendance was required at the spring semester faculty dinner hosted by Principal Norton.

At the restaurant downtown, Molly chose a seat toward one end of the long, narrow table that stretched down the center of the dining room. The table was white-clothed and spotlit. Her chair was hard. Around her, everyone did just as expected, the teachers interrogating their appetizers, the servers pulling corks. How dull it was, how safe it felt. No one here would break a glass, or hurl a napkin, or empty the salt shaker on someone else's head, or jump up and curse and storm out. Even the odors behaved themselves: gentle aromas of garlic and wine, traces of high-priced perfume. It made her throat itch. At the opposite end of the table, Beth Firestein, sipping a martini, looked equally bored.

Around the table, the other teachers complained about school board politics, lamented the price of real estate, and marveled at the massive engagement ring of Gwen Thruwey, whose fiancé had just been made partner at a venture capital firm in the city.

"Well, we knew he wasn't a teacher!" joked Tom Pritchard, and everyone roared. There was nothing these teachers enjoyed more, Molly thought, than laughing bitterly at their own poverty.

She drank. Around her the conversation veered toward the faculty's second favorite topic: the insanity of Mill Valley parents. These parents, said Allen Francher, somehow managed to be not only entitled, intrusive, and demanding, but also negligent. Some of them seemed delusional about their kids' abilities, added Jeannie Flugel. In other words, they were incapable of seeing what pieces of shit their own children could be, said Tom. Worst of all, said Gwen, these parents treated teachers like they were not even professionals, as if they were in the category of babysitters and maids.

"Well," Molly said, almost to herself, "maybe we are." She heard too late the buttery slip of the wine on her tongue, and felt heat rise in her face as the entire table of teachers turned toward her.

"What did you say?" Gwen asked, leaning over a plate of focaccia to glare.

Molly gripped her wineglass, which felt slick and enormous in her hand. "I don't think it matters, that's all, what we call ourselves. What we are doing is very, I don't know, elemental."

"I am a professional person," Gwen said, and the table nodded in assent. "An educator. I don't know what you call yourself."

"That's not what I meant, exactly."

"What exactly do you mean?" Jeannie asked. "You don't seem to think very highly of your own job."

"I just don't think . . . ," Molly said carefully, and paused. She set down her glass and worried the stem. "I don't think you're going to get through to kids if you look at things that way."

Tom Pritchard chuckled. "You don't think, huh?"

"No wonder no one respects teachers the way they should." Gwen gestured toward Molly with open palms, as if toward an exasperating child. "There's attitudes like this coming into the schools."

"Calm down, Gwenny. Have some more wine."

"Shut up, Bill."

"Hold on, everybody." Tom Pritchard raised his hand, then swabbed his goatee with his napkin as they waited. "I want to hear more of what our young Miss Nicoll has to say. Molly, how long have you been teaching again?"

"It's my first year," Molly said.

He nodded. "So, proceed. You were educating us about how to get across to our kids."

"I'm not trying to educate anyone," Molly said. Her blush had steadied, although cold sweat chilled her neck beneath her hair. "I've just found that the most important thing, I mean the way I deal with my kids, is to try to reach them on a deeper level. To really connect. To understand them in the context of their whole lives, in and out of the classroom, even the parts we'd rather not see."

"And I suppose their test scores aren't important," Gwen said. "Whether or not they learn how to read."

"Preparing them for college," Jeannie added.

"Of course that stuff matters," Molly insisted, drawing courage from the compliment Nick Brickston had given her. She'd broken through: the kids liked and trusted her the way they could not like or trust these other teachers, and she knew them in ways these teachers could not. "But you have to look at the bigger picture."

In the silence that followed this declaration, the teachers glanced around the table at one another. Some were smirking, while others merely shook their heads. Katie Norton frowned at her penne. Tom Pritchard fingered his goatee. Gwen Thruwey turned to whisper into Jeannie Flugel's ear; Jeannie nodded righteously in response. Then the table turned away from Molly and toward another topic, and within her the old, eighth-grade feeling flared: she was standing on the platform, she was shrinking to a speck. And yet, remarkably, she didn't care. She did not even care that at the other end of the table, Beth Firestein had set down her martini and had fixed on her a cool, evaluative stare. It seemed like so long ago that she'd run into Beth after having learned the truth about Doug Ellison, even longer since they'd met at the copy machine, Beth so chic and commanding, Molly so eager and insecure. Molly had been a different teacher then, a different person.

Two hours later the dinner was over. It had started to rain. Molly sat in the front seat of her car, warm and slightly dizzy from the wine. She rolled down the window so the air would clear her head. Through her open window she watched middle-aged couples stroll arm in arm and covered convertibles cruise. Fog drifted over the town square, and redwood trees nodded beneficently overhead. The only sounds were the drops of the rain, the clip-clop of boots on the sidewalk, and the whispers of the European engines passing by. What a strange thing, to grow up in this place as her kids had. This lavish peace was their entire world; this was all there was.

THE RIDE

Damon Flintov booked it when he heard the sirens wailing.

Damon was buzzed, but it wasn't that far from Elisabeth Avarine's house in the canyon to his on the other side of town. Mill Valley was tiny and he knew these roads practically by heart—could drive them with his eyes closed. He stayed calm while everybody panicked, jumping into random cars.

In his BMW it was him and his boy Ryan Harbinger in front. Nick Brickston got in back with these three drunkass girls that he was babysitting—Cally Broderick, Alessandra Ryding, and Emma Fleed. Nick sat on one side, Alessandra on the other. Cally rode bitch in the middle. Emma was pretty compact, so she climbed onto Nick's lap for the ride. By this time the rain had taken a breather.

"Okay?" Emma asked Nick. She kind of slurred it through her hair, which was swinging over her face. "Too fat?"

"Shut the fuck up," he told her, and she smiled and pressed her lips to his ear, murmuring something that Damon didn't know but must have been pretty great, because in the rearview mirror Nick started grinning like a motherfucker.

They slid through the night. The car was sick. He drove like a beast. The road was hairpinned and slick but he was relaxed. Steady mobbing down the narrow streets, swerving in and out of his lane, taking curves without even worrying about touching the brake.

• • •

Damon had managed to go six weeks without getting into any shit. So earlier that night, his parents decided to give him back the BMW.

"Not give, *lend*," his mom said, like there was a difference, when he was their only kid left and everything they had would come to him eventually. His mom was a first-grade teacher and liked to use her little-kid voice on him, like she was helping him sound out a word. It made him want to punch the wall. Except he didn't do shit like that anymore.

"Just for the night," his dad said, dangling the keys in his face. "See how you do."

"We really want to trust you again, Damon," his mom said, all earnest, and for five honest seconds he thought about staying home and hanging out with her, baking cookies and watching a Disney Channel movie like they did when he was a kid—those weeks when his dad went out of town for work and that house felt like a place where he could be. But Damon wanted to get to Elisabeth Avarine's function, the last major party of the year. So he just said, "Cool," snatched the key ring, and twirled it on his finger until the keys chimed and clanged.

He went upstairs to get ready. At the bathroom sink he faced his reflection, ran a palm over his buzz cut. He liked to keep it short— liked the shivery feel of the clippers over his scalp and the dents and gleams his skull made in the mirror. He cracked his neck and felt the donut of flesh at the base of his skull. He hated how he always knew it was there. Hated his fleshy belly, his chest like a woman's tits. As a kid he'd worn a T-shirt in the pool. Now he wore bigass shirts and jeans and he just didn't fuckin' swim. He wasn't into exercise, ever since that asshole JV football coach kicked him off the team for grades. He didn't care, he said at the time, loud enough so everyone could hear. Football at Valley was bunk anyway.

His body was what it was, no changing it. But his clothes were bomb and he took care of that shit. The shirt matched the shoes matched the hat. That night, he chose a blazing-purple T-shirt with a neon-yellow swoosh and highlighter-yellow kicks designed to blind. He swabbed alcohol over the silver studs in his eyebrows and trimmed the stray hairs in his nose. Finally, he took out his Swiss army knife that he got for his last birthday, cut his fingernails and scraped the dirt from underneath, jabbed his cuticles with the little plastic stick, snipped his hangnails with the tiny silver scissors. Say what you want about him, he had beautiful fuckin' hands.

He was pumped to get out. He hated being trapped inside his house. Before he got arrested, he'd gone out almost every night with his boys, Ryan Harbinger and Nick Brickston. Ryan was this pretty boy, baseball star asshole who all the girls wanted. And Nick was like an evil genius or some shit—dealt weed and Molly and SATs, always made bank, never got caught. For years they'd gone around town getting chased away by cops. When it was soccer moms sitting around with Starbucks cups, it was called having a nice time; when it was him and Nick with a cigarette, it was loitering. Or Officer Frankel would find him walking home from Ryan's at 11:00 p.m. on a Friday and slow to tail him like a draft car. "Been drinking tonight, son?" he'd yell. "Don't you know there's a curfew in this town?"

Still, Damon preferred the nighttime. In the day he burned too hot. Sometimes it was just physical heat—sweat beading over his eyebrows, T-shirt damp and sticking to his pits—and sometimes it went deeper than that. He'd lope down Camino Alto gripping his waistband so his jeans wouldn't fall around his ankles—the band was cinched around his ass, boxers puffing over like a cloud of smoke—and the old ladies from the retirement home would stop pushing their stolen shopping carts to stare or even glare at him, their faces asking what had happened to their town. Like he was doing some illegal shit just by existing. But he'd lived in Mill Valley all his life—it was his town as much as theirs. He was as much Mill Valley as they were, he thought, in fact more so, because he was the now and the future and they were just waiting to die.

Overall he was just tryna get action. Tryna fuckin' move. Kicking the leg of the dining room table. Snapping his wrist like Ali G. Tipping back in his classroom chair until he hovered on two skinny metal legs. His teachers yelled at him to calm down, be still. *Hush, Damon!* they were always saying. *Focus, Damon! Pay attention!* Since fuckin' kindergarten with this shit. *Stop that tapping! Don't look at that. Don't touch*

her. Don't unwind that paper clip and jab the metal end into your thumb.
Don't pick up that stapler and pry it apart, don't *stick your fingers in to*
wiggle the machinery inside—

His answer was to release the spring, let the stapler's jaws snap shut
with a bang that made the teacher jump. Or the counselor. The therapist. The private educational consultant his parents were paying two
hundred an hour to figure out what was wrong with him. Old ladies
and hippie dudes tryna be down. They kept asking why couldn't he be
quiet and good and listen, and he just sat there counting down the
seconds, thinking he'd die happy if they'd let him get outside.

For example. A few weeks before he got arrested, he got called into
the principal's office, just because he'd called his asshole math teacher
an asshole. In the office he sat and drummed his pencil on Ms. Norton's desk. Out the window there were freshman girls traipsing out to
lunch, their short, wispy skirts flashing shadows on their thighs, and
Ms. Norton, who coulda been hot once but now looked faded in her
uglyass tomato suit, clasped her hands like she was begging him for
mercy.

"Please, Damon, tell me what you need to be successful," she said.
"We all want the best for you, Damon. We're trying to understand,
Damon." Saying his name over and over, like that would prove she
knew him.

His boys who knew him called him Flint. Ryan and Nick—his part-
ners in crime. He loved the motherfuckers. They got how all he
wanted, all he needed, was to make something happen. When they
were bored, they'd go up the 101 freeway to Novato and take turns
lying on the off-ramp, jumping up and running off right before a car
sped around the curve, just to feel the rush of it, the way the blood
thundered in their ears.

Ms. Norton said, "Damon? Damon? Are you listening to me?"

He grinned real big because she had no clue what she was up
against. He started telling her some bullshit story about his favorite
grandpa that just kicked it, but stopped when little clear tears wobbled
in her eyes.

"Oh, Damon," she told him. "I didn't know—"

"Forget it," he told her. "It doesn't fuckin' matter."

Okay, he'd done some shit. Like his dad always told him, he was no angel.

There was that kid in eighth grade. He and Ryan were just fuckin' with the guy, they didn't mean anything. Tristan was a freak to begin with, then he wrote that note going after Cally Broderick, who everybody knew was Ryan's. After it happened, the school came after Damon, but his dad went off on them—threatened to sue the school, the police, anyone in Mill Valley who was gonna accuse his son. Saying Damon had done nothing but act like a normal eighth-grade boy and that he didn't need to be punished because the other kid couldn't cope. Plus, it didn't even happen on school property, so what right did they have? He was only saving his own face, but the school backed down. The worst thing that happened to Damon was he didn't have to go to school for a week.

That was how he knew. That nothing could touch him. And if nothing could touch him, then nothing he did mattered.

Since then, he'd been smoking weed and drinking whatever and for a long time Molly was his jam. It helped him relax. Made his anger melt and transform to love. Love for his friends who partied with him and love for the girls in their silky tank tops and tight jeans, love for the rap on the radio, love for the world. It wasn't a problem till Ski Week, when he and Nick hosted a function and the cops showed at the wrong fuckin' time.

The whole thing was Nick's idea. He did this thing where he found some bigass mansion somewhere that was empty because the people were selling it, then threw a party there, selling hella tickets to all the kids in Marin. He always made bank.

This one house sat high on Mount Tamalpais, spying on the San Francisco Bay, and it was on the market for $5 million. The function was Nick's idea, but when the cops showed, it was Damon outside pissing on the lawn, drunk and high and ecstatic, with the plastic pouch stuffed into his sock. He was having so much fun that he forgot to be afraid. They found the pills in five seconds, hooked the cuffs around his wrists, palmed his head into the back of their black-and-white car. He sat in the cop car and its lights swirled red and blue around the street. He was waiting for Nick to come out in the cuffs, to slide over to make room for his friend's skinny ass. But Nick was too smart for that. He found a way to disappear. Only Damon took the fall.

Damon's dad had a reputation to protect, and he wasn't tryna have a kid in juvie. That's why he worked out with the judge that Damon would go to this special rehab place on Mount Tam. After that he'd be golden, as long as he stayed clean.

When Damon first got to rehab, he was amped. It looked more like a resort hotel than a place to get punished. But as soon as he saw what he'd be doing all day, he thought the jail time woulda been better. At least in juvie he'd just hang out in the yard in his orange jumpsuit or whatever—and the people there would expect him to be what he was, they wouldn't be all up in his face about changing.

At rehab, his counselor was this big, bald black dude named Lance, and it took him a minute just to stop laughing about that. But Lance must have known how faggy his name was, because he didn't get heated about it, just sat back in his swivel chair with one tree-trunk leg crossed wide over the other and scribbled on this yellow notepad he liked to carry around. He must've been writing shit about Damon, but Damon didn't mind. He was used to being sized up—*assessed*. He'd been assessed so many times his mom had a file cabinet full of little papers all tryna explain to her what her own son was like. She must've read them, but it didn't make a difference. The years kept passing and everything kept going on the same.

Lance told Damon about these Four Steps to Recovery that they were gonna do.

"Aren't there supposed to be like twelve of those?" Damon asked, and Lance grinned.

"Different program," he said. "But it's great you know about that."

Lance said the Four Steps were Building Awareness, Finding Support, Learning Vigilance, and Taking Accountability. It sounded like the usual bullshit. Lance said he really believed that Damon could change his life for the better.

Lance didn't try to bond with Damon over sports. He didn't try to impress him with how hard things had been when he was in high school a million years ago. He didn't ask dumbass questions like most adults did: *What's your favorite subject in school? Aren't you excited to be a senior next year? Where are you applying to college?* Lance didn't care about that shit. They just talked about whatever. How Tyler, the Creator, was the best emcee since Hova, and how Damon was gonna flip if someone didn't give him his iPhone and headphones back soon. How the sheets in this place were some common, two-hundred-thread-count shit that chafed your ass at night. How all the food was bunk except the frozen yogurt they brought in every Friday, which, Damon admitted, was pretty bomb.

"I don't know, man, I've never been much into fro-yo," Lance said. "It just doesn't compare to the real stuff."

"Jaws!" Damon protested. "That shit is creamalicious, yo."

Lance laughed. He told Damon his way of talking was hella inventive, kinda like Shakespeare, which his English teacher tried to make him read sophomore year, like on purpose tryna confuse him.

"What can't that dude just talk in fuckin' English?" Damon said. He waited for Lance's reaction, thinking maybe he liked Shakespeare and was gonna get pissed off, but Lance just laughed and shook his head, like he didn't get it either.

Lance started asking Damon all these questions no one else ever had—not Why couldn't he keep still? but What did he care about? and What did he want his life to be? He wanted to know other things too, like what Damon liked to smoke and what he liked to drink and what was happening in his life, and in his head, in the instant before he decided to take a hit. He wanted to know how Damon felt at school, what he thought when teachers yelled at him, and why he'd chosen Ryan and Nick as his crew. How he felt about getting arrested while his best friend got off.

"That's just Nick," Damon insisted. "He's always doing some cutty James Bond shit like that. It's not personal."

Finally, Lance asked how Damon felt about his family. His brother, Max, six years older, who'd left the house at age eighteen and promised never to come back. His mom. His dad.

"Why do you gotta know about that asshole?" Damon said, and plucked a Bic pen off the desk and pried its little plastic handle till it broke.

After a few weeks, him and Lance went outside to hike in the hills around the center. It felt good, after being stuck inside all those beige rooms. It was kinda crazy and Damon wasn't about to admit it out loud, but by that point Lance was his boy. He liked the way Lance laughed big and loud when Damon said something funny, how Lance leaned back in his chair and rubbed his palm over his shiny bald head like he was tryna get a genie to pop out. He liked how Lance's voice was this low, rumbly drawl that vibrated over the airwaves to Damon and made him chill. How he was built like a NFL lineman but didn't need to talk about it. How he didn't give a fuck if Damon messed with the little office shit on his desk, the paper clips or staples or whatever that those teachers were always so worried about. And when he asked Damon questions, he actually cared to listen to the answers.

They hiked along a trail that humped over round hills covered with tall yellow grass. Trees popped up along the edges of the hills, and beyond them a few thin clouds stretched over the San Francisco Bay. The pale blue sky was everywhere. It made him squint and bow his head. His blue nylon basketball shorts hung past his knees and the sun hit the brown-blond hairs on his shins and made them shine. As he stomped down the trail of packed brown dirt, dry grasses slapped his legs. The Timberland boots Lance had loaned him laced up to his ankles and made his feet look bigger than they were and basically he was cool with that. There were no girls there, anyway, so it didn't really matter how he looked.

When the trail narrowed, Lance told Damon to go ahead. As they walked, the air was so quiet he could hear Lance breathing behind him. Their feet beat a rhythm on the dirt. Damon's thumb twitched for his iPhone, but his iPhone wasn't there.

Birds talked to each other over the sky and the wind rustled all the dried-up spears of yellow grass and whispered through the leaves and branches of the green trees ahead. Every now and then something invisible shivered the grass—a snake or a mouse or whatever. The hills looked all meadow-like and still up on the surface, but there was all kinds of shit going on underneath, down in the dirt and the roots, that most people never bothered to know.

All that quiet was starting to fuck with his head. "Man, I'm not built for this exercise shit. Think it's time for some Doritos," he said, glancing back to grin at his boy.

Lance smiled but stayed quiet, letting Damon know to do the same. So Damon cracked his knuckles and kept going. He was hot and sweaty now, T-shirt sticking to his chest, sweat in his eyebrows and dripping down the back of his bare neck, where the glossy tag of his shirt flooded and became a cool square pressing on his skin. The muscles of his legs and ass were burning. His feet ached in the arches. His mind buzzed with boredom. In a minute, this endless trail and these invisible bugs humming in his ears and these little grasses swatting his legs were going to start pissing him off.

Lance had told him once that when he felt like this, he should try to pay attention to his own breath and, like, watch it travel in and out of his body. At first Damon had laughed at this idea, like how did you watch breath that was invisible, but Lance had said, *Just use your brain, picture it—like smoke*. Damon had smirked at the smoke part but Lance was dead serious on this. *Like red-hot smoke going out, cool blue smoke coming in. Hold it in your lungs. Ride it. Watch it. Now let it go*. So now, on the trail, Damon tried it. Watched the smoke suck into his nostrils and lungs, caught it there, held it, then watched the smoke stream slowly out.

He kept on walking and watching his breath. And then he was ready to talk.

What he told Lance—which he'd never fully told anyone else—was the truth about what his father did to him.

Damon's dad was a big shot. Big like Damon, with light blue eyes and light brown eyebrows and light brown hair cropped close to his head. A big-time corporate defense lawyer in San Francisco. He gave thousands of dollars to the school foundations and fire and police groups every year, and went to the charity auctions and bought paintings and spa packages and shit, and got his name printed up on all the little flyers. He was loud and funny and throwing bills and opinions all over the place, and everybody loved him or was scared of him or both.

The last time it happened was the night before Damon got arrested for Nick's party.

When school got out that afternoon, Damon drove by 7-Eleven for a couple bags of Cheetos and Rips and some ninety-nine-cent AriZona Iced Teas. Then he went home, which was a mini-mansion tucked between the freeway and a hill where people let their horses graze. It was early, and his parents were both at work. So he dropped his backpack on the floor and sat down on the leather couch in the great room, emptied his Sevvies bag on the coffee table. He'd opened one of the Cheetos in the car and it was already down to Day-Glo dust. There was dust on his fingers too that he licked off and wiped on the couch. He sat back with his legs spread wide, stayed like that for a minute and ate, sprawled out, enjoying all the space.

When he was done, he grabbed the second AriZona and went upstairs. Got into his room and flicked the light off, shut the blinds, locked the door behind him. He turned on the TV and Xbox, and scooted his fat leather beanbag chair up to the screen. Then he grabbed the controller, upped the sound until it felt like he was sitting inside it.

The game he was working on was Call of Duty: Black Ops II. In the middle of the screen were two white hands holding a handgun. His hands. His gun. He started stalking through some farm that was on fire. All charred-out barns and shit and darkness. Jolly cowboy music echoed in the background. Then zombies started coming out of shadows to veer toward him, eyes blazing. One came too close, so he swapped his gun for a knife and stabbed its chest. It groaned and screamed. Then another zombo came toward him and he stopped it with three gunshots: *pop-pop pop*. Blood spurted out of the hole where its head was.

When his mom had got him this game, she'd asked him, Was it like Mario. He said Sure, but of course that was a jaws. In this game, there weren't gold coins you got or anything. The only point was not to die.

The screen changed. Now he was in a town that was set on fire just like the farm had been. The air all dark and smoky. Ground torn up. Fancy burned-out cars and broken windows. Flames jumping up everywhere. Embers hanging in the air like fireflies, and horror-movie music swelling all around him. A girl zombo came at him waving its arms around like some hella fucked-up dance routine. He shot its face and blood washed the screen dark red. Another one got too close and swiped him. He fell on the pavement and dropped his gun and this cheery-ass song started blasting.

"Motherfucker!" he yelled. But it didn't really matter. He got another life. Same busted town, but the zombos in this one started running at him. If he capped them in the head, they'd die faster. And sometimes the head exploded and shot fireworks of blood and bone into the sky and for a minute he felt hella raw.

Damon's problem was, his dad was so fuckin' loud he could hear him even with the game turned up as high as it would go. Whatever he did, there was always his dad pushing through, hollering the same old shit, like *Get your ass downstairs.*

Damon paused the game and went down.

His parents were waiting in the great room. His mom in an armchair and his dad at the foot of the staircase in black suit pants and a shirt the color of fogged-in sky. A glass in his hand—rye whiskey, had to be. His tie was off. How many had he had already? Two? Three?

"You want to explain yourself?" his dad said, pointing to the coffee table where there were crinkled-up Cheeto bags and cellophane, an empty AriZona can, little twisted papers from the Rips.

Damon shrugged.

"Don't be an asshole," his dad said.

"Fuckin' chill," Damon muttered.

"Excuse me?"

"Nothing."

"That's right nothing. You better believe it nothing."

Damon stuck his hand in his pocket. His Swiss army knife was there like always, and he flicked its small blade up and down, sliding his thumb against the steel. He said, "Yes, sir, Drill Sergeant, sir."

"That's all you have to say to me?"

"The fuck else do you want?"

"What do I want?" his dad said. "What do I *want*?" Then he started yelling shit Damon wasn't tryna hear. How Damon was always pissing everybody off, how his dad had given him everything a kid could want and he'd done nothing, not one single thing, to deserve it. How he was the luckiest kid on the planet and he didn't even know it. "And I want to know. When are you going to grow up? Learn to act like a goddamn human being?"

Damon's mom stood up, crossed her arms. "Hey. Cut it out, you two."

Damon's dad said, "How much money have I wasted already, trying to set you straight?"

"What are you even talking about?" Damon said. What was money? It came, it went. It always came again. "Who gives a shit?"

"Okay, smartass." Damon's dad waved his glass around the great room—plush leather furniture, huge stone fireplace, giant-sized windows with fancy silk curtains—as if Damon gave a shit about any of it. "You like your life? How bout that Xbox? Those ridiculous clothes?" His eyes moved over Damon's oversized baby-blue T-shirt, his jeans sagging over his crotch, his coordinating blue and green Adidas. "For Chrissake, why don't you pull your pants up for once. The world doesn't need to see your ass hanging out twenty-four/seven."

Damon glanced at his mom, but she ducked her head, studied her fingernails like she'd just now noticed they were there.

"Why, so I could look like you? Fuckin' fatass."

His dad's face flared red. His mom stuck her palms up, like *I surrender*. She went into the kitchen and the next sound was water blasting in the sink.

His dad went and clattered his glass on the marble-topped bar; the ice cubes cracked and smacked together. He came back. Stepped to Damon to show how he was still the bigger man. "You will not talk to me that way. Not in my house."

"Your house is a prison cell with curtains," Damon said, getting in his face. "I can't wait to get out of here. Fuck, you ever wonder why Max hasn't been back here once since graduation? Not one time? You think that's fuckin' normal?"

For an awful moment Damon's dad just stared. Then he laughed, hard, mirthless. "You think high school is so hard?" he said. "See what it's like out there for one day, you little shit. One fucking day."

It was evening, and out the window the palominos grazed Horse

Hill against a wide and purpling sky. Their necks, silhouetted, stretched for grass, and there were the beautiful swirls of their tails as they flicked the air.

"Anytime, asshole," Damon said, and pulled his face into the fuck-you grin he knew his dad couldn't stand.

That was all it took. His dad threw a punch and Damon jerked back. The fist flew past his face, sloppy. Then his dad checked his balance and bobbed back, fists up. He bent his knees, hunching his shoulders like this shit was official. Damon's muscles twitched to squeeze his hands to fists, but he held them still.

"Get your fists up," his dad said, "what's wrong with you?"

Damon ground his teeth. Blood throbbed at his temples. He stretched one hand and closed it. With the other he thumbed the cool edge of the knife in his pocket. And it took all his energy to hold himself still in that moment. To pay attention. He knew there was only one way out of this. Like that dumb song they made him memorize in preschool—*Can't go over it, can't go under it, gotta go through it.* Why was he thinking of that now?

He put up his fists.

His dad smiled and swung. Damon wasn't fast enough this time. His dad's knuckles cracked on his jaw. A flash of pain. Blood rushed up his neck, into his cheeks and his ears. Before he could think, he ran at his dad, bear-hugged him, and threw him on the couch. Damon landed on top, and him and his dad grappled on the leather cushions, his dad struggling beneath, Damon slamming him against the couch, exhaling, "Fuckin' asshole. Motherfucker." Damon's dad grunted and struggled as Damon pummeled him, searching for soft spots, hitting whatever he could reach, neck, ribs, kidneys.

"Fuckin'. Asshole. Mother. Fucker."

But his dad had stopped resisting. Breathing heavy.

Damon stopped. Pulled back. His dad was sprawled across the leather cushions, pants twisted under the slick black belt, shirt untucked to show a triangle of fleshy belly. His eyes were closed, his forehead damp. Across his cheeks a ragged flush like sunburn, and a fault line of blood on his lip. He opened his eyes. They were this round, watery blue like Damon's, and there was a thin pink skin over the whites. It was how you looked when you were wasted, but also when you cried.

Holy shit, Damon thought. *What just happened? Like, what did I just do?*

Then his dad broke. Fell back laughing. "Your face," he said.

"Fuck you." Damon got up and shook out his fist. His jaw hurt but he wouldn't touch it.

Damon's mom was standing in the doorway of the kitchen with her hand over her mouth like after all this time this shit still had the ability to shock.

Then she ran up to touch his dad's cheek.

Damon turned, and got out the front door.

He walked to the end of the driveway and to the end of the street, then hiked up Horse Hill where no one would find him. Since he was a kid he'd loved those horses, and whenever his dad was done doing his thing, Damon would go up to tell them about it. He sat down in the grass and pulled a blunt from his sock and blazed it. He could text Ryan and Nick to come swoop him but didn't feel like it yet. The horses were busy chomping yellow-green grass and he knew they couldn't talk back, but he felt like they got him anyway. They kinda shuddered their flanks when he told them, and when he reached out to touch them they didn't even spook, just whipped their coarse mane hair against his hand, like they knew exactly who he was. Like they wanted to tell him that he'd be okay in the end, that there would be an end to this.

When Damon got home from rehab, he was ready to be different. He remembered what Lance said: Always breathe. Catch the anger before the switch flips and it's too late. Though he might feel like he'd been dealing with this shit forever, in the story of a whole life he was just in chapter one. If he kept it together for one more year, he could leave and have a different life. Never see his dad again if that was what he chose.

When Damon got back from rehab, he got out of bed when he was supposed to. He went to class when he was supposed to. He didn't start shit that didn't need to be started. For example. His mom said he couldn't have his BMW back, but he didn't let it get to him, just told her, "I could get a ride from Ryan."

His mom relaxed, like the storm she was bracing for was gonna pass by after all. Then she smiled. "Why don't I drive you? Remember how much fun we used to have cruising around together?"

"Not really."

"When you got cranky, I used to buckle you into your car seat and drive you around and around. We'd listen to the Mill Valley theme song, remember? You used to bounce along to the chorus and kick your little chubby legs."

"Whatever," he said, skimming through texts on his phone, but there was a glimmer of memory there. That song that sounded like carnival music, something they played while you zipped around in circles, then hurled your corn dog off the side.

"Well, you loved it," his mom said.

He didn't fight her. Just got in the car and let her drive him to school. It was weird to be back, but good. It was where he belonged. In first-period English the whole class was pumped up to see him, and his teacher Miss Nicoll—who always used to eye him like she had one finger cocked on her pepper spray—came up and gave him this bigass hug in front of everyone. It was weird as shit, but in a way he didn't hate it.

After sixth period, he went to the tutoring place down the street. The tutors there hated him. They hated him because the old Damon would mess with them at every session. For instance, when a tutor tried to talk to him, he'd tip his chair back on two legs, wave to his friends across the office and yell, "Yo, Jonas, where the function at tonight?" or "Hey, Ry, you jerking off in here again?" Or he'd throw pencils at the back of some dork's head who was pushing his face right up to the computer screen to type. Sometimes he'd just sit there munching Cheetos loud as possible, lick the dust off his fingers and wipe them on the sides of the chairs. If he was tired, he'd act like a retard until the tutor gave up and just told him the answers. And the last time he'd had the cute-ass college chick, Jenny, as his tutor, he'd huddled over his paper and scribbled real careful until she asked to see his work—then he showed her his sketch, which was just of some bitch naked, and cracked up when her cheeks got all red and she jumped up and huffed out of the room. He'd watched her leave, tipped back in his chair, and grinned real big 'cause no one was gonna make him do shit he didn't feel like doing.

This time it was gonna be different.

The front-desk lady saw him and sighed. "Jenny?" she called over her shoulder.

Jenny appeared from a back room. She was about five feet tall and had these glittery earrings on and a bright purple hoodie and green Converse. At first she did the glance thing, like *Really, you're doing this to me again?* but when she realized Damon could see her, she smiled. She had dimples when she smiled and it almost made him forget how she'd looked when she thought he couldn't see her. He knew it was her job to be nice to everyone, but still.

"Hey, Damon. Did you bring your stuff with you?"

"Yeah." He unzipped his backpack and held it out so she could see it was actually full of books: U.S. history, physiology, English, intermediate algebra.

Jenny just stood there looking shocked, so he said, "So? And?" Then stopped himself because Lance would say that was the attitude he used to push away people who were tryna help him and he didn't have to do that anymore.

Jenny cocked her eyebrow like *Is this some kind of trick?* Then she said, "Okay. Well, good. What are you working on today?"

"I got math. I tried to look at it already, but it's fuckin' bullshit—"

Someone cleared their throat. It turned out to be a mom standing behind him with her hands on the shoulders of two little kids. The kids' eyes were saucers and the mom was glaring.

Damon turned back around. "I mean," he said, "could you, like, help me."

"Come on back," Jenny said. She led him through the office toward the little isolation room they always made him go in, the one with the glass wall that looked out into the main room where everybody else got to be. In the main room was a circle of computers with kids and tutors sitting all around.

"Yo, Flint! My *nig*!"

"Hey! Language," Jenny snapped.

It was Ryan. Sprawled back in a cushy office chair sucking on a Big Gulp while his tutor was asking him questions and typing. Damon thought, This was exactly what his life was like. He got put in the isolation room with Jenny who expected him to work, while Ryan got to chill at the computers with a tutor who acted like his secretary.

"Ryan. Hey, man. We've talked about that word," Ryan's tutor said, all earnest. This fuckin' weirdo. Pale and bony with a ponytail drooping down his back and a neck so skinny his Adam's apple looked like an elbow jerking up and down.

"Yo," Damon said. "You do the Decker homework?"

"Naw, I'm in advanced, remember?"

"Yeah. Sucks to be you." He always forgot Ryan was in advanced algebra, not intermediate like him. Ryan wasn't smarter or anything. But the day that Nick was gonna help them cheat on the placement test, Damon had forgot and dipped math class. When he came back, he had to take the test legit. It didn't go too well.

Didn't matter. Didn't matter. Lance said fuck the past. Lance said the present was the place to be and the future a place you made up as you went along.

"Come on," Jenny said now. She pushed Damon into the isolation room. Her small, warm hand on his shoulder. She was little but strong. He wondered what she looked like out of that hoodie and jeans but couldn't really picture it. She didn't touch him again, just pointed at the chair and closed the door behind them. It was a stupid setup because him and Ryan were still facing each other through the wall of glass, but he didn't say anything. He thought, *She's, like, a professional tutor, she should know better by now.*

"Okay," Jenny said, taking a breath. "Let's find out which problems you're supposed to do. Where's your planner?"

"I don't know."

"You lost it?"

He shrugged.

"Damon. We talked about this. How are you going to do your homework if you don't write down the assignment?"

It was starting to feel like the old days. He could feel the slide back, like when he was a kid and his big brother, Max, pushed him down the plastic tube at the playground—he was sliding and sliding and tryna stop himself by holding on to the staticky plastic but there weren't any edges to grab.

To stop the sliding feeling, Damon opened his backpack and pulled out a piece of binder paper. Unfolded it and pressed the wrinkles out on the table. On the paper he'd written the numbers of all the problems Mr. Decker said to do that day in class and the first couple that he tried to do by himself during tutorial. Which meant one actual answer and then a lot of shit he'd penciled in and crossed out.

"I wrote it here."

Jenny was shocked. "Damon, you did this?"

"At tutorial."

"You did *work* during tutorial?"

"So?"

"That's amazing, Damon. I mean it. Really great." She looked like she might be in love with him. Just for a second. She wasn't that much older.

"I guess."

"Right on. Okay. Let's do this." Then she did this crazy thing. Usually, she stayed across the table from him and they kinda stared each other down until he gave in and did some work or she got pissed enough to leave. This time, no. This time she got up and pulled her chair around next to his and reached across him to slide the algebra book between them and she smelled like grass after the rain. "You ready?"

He nodded.

Then she helped him. For every problem, she had him write down the numbers that mattered and then they worked it out together. It was boring as fuck and most of the time he had no clue what she was talking about, but there was something different when she was sitting there next to him and smiling and tucking her hair behind her ear and talking to him like she liked him and there was the jingle of her silver bangles when she wrote and a little whiff of coffee on her breath.

Out the glass wall, there was Ryan tipping back in his chair, throwing a Koosh ball straight up in the air and catching it, and when he saw Damon looking he stopped the ball and made like to throw it Damon's way, jumping his eyebrows and sticking out his tongue. It was hilarious how his tutor didn't notice and kept right on typing Ryan's homework, and the old Damon would have seen it as an opportunity. He would've jumped up and run out to catch the ball, or even just raised his hands and hollered, "Blast that motherfucker!" through the glass, even knowing those little kids were doing their ABC's two tables over. Every inch of his body was itching to get out of that hard plastic chair.

Lance said stop and feel what he was feeling. Breathe his way through it. Wait. So Damon watched the imaginary smoke move in and out of his body. Red and blue, hot and cool. The plastic clock ticked on the wall. Then Ryan's tutor woke up and took the Koosh away, and the moment was over.

By the end of the hour, Damon still didn't give a fuck about any kind of algebra and had tried to visualize six or seven times what Jenny'd look like naked sucking dick. But the homework was done.

"Awesome! Damon, you did it!" Jenny said. He thought if Mill Valley had cheerleaders she'd be one.

"Cool," he told her, and stuck the paper in the front of his math book and shoved the book in his backpack. Thinking about Cool Ranch Doritos and gummy worms and how many zombos he was gonna kill when he got home.

"Cool. So what else do you have to do tonight? Let's make a list."

Fuck. What *else*? The clock on the wall said 5:45. Jenny started looking through his backpack and writing down a list of all the other homework he already forgot. Read two chapters for English. Write a three-page paper for U.S. history. Do the study guide for the quiz tomorrow in physio. Then there was the late work he could maybe still get credit for. And the electives. Spanish. Art. Motherfuckin' *PE*. He stopped looking. It just went on and on. Lance would have said it was his choice to do it or not. It was his choice but there was consequences either way.

"Damon. You can do this," Jenny said. Like she was right in that plastic tube with him. Like she saw him sliding down.

"I know," he told her.

She let him out of the isolation room.

Ryan gave him a ride home. "We got the hookup," he said. "Nick's supplier came through. You down?"

Damon thought, *I could do the rest of this shit tomorrow before school. Get up hella early, bomb through it. I could say I did it but I lost it. I could say I forgot it. I could do it tomorrow night. Hand it in late for half credit. I could not do it. Toss my backpack in the back of Ryan's Expedition and forget it. And for a few hours out of twenty-four do what the fuck I want to do.*

"Naw, not tonight," he told Ryan. "Fuckin' washed, bro."

"Whatever, chag," Ryan said.

When Damon got home, he went straight to his room. He turned on the desk light and shoved the sweatshirts and candy wrappers and broken pens and DVDs onto the floor. He scrolled through his phone to look at funny shit on Vine but didn't even stay on five minutes. He got all his books out and Jenny's list and for the first time ever he did everything on it. Not even joking. Every last thing.

After a couple weeks, it got to the point where Jenny didn't even cringe when he came in. He was turning in work, and his math grades had gone up to C's instead of F's. And he was feeling different. Not smoking or drinking, so his head got clearer. He was still killing zombos on Xbox but it wasn't the first thing he went to, and he didn't lose those hours that used to go by before he was even aware. Now mostly he played at Ryan's or Nick's place. It was better than playing alone and they were mostly cool with him not smoking. Most of all, he was doing better at what Lance said, like not getting so heated when teachers glared at him, and breathing when he felt cooped up. At the tutoring place, Jenny started leaving the door to the isolation room open so he could hear the buzz of kids outside. She said pretty soon they'd be out in the main room and he'd get to use a computer again. She didn't even mind when he came in—came right up to him and asked to help without glancing at anyone.

The night of Elisabeth Avarine's party—the night he got the BMW back—Damon went and picked up Ryan. As they bombed down the half-empty streets toward Elisabeth's house, they were slapping old-school Tupac loud enough to shake the seats. He didn't know what was gonna happen that night, but he hadn't had a drink in weeks and he didn't think he needed one. He was good. He was back.

Elisabeth Avarine lived in one of those big old ghost-story-looking houses in the canyon behind Old Mill Park, on a street that was like two mountains sucking in so cars and people could sneak through. Damon slid the car into a little groove next to a redwood tree and stepped out feeling pretty good—considering he hadn't had a car in months, he still parked like a fuckin' pro. He didn't bother to lock it because this was Mill Valley and anyone who'd be tryna take a BMW was going to be inside the party with him. And people would be getting too wasted to be running around stealing cars and shit.

The house was jammed into the side of the hill, so he and Ryan had to hike down this cutty staircase in the dark just to find the front door. As they descended, Damon's heart started punching his ribs and he thought of what Lance said, like how it's never too late to change the game. People were starting to look at him different. Not everyone—most adults still kinda flinched when he walked in a room—but some. Like Jenny. Like his mom, who was acting just a little more relaxed lately. Not like his dad, but who gave a shit about that asshole. That's what Lance said. "You've gotta adjust your expectations," Lance said. "Don't expect him to be different. And if he comes at you, stay cool. Don't take the bait." Lance said a lot of dope shit and Damon tried to remember it all, running the lines through his brain on a loop. Instead, there was that thing his dad said earlier. *Just for the night. See how you do.* Shaking the keys in Damon's face. Why did he have to do it like that? Why couldn't he just be decent and say, *Good job, Damon, you're not a fuckup after all, you're doing all that homework and not doing nothing to chill yourself out, not drinking, not smoking, not even when your body's screaming at you to give it some relief, and in the three months you've been home the teachers haven't complained about you once?* Instead he had to shake those keys like Damon was a dog begging for a walk and raise that eyebrow like he was a hundred percent sure Damon was gonna fuck it up. Like he wanted him to. Like he'd rather be right than have a son he could actually try to like.

As they walked down to Elisabeth's front door, Damon still had his dad in the back of his head, not his words but his face, that smirk like *I know who you are*. Damon tried to put Lance's words on top, to remember that the past was not the future, he could be anyone he decided to be. But when they got into the party, the music wrapped them up, and there were girls and red cups scattered everywhere, and he knew this was where he belonged.

Damon and Ryan walked through Elisabeth Avarine's living room and out to the redwood deck. The deck glowed under yellow spotlights and beyond the rail there was nothing but black trees and the canyon underneath, the earth skidding down to a creek that was shushing along below.

Nick was over in the corner, just chilling with these girls in a circle of cushy patio furniture. He sat in a chair with a freshman perched on one arm; three more girls spooned each other in a long chair next to him, and there were two more armchairs with dudes who jumped up and disappeared when they saw Damon and Ryan coming.

"Yo, Ryan! What up, Flint!" People called to them from all around the deck. Everyone happy to see them. Which was just how it was when they walked into a function together. And when Damon and Ryan settled into their chairs, the energy shifted—like everyone took a few steps to the left without even knowing they were doing it. Not even wanting to, just sensing shit was about to get interesting because the right people had arrived. This was how Damon knew what actual power felt like.

It never worked when he was alone. It was the power of the three. Damon, Ryan, Nick. They'd figured that out back in eighth grade, and that was why they stuck together. If they split up, would they ever feel this kind of power again? Would they have to go through life without it? That was the most depressing thought possible.

"Want something?" Nick asked them, flicking ash from his cigarette. He'd come early to set up. *Must be making a play for Elisabeth Avarine,* Damon thought. Nick wasn't afraid of anything. It was crazy how he never had an issue getting girls, even though he was beanpole skinny with a razor-blade face. It was probably 'cause he always thought of funny shit to say, or because he made their fake IDs.

Ryan took a cigarette and said, "Fuck yeah." Ryan got even more girls than Nick and didn't have to say or do anything. He just looked like Justin Bieber and played like Buster Posey and it turned out for most girls that was enough. And like they were reading minds, two freshman girls (both flat-chested, one had braces) jumped up from the long chair and scurried inside to get them drinks.

"This house is sick," Ryan said, exhaling smoke. "Elisabeth's got bars."

"No shit," said Nick.

"Have you seen her mom? Fuckin' MILF."

"Hell yeah," Damon said. "I'd hit that."

But they all looked at him like, *What?* and then cracked up. Like, *Who the fuck are you kidding, Flint? Like anyone would want to get with your fat ass.* Ha-ha. Damon was laughing too because it was fuckin' funny, or he was used to it.

The freshman girls got back. One carried red cups for Ryan and Nick, and the braces one had a forty that was supposed to be for Damon. He wondered what bet she'd lost, ending up with him. She walked slow, smiling all shy and scared, and kept tugging at her tube top that she didn't have the tits for, but he had to give her credit, she came right up to him.

"I wasn't sure what you wanted." She smiled in that braces way, halfhearted, pulling her top lip down over her teeth to hide the metal he could obviously tell was there.

"Cool," he said. He wasn't gonna drink it or anything, but this chick had got it for him and if he said he didn't want it, she might, like, run to the bathroom to cry (every function, somebody always did), and if he said the whole thing about rehab and Lance, she'd just think he was gay. So that was why he took it, sliding his fingers over hers and around the cold, wet glass. Plus it gave him something to hold on to.

The freshman blushed and went back to her long chair where the other girls were crushed, giggling. Damon spread his legs and lounged back in his chair. Arching his neck, he looked up at what sky he could glimpse through the arms of the trees. The sky was clear navy, but the trees were thick and black and waving just enough he knew it wouldn't be clear for long. There was the hum of people mingling and talking and drinking and smoking and shouting at each other across the deck. And everyone a little unsure 'cause they were at Elisabeth Avarine's, so it was a distinct possibility the function could turn out to be bunk.

Damon thought that if Nick was tryna get with Elisabeth, he'd better do it already. But she was probably cowering in the kitchen like she was when they walked in, with a look on her face like *What did I just do?* This chick was hot as fuck but still. No wonder she didn't have any friends.

Damon tried to relax. He watched the sky and held on to the forty that dripped dew into his palm. The sky he could see was so minimal. That deep in the canyon, it was all just trees. He could hear the creek splashing along in the darkness down below. Over the edge of the deck, there was nothing, and he felt like an astronaut, staring down the kind of black that didn't end. It was some spooky shit. If he tried to bring his horses, they'd be like, *Fuck no, you can stay, we're getting up out of this bitch.*

He started picking at the label on the bottle. He held it up to his face and scratched at it with his fingernail. Shit stuck to his fingers, but he got a few good strips off and shook them onto the deck. Like Lance said, living in the moment. His boys kept up the conversation and the braces girl blushed in his direction and the night was fine (but the air kinda tingly and strange, a rim of a cloud at the edge of the sky) and everything was chill. And then out of nowhere the rain came down.

Hammered them like a motherfucker.

They ran inside. Damon and Ryan were fastest and claimed the two white couches in the living room while Nick went to handle the stereo. Ryan took the shorter one, but the girls flocked around him in two seconds, even the braces girl from the deck, and the ones that didn't make it sat around him on the floor. Most were freshmen and sophomores, but there were a few juniors too—like Emma Fleed, who was short and on the thick side actually, but okay looking, and pretty much DTF with whoever but especially Ryan. And he had the hottest freshman, little Asian-looking chick Emily, perched on the edge by his head and Damon gave him a look like *Get there.*

Damon's head and face were wet from the rain. He grabbed a fuzzy white blanket from the back of his couch and rubbed its soft face on his. "Fuck, I gotta get me one a these," he said. "This shit is the bomb."

"Ima get one a these couches in my dorm room," Ryan said. "And put like cozy-ass shit all over it. Ima have all the bitches up in there."

"What dorm room?" Damon said.

"Fuckin' college?" Ryan said. "Hello?"

"You're going to college," Damon said, and laughed.

"Fuck yeah I'm going to college. My grandpa's on the board at Pepperdine. Know where that is? Malibu, motherfucker. Ima do my classes at the beach."

Damon's heart began to disturb his ribs. Like, *When the fuck did this happen?* He tried to have his face not show it.

After Ryan, everyone started bragging. Jonas Everett was going to CU Boulder to snowboard. Nick could get in anywhere, everyone said so, but wanted something in The City. Abigail Cress was talking East Coast Ivy League. Dave Chu had scraped the SAT and seemed pretty sure about Berkeley. Emma Fleed had some dance thing in New York. They all knew their GPAs by heart. Took the SAT two, three times already.

Like, *When the fuck did this happen?*

Out the window the beach kids were crazy dancing in the middle of the storm. Cally Broderick and this hot piece Alessandra Ryding and these weird-ass hippie dudes he knew but didn't know. They all were soaking wet and the girls' shirts turning see-through like some kinda magic and it was a good distraction from the inside conversation, Alessandra's little brown nipples and Cally's broader pink ones perking through as they spread their arms and licked the sky. Were they going to college too? he wondered. Were they in this secret get-your-shit-together club like everyone but him?

No one had talked to Damon about the SAT. His parents had talked a couple times about the community college that was fifteen minutes away. And he'd said, "Whatever." Who cared about college, anyway. Sounded boring as fuck.

Now he saw it. Everyone was going but he was not. This was the last big party of the year. It was gonna be summer, then senior year. It wasn't too late to apply to places, but D's and C-minuses weren't getting him anywhere good. Plus three years of summer school. Getting wrapped. Going to rehab. Not even taking the SAT—was it too late? Could he take it in September? He was so far behind already.

He was an idiot. The fuck did it matter if he did this little homework assignment or that one. Big deal he could stay sober for twelve weeks. Like that meant anything to anyone.

There was one year left before his friends left him behind. Even Ryan, who wasn't any smarter than him—Damon always thought they'd get an apartment together, hang out and host functions and get all the girls from there to Terra Linda with no problems. And have the time of their lives. But no. Ryan out of nowhere was going to some school on a L.A. movie set. Ryan all of a sudden had a plan. Now he was talking about going to visit. Talking actress girls everywhere, hot tub parties, bonfires on the beach.

What was Damon working so hard for? Since rehab he'd been torturing himself, for what? He cocked the forty to his lips and drank until he felt like his gut and heart and lungs were full of it. Wiped his mouth with the back of his hand. "Let's get *housed*!" he yelled, and all around him a cheer went up.

Then he was jumping in the BMW with Ryan in front with him and Nick in back with Cally Broderick, Alessandra Ryding, Emma Fleed. He was driving the dark, curvy streets in full confidence, skimming his thumbs on the leather wheel, kicking back and enjoying the feel of the driver's seat he'd been kicked out of for so long.

When they got out of the canyon, Cally said she saw a cop, so Nick pushed Emma down and over until she was lying with her head on Alessandra's lap and her torso stretched over Cally, who petted it. Emma's ass and legs were still on Nick and she was wearing this, like, ballerina skirt and in the rearview Nick slid his hand under its ruffly hem and she let out a little animal moan and was quiet.

In the passenger seat, Ryan put on this rapper Earl Sweatshirt. He was their age only he was a fuckin' genius. His voice was deep and it stretched out of his throat like thick black paint pulled over glass, filling all the empty silent spaces that none of them could stand.

"Crank that shit," Damon said, and Ryan pumped it till there was no room left to think.

In the backseat, Alessandra started to bitch. "Ugh, no. This song is so sexist, you guys."

Ryan turned it up. The bass shook the car and thrummed in Damon's chest. "That's what I'm talkin' about!" he said, riding the beat. "That is the fuckin' bee's knees."

"Fuck you guys, he's talking about fucking rape!" Alessandra yelled.

"Turn it off, asshole!" Cally said.

"Why do you always gotta be such a bitch?" Ryan yelled back, and Damon remembered how he and Cally had a thing back in eighth grade, which suddenly seemed so long ago he had to squint to remember it even existed.

"You're a pig," Alessandra said.

Emma said nothing. Nick's eyes were closed and he was making this math-test grimace and Damon wondered what it was that he was concentrating on.

He swerved before he knew it was there. Cally screamed. A deer in the road, standing there staring at him with its shiny eyes. Veering right he felt a thud, a far-off crunch of metal and cracked glass, a push against his seat, a thrust, a tree trunk glossed with rain, a balloon exploding in his face.

Then he was ice calm. He thought, *Oh shit, someone got in an accident.*

Behind him, Alessandra started yelling, "Oh my God, oh my God!" Ryan was hugging his airbag like a teddy bear and it was funny as shit but it wasn't. Cally was crying and screaming and Nick was holding up his hands now, staring at his lap. Dark blood sliced his forehead. Damon wondered what he was looking at.

It could have been the sirens he heard or just his memories of them echoing. He didn't wait to find out. He rolled out the driver's-side door, took off running through the rain, and didn't look back.

On the morning after the faculty dinner, Molly scanned the news online. Dutifully she checked the *New York Times,* although its violent photos and stern headlines had seemed over the recent months increasingly distant and unreal. Then she clicked over to the local *Marin Independent Journal:*

May 26, 2013

Mill Valley Crash Injures Five Teens, One Critically; Driver Arrested on Suspicion of DUI

by Nathan Hanlon

MILL VALLEY—One juvenile has been detained by police and another is in critical condition after their 2012 BMW 5 Series sedan slammed into a tree at high speed early this morning, officials said. The crash occurred at approximately 1:30 a.m. on Throckmorton Avenue in Mill Valley, Mill Valley Police Department spokesman Dan Cisco said.

The critically injured teen, a 16-year-old female, is being treated at Marin General Hospital in Greenbrae. Four additional passengers were treated for minor injuries and released this morning, hospital officials said.

According to Cisco, the car was driven by a 17-year-old juvenile of Mill Valley and registered to his parents, also of Mill Valley. Cisco added that the teens were fleeing a Cascade Canyon house party that had "spun out of control." Officers were called to the party scene by a neighbor who complained of "disturbing and excessive noise," Cisco said, and the accident occurred as the teens exited the canyon and headed toward Lytton Square in downtown Mill Valley.

It is believed that alcohol as well as marijuana and possibly other illegal substances were present at the party. The MVPD is still investigating how the teens obtained the alcohol, said Officer Aaron Shmersky. Several witnesses who wished to remain anonymous indicated that all of the teens, including the driver, had been drinking prior to the accident.

Cisco said the car may have been going as fast as 55 miles per hour through this quiet residential neighborhood when the driver lost control of the vehicle and crashed headfirst into the tree, an old-growth redwood native to this region.

Immediately following the crash, the driver attempted to flee the scene, Cisco said. He was pursued on foot by an MVPD officer who observed the accident from his patrol car. The officer was parked a block from the crash site, near the intersection of Throckmorton Avenue and Olive Street. According to Cisco, the driver's blood alcohol level was measured at 0.16 percent. (The legal limit for adults is 0.08 percent.)

"This incident underscores the need for stricter enforcement of our citywide curfews," said Mill Valley City Council member Sandra Smith-Wolinsky. "As we have seen in this case, teenagers allowed to roam our community freely and unattended are likely to pose a danger not only to themselves, but to all of us."

COMMENTS

Al Blackburn: Just more stupid Marin kids taking
peoples lives in their hands.

Dianne P.: Don't teenagers have parents anymore?

Cheryl Yamhill-Brooks: Kids' brains don't develop
until they are in their twenties. thats why they need
guidance to learn about the DANGEROUS affects
of drug and alcohol.

steven p.: tax payer money being used to send
these iresponsible rich kids to rehab? I DON'T
THINK SO.

Greg Hill: What are these parents thinking giving
that kid that nice of a car???

Janis W.: I don't understand why did this happen?
When I was a kid I had to buy my own car.

cynthia y.: lock this kid up NOW before he hurts
somebody else!

1MarinView: This is not even half the story.
Get all the details and REAL reporting at
www.onemarinviewblog.com!

Molly ventured down the Internet rabbit hole. She typed in the blog's
url. Here names were named. Screenshots were posted from the night
before: reposts from teenagers' accounts on Facebook and Instagram
and Twitter and Vine. She read about the ransacked house of Elisabeth
Avarine and the arrest of Damon Flintov. Everywhere were names she
knew, and faces. Faces she knew drinking and smoking and grinding
and stripping, names she knew—even Nick Brickston—spouting obscenities and humiliating the weakest among them. In dull horror she
scrolled through nearly naked photos and videos of the injured Emma
Fleed, a popular girl who'd eaten lunch in Molly's classroom but whose

name Molly hadn't known. The kids had posted all this online with apparently brazen indifference, and the Internet had refreshed their posts over and over again, until it seemed the night had occurred not just once but an infinite number of times.

Alone in her apartment, Molly was powerless. She hated the feeling. After an hour of pacing, she gave in to impulse: she picked up her cell phone and dialed the number she had.

"Nick," she said to his voicemail, "it's me, Molly. Miss Nicoll. I've just seen the news. It's so horrible, I can't believe it. What happened last night? I mean, I can see—I know what happened. Everyone knows what happened. But why?" Her voice threatened to crack—she hung up. She sat on the edge of her love seat still vibrating from the call. In her head she heard her message as Nick Brickston would, and she sounded unhinged.

But she was unhinged. These were her kids, and their darkest moments were playing out on a public stage—there had to be something she could do.

She went to Facebook and logged on. She went to Nick's wall, then Amelia Frye's, Steph Malcolm-Swann's, Ryan Harbinger's, Damon Flintov's, leaving comments everywhere.

> **Molly Nicoll:** I can't believe this is happening. What did you guys do??
>
> **Molly Nicoll:** You know you should have called me! That poor girl who was hurt.
>
> **Molly Nicoll:** What is the girl's name? Emma? Who's her English teacher?
>
> **Molly Nicoll:** Emma Fleed, I'm so sorry this happened to you.
>
> **Molly Nicoll:** Damon, you are on my mind. Please msg me if you need to talk.
>
> **Molly Nicoll:** Ryan, have you spoken to Damon? Is he all right? Who let him start drinking again?
>
> **Molly Nicoll:** Sorry if you are too shaken up to an-

swer questions. I'm just worried about you. All of
you.

Molly Nicoll: What can I do to help?

Molly Nicoll: Love you guys no matter what. I'm
here for you.

Molly Nicoll: Let me know!!!

THE DANCER

Emma Fleed danced alone. A vast stage. Shafts of light beamed against her body, warming her face and dazzling her sequined skirt. It was a ballet she did not remember learning, yet her body eased into the movements like it had known them all her life. Oddly, she heard no music, just a steady humming through her body, through the room. The audience was a red-black sea beyond the footlights. She rolled onto the boxes of her toe shoes, rose *en pointe*. Driving her toes into the floor, she steadied her ankles and flexed her calves and stretched out of her feet, arms above her head, until it felt like floating. Then she stepped and leapt, splitting her legs in the air, and landed with such lightness that only she could hear the soft thud of her slippers on the wood. She set, pirouetted, spotting a point beyond the lights. Rising and spinning, holding her head in perfect stillness before whipping around at the last possible second. Applause shook the room. Her center was holding. Her legs were strong. In this moment, she was exactly where she was meant to be.

Then she woke up. She squinted against stark white light. The air was cold, antiseptic.

She turned her ankles, one and then the other, and they were intact and yet something was not right. The world was not the world she went to sleep in. There was the ambient clatter of metal instruments, and a machine that measured something—possibly her heart—beeped randomly.

A silver-haired doctor—white coat, blue scrubs—approached her bed. A nurse followed, took Emma's hand and flipped her wrist, pressed two fingers to her pulse and there was the strange urgency of her blood as it throbbed against this stranger's skin.

The doctor peered into her face. His eyelids sagged, and pink webs fractured the whites of his eyes.

"Emma? Can you hear me?" He spoke like he was announcing something to the room. "This is Dr. Kopech. Do you know where you are?"

No, she did not. The last thing she remembered was lying down, the backseat of a moving car. A beat that shook her shoulders. Voices fighting above her. Hands moving under her skirt, or just the memory of hands, sliding under her underwear's elastic seam, her head on someone's lap and smells of laundry detergent and leather and beer. She was trying to be where she was but the world was falling from her, she was dropping through darkness and the music pulsing harder in her bones and all she wanted in her life was to be allowed to go to sleep. She was in the car with other people—friends or almost-friends—and now she wondered, What had happened to them?

Her mother appeared at the side of her bed. "Emma?" she said, stroking her hand as though afraid to break it. (A plastic tube snaked from the vein.) "Baby?" Her mother's body was small and swaddled in deep-green pashmina. Her mascara washed to shadows at the edges of her eyes. The light showed every hairline wrinkle in her face. It sallowed her cheeks and forehead, the green emitting from the skin as if this was truth, what had always lain beneath.

Then her father was there, in faded plaid, tall, unshaven, on the other side. Unshaven, hunched over—he was not himself. She should comfort him.

The doctor squirted gel onto his palms—Emma swooned, for it reeked of alcohol, a familiar, sickening stench. He rested one palm on Emma's shoulder and the hand was heavy, cold. "How are you feeling?"

She nodded because it was all she could do. She wanted to ask how much time had passed, but her lips didn't have the energy, her tongue lay slack in her mouth. Her throat ached. Her head ached. Her feet under the starched sheets felt distant and strange.

Her dad lifted her hand and clasped it between his palms. His hands were big and hot and he was holding her too hard. She wanted to pull away but he kept squinting and not talking, so she didn't. Her mom reached out and tucked Emma's hair behind her ear. Emma flinched. She didn't mean to. There were too many hands and she felt they had been everywhere, all over her body, while she had lain asleep.

The doctor made his speech. It went on and on without inflection, like something he'd rehearsed the night before. The ambulance had brought her in at 1:55 a.m. (Ambulance—she did not remember.) The CT showed internal bleeding, and they had operated in order to locate the source. (Surgery—she did not remember.) Her spleen had fractured, and they had made the repair; they did not know, yet, whether it would be necessary to remove it. (Spleen—she had seen an illustration in her physiology textbook: a purplish, pulpy organ filled with branching veins. It had something to do with blood, was that it?)

Her mom's breath caught on the phrase *remove it*. "I still don't understand, what does the spleen do?" she said. "Doesn't she need that?"

The doctor said, "It's amazing what the human body can learn to live without." The doctor said that, as he'd told her parents earlier, in addition to the fractured spleen Emma had a cracked pelvis and a concussion. There would be rounds of antibiotics, exercises, rehabilitation.

Emma's mother asked, "When can she dance again?"

The doctor told them Emma was lucky. She had not been wearing a seatbelt, and she might have been thrown from the car. She might have died. She might have gone straight through the windshield. She might have died. Had she been sober, her body rigid, she might not have absorbed the blow so well. She might have died. Through the fog of medication Emma tried to understand this.

Emma was sixteen and special, her teachers said: gifted. All week, her life coiled tightly around this gift—dance rehearsals, training, turning out, stretching, sitting in Chinese splits, legs spread, chest pressed to the floor and cheek turned to the waxed wood, or cycling through positions at the barre as her ballet teacher, Miss Celeste, paced the studio, pausing to press hips and rib cages into alignment, to correct the inelegant angles of arms, the placement of fingers.

Emma's feet were her true gift. God-given. Strong and arched and perfect. Cracked and bloodied and bruised from years of toe shoes. Every day, she wrapped them in tape and lamb's wool. She grew thick calluses on her toe pads and heels. Still, her feet swelled. Corns formed between her toes. In time, the corns became ulcers, seeping yellow pus. Her toenails thickened. Skin hardened in the nail beds. Sometimes a nail broke off and the exposed skin cracked, dark blood pooling in the pink silk of her toe shoe. Bunions formed and bruised, sometimes blackened. The skin blistered. The joints of the toes inflamed. Once, she had broken a metatarsal in the middle of a recital—a crack, a flare of pain—but this had not stopped her from dancing.

On weekends, though—endowed with that most dangerous of teenage possessions, *free time*—she released. And this, among her classmates, was how she was known. Party girl, fun girl. Down for a good time. Miss Celeste told Emma that her body was a temple, but Emma did not believe this. She believed it was an instrument: it did what she asked it to do. Performed as required. She wouldn't coddle it. Indulge it, yes. Pleasure was the purest of pursuits: she was not ashamed to want it.

She was slightly chubby for a dancer, she knew, but cute. Compact. When she was a child, other, bigger kids would pick her up and adore her, place her on their laps, treat her as their baby. Her eyes were large and warm and her cheeks permanently plumped by baby fat. They petted her, prized her, fought to determine who might claim her for the hour of recess, for the day, for the term. Not understanding that it worked the other way: she had, in fact, claimed them.

All her life, Emma had lived with her parents in an A-frame in Mount Tamalpais State Park. Slanted roof, tall windows, wood-paneled walls. In the evenings, in the center of her mother's kitchen, Emma would practice her pirouettes. Spinning past the sunset view of gold, tree-stippled hills—finding her spot on the blue bowl of the Pacific

Ocean beyond. This was a point on which to focus as she spun. A point to return to again and again. And this was what dance had always been for her. The point on which to focus, to stop the world from spinning. What did people do with their lives, she'd often wondered, when they didn't have that spot?

On the second day, Emma opened her eyes to the white light and remembered: Accident. Surgery. Spleen. Pelvis. Damaged. Lucky.

Trapped. Cut off.

In the hospital room she lay alone, her door cracked to the hallway, rubber soles of strangers squeaking past. She wanted to know where her parents were, what had happened to the others in the car, what had happened to her phone. She sat up, opening her mouth to shout. But her body shrieked in pain that shut her lungs, and she fell back against the pillows, closing her eyes and evening her breath until the pain's pitch lowered to a deep and steady moan.

The room's ubiquitous plastic radiated a faint artificial smell. Like the Vacaville Walmart where she and Abigail Cress had stopped last summer on their way to Abigail's Lake Tahoe cabin—the store a monolith that Emma's mother forbade her to visit (its owners were "those big-corporate, human-rights-violating, air-polluting jerks") and which Abigail's mother simply dismissed as "that nightmare." Emma and Abigail had wound through the aisles of flimsy melamine furniture and tacky polyester clothes, clinging to each other as they giggled in fascination and horror at this newly discovered yet essentially unknowable corner of the universe.

Where was Abigail now? A memory returned, a bright balloon she grasped for as it floated past:

At Elisabeth Avarine's party, Emma had gone into the kitchen in search of more to drink. Bottles and cups littered the counters, and a sour stench drifted from the overstuffed trash bag that slouched below the sink.

Abigail had followed her. "Do you think you should?" she asked.

Emma shrugged. She found a partially full handle of vodka on the counter and unscrewed the cap. Sniffing it, she scrunched up her nose: it was cheap stuff, like medicine. Still she poured most of what was left into a red plastic cup, then added Sprite until the liquid foamed and shimmered at the rim.

"Why do you let him do this to you?" Abigail said.

"Let who do what?" Emma said, and drank. The burn slid down her throat and warmed her stomach. She felt steady, then a pleasant dip, like the first drop of a roller coaster.

"Seriously," Abigail insisted. "Don't you think you've had enough?"

"Dude. Are you my mom?"

"I'm just saying."

"Everything's fine."

"I know. I just think—"

"Seriously, Abby. Fucking get over it, okay?"

"Excuse me?"

She went back to the bottle. "Why don't you have a drink and, like, relax for once in your life?"

"What is that supposed to mean?"

"Nothing," Emma said, refilling her cup.

In the living room, lounging on white couches, Ryan's friends were glancing at her, smirking. Damon Flintov said, "Yo Ry, did you just get some ballerina ass?" and Ryan shrugged. The freshman girls were back; they glommed on to him like metal shavings to a magnet, and not one of them understood him the way she did.

Emma didn't care. Dance was the real thing in her life, the core of it. School was something to do beforehand. The weekend was the way to unwind after. And Ryan Harbinger was only a "distraction" (so Miss Celeste would say), a "harmless crush" (so her mother believed), or an "idiotic, misogynistic waste of time" (so Abigail told her, whenever she found out that Emma and Ryan had hooked up again). He was most certainly not a boyfriend.

Abigail flipped her middle finger at Ryan and his friends. "He's such an asshole," she said.

"So what," Emma said.

"I'm just saying. You deserve better."

The vodka was gone, so Emma found a fresh bottle. She thought about the cup but why bother. She pressed the bottle to her lips.

"I'm just saying, you can't, like, expect these guys to give you respect. They want what they want and the truth is they don't give a shit about us. So you have to protect yourself, Em. I don't want to see you get your heart broken. Especially not by an immature asshole like Ryan Harbinger." Abigail paused, crossed her arms. "And look, I'm sorry, I really don't think you need another drink!" She grabbed at the bottle in Emma's hands.

"Oh my God, Abby!" Emma jerked back, and the vodka sloshed onto her wrist. "You fucked one teacher. That doesn't make you an adult!"

Only in the silence following this outburst did Emma realize she had yelled. Around them the silence spread outward in slow, awful waves. And everyone—whether milling in the kitchen, playing flip cup in the dining room, lounging in the living room, or huddling in the doorway to the deck—stopped and turned to stare.

Abigail blinked at Emma, a permanent hurt in her small gray eyes.

"Fuck," Emma said, dropping the vodka bottle on the counter. "Abby. I didn't mean—"

"You don't know what the fuck you're talking about," Abigail said evenly.

"I'm sorry." She didn't know what to say. "I just meant—"

"You know what?" Abigail said. "Fuck you, Em, okay? Find your own ride home."

Emma's parents returned to the hospital room bearing cafeteria coffee and strained smiles. Their anxiety emanated from their skin. It flowed outward like the electricity in textbook illustrations and made Emma squirm in her bed, her pelvis yelping in protest. (That was what it was—a pelvis. She was never so aware of the presence of a bone. Of its precise location within her center, where Miss Celeste said she derived all her power—not from the legs, but from the core. *Make yourself as light as a bird, Emma. It is up to you to lift yourself up.*) She wanted to go to rehearsal. It was torture to lie there, flexing and pointing her toes under the thin, tight sheets, with nothing to do but think. She wanted her phone, the portal to life outside this room. She wanted her phone, her missed texts, her Facebook, her friends.

Her parents answered her questions with questions of their own:

"The other kids are fine, sweetheart. Tell us, please, what do you remember?"

"Why did you get in that boy's car?"

"Did you know that he was drinking?"

"We always told you to call us if you needed a ride home—even if you had been drinking. Were you scared to call us? Did you think you'd get in trouble?"

"Honey, why didn't you call?"

"Honey, tell us, *why did you get in that car?*"

She had no answer for them. What she remembered of that moment they could not possibly want to hear:

She was puking at the feet of the redwood trees that lined Elisabeth Avarine's driveway. Cold sweat broke on her forehead, and although the rain had stopped, the trees dripped on the back of her neck. The air smelled of wet pavement. Someone was holding her hair back. Pulling her up, leading her away from the house. Had her by the arm and was guiding her out toward the street, into the dark and the wet. She didn't want to. She wanted to lie down, to sleep. The earth reeled beneath her and the house was slanting sideways, tilting on its stilts.

"Come on, hurry, you have to get out of here," said the boy who held her triceps in his grip.

She dropped her head on his chest. "I just wanna, let's sit here a minute." Let her weight sag against his body, pulling him down. "Let's sit and look at the stars and just rest. Okay?"

The clouds had passed over and stars strained to blink between the redwoods. They were deep inside that dark and winding canyon; branches shielded much of the sky.

"You have to go," the boy said, his voice panicked.

She laughed. The laughter rolled over her body in waves that picked up speed and power until she felt she would drown beneath them. She was drowning already, doubled over now, gasping for air. (A boy had drowned once, or almost drowned, in the Valley Middle School swimming pool as the rest of the eighth grade had watched—was that right? His fat arms stirring the water, blond head pulsing frantically under another boy's hand? Was this a true memory, or only a trick of her mind?)

• • •

After a week of quiet, a nurse knocked on her open door. "Emma? You have a visitor."

"Come in," Emma called, relieved. She propped up on her elbows, gritting her teeth through the now-familiar pain, prepared to apologize as soon as Abigail appeared.

But it was Elisabeth Avarine who followed the nurse into her room. Elisabeth was model-tall and perfect, but slouched when she walked. Miss Celeste would have pushed her shoulders to the wall, tipped her chin up with two fingers, told her, *Posture, darling, posture. Who will stand you up in this world if you will not do it yourself*?

"How are you feeling?" Elisabeth asked.

"Okay, I guess. I don't know. I don't really want to talk about it."

"I'm sorry."

"It's not your fault."

"I know. Still." She glanced at the monitor by Emma's head. "Is it okay in here?"

"I guess. The nurses are nice. The food is fucking foul."

Elisabeth smiled. There was an awkward pause as she looked around the room; she seemed to be searching for something to say. Finally she asked brightly, "Who else has come to visit?"

Emma thought of Abigail, Ryan, Nick Brickston, Dave Chu, Jonas Everett, Lexie Carlton—her circle of friends was wide. She knew they loved her. She hadn't heard from any of them yet. This thought caught in her throat; she shook her head. "What's going on at school? What did I miss?"

"You know."

"Did Damon get in trouble? They told me everyone else was okay."

"He's in jail, I think. The police came to my house—they had all these questions—I didn't know what to tell them."

"Did your mom flip her shit?"

"It was pretty bad. But good, too, in a way."

"Serious?"

Elisabeth shrugged.

"That is fucking incredible," Emma said. "I can't believe she didn't murder you."

Elisabeth reached into the back pocket of her jeans and pulled out Emma's iPhone. "I almost forgot, I found this in the Red Room— I mean, that's what we call the guest room."

The Red Room, Emma remembered: the color of the walls recalled the meat of a beating heart. Emma had perched on the edge of the bed, the down mattress exhaling underneath her. The walls cast pink light on her hands. Ryan Harbinger lay before her, stretching to fill as much space as possible, just like boys like him always did, without even noticing. Above him hung one of Elisabeth's mother's art experiments: a grotesque yarn macramé, maroon, that looked like sinews torn and stringing down the wall. Ryan's eyes were closed and his caramel-colored hair, which usually swept low over his forehead, now fell back to reveal a secret band of untanned skin, and a cluster of tiny, gleaming whiteheads at his hairline that no one, she was sure of it, had ever seen but her. She wanted to pop them, one by one. He opened his eyes.

"Hey," she said.

"Hey." He smiled sleepily, fingered the skin at the small of her back.

Leaning down, she kissed him. He returned the kiss, flattening his palm, pressing her toward him. Urgent, awake. She wanted more. She wanted to taste him all over. She wanted the salt on his palms and the sweat between his shoulder blades. The spice of tobacco on his finger-tips. The tang of beer on his tongue. She pushed her palm over his hair, finger-combed the waves. He sat up, pulled off his T-shirt and dropped it on the floor beside the bed. She pushed him back to the pillow. Lay beside him and connected the dots of three small moles on his shoulder, each perfectly round and flat, the color of dark chocolate. Raked her fingernails from the curve of his elbow to the seat of his palm, trailing goosebumps. Tongued his belly. His fingers. Sucked on his bared neck, the blood pumping frantically under her mouth. He moaned. Gripped the cords at the back of her neck. She gasped, re-leased him. Opened his mouth with her fingers and kissed him softly there. He pushed back. He unbuckled his jeans and kicked them to the floor. He was the only boy she knew who wore briefs, not boxers— they were electric blue and clung closely to his hips. She liked them.

She slid her fingers under their elastic band and giggled as she snapped it, leaving a shocked pink strip of skin. He bucked. Grinned. Let her do what she would. He didn't tell her he loved her or even that she was beautiful, but she knew that he liked it. She knew that she was wanted.

She didn't remember all of it, but she remembered that he came. She did too. It didn't always work that way—Abigail had said a lot of girls couldn't get off ever. (Had Mr. Ellison told her this? Disgusting thought.) So what was the point of doing it then, Emma had asked her, because since losing her virginity to Jonas Everett freshman year, she'd hooked up as much for her own pleasure as for any boy's.

In the hospital room, Elisabeth handed Emma her phone. "I charged it for you," she said.

"Thanks." The smooth white phone, nestled in Emma's palm, had a comforting, familiar weight. She curled her fingers around it.

As soon as Elisabeth left, Emma scrolled through her missed texts. She stopped on a series from her mom, from that night:

> 11:32 PM: Hi honey, where are you? Are you at Abigail's? Everything OK?
> 12:05 AM: Hello? Do you realize it's an hour past curfew?
> 12:12 AM: Time to come home now.
> 12:12 AM: We will talk about this when you get here.
> 12:32 AM: Emma Jane. This is your mother. Please do not ignore me.
> 12:48 AM: Text me or call NOW, please!
> 1:01 AM: Now I'm beginning to worry . . .
> 1:06 AM: I just want to know you're OK.
> 1:13 AM: OK I'm calling again. Pick up your phone!!
> 1:15 AM: Honey?
> 1:15 AM: You didn't answer.
> 1:33 AM: Where are you.

1:34 AM: Are you OK??

1:35 AM: Answer me

1:35 AM: Text me

1:36 AM: Call me I'm trying you again

1:41 AM: Baby?

1:42 AM: Please

Emma dropped the phone. The naked desperation in the messages made her ache—an ache deeper than her injuries, centered in the hollows of her bones. Her mom was her mom, no matter her faults.

No matter that when Emma was thirteen, her mom would gather her parents' friends in the living room for drinks, then pull Emma to her lap and hug until it hurt. "This is my favorite girl, my best girl," she said, squeezing her, kissing her neck. "I love you, Emma-Bear, I love you, I love you." While everyone was watching. The grown-ups with their glasses tilted over their faces smirking because they knew her mom was drunk.

Emma kissed her mom and said she loved her too. Then she squirmed away and went back to her bedroom. But the party people's voices carried through the walls, hippie music on the stereo and plates crashing on the hardwood floor and bodies thumping into walls and Emma knew that they were dancing. Not dancing like she did, not real, just bodies lurching senselessly around the room. It was no use trying to sleep. She was missing everything. Rubbing her eyes, she pulled her hair into a topknot and went out in her pink cotton nightgown to join them.

The grown-ups careened around the living room. Emma's mom spun in Randall Neal's arms. Threw her head back, laughing. "Emma-Bear, you're up!" she said. "Come here, honey. Dance with us. Emma is the *most* amazing dancer," she announced, and Emma blushed with pleasure and embarrassment.

"Jesus Christ, Debra," said Bob Simonsen, "we know, we know!"

"My little ballerina girl," her mom said, breaking away to come to Emma, brush her hair back from her face. "When she dances, it's a— what's that called, like a religious experience, like a thing you can't believe—"

"A miracle," Emma's dad broke in. He was at the wet bar, pouring drinks.

"Yes!" Emma's mom leaned down to Emma, who was small for her age, pulling her against her chest. Her cotton blouse released the familiar, heady scent of patchouli and red wine. "It's like a *miracle*. God-given, I'm telling you. Her father and I had nothing to do with it."

"No kidding," said Phil Monroe.

Emma was pleased and embarrassed, embarrassed and pleased. She said, "Mom, get off, you're crushing me." She untangled herself, went and opened the door to the kitchen.

"Em, while you're up, bring us a refill?" Her dad picked up an empty gin bottle and shook it. "Should be another in the fridge."

In the kitchen, glassware scattered over the butcher-block counters. Half-drunk martinis and glasses of wine. She picked a martini glass still heavy with gin. Sipping the bitter liquid, she circled the kitchen and stopped at the sink. The gin made her head swim gently, pleasantly. Out the window were swirls of misty silver. Mill Valley lay below them, but she couldn't make out its glitter of lights; they were floating on acres of fog. It was like gazing out the window of an airplane after ascending through a cloud—the span of clear, dark sky above, the roiling gray below. Hilltops broke through here and there, stippled with houses, but these were the only signs of any kind of life below them, any other humans in the universe.

In the hospital, Emma scrolled through the rest of her texts:

> **Lexie Carlton:** omfg em r u ok I cant beleive this happened!!
>
> **Jonas Everett:** Emma just want u to know Im here for u whatever u need. Sorry this sux so hard.
>
> **Dave Chu:** Emma, I'm sorry abt what happened. Are you having more surgeries? My mom says Get well soon and We're thinking abt you.
>
> **Kai Alder-Judge:** Emma Fleed. This truly blows I am so sorry. Stay strong and keep a Positive Out-

look. Remember its the struggles in life that help us grow. Peace and Love.

Annalynne Schmidt: Luv u to the moon and back, lets do something soooon!

Alessandra Ryding: Miss ur beautiful face girly. <3 See u soon.

Nick Brickston: Yo ima try to get there to see u asap. hang in there girl.

Ryan Harbinger: Dear Emma, Get Well Soon. My parents said we should all come visit you so maybe thatll happen, lol well see. Anyways hope you feel better soon.

Steph Malcolm-Swann: Luv u hope u r doing better. I cant wait to visit u babe!!!!

Abigail Cress: I texted your mom and she said u r ok. I'm glad.

Abigail Cress: It's not that I'm not thinking of u. Believe me I am.

Abigail Cress: I know I should come. I will when I can. I still <3 u Em, promise.

So many declarations, so many promises. Yet she'd been in the hospital for a week and seen no one but her parents and Elisabeth Avarine. It made no sense. If her friends loved her, where were they? If they wanted to see her, why didn't they? Emma knew that she was missing a piece of the puzzle—something must have happened that was keeping them away.

On her phone she clicked the Instagram app. She saw that she was tagged in sixteen photos. Dread settled in her chest—there were too many hours she couldn't remember. She was scared to see the pictures, but it was more dangerous not to know.

She clicked on the first—it filled the phone's small screen—and exhaled when she saw it was harmless, a crowd scene, Emma barely visible in a cluster of junior girls. Next there was a selfie with Abigail: they posed with eyes wide, cheeks sucked in to sharpen cheekbones, lips glossed pink and pursed.

The photos that followed told the story of the night: Emma posed on Elisabeth Avarine's glass coffee table. Mid-swing, her hair strung over her face, and bra straps dangled down both arms; her tiered chiffon skirt swung up to flash a strip of muscled thigh. In another, she bent forward to reveal a dip of cleavage, a black push-up bra, a dark slice of nipple. In the third, she sprawled across a white couch, eyes closed, head cocked on her shoulder, legs dropped open to reveal a pink vee of underwear under her skirt. On Facebook more photos were posted—the same poses shot from different angles, by different kids—and beneath them were strings of comments from people she called friends, the same kids who had texted her afterward, professing love and promising to save her from her solitude. Then there was the blog post that popped up when she Googled her name, and Twitter posts from people she had never even met:

http://www.onemarinviewblog.com

Marin County Teenager Injured After Night of Hard Partying Recorded on Social Media

posted by admin

5/27/2013

A Marin County teen is in the hospital today after a drunken car crash near downtown Mill Valley early Sunday morning. The girl, 16-year-old Emma Fleed, will have to cope not only with the serious injuries she has suffered, but also with the nightmare that has been raging online ever since the news of the crash got out. Facebook and Instagram posts from the party that preceded the crash are all over the Internet, and they are disturbing. But they do give us a glimpse into the reality of teenage life in Marin today:

> **Nick Brickston:** Everybody in mv get to elisabeth avarine's shes throwing down
> **Ryan Harbinger:** yee
> **Emma Fleed:** yeah its bout to be fat
> **Damon Flintov:** lez do it

As the night wore on, signs of trouble began to emerge. There is a photograph of the driver of the BMW, Damon Flintov, kneeling on a kitchen floor, a bottle of Smirnoff Ice cocked at his mouth:

> **Nick Brickston:** Damon getting iced
> **Ryan Harbinger:** chag ro
> **Ryan Harbinger:** fuckin goon
> **Damon Flintov:** Ha ha flints back bitches
> **Jonas Everett:** ohhhh shit

In another photo, Nick Brickston, one of the passengers in the BMW, gives a sexually explicit hand sign kids refer to as "The Shocker":

> **Ryan Harbinger:** its the shocker!!
> **Emma Fleed:** ohh yaaaa
> **Damon Flintov:** yo nick brix got the hooks

The night progressed and Emma Fleed, the primary victim of the car accident at Throckmorton and Cascade Canyon, was video-recorded on a mobile phone as she danced on a glass coffee table, apparently unaware of her surroundings, likely intoxicated (or "turt"). The video was posted on Vine, a popular social networking site where short videos play on never-ending loops. Here, the kids' comments take a darker turn:

> **Nick Brickston:** majestic
> **Steph Malcolm-Swann:** he he
> **Damon Flintov:** woah woah woah. this chick is so ratchet
> **Lexie Carlton:** luv u sexxxy 😊
> **Ryan Harbinger:** drunk off her ass ha ha
> **Annalynne Schmidt:** wut the fuck is this girl doing??? lol
> **Nick Brickston:** Emma Fleed is so wasted Lindsay Lohan just told her to get it together
> **Jake Rambelli:** is this girl getting naked or what?

The kids continued to take advantage of Emma Fleed's vulnerable state, posting additional photographs and videos of the young girl on the table, her skirt and top disheveled so as to reveal her thighs and underwear:

> **Jonas Everett:** this girl is fcked UP
> **Jake Rambelli:** thirsty trick
> **Steph Malcolm-Swann:** this is so hilar
> **Dave Chu:** what if that was your daughter
> **Ryan Harbinger:** what if it was my fuckin little sister
> **Damon Flintov:** it wouldn't be tho. she wouldn't do that.
> **Ryan Harbinger:** real.

Jonas Everett: Emma Fleed is DTF whose ready??

◉ CHRIS NGUYEN and 6 others

Finally, the victim is shown as she lay passed out on a soiled white couch, her hair disheveled, her skirt hiked up to reveal pink underwear. Though at least five other kids took and posted photographs in this moment, it does not appear, from the photos, that anyone stepped in to help the girl. To the kids it seemed to be a kind of terrible joke:

Damon Flintov: she is so fucked right now

Corie Narlow: who is this sloppy drunk bitch?

Brian DeAngelo: cumbucket

Jeremy McCreigh: some people deserve to get raped

Damon Flintov: u r one sick fuck

Jeremy McCreigh: ☺

http://www.twitter.com
5/25/2013–5/26/2013

@sflover_08: @1marinview *It must suck to be that drunk slut everyone's tweeting about #mvcrash #partyfouls #sloppydrunkbitches #kidsthesedays*

@aliciababe8: *Girls need 2 stop putting thmselves in dangerous situations like this. #mvcrash #kidsthesedays*

@mvdad94941: @aliciababe8 @1marinview *What so now it is her fault the other kid was driving drunk?? #mvcrash*

@anniebansie: @mvdad94941 if u act like she did
ur asking for things 2 happen 2 u. Its common
sense, this is the world we live in. #mvcrash

@ericdracula2: Stupid bop gets what she
deserves. Maybe now shell see dont get in cars
with ppl who r drinking!! #mvcarcrash
#sloppydrunkbitches

As Emma read, her heart beat faster. This was her (could this really be her?) that they were talking about. She had always been popular, among kids and adults. Now she was worse than a slut or a trick—she was a victim to be judged, pitied, and avoided. Even Abigail, her best friend, did not want to be near her. No one did.

In restless dreaming she was standing on the wet deck at the party, in a circle of basketball players. One of them, Chris Nguyen, she'd given a blow job after the MCAL finals. Now they flirted in the semi-dark and Emma let him kiss her because why not. When Rihanna soared through the stereo, Emma's of-the-moment favorite, she didn't need a partner to start dancing.

And she drifted to an earlier performance, years before:

The other kids were playing in the tents or crawling over the fence line or turning cartwheels at the edges of the grass, but in the center of the lawn Emma practiced her dance for the grown-ups. The recital was just two weeks away and she'd been rehearsing constantly. The music wasn't playing, but she felt it in her body. She was small, but she stretched to draw the lines the dance required. The adults sat around the campfire chewing on their ribs and pasta salad; her dad had a picked bone in his hand and reddish juices smeared at the corners of his mouth. The adults turned toward her, but they didn't know how to be an audience: they laughed at the parts that were serious, *oo*hed and *aah*ed at the parts that were easy, glanced away from the parts that were hard. As Emma leapt into a *grand jeté*, her mother spilled a glass of red wine across the picnic table's cloth and cursed, and everybody jumped up screaming and laughing as the wine skimmed over the table and flowed off the edge. "Time to cut her off!" Emma's father yelled, and her mom fake-slapped him as she stumbled toward the house.

The next day, although Emma could not yet walk, Dr. Kopech promised that she would. She'd have to work at her physical therapy, he told her and her parents, but all would heal in time. Her body was young and strong, had bounced back remarkably, and would recover completely.

At this news Emma felt a tightening in her chest, a quickening. "I'm going to be able to dance?" The doctor nodded. Emma's mom started crying, messy, sniffling sobs; she covered her face with her hand. "Oh, Emma-Bear," she said, and enfolded Emma's hand in hers. Emma shook her off. Her mother's blatant joy annoyed her, though she didn't know why. She would heal, she would recover her legs, her feet, her turnout—and yet something disturbed her. It was something to do with the stage and the freedom she'd once found there, something to do with the texts and tweets and online posts that had come to define her to the world outside this room, and something to do with the understanding that, in spite of his smug hands and satisfied smile, the doctor was as powerless as everyone else—powerless to recover her in the way that really mattered, powerless to erase the record of her shaming, powerless to bring her back to that night and undo what had happened to her.

After two weeks in the hospital, Emma was released to a rehab center.

On the way there, Emma's dad pulled his Mercedes convertible into the parking lot of the shopping center across from school. "I've got to pick up a couple things for your mom," he said. "Just hang tight, okay?"

Her crutches were propped in the backseat, announcing themselves, waving hello. "Where am I gonna go?"

The parking lot was rimmed by trees, but the convertible sat in full sunlight. The heat made her elbows itch. Her seat was glossy and hot to the touch, and the white leather perforated by tiny dots; the pattern blurred her vision when she stared at it too long. She hoped no one would notice her there. None of her friends had come through on their promises to visit, and she didn't know how people from school would react to seeing her. Nor was she sure what she wanted to say to them. She wore pink Victoria's Secret sweatpants and a black cotton tank top that absorbed the heat. She had oversized sunglasses and ponytailed hair. No makeup. She found a lip gloss in her purse and dabbed it on in the rearview mirror. Her skin looked sickly, as if the hospital's white light had seeped into the pores.

The stillness hurt. She tilted her seat back and raised her hips, pushed against the leather to ease the pressure on her pelvis. With every adjustment, hot knives stabbed at her core. She kept rearranging her body in the seat but she wasn't dulling the pain, only shifting it from place to place. She was sweating under her arms and there was a strip of it along her belly, a wet line through the black cloth. Her hot-pink bra strap tangled in the skinny black strap of the tank top, and she wondered, for the first time ever, if it mattered that the bra strap showed. If this said something essential about her. If it was true, after all, that she was what they said. *Slut. Cumbucket. Victim.*

Her life had now been split. There was the girl waiting alone in this open-air car, roasting in the sunshine of a June afternoon in Mill Valley. Then there was the girl on the Internet, the girl in the pictures.

Fifteen minutes passed, and her dad did not return. She picked up her phone and texted:

Dad where R U? Boilling to death out here!!

She waited. Of course he didn't answer. Parents could be counted on to respond to texts about thirty percent of the time, and often hours or days late or right in the middle of class.

Then, across the parking lot, an army of her peers spilled onto the pavement. She hadn't realized it was lunchtime. Crazy how she'd been out of school for only two weeks and discovered the rest of the world went on during those eight hours. Strange how she'd already forgotten the rhythm of classes, the regular running of bells. They were headed her way.

Emma watched as the kids crossed the lot. She knew most every-one. Even the kids she didn't know most certainly knew her. But the ones who knew her before may have forgotten that person and re-placed her with the girl on the Internet, the girl in the pictures. This thought made her sick: she was the girl to be leered at or pitied or defended or mocked. The piece of news. The hashtag. The girl that some adults were condemning outright. Holding her up as a symbol of "What Has Gone Wrong with Our Kids."

They had said it on Twitter, on Facebook, on blogs: Emma Fleed was a rich girl. A privileged child for whom this whole town had been orchestrated so that her life might be easy and safe. Whose tragedies were petty and self-inflicted. Avoidable, if:

She hadn't stepped into that car.

She hadn't had so much to drink.

She hadn't danced in the living room.

She hadn't dressed in a skirt.

She hadn't gone to that party with a good friend to watch her but stayed at that party alone.

A girl like Emma, the people determined, had no claim on heart-break. She ought to be counting her blessings.

Just last month, Emma's English teacher had asked her, during a "reflection period," *But why do you think those children ended up in Rwanda and you ended up here? What if you had been born there and they had been born here?* And Emma had stopped texting long enough to cock her eyebrow at the teacher, like, What did that even mean? Why was she in Mill Valley and not Rwanda?

"Because this is where my parents live?" she'd said. Was she sup-posed to feel bad about the life she was born into? Was she supposed to go live in Rwanda? Or was she just supposed to know? That she could just as easily have ended up anywhere else. That it could just as easily have been some other girl sitting in the back of this shining Mer-cedes, watching her friends travel past her in packs she last week be-longed to and now sat apart from, wondering, *Am I a victim? Am I a slut?*

• • •

Emma couldn't sit in that open convertible—exposed, pathetic, trapped—while all of Valley High paraded past. What if people stopped to talk to her? What if they didn't?

She'd taken her painkillers. She'd practiced walking with the physical therapist in the hospital. She thought she was strong enough.

She pushed open the car door. Reached into the backseat (stabbing pains in her gut and hips; she gritted her teeth), grabbed her crutches and lifted them over the edge, stood them on the asphalt, leaned against the car. Then she turned, clutched her thigh, and lifted her leg out, setting her foot on the ground. Every movement hurt. She stopped, breathed until the knives relented. She reached for the crutches and pulled herself up, dropped her weight on the supports under her arms. The pain was a shock. She fell forward on her crutches and the world washed in black for a second. She had not lost consciousness. She blinked the sun out of her eyes. Breathed in and out, in and out, until she had the strength to move again.

Now she saw that the crowds had passed, and heads turned back to stare as she swooned on her feet. Freshmen mostly: nobody she could allow to see her fall on the asphalt, or drop back into that car, or cry. There was nothing left to do but to lift her chin, to feign a sense of purpose, to hobble with as much dignity as she could muster toward the fluorescent bustle of the grocery store. She had to find her father, and get out.

Emma's former friend Cally Broderick lounged with the beach kids on stone benches around the entrance to the store, their faces to the sun and eyes shielded by Ray-Bans. They were, as usual, in some other dimension and it was easy to avoid them as she went inside. There, the mood was jovial, frantic. Kids everywhere, shouting, laughing. Cutting lines that snaked back through the aisles, angling for position. Clustering at the deli counter, behind which middle-aged ladies in white aprons cupped their ears, straining to hear shouted orders. Boys strolled around with their fists in bags of Cheetos, cellophane crackling. Girls huddled together, clutching tubs of sushi, gazing into iPhones. Talking to each other, texting people elsewhere. They had only forty minutes before they would be locked up for the afternoon. They had to cram their lunches quickly, their socializing too. They had to find out what was happening before they were cut off from each other again, corralled in classrooms, forced to text half-blind with iPhones hidden in their laps. Then there were scattered adults who, like Emma, had forgotten that it was the lunch hour, who edged around the crowds, wary as gazelles while skirting a pride of lions.

Emma searched for her father's head above the crowd. Two freshman girls by the soda case saw her and giggled, huddled over their phones. Then. It was as subtle as the ripples from a cast stone: around the store, phones trilled and were pulled from pockets, one by one, eyes scanned texts, eyes lifted to follow Emma as she passed, then looked away when she stared back.

She shouldn't have tried to walk so far. With every step, her core seized up. She kept moving, breathed through it as Miss Celeste had taught her to do, knowing she had underestimated the power of this pain.

"Emma Fleed!"

Emma turned toward the older woman's voice, a familiar rasp that she could not exactly place. Neither could she place the image of the woman rushing toward her—fat and freckled with frizzed red hair, enrobed in a peacock-printed blouse whose wispy arms fanned out like wings. But when Emma saw the ribbon pinned to the woman's blouse—royal blue, positioned just above her heart—she knew.

The pain at her core cooled to dread. She had known Tristan Bloch's mother in middle school—she came to school so often that everyone had—but hadn't said a word to her since Tristan jumped from the bridge. She wondered if Mrs. Bloch blamed her—Emma's name was on the Facebook page, she had thought the comments were funny, she had been only thirteen years old.

"How are you feeling, hon?" Tristan's mother's face up close was broad and furred with translucent hairs. Her eyes were naked blue and needed liner; they had the gloss of tears though she wasn't crying. "I read about what happened."

Tristan's mother's breath smelled of the dregs of black tea and honey. Emma imagined her alone at a broad kitchen table, the mug between her palms. She forced herself to smile, to speak. "Okay. Thanks."

All around them people were stopping and staring, but Tristan's mother went on—Emma guessed she was used to it. "Should you really be trying to walk this soon, sweetheart? What did the doctors say? How are your parents holding up? I've been leaving messages for your mom, wondering if there's anything at all that I can do. . . ."

Tristan's mother's voice seemed to be growing louder. Emma was desperate to run. Instead she hunched on her crutches, the supports biting into her armpits, and leaned on her right hip with her left foot cocked, her toe just grazing the ground. She shifted back and the hot knives stabbed at her core. She gripped the metal handles of her crutches, bearing her weight in her shoulders. As Tristan's mother talked, Emma glanced over her shoulder. Everyone in Mill Valley, it seemed, had crammed into this crush of checkout lines—where was her father?

Tristan's mother worried her eyebrows, tilted her head. "Oh, honey," she said. Her eyes traced Emma from head to toe, and Emma tried to read the expression on her face. Judgment? No. Pity. The face that everyone had made for Tristan Bloch, after he was dead.

Emma leaned on her left crutch and yanked up her tank top, which had dipped to reveal a slice of hot-pink bra. Needles of pain all over. Then Tristan's mother reached out, closed her plump, dry palm over Emma's fist. Her skin was unbearably soft.

Instinctively Emma pulled back, but Tristan's mother gripped her harder. Insisted on the intimacy. Shaking Emma's knuckles for emphasis, she said, "If you need someone to talk to, a friend, if you need *anything*—"

Emma glanced around, looking anywhere but into Tristan's mother's pitying, pitiable face. Accidentally she caught the eye of a man her dad's age who hovered behind the candy display, and on his scruffed face a smile flickered to life. A sickness centered in her gut and pulsed out. *Did he know? Had he seen?*

Emma was still trapped by Tristan's mother when Ryan Harbinger strode through the automated doors. Nick Brickston shuffled in behind him. She wondered where Damon Flintov was before remembering. Juvie. She tried to conjure it: jumpsuits, steel bars, bulletproof glass. But it was an unimaginable thing—like falling off the face of the earth. Had she been the one to push him over?

The boys came nearer. Emma pulled away from Tristan's mother. "I have to—I have to go," she said.

"Are you okay?" Tristan's mother said. "Are you sure?"

Emma hobbled back as fast as she was able. "I'm—thank you. I'm sorry."

She turned, and found herself face-to-face with Ryan. Behind him, Nick trained his gaze on the floor.

"Hey," she said.

"Oh," Ryan said. "Hey."

"What are you guys doing here?"

"They took my car. It won't last, they don't want to drive my ass around. I thought you were—"

"I was. They just let me out. I'm going—"

"Cool. How are you—"

"I'm heading home now. We just stopped to get some—"

"That's good."

"My dad's here, somewhere—"

"Yeah. Oh." Ryan glanced over his shoulder.

"Do you think—?"

"Um. Yo. I've got a—" Ryan pulled his phone from his pocket and scanned the screen. "Yeah, sorry. We gotta go." He nodded to Nick, who nodded back. "I hope you, you know, feel better, or whatever," Ryan said. Then they turned and walked away.

This hurt, and yet she understood. They did not want to be associated with her suffering. They did not want to be reminded. Two weeks earlier, she might have done the same thing. It was something she might have done, for example, to Tristan Bloch, whose love note to Cally Broderick and the Facebook comments they'd all made about it had been so riotously funny up until the moment that they weren't.

Tristan's mother had walked away and Emma stood like an island in the middle of the store, shifting from foot to foot. Kids clustered up, cut lines, held hands, shared sips of soda, knocked into one another, play-fought, but around her they carved a wide circle.

From the cover of a magazine a pink headline blared: KIM KAR-DASHIAN SEX TAPE SHOCKER. Kim herself, airbrushed to a poreless sheen, gazed sadly out. It seemed to Emma that the star's humiliation had been perfectly arranged: she was sexy and pretty and perfectly piti-able and you wanted to be her. You hated her and yet you wanted to be her. You thought her life was constricted and her sex tape degrading and yet you saw, behind her tragic eyes, a small, triumphant smile.

Emma's humiliation had no glamour. No one wanted it. There was nothing desirable about standing there among her former peers, scraped of makeup, hobbled and hunched and wincing in pain, as eyes darted away from her or lingered too long. It was too painful to move, so she slumped against the magazine rack and waited for her dad to appear or her strength to revive.

In her body the knives awakened, fierce and fast, rhythmic stabbing at her pelvis and hips and legs, a musical fury that halted her breath. A black curtain dropped over her eyes and lifted. She blinked at the scuffed floor and forced herself to stand upright, to lift her head. Her stomach started churning; acid tickled at the bottom of her throat. She longed to collapse on the linoleum, to drop into oblivion. She did not. She stood on her crutches and breathed in and out. She knew how to control her breath, and she had always commanded her body; she would command it now. She would hold herself up. *Who will do it if you will not do it yourself?* Miss Celeste had always told her. She held herself up until the black curtain dangled at the edge of her eyes, threatening to fall and take her under, held herself until, at the very last second, mercifully, her dad appeared and scooped her up, his strong arms underneath her, and looped her arms around his neck and she crumpled against him, crying into his flannel with embarrassment and hurting and relief, and yes, she thought, as her world set once more to spinning, she would let her father hold her, for a little while more.

As Molly stood outside the principal's office in her Fresno State sweatshirt and skinny jeans, it was impossible not to feel like a teenager in trouble.

As a high school freshman, she'd been sent to the office of the humorless Principal Boyd for the sin of reading in class—worse still, reading books unapproved by the Fresno Unified School District. Her father had been called, and had seethed through the meeting, waiting till they were alone to unleash: *Jesus, Moll, why can't you just do what they tell you?* Molly had apologized, though she didn't believe she'd done anything wrong. Wasn't reading the whole aim of school? Oh, how adults missed the point—how they seemed to do it on purpose, to delight in their obtuseness—over and over again!

She knew she'd been summoned now because of Elisabeth Avarine's party. She was sick about it; since seeing the posts online Sunday morning, she'd hardly eaten or slept. She'd spent the day refreshing her browser, hoping for new information that would somehow make the previous night's stories untrue, so that she would not have to believe that the funny, friendly, utterly human kids she talked to in class each day were the same as the heartless avatars she'd seen online. Nick hadn't called back; the kids hadn't answered her Facebook posts. She guessed they were embarrassed to face her. She was embarrassed to face them too. But this all felt like her own private horror. What did Katie Norton want?

Molly knocked on the office door. "Come in!" came the call in response, and she stepped inside.

The office was overstuffed, cluttered, and forcedly cheerful: among the too-large furniture and stacks of files were globes of pink and purple roses placed in what seemed like strategic disarray around the room. Katie Norton sat behind the desk smiling tightly. Across from her, straightening a sheaf of papers, was Beth Firestein.

"Molly, thanks so much for coming." Katie shifted the roses on her desk. There was a royal blue awareness ribbon pinned to her lapel. What was it for? It seemed not the time to ask.

"Of course. Why did you want to see me?"

Katie gestured toward the seat beside Beth's. "Why don't you have a seat?"

Molly sat, wondering why Beth was even there. Beth looked straight ahead, holding her papers to her chest.

"First of all," Katie said, leaning forward to clasp her hands upon the desk, "we want you to know that we recognize your deep engagement with and investment in your students. We appreciate that. We really do."

What did this have to do with the party, the accident? And who was *we*? The administration? Katie Norton and Beth Firestein? Molly forced a smile. "That's nice to hear. Thanks."

"So, we're coming up on the end of the semester, and I believe constructive feedback is always valuable, even if it isn't always appreciated at first . . ." Katie trailed off. She glanced at Beth, then nodded. "Here's the thing. There have been some questions raised by certain members of the staff, questions about your pattern of behavior. It seems the tone that has been set in your classroom, I mean as far as student learning objectives are concerned, has not been especially productive. It has been suggested, and unfortunately I can't disagree, that in fact it has not seemed entirely appropriate. And now it has come to our attention that there has been some activity on your part that has been found to be, for lack of a better word, *untoward*. Isn't that so, Beth?"

Still Beth Firestein did not look at Molly. She didn't say a word.

Molly stared back at Katie Norton—her gamine haircut, her cheerleader face—and struggled to untangle the maddening grammar of principal-speak: the convoluted scramble of ambiguous vocabulary, the passive construction that obscured any meaning. She still had no idea what this meeting was for, and she wondered if Katie and Beth somehow didn't know about the weekend's events—if her colleagues were really that clueless. Finally she asked, "Have I done something wrong?"

"No one's here to place value judgments," the principal said.

"I don't understand," Molly said.

"Katie," Beth Firestein said, raising her hand, "why don't you let me take it from here?" And Molly watched, amazed, as the principal nodded and stood and ceded her own office to Beth Firestein, shutting the door quietly behind her.

Without speaking, Beth took the papers she'd been holding and laid them out, one by one, across the desk. Molly froze. They were screenshots from Facebook, arrayed like evidence, but not the kids' posts. Hers.

Molly had known in the abstract that her online comments were public, yet she'd believed that what she and her kids had shared there, like what they had shared in her classroom, was protected somehow. It seemed perfectly obvious but had simply never occurred to her that a person like Beth Firestein would have the means, or even the inclination, to so easily access the students' world—a world it had taken Molly months to penetrate.

"What you've done here is highly inappropriate," Beth said. "You know that."

Molly stared at the papers, unable to speak.

"We all feel for the girl who was hurt." So Beth did know. Her tone was calm and measured; she might have been describing the casualties of Gettysburg or the famine of some distant country, a tragedy too far away to feel. When the trouble was here, it was all around them.

"Emma Fleed is her name," Molly said.

"It's clear you were affected by her situation."

"I'm still affected. We're all affected, aren't we?" Molly heard her voice grow strident but didn't care. "She's one of our kids. So what are we going to do to help her?"

"Molly, listen to me now," Beth said levelly. Her eyes were luminous and dark. "These are not your kids. These are your students. Last year they were someone else's, next year they'll be gone. You can't be their mother. You certainly aren't their friend. You are the person who gives them grades. And if you go on caring for them in this way, you won't survive."

"But isn't it our job to care?"

Beth smiled, pityingly. "Of course not. It's our job to teach." When Molly didn't answer, Beth went on. "I'm going to tell you something that might help you. Several years ago, I was convinced to assist with a tutoring program at the middle school, one of these feel-good endeavors meant to help eighth graders prepare for the rigors of high school. I worked there once or twice a week after school, sitting one-on-one with students and attempting to wring educational value from the insipid assignments their English teachers gave out for homework. It was a dreary project. The lessons were tedious. The students were not quite people yet, not quite cooked. Their problem was not that they were unprepared for high school; their problem was that they were thirteen years old.

"There was one boy who did not bore me. His teachers told me that he was very sweet and very smart, but somewhat odd. They said that he had trouble remembering to turn in his assignments. I soon learned that he was not at all forgetful, but that he simply chose to pursue passionately what interested him, and to disregard the rest. Although this would have been a disastrous approach to high school, I thought it was an excellent approach to life, and I respected him for it. His teachers would not accept this. They continued to pathologize him. The main problem, his resource teacher claimed, was that he had a hard time 'fitting in with his core peer group.' What she meant was that the other kids disliked him. I knew what this was like; I had not been all that popular in school either. I believed this boy was someone who, if he survived his public education, would find some strange and intelligent obsession in college, some strange and intelligent friend, and end up all right. Still, I wanted to help him. I tried to know him better, to talk to him about his life. One day he admitted he was lonely, and I said—it was quite offhand, really—'Well, why don't you do something about it?'

"Three months later, that boy was dead. He had jumped off the Golden Gate Bridge. They said that he had been tormented by people on the Internet—'cyberbullies,' they are called, as if they're characters in some ridiculous video game. He had written a private letter which his classmates had posted online. They had laughed at his humiliation, berated and insulted him. They told him to shoot himself, and that no one would care if he died. Would you like to know who those classmates were?" Beth paused. Molly could not speak. She felt hollow and ill. She did and did not know who the bullies had been, why Beth was telling her this story now. "They're your students, Molly. The ones you know so well."

Molly stood on the mostly empty front lawn, looking down on the grass and the stucco arches and the slow and steady traffic on the road. White fog shielded half the sky; she squinted against the glare. She thought of the sneers of Damon Flintov on her first day; the daily disdain of Abigail Cress; the smirks of Ryan Harbinger on their seventh consecutive night without homework; the awkwardness of Nick Brickston in her car; the haste with which Calista Broderick had fled from her classroom as soon as she had been allowed. Fled from Molly who had poked and prodded, who had been so painfully desperate to connect. She felt like a character in an old cartoon—having run off the cliff's edge, glancing down to see the air beneath her feet.

The afternoon bell rang, signaling the end of her free period and the end of the school day. She headed inside to gather her things. As she walked toward her classroom, the tide of students pushed the other way. She heard and felt but hardly saw them. She did not stop until she'd reached her room. There she grabbed her satchel and sweater and keys, then locked the room and hurried down the back steps to her car. She had to be alone, to think. How could the things that Beth had told her be right, and how could Molly have been so wrong?

She was stopped at the long red light in front of the school. The kids filled the front lawn; some filed under the arches and spilled onto the sidewalk. A few girls and boys crossed the avenue, the girls tugging down their miniskirts, the boys tugging up their sagging jeans. But most massed in front of the school, huddled in conspiratorial circles, the shells of their backpacks turned toward her. She peered through the windshield; she could not tell the ones she knew from the ones she didn't know. She might have seen Calista Broderick's caramel waves of hair; she might have seen Nick Brickston's narrow shoulders. Prior to this weekend she would have thought she'd know them instantly. Now she could not be sure. She could not be sure of anything. She thought she saw the tide of students ebb, prepare to dissipate. As the light turned green, the circles shifted. The students moved away from her, and she drove on.

Senior Year

THE PRETTY BOY

It should have been Ryan Harbinger's season. He should have spent his summer at the beach, should have jumped in the Expedition every day after baseball practice, swung by for Nick and Flint, and mobbed over Mount Tam to Stinson Beach. They'd surf or swim or just sprawl on the hot sand and chill as gulls wheeled and cried overhead and the waves shushed them into a kind of trance. Blaze a couple blunts and pass them around and wait for the world to lift from their shoulders, to evaporate, breezes carrying kelp smells and faint sprays of salt. Sun glazing his skin and then burrowing under. He'd feel his cells splitting, molecules dancing. His skin tingling, each breeze raising the fine brown hairs on his arms and legs.

But in the weeks after the car crash, Ryan suffered from whiplash, bruised ribs. Stiffness in his shoulders and neck and torso, a deep ache in the muscles he used to laugh. Flint was somewhere he didn't even know, in jail or at the far-off wilderness boot camp that was his parents' last-ditch effort to make him what he wasn't. Without Flint there to laugh at their jokes, Nick and Ryan were uneasy with each other, not enough to kill their friendship but just enough, along with the memory of the accident—Ryan's crying and Nick's bloody face—to make Ryan hesitate to call.

After school each day, in the three weeks between the accident and the last day of school, Ryan's mom picked him up and took him home and sent him to his room. He could walk, but she encouraged him to eat in bed, where she served him bowls of tomato soup, plates of steak, even racks of ribs. She'd wet and microwave an old bath towel, spread the hot, damp towel over a cool, dry one on his lap and let him tear into the food until his plate was clear, then drag the damp towel across his mouth and scrub his chin and hands.

"Jesus, Mom, get off!" he'd yell, pushing her away.

"Now, what else do you need?" she'd ask, determined, unde-terred.

Even as his parents coddled him, they punished him. Took away his car and grounded him. They wanted him home. To reflect. He would be forgiven, they told him, but he had to understand what he had been a part of on the night of Elisabeth Avarine's function.

"Think of what might have happened to you," his mom said.

His dad said, "Think of that poor girl lying in the hospital."

But Ryan did not want to think about Emma Fleed. He had seen her after the accident, in the store across from school, his ribs still swaddled in Ace bandages. Hunched on her crutches, she'd looked up at him with uncharacteristic pleading in her eyes. Girls had often looked at him this way: as if there were something they desperately needed from him but couldn't even name. Some answer. Some pur-pose or somewhere to land or some making sense of their unsteady place in the universe. They wanted him to what? Claim them? Protect them? Tell them what to want and what to do? Tell them that he loved them? He didn't, of course—and they didn't love him—so why did they expect it? Why did they ask him to lie? He was sorry that he'd had to walk away from Emma, that he'd left her there when no one else would look her in the eye. Basically, he liked her. But in the middle of that store, her body bent and broken, she was a damaged object that he didn't have the tools to repair.

After Flint's BMW had slammed into that tree, and Ryan's body had slammed against the airbag, as the world ground to stillness and he struggled to breathe and Flint blinked at him out of a shocked, drained face, in the clamor of Cally Broderick's screams and Alessandra Ryd-ing's calls to God, Ryan realized that the nauseating thud against his seat had been a human body, Emma, and he had not looked back to see her. He had not looked back in that moment, and he could not look back now.

Starting in the last week of June, Ryan's summer league team met at the Valley High baseball diamond. The ball field had been built, they said, on top of marshland, and was sinking perpetually yet imperceptibly under Ryan's feet as he stood on the pitcher's mound, waiting for the next at-bat.

He squinted against the summer haze. The sky was drawn in pastel crayon. Bugs like tiny tangles of fishing line dangled in the air, flickering against the bare skin of elbows and temples and ears. He swiped the sweat from the back of his neck as Dave Chu—his teammate during the regular season—emerged from the dugout and strode toward home plate. Of course they were putting up Dave, a top-of-the-lineup kid, who could be counted on for a base hit or a walk, setting the table for better players to come up after him and drive him home.

Now Dave stepped into the batter's box and stared directly into Ryan's eyes, furrowing his eyebrows. He backed up and knocked the red dust from his cleats, then took a practice swing and stepped back into the box. Something was different about him. It had been there since he'd hooked up with Elisabeth Avarine after the function—a feat that had amazed them all.

Across the field, three girls scaled the silver bleachers and settled down to watch them. New girls, always new girls, eighth graders who'd be freshmen in the fall. They already knew who he was. They'd already made up their minds. Touching temples and giggling into their palms as they looked him up and down. He might fuck one or all of them next year, at some party, and then never speak to them again. That was what they expected of him, and maybe what they wanted.

Beyond the outfield was the road, and beyond the road the marsh, through which a bike path wound southward toward Sausalito and San Francisco.

This was the path, they said, that Tristan Bloch had taken to the bridge. The kid had been weird. The kid had made everyone twitchy.

There'd been the fight at the swimming pool (which, no one seemed to remember, Tristan, not Ryan, had started). And then he had written that note. Cally Broderick herself had delivered the note to Ryan, begging him to do something—anything—gazing up at him with that *Save me* look, extending her palm, the note tucked inside like a bomb to disarm—and Ryan had taken it. Had done what she wanted him to do. At first the note had merely shocked him, made him laugh out loud. Then he had reread the note and seen it for what it was: an act of aggression. Tristan Bloch, grade eight, had made an open declaration of love—*love!*—with no euphemism, no qualifiers, no self-protective irony, no restraint, no regard for the laws of modern courtship or middle school.

Afterward, Ryan had been suspended and grounded, and his parents had made him shut down his Facebook account. He'd set up a new account days later, using a fake name until he felt it was safe, and waited out his punishment (three weeks only—his parents were sick of it before he was) and went into high school and stopped talking to Cally Broderick and rarely thought of Tristan Bloch again.

And when he found himself awake in the middle of a night too hot to sleep, Ryan would roll from his bed and open his closet, kneel down and scrape the shoebox of baseball cards along the floor, lift the lid and sift the cards to find the square of binder paper underneath, and unfold it, the paper worn soft at the creases, the handwriting faded, pale blue ink—*Dear ~~Cally~~ Calista Broderick. You might not think I watch you but I do*. Only on these rare occasions did Ryan allow himself to ask why Tristan Bloch had written this. To wonder, briefly: How was it possible to go through life so blind, so unafraid?

On the pitcher's mound, Ryan set and glared at Dave Chu, holding his grip on the ball.

Dave Chu didn't flinch.

Ryan tugged his cap over his forehead. He imagined himself from the outside: a knife blade of shadow shielding his eyes. Hair burnished gold beneath the cap. Body tall and trembling with potential energy, muscles tight, developed and defined, strong jaw raised as he scanned the diamond. The ball nested in his glove. He brought his fists to his chest, as if in prayer, and tried to appear not only desirable but formidable to Dave, who waited, bat cocked, at the plate.

Ryan turned his head and spat. Tobacco tingled in his lower gums—he'd told Coach Gifford it was Big League Chew and Coach Gifford had been happy to look the other way. Now, behind the first-base line, Coach was showing Grayson Paul, a scrawny sophomore, how to hold a bat. Where to place his fingers, whether to choke up, something so instinctive to Ryan that he had never needed to learn it—in T-ball someone had handed him a bat and he had imitated the players on TV, and the bat had instantly belonged to him.

Mill Valley sports ran on an unspoken rule: *Don't favor the kids who are talented, because this will make the untalented kids feel bad*. Despite this bid for equality, this enthusiasm for mediocrity, the untalented kids always knew who they were. The whole thing was pointless, maddening. Infuriating that Ryan should fight for attention with the likes of Grayson Paul—that Coach should focus on this kid who was clearly on the express train to accountant-ville, while Ryan, who had the potential for actual greatness, stood neglected on the mound.

Ryan slapped the ball into his glove. Cracked his neck once, twice. Dave Chu waited. Behind him, the catcher, Jonas Everett, crouched and started flashing signals between his legs. *Curveball. Slider.*

Ryan shook his head. Split-finger fastball was what he wanted, his specialty. He wanted to hurl the ball down the center of the plate, to rip a gash in, tear the fibers of, that perfect summer day. Jonas finally gave the signal for the splitter. Ryan nodded.

Ryan wound up and lunged forward, energy flowing from the muscles of his legs and back to the arched tips of his fingers as he released the ball and it spun straight toward the plate and dropped abruptly before finding the catcher's mitt. It was a perfect pitch. Had it been slower, even a girl could have hit it. But it was fast, and Dave Chu, for all his newfound confidence, was not its match—he flailed at it, too high and too late.

Ryan turned to the dugout, but Coach Gifford wasn't watching. He stood with his back to the diamond, and laughed at Ryan did not know what, and slapped the skinny ass of Grayson Paul.

• • •

When Ryan's parents sent him to his room each night that summer, still stubbornly punishing him for the function and the crash, they didn't think to take the laptop out. So he was never really alone at all.

He met Martin Cruz online. His Facebook picture was a Hollywood abstraction, a profile obscured by square black Ray-Bans and bleached by sunlight, a convertible Infiniti with a teal smear of ocean in the background, a thick, tanned thumb on the wheel. His location: *City of Angels*. Occupation: *Starmaker*.

He sent the friend request to Ryan just before school let out for summer, with a brief message attached:

LIKE TO GET TO KNOW YOU BETTER.
THINK YOU COULD BE SOMETHING SPECIAL.
—M.C.

Ryan thought, *Fuck this fag, this perv, this pathetic lurker.* His cursor moved to the "Ignore" button and hovered there. But at the last moment he shifted over, and clicked "Accept."

A queasy thrill turned his stomach. Some hidden chord within him strummed, sending low vibrations through his body. These things were sometimes as simple as this: he wanted to see what would happen.

The first messages between them were short and friendly, with a competitive sheen that made them feel familiar and fraternal and benign: NorCal versus SoCal, Giants versus Dodgers, Tyler versus Earl. After three such exchanges, Martin changed the subject.

YOU KNOW THAT YOU COULD BE A MODEL?
he wrote.

Naw I'm not a homo, Ryan wrote.

JUST SAYING. THERE'S TONS OF $$$ OUT
THERE FOR A GUY THAT LOOKS LIKE YOU.

Ryan paused. Then: Real?

YEAH DUDE. YOU COULD BE DOWN HERE
RIGHT NOW. LIVIN THE LIFE.

Yeah.
To bad I got school tho.

SUMMER JUST STARTED, DIDN'T IT? THREE
MONTHS OF FREEDOM.

More like 2.

NOT MUCH TIME.

Nope.

BETTER MAKE THE MOST OF IT.

"Hey, I've got an idea," Martin said, midway through their first video chat. His face filled the screen of Ryan's MacBook. Dark-chocolate eyes. Tanned skin wrinkled in the soft spots: eyelids, neck. A broad, clean smile. At his edges were generic slices of room: dull white walls carved by vertical shadows, a black plastic floor lamp, a flat-screen TV. "Why don't you let me see you?"

Fine needles pricked Ryan's spine, climbing upward, groove to neck. "See me how?" he said.

"Stand up, stand back from the screen a little bit."

"Like this?"

"That's good. That's good."

Ryan waited for more. "This is fuckin' weird, bro."

"It feels that way at first. You're doing great. Now just—"

"Yeah. I dunno."

"You want to be a model, right? Start stacking those bills?"

"I guess."

"Well, this is what models do. I pegged you for the kind of guy that could handle it. Was I wrong?"

Ryan shook his head. "Naw."

"Awesome, man. I didn't think so." He paused. "Want to keep going?"

Ryan shrugged.

"Okay. Cool. Now, just go ahead and pop your shirt off. So I can make sure if you'd pass."

"You want me to take off my shirt?"

"To see if the agency would take you. Standard stuff."

Ryan hesitated.

"Look," Martin said. "Let's forget it. It's not that big a deal. I don't want you doing anything you're not ready for." He leaned back, hammocking his head in his hands, and his dark gaze flickered from the screen.

Ryan closed his eyes. He took a breath and released it. Then, swiftly, before he had a chance to change his mind, he pulled his T-shirt over his head and dropped it on the bedroom floor.

"Look at me," Martin said.

Ryan looked.

The man's face zoomed closer to the screen. There was the tiny square of light reflected in each iris. The pink bulbs in the corners of his eyes.

Ryan's heart hurled itself against his ribs, a desperate prisoner. "What now?" he asked.

Martin grinned. Drew a slow circle with his finger on the air.

Ryan nodded. He clenched his fists to keep them still. Cleared his throat and started turning, looking back over his shoulder to see what Martin was seeing, his body small as a doll's, glowing in the inset square in the corner of the screen.

Martin nodded, pleased. "Like I thought, man, you're a natural," he said. Almost whispered: "Man, that is so, so good."

That night, stripped, Ryan locked the bathroom door and stepped into the crash of shower water. Slid the glass door shut behind him. Turned the tap till his feet screamed and steam billowed at his ankles. Gasped but kept it up as hot as he could stand it, arching under the furious stream till it soaked his hair, then closed his eyes and gaped his mouth, the hot water pooling in his lashes and gums.

He spat. Stepped back. Water drilled his chest. He pumped satiny soap into his palm. Lathered the soap over his torso, reloaded and scrubbed his pits, his belly button, the tapered trail of dark blond hair, and continued moving down.

Think of something normal.

Kim Kardashian. Mila Kunis. That what's-her-name from *Sports Illustrated*, bikini model, stacked blonde—Kate Upton. He thought of all three at once. Caught his tongue between his teeth and saw them in the shower with him, bare and gleaming and bloodrushed and wet, running hands over his shoulders and lats and ass, one wrapping him up from behind, one nuzzling his neck, the third sinking slowly to her knees.

He knitted his eyebrows, fought to concentrate. He had to hold the scene in his head until it worked. But something kept intruding. A shadow in the corner of the room. A dark figure behind the fogless glass. A black, rapt gaze.

Ryan shuddered, came. He deleted every new message from Martin Cruz for two weeks.

Martin Cruz persisted. He wrapped his gifts in brown paper. A baseball card, a video game. Modest treasures, small enough to hide. Then, one day:

"What is this?" Ryan's mom said, pushing into his room with a brown paper package in her hand, the paper ripped open.

Ryan reached for it, but she pulled back. Cocked her head at the return address.

"Who do you know in Los Angeles?"

"No one," he said. He grabbed at the package again.

"Oh, no," she said, holding it against her chest. "You are going to tell me where this came from."

"Jesus, Mom. The fuck should I know? I can't like control who decides to send me stuff."

"Ryan Michael Harbinger, you are going to tell me where this came from. Right. Now."

"Lemme see it."

She hesitated.

"Lemme *think*," he said.

She handed him the package.

He pulled off the torn paper and tossed it to the floor. Opened the plain white box and reached inside.

A baseball glove. Not just any glove—the new Rawlings Primo. Four hundred dollars. Ryan had three or four gloves already, but this one was expensive to the touch, smooth and supple, saddle-brown Italian leather. Leather laces crisscrossed the fingers and the palm was trimmed in a complex and beautiful braid. He brought the glove to his face and inhaled it. That rich blend of cowhide and lanolin, that miraculous, delicious smell.

"Hello?" his mom said.

"Hold up." Ryan worked his left hand into the glove. Slid his fingers and thumb into the tight, new grooves. He stretched his palm open and closed, the leather softly creaking. As soon as he broke it in, oiled and stretched it, it would fit perfectly. As if it were made for him. He needed to keep this. His mom was tapping her foot and Ryan stalled, turning the glove over to examine the logo embroidered on the wrist, cycling through lies he could tell her. He wished Nick were there. What would he say?

It came to him. "Oh yeah," he said. "I forgot. I ordered it. It was, uh, eBay."

She narrowed her eyes. "How did you pay for it?"

"Uh, Visa? PayPal?"

"Ryan. How many times do we have to have this conversation? That card is for food and emergencies only."

"I needed a new glove. It was an emergency."

She stood back and eyed him. "You know, when you do things like this, it makes me wonder whether you can handle this kind of responsibility." This was an encouraging sign. She had been wondering whether he could handle the responsibility of a credit card for at least the last year and a half.

"Whatever," Ryan said, shrugging.

"Or maybe we'll just send this back," she said. She plucked the white box off the floor and rifled through it. "Wait. What's this?" She pulled out a small index card, blue, unlined. In black, boxy letters, anonymous as a ransom note, was written a single line:

A THING OF BEAUTY IS A JOY FOR EVER. —M.C.

"What is this?" she said. "Who's M.C.?"

"How am I supposed to know? What, you think I asked for some creepy-ass card?"

She waited for more.

"Maybe it's, like, his slogan or something," Ryan said. "Anyway. I can't return it. The guy said no refunds. If it bothers you that much, I'll pay you back."

She laughed. "With what money?"

"Look, I will, okay? Could you just fuckin' chill?"

Ryan's mom intruded on his life at every opportunity: logged into his Home Access account to check his homework and grades, typed his papers, emailed his teachers and tutors, made his excuses, selected his college (Pepperdine, where both she and her father before her had gone), colluded with his coaches, gossiped with the mothers of his friends and hookups, made his lunches and monitored his dinners, asked about his exercise, glimpsed him from the hallway as he slept. And the older he got, the more invasive her actions became, as if she could sense his shifting away from her and grew ever more desperate to pull him back. And yet, for all these efforts, she knew nothing. Knew nothing of the whirrings of his brain, the anger in his heart, the desire for he knew not what, or the knot at the floor of his stomach that had been there for as long as he could remember, telling him that something was not right.

At school, he folded up inside himself. He wailed on freshmen. Fucked with girls who worshipped him. Spit words at teachers. His boys, Nick and Flint, had known him so long they didn't expect him to be any other way. "Man, don't take it personal, that's just Ryan," they'd explain. They said this to show their loyalty and love, they didn't know it felt like a life sentence.

Ryan's mom didn't speak, just watched him, and there was a shimmer in her eyes that made him wonder if she saw it now, could understand and possibly accept, not who he actually was but how little she actually knew. She seemed about to ask him something. But then Ryan's little sister, Nell, ran into the room, snot-nosed and shrieking, and grabbed his mom around the waist. Ryan didn't try to listen to her whines. She was hungry, she was hurt, she wanted, she did not have. The same old Nell routine.

As she was dragged off toward the kitchen, Ryan's mother called over her shoulder, "One of these days, kid, we're going to talk about that attitude of yours."

He went back to the webcam. He just didn't think about it. Whether it was weird or not. Whether he liked it and what it meant if he did.

At night he would open his laptop, peer into the webcam's tiny eye. His body in the bedroom filled the small square in the corner of the screen. Amazing how his world could be compressed in this way—how small it was, how insignificant. Grinning, he tilted the screen until it cut off his head. Above the elastic line of the little-boy briefs his mom insisted on buying him, his torso, slim and tan from an early-summer surge at Stinson Beach, looked alien. It was like watching a stranger strut around a room that once was his.

His body fascinated. Martin's greedy face filled the screen. His jaw and the broad banks of his smile. Although he'd said he was close to Ryan's age, his eyes revealed him—he was in his thirties at least. Ryan didn't care. If Martin was older, it was probably better. It meant he'd have more to give.

Ryan posed. Messing around at first and then working his body in earnest, stealing glances at the corner of the screen in order to see what the man was seeing, sweating slightly in his armpits and along the furred small of his back as he sought out the ideal angle of his beauty. His mother's anxious presence pressed toward him through his locked bedroom door, but he knew she knew nothing of what was going on inside. No one did.

He did like it. He liked turning the lock on his mother, liked watching himself in the corner of the screen, liked the little presents Martin sent in unmarked envelopes. He even liked sneaking out to intercept the mailman at the curb, beating his mother to it, just in case.

Martin Cruz returned to watch him again and again. The truth was that he asked for hardly anything. He said he wanted to know what Ryan would be doing if he were all alone. That was the phrase he used, "all alone," like he was talking to a child.

Then, one night:

"Have you ever been to the city?" Martin asked. "Are you ready to see what life's like for a star?"

Los Angeles was six hours south. When Ryan's family had driven to Disneyland three summers ago, he'd crowded into the backseat with his snoring sister and pressed his temple to the window as the I-5 landscape paled and dried, the sky's precious Northern California blue gritting and bruising purple in a way that felt portentous and magic. As they descended into the city, he thrilled to its chaos and its ugliness, its dirty laces of streets, fast-food neon, power lines slashing the sunset like scars.

Ryan knew what Martin meant, what kinds of movies they made in the grim stucco cloister of Martin's real hometown, Van Nuys (which he'd seen on Google Earth, his cursor tracing the bleached streets). The idea intrigued him. The cut would be swift and total. In this way, he would free himself from the perfect shackles of his life.

The strange, hot June ceded to a foggy July and a temperate August.

With his backpack hanging from one shoulder, Ryan walked to the Miller Avenue stop and boarded the bus to San Francisco. Planning the trip was easier than he'd expected: it turned out buses traveled the California spine each day, San Francisco to L.A.

As Ryan stepped onto the bus, the air conditioning blasted him with dry cold and the faint smell of rubbing alcohol. Mill Valley didn't believe in air conditioning, nor need it, usually, so this smell took Ryan to lesser places rarely visited: a McDonald's in Orlando, his grandfather's condo in Seal Beach. The bus driver creaked the springs in his seat. Nodded in Ryan's direction, fixing his eyes on the road ahead. Ryan's heart picked up its pace. It was happening. He'd never traveled alone before, and it was incredible how he could just do this, get on a bus and go somewhere, flash his iPhone with an email that said someone had paid for him, some adult somewhere was responsible for this, take a seat and let this dull-eyed old stranger drive him out of his life.

Ryan scanned the dim corridor of the bus and headed down the aisle. It was the middle of the day, a week before the start of school, and the bus was sparsely populated. There were a couple of white guys with dreads and headphones, and behind them an old man sleeping, head dropped on his chest. The old lady beside him wore a flowery T-shirt with fluttery sleeves, opened one eye to follow Ryan as he passed but kept quiet, with her hands crossed placidly over her belly. Next there was a woman about his mom's age but nothing like his mom: this one was buttoned into a cheap-looking suit, hair clamped back with plastic jaws, blue smears over her eyes. He thought she'd say something, start asking questions, but instead she nodded at him, smiled, ducked her head.

He passed her. Next there were four Hispanic guys spread across one row, talking to each other in indecipherable Spanish. (Ryan had gotten a B+ in Spanish 5-6 last year, but his repartee was limited to *"Hola!"* and *"Qué pasa?"* and *"Por favor, Señora O'Shannahan, puedo ir al baño?"*) The men glanced at Ryan as he walked between them, but then went back to their conversation. They weren't interested. Only then did it become real to him, only then did he understand:

No one was going to stop him.

He chose an empty row. Set down his backpack, scooted down in the seat and plugged his earbuds in his ears. It was Flint's favorite: Tyler, the Creator. (He thought of Flint, trapped now, awaiting his fate.) The beat pounded Ryan's eardrums. The voice shuddered his heart and tightened his throat—that slow, thick bass, saying whatever the fuck it wanted.

The bus coughed and rumbled to life. His seat quivered beneath him. He rested his head on the scratchy fabric and turned to watch out the window as they pulled away from the curb and headed south on Miller Avenue. They passed the baseball field. His teammates were white stick figures warming up. It was like watching himself on that field, a dozen copies of the boy he'd always been.

The bus traveled out of that little green valley that had been his whole life, that small town circumscribed by mountain and bay and fortresses of ancient trees, and wound toward the freeway, out of the gentle fog and into the hard blue sky, the open expanse of the land. He didn't really know what he was going to, but he didn't care. The main thing was that he was going. Was this how Tristan Bloch had felt, he wondered, while on his journey to the bridge?

Ryan's life was opening all around him, whirling and spinning, whispering into his ear all the things it was going to be. And who he was going to be in it:

Anyone.

Anything.

He was a prisoner of the heat. Sweating little rivers in his palms and through the hair curled at his temples, in his pits beneath the borrowed robe and in the crease of his ass beneath his briefs. Cream makeup spackled and suffocated the pores of his face. Two fans limply spun as he waited on the teenage-bedroom set that looked weirdly like his own but not—it was some adult's best guess, a twin bed with a blue plaid blanket, a desk with a cardboard box painted to resemble an ancient computer, a hair-band poster hanging cockeyed on the wall. A bored-looking girl in sandals and shorts reflected light into his face with a silver screen. The cameraman crouched behind his blank machine. The director yawned in his chair. Only Martin, hovering in the darkness beyond, watched Ryan's every move with a fierce attention that felt like love.

Beyond the camera was a fluorescent hallway leading out. Ryan squinted to see, but the girl kept flicking silver light into his eyes and he knew now that Out There was nothing but hot smog and noise. He took off his robe. His little-boy briefs embarrassed him, but Martin's voice carried out of the gloom to tell him they were perfect, he was perfect, he was beautiful, special, there was no one in the world like him. His costar, steroid-bulked and buzz-cut, marched on set yelling into a cell phone, guzzling a Coke. When he saw Ryan, he hung up, hawked into his can.

"Let's do this," he said.

As Ryan sat on the edge of the bed, the costar kissed him. Ryan had thought about this but he wasn't used to it, he was used to girls, the sweet, waxy taste of their lip gloss and gum, the way their soft lips faltered and nipped. The costar led with his jaw, his lips chapped with sharp crusts of skin, and he pushed until their teeth clanged and then forced his tongue inside. Ryan's heart was kicking, a small caught animal inside his chest. He was backing away, or being pushed, and he was getting hard like he didn't know he could and didn't want to but it was too good and too bad and too fast to stop. The costar released Ryan's face and the sudden light stunned and dizzied him as the costar moved down, pulling at the waistband of Ryan's briefs. Ryan let him. He closed his eyes until out of the shadows Martin said, "Don't." So he opened them, and stared into the dark, gleaming tunnel of the lens.

It ended eventually. His payment in his pocket, eight hundred dollars in cash. He'd had money before, always, but this money belonged to him.

Outside, the sky lay low and smoggy and soft, and stucco buildings glared white light. Grit scattered in the street. The sidewalk was empty, and cars sped by not seeing him.

He wanted to check Facebook but his iPhone was off, untraceable. A pay phone was across the street, clawed to the side of a squat motel. He'd heard of these things but never used one. He crossed and read the ancient instructions, dug for quarters, dialed the only number he knew by heart.

As it rang, he wondered what she'd say. What her voice would sound like small and jagged and scared. *Ryan, is that you? Where are you, baby, we're going crazy here worrying—*

She interrupted him. "Hello! You've reached the home of Ellen, Steven, Ryan, and Nell! We're four busy bees, so leave your message at the tone!"

Her voice was bright, smooth, oblivious. Contained in the machine, it was like another person's mother in another person's life. At the same time, he heard it in a deeper place and with sudden force remembered being small, the sweat and powder of her body as she'd opened her robe in the morning and he'd wrapped himself inside, pressed his ear to the soft cotton nightgown to hear the steady throbbing of her heart. He knew her, a determined kind of woman: given the slightest clue to follow, she would never stop searching for the boy he wasn't anymore.

He believed that it would be his first unselfish act, his kindness, to lay the phone in its cradle and walk away.

In the deal that was struck, Molly was allowed to keep her job but not her classroom. The following fall, she was relocated to the school's most modern building: two stories of steel and glass, gray walls and bright hallways. Her classroom was large and air-conditioned and more functional in every way, yet Molly missed her old home in Stone, that musty, sunny, hundred-year-old hall.

She now taught next to Beth Firestein, who would observe Molly's classes several times every term while Molly, as Katie Norton put it, "worked on getting back on track." Molly had swallowed this, as she'd swallowed the censure by Katie, the note in her file, and the not-entirely-voluntary deletion of her Facebook account. At least for a while, she'd reside in the land of the actual, where she might discover who her real friends were. Where she might discover herself.

On a sunny Monday morning, Molly strolled into her classroom in black pants and a crewneck sweater and dropped her satchel on the desk. Her class was a new crop of juniors. They were reading *The Great Gatsby,* just as last year's juniors had. The kids were gossiping about a party from the weekend. There was some dispute about a student who'd been arrested or almost arrested or merely grounded.

"Hey, guys," she said. "Quiet down, please. Take out your homework."

The kids groaned and whined. Three hands shot up; she knew what this meant and preempted. "If you didn't do it, I don't need to know why. Just bring it to me tomorrow."

The hands sank. The papers were passed through the rows to Molly's desk at the front of the room. She scooped the pile into her satchel and pulled out a stack of first drafts handed in the week before.

"Peer edits," she said. "Partner up, everybody."

Again the kids shifted and groaned. "Seriously?" one asked.

"Seriously."

There was a murmur of activity as her students paired up and shoved their desks together. She distributed their papers, then sat at her desk and sorted her faculty mail: payroll statements she filed away, department memos she tossed in the recycling bin. At the bottom of the stack was a paper, typed and stapled, but nothing that she had assigned. It was a short story written by Calista Broderick.

Molly picked up the story and riffled the pages. The paper was unthumbed, unstained—this had been printed for her. It surprised her. Since the start of the school year, she'd seen Calista in the halls several times, but they'd swept past each other like strangers in an airport, hurrying toward distant destinations.

Molly recognized Calista's story, of course. It centered on a group of kids at Valley Middle School, in particular the class outcast, who writes a love note to an insecure girl who cannot be trusted with it. She shares the note with her friends, who share the note on Facebook, and the boy is cyberbullied until driven to jump from the Golden Gate Bridge. It was the story Beth had told her, but with Calista Broderick as protagonist and villain. No wonder the girl had been blowing off classes, getting high, spacing out: she was carrying the weight of this.

Molly got up and went to her classroom door. Her students stirred in their seats; she shushed them. In the mostly empty hallway a few seniors were chatting. Seeing Molly, they scuttled into the girls' bathroom. The one she cared about, Calista, wasn't there. An old, familiar impulse flared: she wanted to find Calista, pull her in and sit her down and talk until they had unraveled every detail—then help the girl, somehow, to move past it. She returned to her desk, uncapped her red pen, and turned to the story's final page.

THE SLEEPING LADY

Cally Broderick had gone through middle school with Abigail Cress and Emma Fleed on either arm; she started high school on her own.

She walked through the Valley High School gates and passed Abigail and Emma and her other former friends clustered on the lawn. They saw her too. She passed them by. She'd hardly spoken to any of them since she'd done what she had done.

She knew the boy was dead because of her. A series of small decisions she had made, each of which had seemed inconsequential at the time, all of which had combined to bring the end of Tristan Bloch.

Tristan had died, and Cally's mom had recovered. The combination of radiation and chemotherapy and mastectomy had nearly killed her and then allowed her to live. So Cally had a mother again—hollowed, bowed, yet present. Her father returned to work, and the living room, cleared of insurance papers, became a living room again. Peace and order restored, life returned to normal. It was Cally who had changed.

Through freshman year, she kept mainly to herself. And it seemed right that she should be alone. A kind of penance.

Her parents didn't understand why the suicide of "that poor, strange boy" should affect her so deeply. They sent her to a psychiatrist she knew they couldn't afford. In session Cally talked about the things that didn't matter—the stress of high school, the challenge of making friends, the pressure to be exceptional in a town where nothing less was tolerated—and the doctor seemed pleased with her answers. He prescribed pills meant to dull Cally's emotions, make her lighter, more pleasant and pliable—Cally took them home and dumped them down the bathroom sink, watched them swirling in the drain.

The months came and went, yet she could not avoid the scattering of small reminders.

A Facebook post.

A blond head.

A red bicycle.

Blue ink on lined paper.

A crane, or really any bird, shrinking to a black speck in the sky.

Tristan himself would haunt her dreams, a broken body floating on the current of the bay. She'd thought nothing could be worse than her nightmares, so she Googled once for details: *What happens to a body after jumping from a bridge?*

But the truth was worse. The truth was that it could take minutes for death to arrive. The force of impact caused organs to tear loose, bones to snap. Spleens, livers, hearts. Ribs, clavicles, pelvises, necks. People thought that jumping off the Golden Gate would feel like flying into Heaven, the Marin County coroner said, but it didn't. It was multiple blunt-force trauma. Like being hit by a car but worse, because even if you survived the fall itself, you'd likely drown. Sometimes jumpers could be spotted thrashing in the water, too weak to swim because their organs were bleeding out. By the time the Coast Guard reached them, these jumpers were usually dead. The sailors would pull a body from the water and lay it dripping on the deck. Sometimes mucous bubbled at the nostrils. In almost all cases the body was purple all over.

Cally would wake sheet-tangled, shaking, and soaked in cold sweat. Sometimes she hated Tristan. Cursed his selfishness. Middle school had been close to over—he could have waited it out. Sometimes, strangely, she missed him, imagined him with her and some new group of misfit friends. Was it too much to believe she could have talked him out of sweatpants, convinced him to grow out his hair and keep his tongue inside his mouth and his mom out of the school? Was it a fantasy to think he could have learned to be a little cooler, to care a little less? It was too late, anyway.

Sophomore year, Cally took to eating lunches sideways on a splintered wood bench in the outdoor amphitheater at the outer edge of campus. Here she met Jess Steinberg, Kai Alder-Judge, and Alessandra Ryding. They were so-called Bo-Stin slackers, Bolinas and Stinson Beach kids who were bused over Mount Tam every morning. They all took drama, and Alessandra was president of the HIV Awareness Club, but that was the extent of their participation in life at school. During spirit rallies they slept behind Ray-Bans in the uppermost rows of the theater; at morning break they wandered off campus to smoke. Often they ditched their afternoon classes and drove up the mountain to Sunset Ridge; they'd photograph one another in halos of sunset, and drink until the sky swam over their heads. Sometimes it seemed that they were the only ones who realized this was a paradise they lived in.

"How could you sit in a classroom all day," Jess wondered one late afternoon, pinching his blunt between two fingers, drawing its bright tip across the mountain's green-gold panorama, the pink-striped sky over hazy water far below, "when this is all around you?"

"Fuckin' insanity," said Kai.

"Eyes wide shut," said Alessandra, stretching her arms overhead. Then they all nodded knowingly, Cally silently longing to be told what this meant.

Cally grew to love to hear her talk. Alessandra had plans. She was going, for one thing, to start visiting Christian centers for pregnant girls, to infiltrate and investigate.

"You know, Calista," she said as they faced each other cross-legged on a bench, sharing lunch (a salty baguette, a plastic crate of strawberries). She had small, perfectly round brown eyes and long lashes. "Those places advertise in *our* school paper, promising pregnant teenagers help and guidance and, like, *all* the *options*"—she pulled the school newspaper out of her tote bag and shook it fiercely—"and then, when you go there, it turns out they just want to lecture you about Jesus and, like, indoctrinate you and make you look at pictures of tiny aborted fetuses and their tiny aborted limbs and scare you into keeping yours. It's so deceptive. It's, like, criminal."

Cally sucked on her strawberry, listening to Alessandra's emphatic voice. It amazed her that Alessandra believed the world could be a better place in this one specific way, and that she herself could make it better.

The fall of Cally's sophomore year drifted toward the winter. A collection of small moments let her know she was no longer alone: Cally sat passing a flask between Kai and Jess in the school theater, watching Alessandra beam heat from the center of the stage. (She always played some tragic woman—Lady Macbeth or Antigone or Tamalpa, daughter of the mountain witch, whose story Tristan Bloch had referenced in his note.) Alessandra looped her arm in Cally's as they wandered off campus together. Cally and Jess lay side by side on the mountain, smoking and watching the fog roll over the sky, when he reached out to caress the silver chain that Cally wore around her neck. In his car Kai leaned in close, pursed his lips, and blew a fallen eyelash from Cally's cheek. At Muir Beach after midnight, Alessandra stripped off her skirt, thighs ghostly beneath her oversized shirt as she ran into low waves laughing and calling—*"Calista!"* Once or twice they'd all made out at parties. Casually, giggling all the way. Jess snuggled her in doorways or nuzzled her on couches; Kai kissed her briefly, softly, on the lips to say goodbye. Never a discussion of what any of it meant.

By the end of that school year, Cally was one of them. Her hair faded and tickled the scoop of her spine. She threw away her lip gloss and mascara; her skin took on a gentle tan. She let Alessandra draw elaborate, vaguely Asiatic patterns on her forearms and hands, painted her fingernails putrid green, stacked silver rings on her thumbs and hammered-silver bangles on her wrists, went to the Salvation Army and covered her body in costume: short, flower-splattered dresses; silk vests and patched denim; gauzy lingerie; dead men's shoes.

Junior year. She was high most every day. She drifted through her classes. The teachers just kept passing her along. Some, young and earnest like Ms. Flax had been, would stop to pull her into classrooms, tell her she was *wasting her potential.*

"You are a perceptive, intelligent girl," her English teacher, Miss Nicoll, told her one day during lunch. "Why not try?" With her deep brown eyes and optimistic blazers, Miss Nicoll seemed so innocent, so hopeful—Cally couldn't bear to tell her who she really was, or what she'd done.

Miss Nicoll worried, Cally's mother worried, her father worried. One brother, Jake, called her a freak, while the other, Erik, began to watch her with a new, grudging respect.

On school days, Cally daydreamed through the morning and at lunch went into an abandoned potting shed behind the school to smoke weed with Jess and Kai and Alessandra, then swam through the day till the day was done. She hated being trapped at school. The English classes were the worst. *Romeo and Juliet, All Quiet on the Western Front, A Clockwork Orange, The Great Gatsby, Macbeth.* Did the teachers realize that all their books were obsessed with death? Giddy with it. The why and the how of it. People thrusting knives into each other, severing heads, crushing each other with luxury cars, blasting off limbs in the name of God and country, stabbing their hearts in the name of love. Cally preferred poetry:

> The memory throws up high and dry
> A crowd of twisted things;
> A twisted branch upon the beach
> Eaten smooth, and polished
> As if the world gave up
> The secret of its skeleton,
> Stiff and white.

She couldn't get Eliot's poem out of her head. The music of the syllables. The permanent stillness of that calcified branch. Once, she sat down and tried to write about it, to work out her obsession:

The image of the branch on the beach represents . . .

The branch on the beach is important because . . .

She stopped. Out her bedroom window was the old, familiar view:

the undulating lawns and willow trees of Bayfront Park, where a life-time ago they'd run the mile in PE. Mount Tamalpais loomed above, bluish in the fading light as if it had been dipped under water. She wrote: *The branch on the beach means nothing.*

The end of junior year was Elisabeth Avarine's party. Cally went with Jess and Kai and Alessandra. They showed up high, then shared bottles of beer on the crowded deck. When the storm hit, most people ran to take cover inside. But Cally danced with her friends in the rain, stretching her neck to it, drinking it, letting it batter her shoulders, wet her hair till it glistened and curled. Then she was led down a hallway, to a purple bedroom and the promise of a better feeling, and this she did want: the capsule that Jess dropped in her palm. There was one hit of Molly for each of them. She moved to place it on her tongue, as she'd always done before.

"Wait," Kai told her. "It's better if you rail it."

"Real," Alessandra said, and tapped her nose.

Cally nodded. She set the capsule on a precalculus textbook on the floor. With a kitchen knife Jess chopped her capsule into three clean lines of powder. Cally leaned over the first line, closed one nostril. Just a second's hesitation and she forced herself to do it: inhaled fast and sharp so her sinuses burned—she cried out from the shock and the pain of it. Alessandra knelt beside her, offering a glass of water. Cally drank it fast, prepared to disappear.

After a few minutes, everything was clear. Alessandra climbed onto Jess's lap at the edge of the bed and Kai wrapped his arms around Cally, his body warm against hers. On the bed Jess whispered into Alessandra's ear; her giggles floated weightless in the air. Alessandra's power came out of her body, the arcs and shapes she made as she dis-entangled from Jess and stood and swayed around the room. They wanted to see her bare arms luminous against the walls of purple, her pupils wide and dark as she exclaimed, "I love you guys, all of you, everyone!" They laughed. Their laughter had a movement of its own, a texture—together they created a soft, supple space in the world. Cally curled on Kai's lap and it was expansive, a throne. She found bal-ance in her flimsy dress, rough denim against her thighs. Shifting side-ways, she looped her arms around his neck and tucked into a ball. She was so small and he was so big. This feeling familiar and warm. She could lose herself in him if she wanted to—he would give her the gift of completely overtaking her. She pushed closer, her head against his chest so she could watch Alessandra at an angle, skewed. Cally was part of him and part of them, all of them one being. Here she was, here here here. This moment was the only moment there was, this place the only place.

They needed to move. So they were up and running to the living room, where music burst upon them, a joyous crowd of noise. Oh, the rush of those guitars, electric, the singer bratty and loud. The room was crowded and hot, so they ran out to the deck to dance. Reaching for a hand, Cally found one, Alessandra's, tiny dark freckles scattered along the fingers. They were dancing, singing, though they didn't know the words. Jumping and dancing and shaking their hair, bodies strummed by the song. They were holding everybody's hands. Cally's body turned liquid. Her heart was beating harder and nothing would ever stop it. Nothing new would ever happen. Everything in the world was exactly right now.

Later, as the drug's effects began to fade, Cally climbed onto the narrow redwood railing of the deck. Stood shaking, winged her arms. The rain slowed to a patter along her naked arms, but she didn't feel the cold. In fact she felt a warmth that radiated from inside, and as her friends cheered and hooted below, she began to walk the rail. On one side was the safety of the deck, and on the other, nothing: canyon that yawned into the black mass of redwood trees, smashed tracks of deer, the creek whispering over stones and dirt and chokes of weeds below. A strange thought took hold: the whole creek was moving, not just the water on top but the water beneath and the fish and the pebbles and sediment and dirt. All of it was moving, all the time, and never stopped. This thought distressed her; she wasn't sure why. There was something unrelenting, cruel, in the water itself. How it could break a person's bones, or slide inside and drown the lungs. How soft it sounded. How hard it was.

Cally stood on tiptoe and teetered left and right, shifting her weight, pulling herself up again. To her friends on the deck, it was a game. They believed that she was like them, careless and brave. To her it was a thrill to stare down the canyon, to know that if she were to fall into it, no one would think that she'd jumped. They'd consider it an accident, a tilting of her body into blackness. It was a joy to think of it, a relief to think of it. A relief to think it could all be over in an instant, that she might fly from her guilt and evaporate to nothing, and no one would blame her.

Arms extended, Cally pirouetted on the slick and narrow beam. Across her field of vision swept darkness from the canyon and light from the house. She closed her eyes and listened to the whooping of her friends. Wavered once but held her center. This was it, she felt: the time to let go. She took a breath—air fresh from the rain—and released it. As she began her slow tiptoe across the beam, her mind was very clear. She thought, *If I am going to do this, I am going to do it now*.

But she was not like him. She was afraid.

Later that night, she heard the sirens shrieking and climbed into the backseat of the first ride heading out: Damon Flintov's BMW.

Alessandra and Nick Brickston jumped in on either side, and Emma Fleed, eyelids fluttering and skirt askew, lay across their laps as if to sleep.

Ryan Harbinger blasted a rap song in the front seat. He was the only person she truly hated, a brutal force in the universe. It was all that was wrong with the workings of life, that he should be grinning and dancing while she sat there trapped in her misery, while Tristan Bloch's body lay under the ground. The fact that she had once convinced herself to kiss a person like Ryan now nauseated her, and made her hate him with the fiercer intensity of putrefied lust.

They sped through the canyon. With each curve Cally was thrust from Alessandra's shoulder to Nick's. She closed her eyes, pulled her seatbelt down across her chest and buckled it. Moments later they crashed. In the aftermath Cally looked down at Emma Fleed, whose body was twisted at a sickening angle. Emma didn't move. Dead? Eyes shut, spine twisted. Yes, Cally thought, dead.

When that car hit the redwood, Cally herself should have gone straight through the windshield. She should have been injured even more seriously than Emma was, or killed. Just hours before, on the railing, she'd wanted to die. In the car, she had fastened her seatbelt.

Intention was one thing; it was the smallest decisions that made any difference.

"Oh my God," Alessandra told her one day in the fall of senior year, as on the serpentine roots of a redwood tree they sat shoulder to shoulder, sharing lunch (a cup of key lime yogurt, a bag of salted pretzels), "you *so* need to do this."

"What is it?" Calista asked.

"Write me a play. For the One-Act Festival."

"I'm not a writer."

"That's negative energy. Totally unproductive. How do you know?"

"I've never written anything in my life."

"Yet."

"You're crazy."

"I need a good part. Otherwise I'll just get cast as a prostitute again, and I'm so over that. I'm so over the systematic subjugation of women by these chauvinist writer-directors I can't even tell you."

"Why don't you write it yourself?"

Alessandra scooted closer, crossed her slim, bare leg over Calista's. "Oh, sweet Calista, my darling, my love, the muse doesn't create. She inspires."

Calista spent the next few weeks writing. On school days they'd pile into Kai's old Land Cruiser and drive to the beach, to Sunset Ridge, or to the cemetery in the hills above Mill Valley.

At the cemetery they'd gather at the feet of a wooden Buddha in a clearing at the curve of a one-lane road. The Buddha faced away from the hill with its imperfect patchwork of graves, toward the clutch of coast oaks and eucalyptus in the canyon. On the air was the chatter of songbirds, the echoes of car horns far below. Above them stretched a pale blue sheet of sky.

Calista circled ground that was blanketed by wood chips, strewn with yellow leaves. They reminded her of Robert Frost: *And both that morning equally lay / In leaves no step had trodden black.* Breezes shifted her hair and the leaves on the trees. She settled on one of six tree trunks arranged around the Buddha, each flat-topped, solid and smooth. It was clear someone had cut and arranged the trunks exactly, and yet she felt there a sense of eternity, of this place having risen intact from the land. The Buddha was said to be powerful, magic, and as they visited again and again through the spring, Calista began to believe that it was. In yellow-toned wood were carved the intricate folds of his robe and the buttons that covered his head. His eyes were closed in a face that was human and beyond human. His right hand was raised with palm facing outward, the second finger bent to meet the thumb. *"Karana mudra,"* Alessandra explained once as Calista examined the Buddha's hand. "He's warding off bad energy, bad spirits."

There was a hollow in the tree trunk on which the Buddha sat. The hollow was filled with offerings, small, significant: a gourd, a pair of sunglasses, a string of beads. There were school pictures of girls who had overdosed and boys who had driven off cliffs. The offerings were for them. The rule was, you could leave things but not take things away.

Her journal open on her lap, Calista wrote as the others talked and smoked and dozed. She wrote the only story she had to tell.

Tristan Bloch had been smart. After the torment had started, he'd known it wouldn't end. He'd known that his world would continue to constrict, like those finger-trap toys sold in Chinatown: you stuck your fingers in the ends of the tube, and the more you moved, tried to jerk free, the more tightly the tube closed around you. Mill Valley was so specific in its beauty, in its limits. Kids like Tristan and Calista would never forget how this world had been created for them, how they had been born into this perfect nest and still they had insisted on unhappiness. At thirteen, Tristan could only assume that wherever he traveled, that darkness would travel with him.

In their eighth-grade class photo, Tristan was baby-blond and roly-poly, squinting into the sun and grinning wide. Calista and Abigail and Emma posed in tank tops and miniskirts and scribbled-on Chuck Taylors, with bony chests and push-up bras, coltish legs, baby cheeks. Dave Chu was gawky and lean, in a red polo shirt that hung like a drop cloth on his narrow shoulders. Nick Brickston's neck was too long for his torso, and his smile was cluttered with metal. Elisabeth Avarine almost disappeared: she was a child's flyaway ponytail, a blurred face avoiding the camera. Damon Flintov was adorable, chubby under his oversized T-shirt and jeans, eyes big and innocently blue though he jutted his chin to show toughness. Ryan Harbinger was cherubic, dark-gold hair tangled, tanned forehead shining with sweat because he'd recently been playing. It was shocking, how they all just looked like children.

On one of her long and lingering afternoons in the cemetery, before she left the feet of the Buddha, Calista left an offering of her own. She wanted something unobtrusive, a small token to nestle with the others in the hollow of the trunk. She chose, of course, the origami crane of silver paper, precisely folded, gleaming still.

When Calista had finished writing, she changed the names and submitted the draft not to the One-Act Festival but to her English teacher from the previous year, Miss Nicoll. She didn't know what she expected. Miss Nicoll seemed smart and open. Last year, Calista had often seen the teacher talking and laughing with Calista's classmates, during breaks and after school. And she had seemed interested in Calista, once. After graduation, Alessandra and Kai were going to plant trees in Ecuador and wanted Calista to go with them, but she hadn't committed; a small but urgent part of herself envisioned an ivy-covered college on the East Coast, a small class gathered on a warm lawn, poetry piled at her feet. Maybe Miss Nicoll would read Calista's story and show her how to move beyond it, to reach this other place. For a week she waited, allowing herself to dream.

Miss Nicoll found her in the hallway. The teacher looked different, somehow—her hair cut short, her outfit unfussy. Her manner was relaxed too; she wasn't searching Calista's face as she used to do, with that hopeful, desperate need.

"I'm so glad you shared this with me," Miss Nicoll smiled, handing Calista her story. "Thank you. I have to get to class now, but I've written you a little note on the back."

Calista thanked her, then hurried to her locker to read. The note was there as promised at the end of the story, handwritten in red cursive:

Dear Calista,

Thank you for sharing your writing with me. I would
like to congratulate you on your lovely natural writing voice, which I recall from when you were a student in my class. There are many beautiful metaphors
and similes in this story.

However, there are a few issues that I hope you
won't mind my pointing out.

1. I am wondering if the tone and vocabulary of
the story match the age of the protagonist. If this girl
is only thirteen years old, would she really know advanced vocabulary words such as "calcified" and "indelible"?

2. In one section of the story, the protagonist de-
scribes, in great detail, the little boy's bike ride to the
Golden Gate Bridge. Well, I am wondering, how
could she possibly know all these details if she wasn't
there? It seems very unlikely. Is there any way this can
be explained, such as having the boy leave a note explaining what he did? Or perhaps you might delete
this section altogether?

3. There is an awful lot of foul language, especially
for eighth graders to be using!

Calista, I truly wish you all the best. You are a
very fine writer.

Warmly,
Molly Nicoll

On the last Saturday of senior year, Calista stood with Jess and Kai and
Alessandra on Mount Tam's Sunset Ridge. In a clearing they'd stoked
an illicit fire—Alessandra's idea to torch their textbooks and note-
books, a gesture to show that their old lives were over.

The yellow hills dipped to shadows—below them lay Muir Woods,
a famed redwood grove strictly for tourists. Beyond the western ridge,
the sun dipped into the Pacific. Calista's friends were sharing beers and

blunts around the fire, but she was only watching, taking pictures on her phone to freeze the moment.

In a few months more, Calista and her classmates would all be gone from there. Calista would be pulled by Alessandra's enthusiasms across countries and continents. Her former best friend, Abigail, was off to Dartmouth. Dave Chu and Elisabeth Avarine were going together to UC Berkeley. Nick Brickston was moving to San Francisco to do who knew what. Some of them had already gone: Emma Fleed had transferred to the alternative high school after the accident, and from there had vanished in the miasma of Central Marin. Damon Flintov had been sent to juvie, then to a wilderness boot camp in some wild and faraway place—Idaho, Montana, West Virginia. And Ryan Harbinger had disappeared just before senior year, leaving a wake of wild rumors behind him.

Across the fire, Alessandra tucked a lock of hair behind Kai's ear and they lay back in the grass and began to kiss.

Calista stood and, with no particular direction in mind, turned and hiked up the hillside in the gathering dark. She went barefoot over sun-baked dirt. The trail dipped under giant redwoods; the ground turned cool and damp. A familiar dankness took her, without warning, back under the deck at Abigail's—the sharing of bad beers, the buzzing in her blood, how they had laughed and laughed, nothing had ever been funnier. And she felt her heart untether in her chest. It began to melt, she could not hold it. It was like trying to pool streaming water in her palms. She was crying. She blamed it on the withdrawal of drugs from her system, on the sight of Alessandra's fingers in Kai's hair, on the knowledge that this was their last night all together as they were right now, on the darkness of these woods, on their unrelenting beauty. At a clearing in the trees, she lay her head on the dirt. The stars wheeled above her in a twilit sky.

No magic in it, but as she closed her eyes Calista felt the mountain around her. The screams of red-tailed hawks, the creaks of grasshoppers, wind shivering the redwoods behind her, whispering through grasses at her ears. As life whirled on without her, she lay there and listened.

It came from the mountain or it came from within herself. There was no meaning in lying down. There was no explanation, no relief, in anything anyone else might tell her. She wanted to die for what she had done, but she was eighteen years old: she wanted to live.

There was only the decision to get up. There was only standing and brushing herself off, only turning and hiking back to her friends whose hoots and laughter carried through the trees, to her friends who were flawed but, yes, living; there was only digging through her bag for the last remnants of high school, throwing them into the fire. As the flames ate the papers to curling black, she knew there was only this, and whatever moment would come after, only Calista Broderick going on and trying, like everyone, to live in this beautiful world.

ACKNOWLEDGMENTS

My sincere thanks to:

Susan Golomb, constant ally and wisest guide, who plucked me from the slush and changed my life. Noah Eaker, who has been the editor every little girl dreams of (or maybe that was just me): brilliant, relentless, and always kind. Susan Kamil, who lent her editorial advocacy, her inspired ideas, and her shawl when I was cold. The Random House and Writers House families, especially Gina Centrello, Avideh Bashirrad, Jessica Bonet, Maria Braeckel, Sanyu Dillon, Deborah Dwyer, David Ebershoff, John Hastie, Cynthia Lasky, Wade Lucas, Leigh Marchant, Sally Marvin, Steve Messina, Bridget Piekarz, Ron Shoop, Theresa Zoro, Nina Arazoza, Emma Caruso, Allyson Lord, Caitlin McKenna, and Scott Cohen. And to Soumeya Bendimerad Roberts, who sent these California teens around the world.

The Rose and Thistle Writers—Kate Hope Day, Kevinne Moran, and Rita Michelle Pogue—who shepherded this book into being with their unfailing support and unfailingly honest critique (and who are always right). Mitra Parineh and Melanie Catherine Nead, bright lights and kindred spirits, on whose sublime optimism and profound empathy I have come to rely. Margo Beth Fleming, most trusted reader of manuscripts and queries, whose counsel has steered and steadied me. My teachers at UC Davis and the University of Southern California—especially Elizabeth Davis, Janet Fitch, Gina B. Nahai, Gabrielle Pina, and Rita Williams—who gave me the tools for a writing life. My teachers at the Attic Institute of Portland, Merridawn Duckler, Karen Karbo, and especially Jennifer Lauck, who opened a window. Anthony Doerr, who bestowed his generous enthusiasm and sage advice when this book was little more than a list of ideas. The Portland Writers' Dojo, the Tin House Writers' Workshop, and the Squaw Valley Community of Writers, which provided much-needed community, and the Panera bakery-cafés of Beaverton, Oregon, and Culver City, California, which allowed me clean, well-lighted space to write. Neelanjana Banerjee, Katrina Carrasco, Matt Cunningham, Jenée Desmond-Harris, Alex Espinoza, Michael Fleming, Jason Harris, Joy Johannessen, Dorothy Johnson, Chris Lacroix, Maggie Heaps Lauffer, Zoe Vandeveer, and Heidi Williams, who gave vital notes and encouragement along the way. Jaime and William Heaps, teenager whisperers, who made this book possible, and so much more. Seth Greenland, who read all the bad drafts, and waited a decade for me to just tell him a story.

My husband, Ben DiPardo, whose abiding love sustains me, and whose unwavering support inspires me every day to work harder, to do better, to be more, and to be more myself. (You are the best good.) Anne and Mike DiPardo, who welcomed me into their family with open arms and conversation about books. Ardyce and Jay M. Johnson, Meredith Johnson Sagolla, Tyler Johnson, Erica Ireland, Linda and Jeff Lockwood, Linda Mai, Ashley Sanders, Laurel and Holly Shear, Gina Uriarte, and Lindsay Van Syckle, whose friendship and faith have bolstered this writer for years longer than was reasonable or, possibly, deserved. Austin Bah, who took my writing seriously when I was fifteen years old (and that made all the difference). And my parents, Susan and David Johnson, who made me believe—not that this could happen, but that it would.

Finally, I am grateful to the teenagers of Marin County, who brought me so much joy.

ABOUT THE AUTHOR

LINDSEY LEE JOHNSON holds a master of professional writing degree from the University of Southern California and a BA in English from the University of California at Davis. She has served as a tutor and mentor at a private learning center, where her focus has been teaching writing to teenagers. Born and raised in Marin County, she now lives with her husband in Los Angeles.

ABOUT THE TYPE

This book was set in Galliard, a typeface designed in 1978 by Matthew Carter (b. 1937) for the Mergenthaler Linotype Company. Galliard is based on the sixteenth-century typefaces of Robert Granjon (1513–89).